SHORT FICTION OF THE MASTERS

SHORT FICTION

Edited by LEO HAMALIAN

OF THE MASTERS

and FREDERICK R. KARL

G. P. *Putnam's Sons*   NEW YORK

Acknowledgments

The editors wish to thank the following individuals and publishers for their permission to use copyrighted material:

"The District Doctor" by Ivan Turgenev, from the Story Classics edition, by permission of Thomas Yoseloff, Inc.

"Midnight Mass" by Machado de Assis, translated by William L. Grossman. Used by permission of the translator.

"The Orphans" by Giovanni Verga, from *Little Novels of Sicily* by Giovanni Verga, translated by D. H. Lawrence. Copyright 1925 by Thomas Seltzer, Inc., 1953 by Frieda Lawrence Ravagli. Reprinted by permission of the Viking Press, Inc. and Laurence Pollinger, Limited.

"Il Conde" by Joseph Conrad, from *A Set of Six*, by permission of J. M. Dent & Sons, Limited.

"Tit for Tat" by Sholom Aleichem, from *The Old Country* by Sholom Aleichem, translated by Julius and Frances Butwin. Copyright 1946 by Crown Publishers, Inc. Used by permission of the publisher.

"The Madness of Dr. Montarco" by Miguel de Unamuno, from *Abel Sanchez and Other Stories* by Miguel de Unamuno, by permission of Henry Regnery Company.

"The Soft Touch of Grass" by Luigi Pirandello. Copyright © 1959, from *Gli Eredi* di Luigi Pirandello. Reprinted by permission of Simon & Schuster, Inc.

"Twenty-Six Men and a Girl" by Maxim Gorki, translated from the Russian by Emily Jakovlev and Dora B. Montefiore, copyright by Gerald Duckworth & Co., Limited. Used by permission of the publisher.

"The Melancholy Summer of Madame de Breyves" by Marcel Proust. From: *Pleasures and Days* by Marcel Proust. Reprinted by permission of Librairie Gallimard and Doubleday and Co., Inc.

"Little Lizzy" by Thomas Mann, reprinted from *Stories of Three Decades* by Thomas Mann, by permission of Alfred A. Knopf, Inc. Copyright 1936 by Alfred A. Knopf, Inc.

"Within and Without" by Hermann Hesse, by permission of Marie Rodell and Joan Daves, Inc., on behalf of Suhrkamp Verlag.

"A Man Without Character" by Robert Musil, translated by E. M. Valk.

[5

Used by permission of the translator and Franz Horch Associates, on behalf of Rowohlt Verlag.

"Counterparts" by James Joyce. From *Dubliners* by James Joyce. Reprinted by permission of the Viking Press, Inc.

"The Judgment" by Franz Kafka. Reprinted from *The Penal Colony* by Franz Kafka, copyright 1948 by Schocken Books, Inc., New York, translated by Willa and Edwin Muir, by permission of Schocken Books, Inc.

"The Man Who Loved Islands" by D. H. Lawrence, reprinted from *The Woman Who Rode Away* by D. H. Lawrence, by permission of Alfred A. Knopf, Inc. and William Heinemann, Limited. Copyright 1927, 1928 by Alfred A. Knopf, Inc.

"The Children's Campaign" by Pär Lagerkvist. From *The Eternal Smile and Other Stories* by Pär Lagerkvist. Copyright 1954 by Random House, Inc. Reprinted by permission.

"In a Grove" by Ryūnosuke Akutagawa. From: *Rashomon & Other Stories* by Ryūnosuke Akutagawa. By permission of Liveright, Publishers, New York. Copyright © 1952, by Liveright Publishing Corp.

"My First Goose" by Isaac Babel, Copyright 1955 by Criterion Books, Inc. Reprinted by permission of the publisher from *The Collected Stories of Isaac Babel* (New York: 1955).

"A Clean, Well-Lighted Place" (Copyright 1933 Charles Scribner's Sons; renewal copyright © 1961 Ernest Hemingway.) is reprinted with the permission of Charles Scribner's Sons from *Winner Take Nothing* by Ernest Hemingway.

"Brother" by Graham Greene. From *Nineteen Stories* by Graham Greene. Copyright 1947 by Graham Greene. Reprinted by permission of the Viking Press, Inc. and Laurence Pollinger, Limited, on behalf of William Heinemann, Limited.

"The Wall" by Jean-Paul Sartre, translated by Lloyd Alexander, from *Intimacy*, translated by Lloyd Alexander. Copyright 1948 by New Directions. Reprinted by permission of the Publisher.

"Yellow" by Samuel Beckett, from *More Pricks Than Kicks*. Used by permission of the author and Grove Press, Inc.

"The Ruin of Humanity" by Alberto Moravia. Reprinted from *Roman Tales* by Alberto Moravia, by permission of Farrar, Straus & Cudahy, Inc. and Secker & Warburg, Limited. Copyright © 1957 by Farrar, Straus & Cudahy, Inc.

Introduction

&

IN attempting to give the reader an anthology of short fiction distinguishable from the numerous other collections of its kind, the editors have been guided by three basic principles. First, we sought to include only the story which is continuous with the author's major work, not the isolated or bizarre piece. For the student who is fresh to these writers, the stories should provide an introduction to their longer and more involved fiction, which he may study later in his college career. For the general reader who enjoys good literature, the stories should reward him with insights into his favorite authors and perhaps suggest aspects of their art that he missed in their novels. For each author in question, our selection presents, in small, what great literature is about.

Second, we considered the intrinsic worth of each piece. We did not choose a story simply because it was representative of the author's work or because it illustrated some principle of the craft: it had to be as well one of the short masterpieces of that writer. In selecting the best, we tried, moreover, to avoid the over-anthologized story, not because the too-familiar piece is necessarily poor but because it often perpetuates merely an accepted or stereotyped view of the author. We have embraced stories which, while central to the writer's canon, are also slightly divergent from the usual run of selections. Thus, instead of Kafka's "The Country Doctor" or "In the Penal Colony," we have included "The Judgment"; instead of Conrad's "The Secret Sharer" or "Youth," we have the relatively unknown "Il Conde"; instead of Greene's "The Basement Room," we preferred "Brother." These selections, we feel, suggest quite successfully somewhat different ideas and views from those in the more common choices. When we had no alternative, either because of a publisher's restriction (with Hemingway) or because no other piece by the author approached his most famous story (with Balzac), we were not reluctant to represent him by the favorite.

Third, we made our selections from authors (with the exception of the Japanese master, Akutagawa) whose work stands at the center of major Western literature and whose reputations are established or growing into major dimension. Hence, authors usually not available in such anthologies—such as Musil, Beckett, Proust, Silone, and Moravia—make their appearance here. As with the older masters, the themes and conflicts in their stories lead into the themes and conflicts common to all great literature. These are not stories merely good of their kind but insignificant or thin when measured against weightier fiction. These stories stand by themselves as literature.

A successful short story shares the substance of all great literature. These thirty-one stories are concerned with the nature of man's existence, with his ability or failure to grapple with the problems of life and to resolve his conflicts. Since great literature is "moral" simply by virtue of the author's honesty with character and theme, these stories are "moral" entities because they create a world of real life. Whether the author is realistic, poetic, or symbolistic in his methods, whether for him a bird is a creature who chirps on a tree or a symbol of freedom and flight, the artistic success of his work depends upon his creation of a world in which *his* view is possible. The moral resolution of our own conflicts—the catharsis that Aristotle spoke about—occurs when the author, for that moment, raises us to his level of insight and imposes his values. At that moment of pity and terror, no matter what the method for seducing us, we recognize the moral justification of all great literature.

The stories in this collection are serious, sometimes even morbid, but most important fiction is serious and often morbid. Serious writing, however, does not preclude the possibility of some leavening, and many of the authors in this collection are in the best sense witty. Nevertheless, any collection of short fiction that pretends to serve as an introduction to the masters must concern itself with the heights and depths of human behavior. These stories, accordingly, raise and lower us, make us respond to the best and worst in man, and, finally, give us a sense of the world with which all of us must come to terms.

Although these stories can speak ably for themselves, we believe that as editors we would be irresponsible if we left the learner rudderless and the instructor empty-handed. We have therefore provided a brief critical biography of each writer before his story and a series of questions after his story. These questions attempt to make the generalizations above less abstract, to show how each writer achieves the atmosphere one associates with great craft. The terminology and method the sensitive student needs to approach and appreciate these stories we have tried to work unobtrusively into these questions. Thus, we hope to induce the student to read closely and carefully, without controlling his response, and to offer the instructor several means of approach without restricting his direction or interfering with his own interpretation of the story.

LEO HAMALIAN
FREDERICK R. KARL
The City College of New York

Contents

Contents

Honoré de Balzac:

A PASSION IN THE DESERT

*One of the most prolific of novelists, Honoré de Balzac was born in
1799 in Tours, France. Before he died of apoplexy in 1850, he had
attempted to complete an all-inclusive panorama of the French society of his day. The dozens of interconnected novels and stories
which constitute this great vision were grouped under the title* The
Human Comedy *and were to occupy him for sixteen years. In the
process of describing and analyzing the passions which have a
devastating effect on men's lives, he used realism and precise docu-
mentation to transform fiction and make the modern novel a compre-
hensive literary form. "A Passion in the Desert" is one of his most
effective accomplishments, for in the relationship between the man
and the beast, Balzac has dramatized the mystery of a man forced
to face his inner self.*

ॐ

"THE whole show is dreadful," she cried, coming out of the
menagerie of M. Martin. She had just been looking at that daring
speculator "working with his hyena"—to speak in the style of the
program.

"By what means," she continued, "can we have tamed these animals to such a point as to be certain of their affection for——."

"What seems to you a problem," said I, interrupting, "is really
quite natural."

"Oh!" she cried, letting an incredulous smile wander over her lips.

"You think that beasts are wholly without passions?" I asked her.
"Quite the reverse; we can communicate to them all the vices arising in our own state of civilization."

She looked at me with an air of astonishment.

"Nevertheless," I continued, "the first time I saw M. Martin, I
admit, like you, I did give vent to an exclamation of surprise. I
found myself next to an old soldier with the right leg amputated,
who had come in with me. His face had struck me. He had one of

[13

those intrepid heads, stamped with the seal of warfare, and on which the battles of Napoleon are written. Besides, he had that frank good-humored expression which always impresses me favorably. He was without doubt one of those troopers who are surprised at nothing, who find matter for laughter in the contortions of a dying comrade, who bury or plunder him quite light-heartedly, who stand intrepidly in the way of bullets; in fact, one of those men who waste no time in deliberation, and would not hesitate to make friends with the devil himself. After looking very attentively at the proprietor of the menagerie getting out of his box, my companion pursed up his lips with an air of mockery and contempt, with that peculiar and expressive twist which superior people assume to show they are not taken in. Then when I was expatiating on the courage of M. Martin, he smiled, shook his head knowingly, and said, 'Well known.'

"How 'well known'?" I said. "If you would only explain to me the mystery I should be vastly obliged."

"After a few minutes, during which we made acquaintance, we went to dine at the first *restaurateur's* whose shop caught our eye. At dessert a bottle of champagne completely refreshed and brightened up the memories of this odd old soldier. He told me his story and I said he had every reason to exclaim, 'Well known.' "

When she got home, she teased me to that extent and made so many promises, that I consented to communicate to her the old soldier's confidences. Next day she received the following episode of an epic which one might call "The Frenchman in Egypt."

During the expedition in Upper Egypt under General Desaix, a Provençal soldier fell into the hands of the Mangrabins, and was taken by these Arabs into the deserts beyond the falls of the Nile.

In order to place a sufficient distance between themselves and the French army, the Mangrabins made forced marches, and only rested during the night. They camped round a well overshadowed by palm trees under which they had previously concealed a store of provisions. Not surmising that the notion of flight would occur to their prisoner, they contented themselves with binding his hands, and after eating a few dates, and giving provender to their horses, went to sleep.

When the brave Provençal saw that his enemies were no longer watching him, he made use of his teeth to steal a scimitar, fixed the blade between his knees, and cut the cords which prevented using his hands; in a moment he was free. He at once seized a rifle and dagger, then taking the precaution to provide himself with a sack of dried dates, oats, and powder and shot, and to fasten a scimitar to his waist he leaped onto a horse, and spurred on vigorously in the direction where he thought to find the French army. So impatient was he to see a bivouac again that he pressed on the already tired courser at such speed that its flanks were lacerated with his spurs, and at last the poor animal died, leaving the Frenchman alone in the desert. After walking some time in the sand with all the courage of an escaped convict, the soldier was obliged to stop, as the day had already ended. In spite of the beauty of an oriental sky at night, he felt he had not strength enough to go on. Fortunately he had been able to find a small hill, on the summit of which a few palm trees shot up into the air; it was their verdure seen from afar which had brought hope and consolation to his heart. His fatigue was so great that he lay down upon a rock of granite, capriciously cut out like a camp-bed; there he fell asleep without taking any precaution to defend himself while he slept. He had made the sacrifice of his life. His last thought was one of regret. He repented having left the Mangrabins, whose nomad life seemed to smile on him now that he was afar from them and without help. He was awakened by the sun, whose pitiless rays fell with all their force on the granite and produced an intolerable heat—for he had had the stupidity to place himself inversely to the shadow thrown by the verdant majestic heads of the palm trees. He looked at the solitary trees and shuddered—they reminded him of the graceful shafts crowned with foliage which characterize the Saracen columns in the cathedral of Aries.

But when, after counting the palm trees, he cast his eye around him, the most horrible despair was infused into his soul. Before him stretched an ocean without limit. The dark sand of the desert spread farther than sight could reach in every direction, and glittered like steel struck with a bright light. It might have been a sea of looking-glass, or lakes melted together in a mirror. A fiery vapor carried up in streaks made a perpetual whirlwind over the quivering land. The sky was lit with an oriental splendor of insupportable purity, leaving naught for the imagination to desire. Heaven and earth were on fire.

The silence was awful in its wild and terrible majesty. Infinity, immensity, closed in upon the soul from every side. Not a cloud in the sky, not a breath in the air, not a flaw on the bosom of the sand, ever moving in diminutive waves; the horizon ended as at sea on a clear day, with one line of light, definite as the cut of a sword.

The Provençal threw his arms around the trunk of one of the palm trees, as though it were the body of a friend, and then in the shelter of the thin straight shadow that the palm cast upon the granite, he wept. Then sitting down he remained as he was, contemplating with profound sadness the implacable scene, which was all he had to look upon. He cried aloud, to measure the solitude. His voice, lost in the hollows of the hill, sounded faintly, and aroused no echo —the echo was in his own heart. The Provençal was twenty-two years old;—he loaded his carbine.

"There'll be time enough," he said to himself, laying on the ground the weapon which alone could bring him deliverance.

Looking by turns at the black expanse and the blue expanse, the soldier dreamed of France—he smelt with delight the gutters of Paris—he remembered the towns through which he had passed, the faces of his fellow-soldiers, the most minute details of his life. His southern fancy soon showed him the stones of his beloved Provence, in the play of the heat which waved over the spread sheet of the desert. Fearing the danger of this cruel mirage, he went down the opposite side of the hill to that by which he had come up the day before. The remains of a rug showed that this place of refuge had at one time been inhabited; at a short distance he saw some palm trees full of dates. Then the instinct which binds us to life awoke again in his heart. He hoped to live long enough to await the passing of some Arabs, or perhaps he might hear the sound of cannon; for at this time Bonaparte was traversing Egypt.

This thought gave him new life. The palm tree seemed to bend with the weight of the ripe fruit. He shook some of it down. When he tasted this unhoped-for manna, he felt sure that the palms had been cultivated by a former inhabitant—the savory, fresh meat of the dates was proof of the care of his predecessor. He passed suddenly from dark despair to an almost insane joy. He went up again to the top of the hill, and spent the rest of the day in cutting down one of the sterile palm trees, which the night before had served him for shelter. A vague memory made him think of the animals of the desert; and in case they might come to drink at the spring, visible from the base of the rocks but lost farther down, he resolved to guard himself from their visits by placing a barrier at the entrance of his hermitage.

In spite of his diligence, and the strength which the fear of being devoured asleep gave him, he was unable to cut the palm in pieces, though he succeeded in cutting it down. At eventide the king of the desert fell; the sound of its fall resounded far and wide, like a sign in the solitude; the soldier shuddered as though he had heard some voice predicting woe.

But like an heir who does not long bewail a deceased parent, he tore off from this beautiful tree the tall broad green leaves which are its poetic adornment, and used them to mend the mat on which he was to sleep.

Fatigued by the heat and his work, he fell asleep under the red curtains of his wet cave.

In the middle of the night his sleep was troubled by an extraordinary noise; he sat up, and the deep silence around him allowed him to distinguish the alternative accents of a respiration whose savage energy could not belong to a human creature.

A profound terror, increased still further by the darkness, the silence, and his waking images, froze his heart within him. He almost felt his hair stand on end, when by straining his eyes to their utmost he perceived through the shadows two faint yellow lights. At first he attributed these lights to the reflection of his own pupils, but soon the vivid brilliance of the night aided him gradually to distinguish the objects around him in the cave, and he beheld a huge animal lying but two steps from him. Was it a lion, a tiger, or a crocodile?

The Provençal was not educated enough to know under what species his enemy ought to be classed; but his fright was all the greater, as his ignorance led him to imagine all terrors at once; he endured a cruel torture, noting every variation of the breathing close to him without daring to make the slightest movement. An odor, pungent like that of a fox, but more penetrating, profounder —so to speak—filled the cave, and when the Provençal became sensible of this, his terror reached its height, for he could not longer doubt the proximity of a terrible companion, whose royal dwelling served him for shelter.

Presently the reflection of the moon, descending on the horizon, lit up the den, rendering gradually visible and resplendent the spotted skin of a panther.

The lion of Egypt slept, curled up like a big dog, the peaceful possessor of a sumptuous niche at the gate of an hotel; its eyes opened for a moment and closed again; its face was turned toward the man. A thousand confused thoughts passed through the Frenchman's mind; first he thought of killing it with a bullet from his gun, but he saw there was not enough distance between them for him to take proper aim—the shot would miss the mark. And if it were to wake!—the thought made his limbs rigid. He listened to his own heart beating in the midst of the silence, and cursed the too violent pulsations which the flow of blood brought on, fearing to disturb that sleep which allowed him time to think of some means of escape.

Twice he placed his hand on his scimitar, intending to cut off the head of his enemy; but the difficulty of cutting the stiff, short hair compelled him to abandon this daring project. To miss would be to die for *certain,* he thought; he preferred the chances of fair fight, and made up his mind to wait till morning; the morning did not leave him long to wait.

He could now examine the panther at ease; its muzzle was smeared with blood.

"She's had a good dinner," he thought, without troubling himself as to whether her feast might have been on human flesh. "She won't be hungry when she gets up."

It was a female. The fur on her belly and flanks was glistening white; many small marks like velvet formed beautiful bracelets round her feet; her sinuous tail was also white, ending with black rings; the overpart of her dress, yellow like unburnished gold, very lissom and soft, had the characteristic blotches in the form of rosettes, which distinguish the panther from every other feline species.

This tranquil and formidable hostess snored in an attitude as graceful as that of a cat lying on a cushion. Her blood-stained paws, nervous and well-armed, were stretched out before her face, which rested upon them and from which radiated her straight, slender whiskers, like threads of silver.

If she had been like that in a cage, the Provençal would doubtless have admired the grace of the animal, and the vigorous contrasts of vivid color which gave her robe an imperial splendor; but just then his sight was troubled by her sinister appearance.

The presence of the panther, even asleep, could not fail to produce the effect which the magnetic eyes of the serpent are said to have on the nightingale.

For a moment the courage of the soldier began to fail before this danger, though no doubt it would have risen at the mouth of a cannon charged with shell. Nevertheless, a bold thought brought daylight to his soul and sealed up the source of the cold sweat which sprang forth on his brow. Like men driven to bay who defy death and offer their body to the smiter, so he, seeing in this merely a tragic episode, resolved to play his part with honor to the last.

"The day before yesterday the Arabs would have killed me perhaps," he said; so considering himself as good as dead already, he waited bravely, with excited curiosity, his enemy's awakening.

When the sun appeared, the panther suddenly opened her eyes; then she put out her paws with energy, as if to stretch them and get rid of cramp. At last she yawned, showing the formidable apparatus of her teeth and pointed tongue, rough as a file.

"A regular *petite maîtresse*," thought the Frenchman, seeing her roll herself about so softly and coquettishly. She licked off the blood which stained her paws and muzzle, and scratched her head with reiterated gestures full of prettiness. "All right, make a little toilet," the Frenchman said to himself, beginning to recover his gaiety with his courage; "we'll say good morning to each other presently," and he seized the small, short dagger which he had taken from the Mangrabins. At this moment the panther turned her head toward the man and looked at him fixedly without moving.

The rigidity of her metallic eyes and their insupportable luster made him shudder, especially when the animal walked toward him. But he looked at her caressingly, staring into her eyes in order to magnetize her, and let her come quite close to him; then with a movement both gentle and amorous, as though he were caressing the most beautiful of women, he passed his hand over her whole body, from the head to the tail, scratching the flexible vertebrae which divided the panther's yellow back. The animal waved her tail voluptuously, and her eyes grew gentle; and when for the third time the Frenchman accomplished this interesting flattery, she gave forth one of those purrings by which our cats express their pleasure; but this murmur issued from a throat so powerful and so deep, that it resounded through the cave like the last vibrations of an organ in a church. The man, understanding the importance of his caresses, redoubled them in such a way as to surprise and stupefy his imperious courtesan. When he felt sure of having extinguished the ferocity of his capricious companion, whose hunger had so fortunately been satisfied the day before, he got up to go out of the cave; the panther let him go out, but when he had reached the summit of the hill she sprang with the lightness of a sparrow hopping from twig to twig, and rubbed herself against his legs, putting up her back after the manner of all the race of cats. Then regarding her guest with eyes whose glare had softened a little, she gave vent to that wild cry which naturalists compare to the grating of a saw.

"She is exacting," said the Frenchman, smilingly.

He was bold enough to play with her ears; he caressed her belly and scratched her head as hard as he could.

When he saw that he was successful, he tickled her skull with the point of his dagger, watching for the right moment to kill her, but the hardness of her bones made him tremble for his success.

The sultana of the desert showed herself gracious to her slave; she lifted her head, stretched out her neck, and manifested her delight by the tranquillity of her attitude. It suddenly occurred to the soldier that to kill this savage princess with one blow he must poignard her in the throat.

He raised the blade, when the panther, satisfied no doubt, laid herself gracefully at his feet, and cast up at him glances in which, in spite of their natural fierceness, was mingled confusedly a kind of good-will. The poor Provençal ate his dates, leaning against one of the palm trees, and casting his eyes alternately on the desert in quest of some liberator and on his terrible companion to watch her uncertain clemency.

The panther looked at the place where the date stones fell, and every time that he threw one down her eyes expressed an incredible mistrust.

She examined the man with an almost commercial prudence. However, this examination was favorable to him, for when he had finished his meager meal she licked his boots with her powerful rough tongue, brushing off with marvellous skill the dust gathered in the creases.

"Ah, but when she's really hungry!" thought the Frenchman. In spite of the shudder this thought caused him, the soldier began to measure curiously the proportions of the panther, certainly one of the most splendid specimens of its race. She was three feet high and four feet long without counting her tail; this powerful weapon, rounded like a cudgel, was nearly three feet long. The head, large as that of a lioness, was distinguished by a rare expression of refinement. The cold cruelty of a tiger was dominant, it was true but there was also a vague resemblance to the face of a sensual woman. Indeed, the face of this solitary queen had something of the gaiety of a drunken Nero: she had satiated herself with blood, and she wanted to play.

The soldier tried if he might walk up and down, and the panther left him free, contenting herself with following him with her eyes, less like a faithful dog than a big Angora cat, observing everything and every movement of her master.

When he looked around, he saw, by the spring, the remains of his horse; the panther had dragged the carcass all that way; about two-thirds of it had been devoured already. The sight reassured him.

It was easy to explain the panther's absence, and the respect she had had for him while he slept. The first piece of good luck emboldened him to tempt the future, and he conceived the wild hope of continuing on good terms with the panther during the entire day, neglecting no means of taming her, and remaining in her good graces.

He returned to her, and had the unspeakable joy of seeing her wag her tail with an almost imperceptible movement at his approach. He sat down then, without fear, by her side, and they began to play together; he took her paws and muzzle, pulled her ears, rolled her over on her back, stroked her warm, delicate flanks. She let him do whatever he liked, and when he began to stroke the hair on her feet she drew her claws in carefully.

The man, keeping the dagger in one hand, thought to plunge it into the belly of the too-confiding panther, but he was afraid that he would be immediately strangled in her last conclusive struggle;

besides, he felt in his heart a sort of remorse which bid him respect a creature that had done him no harm. He seemed to have found a friend, in a boundless desert; half unconsciously he thought of his first sweetheart, whom he had nicknamed "Mignonne" by way of contrast, because she was so atrociously jealous that all the time of their love he was in fear of the knife with which she had always threatened him.

This memory of his early days suggested to him the idea of making the young panther answer to this name, now that he began to admire with less terror her swiftness, suppleness, and softness. Toward the end of the day he had familiarized himself with his perilous position; he now almost liked the painfulness of it. At last his companion had got into the habit of looking up at him whenever he cried in a falsetto voice, "Mignonne."

At the setting of the sun Mignonne gave, several times running, a profound melancholy cry. "She's been well brought up," said the light-hearted soldier; "she says her prayers." But this mental joke only occurred to him when he noticed what a pacific attitude his companion remained in. "Come, *ma petite blonde*, I'll let you go to bed first," he said to her, counting on the activity of his own legs to run away as quickly as possible, directly she was asleep, and seek another shelter for the night.

The soldier waited with impatience the hour of his flight, and when it had arrived he walked vigorously in the direction of the Nile; but hardly had he made a quarter of a league in the sand when he heard the panther bounding after him, crying with that saw-like cry more dreadful even than the sound of her leaping.

"Ah!" he said, "then she's taken a fancy to me; she has never met any one before, and it is really quite flattering to have her first love." That instant the man fell into one of those movable quicksands so terrible to travellers and from which it is impossible to save oneself. Feeling himself caught, he gave a shriek of alarm; the panther seized him with her teeth by the collar, and, springing vigorously backward, drew him as if by magic out of the whirling sand.

"Ah, Mignonne!" cried the soldier, caressing her enthusiastically; "we're bound together for life and death—but no jokes, mind!" and he retraced his steps.

From that time the desert seemed inhabited. It contained a being to whom the man could talk, and whose ferocity was rendered gentle by him, though he could not explain to himself the reason for their strange friendship. Great as was the soldier's desire to stay upon guard, he slept.

On awakening he could not find Mignonne; he mounted the hill, and in the distance saw her springing toward him after the habit of these animals, who cannot run on account of the extreme flexibility of the vertebral column. Mignonne arrived, her jaws covered with blood; she received the wonted caress of her companion, showing with much purring how happy it made her. Her eyes, full of languor, turned still more gently than the day before toward the Provençal who talked to her as one would to a tame animal.

"Ah! Mademoiselle, you are a nice girl, aren't you? Just look at that! so we like to be made much of, don't we? Aren't you ashamed of yourself? So you have been eating some Arab or other, have you? that doesn't matter. They're animals just the same as you are; but don't you take to eating Frenchmen, or I shan't like you any longer."

She played like a dog with its master, letting herself be rolled over, knocked about, and stroked, alternately; sometimes she herself would provoke the soldier, putting up her paw with a soliciting gesture.

Some days passed in this manner. This companionship permitted the Provençal to appreciate the sublime beauty of the desert; now that he had a living thing to think about, alternations of fear and quiet, and plenty to eat, his mind became filled with contrast and his life began to be diversified.

Solitude revealed to him all her secrets, and enveloped him in her delights. He discovered in the rising and setting of the sun sights unknown to the world. He knew what it was to tremble when he heard over his head the hiss of a bird's wing, so rarely did they pass, or when he saw the clouds, changing and many-colored travellers, melt one into another. He studied in the night time the effect of the moon upon the ocean of sand, where the simoom made waves swift of movement and rapid in their change. He lived the life of the Eastern day, marvelling at its wonderful pomp; then, after having revelled in the sight of a hurricane over the plain where the whirling sands made red, dry mists and death-bearing clouds, he would welcome the night with joy, for then fell the healthful freshness of the stars, and he listened to imaginary music in the skies.

Then solitude taught him to unroll the treasures of dreams. He passed whole hours in remembering mere nothings, and comparing his present life with his past.

At last he grew passionately fond of the panther; for some sort of affection was a necessity.

Whether it was that his will powerfully projected had modified the character of his companion, or whether, because she found abundant food in her predatory excursions in the desert, she respected the man's life, he began to fear for it no longer, seeing her so well tamed.

He devoted the greater part of his time to sleep, but he was obliged to watch like a spider in its web that the moment of his deliverence might not escape him, if any one should pass the line marked by the horizon. He had sacrificed his shirt to make a flag with, which he hung at the top of a palm tree, whose foliage he had torn off. Taught by necessity, he found the means of keeping it spread out, by fastening it with little sticks; for the wind might not be blowing at the moment when the passing traveller was looking through the desert.

It was during the long hours, when he had abandoned hope, that he amused himself with the panther. He had come to learn the different inflections of her voice, the expressions of her eyes; he had studied the capricious patterns of all the rosettes which marked the gold of her robe. Mignonne was not even angry when he took hold of the tuft at the end of her tail to count her rings, those graceful ornaments which glittered in the sun like jewelry. It gave him pleasure to contemplate the supple, fine outlines of her form, the whiteness of her belly, the graceful pose of her head. But it was especially when she was playing that he felt most pleasure in looking at her; the agility and youthful lightness of her movements were a continual surprise to him; he wondered at the supple way in which she jumped and climbed, washed herself and arranged her fur, crouched down and prepared to spring. However rapid her spring might be, however slippery the stone she was on, she would always stop short at the word "Mignonne."

One day, in a bright mid-day sun, an enormous bird coursed through the air. The man left his panther to look at this new guest; but after waiting a moment the deserted sultana growled deeply.

"My goodness! I do believe she's jealous," he cried, seeing her eyes become hard again; "the soul of Virginie has passed into her body; that's certain."

The eagle disappeared into the air, while the soldier admired the curved contour of the panther.

But there was such youth and grace in her form! she was beautiful as a woman! the blond fur of her robe mingled well with the delicate tints of faint white which marked her flanks.

The profuse light cast down by the sun made this living gold, these russet markings, to burn in a way to give them an indefinable attraction.

The man and the panther looked at one another with a look full of meaning; the coquette quivered when she felt her friend stroke her head; her eyes flashed like lightning—then she shut them tightly.

"She has a soul," he said, looking at the stillness of this queen of the sands, golden like them, white like them, solitary and burning like them.

"Well," she said, "I have read your plea in favor of beasts; but how did two so well adapted to understand each other end?"

"Ah, well! you see, they ended as all great passions do end—by a misunderstanding. For some reason *one* suspects the other of treason; they don't come to an explanation through pride, and quarrel and part from sheer obstinacy."

"Yet sometimes at the best moments a single word or a look is enough—but anyhow go on with your story."

"It's horribly difficult, but you will understand, after what the old villain told me over his champagne.

"He said—'I don't know if I hurt her, but she turned round, as if enraged, and with her sharp teeth caught hold of my leg—gently, I daresay; but I, thinking she would devour me, plunged my dagger into her throat. She rolled over, giving a cry that froze my heart; and I saw her dying, still looking at me without anger. I would have given all the world—my cross even, which I had not got then—to have brought her to life again. It was as though I had murdered a real person; and the soldiers who had seen my flag, and were come to my assistance, found me in tears.'

" 'Well sir,' he said, after a moment of silence, 'since then I have been in war in Germany, in Spain, in Russia, in France; I've certainly carried my carcass about a good deal, but never have I seen anything like the desert. Ah! yes, it is very beautiful!'

" 'What did you feel there?' I asked him.

" 'Oh! that can't be described, young man. Besides, I am not always regretting my palm trees and my panther. I should have to be very melancholy for that. In the desert, you see, there is everything, and nothing.'

" 'Yes, but explain——'

" 'Well,' he said, with an impatient gesture, 'it is God without mankind.' "

BALZAC: *A Passion in the Desert*

1. On the literal level, "A Passion in the Desert" suggests an adventure story, but some study will show that Balzac's ambition is not limited to an account of mere adventure. Where do you find clues that this is more than an adventure story? What is the real purpose of the author?

2. In connection with the above questions, what part does the desert play in conveying the author's meaning? Is it more or less pervasive in its importance than Gorki's dough factory, Joyce's Dublin, Lawrence's three islands, or Beckett's hospital?

3. Can you explain Balzac's description of the desert as "God without mankind"? Is this vision fully explicable? Why not? How does Balzac attempt to communicate it? Does his vision have any relation to the vision in Hesse's "Within and Without"?

4. What is meant by this line: "The silence was awful in its wild and terrible majesty." ?

5. What possibilities does the relationship between the Frenchman and the panther suggest? Why does Balzac describe the relationship in terms of a love affair when evidently he means much more than that?

6. Must the beast be a panther? Would a goat or a camel or a dog serve as well? Why?

7. Both Balzac's Frenchman and Sartre's Ibbieta face destruction, yet the reaction of one is vastly different from that of the other. What does this difference tell you about the authors, and particularly about their points of view, one from the early nineteenth century, the other from the twentieth? which one do you find truer to human experience?

Nathaniel Hawthorne:

MY KINSMAN, MAJOR MOLINEUX

Nathaniel Hawthorne was born in Salem, Massachusetts, in 1804. After winning notice with his short stories (collected in Twice-Told Tales*), he entered the Brook Farm Institute, a famous literary and economic community of a Utopian nature. There he came to know Emerson, Thoreau, Margaret Fuller, and other transcendentalists who were shaping New England's intellectual life. Beginning in 1850, with* The Scarlet Letter, *Hawthorne published the somber novels on which his reputation rests:* The House of the Seven Gables (1851); The Blithedale Romance (1852), *which gives a picture of the Brook Farm experiment; and* The Marble Faun (1860). *Approximately a century after his death in 1864, Hawthorne is regarded as one of the greatest American literary figures of the nineteenth century and a powerful influence upon the supernatural themes of Henry James. The following story is characteristic of Hawthorne in its blend of realism and melodrama, and in its preoccupation with darkness, Gothic imagery, and the mysteries of human behavior.*

ᗡᗅ

AFTER the kings of Great Britain had assumed the right of appointing the colonial governors, the measures of the latter seldom met with the ready and generous approbation which had been paid to those of their predecessors, under the original charters. The people looked with most jealous scrutiny to the exercise of power which did not emanate from themselves, and they usually rewarded their rulers with slender gratitude for the compliances by which, in softening their instructions from beyond the sea, they had incurred the reprehension of those who gave them. The annals of Massachusetts Bay will inform us, that of six governors in the space of about forty years from the surrender of the old charter, under James II, two were imprisoned by a popular insurrection; a third, as Hutchinson inclines to believe, was driven from the province by the whizzing of a mus-

[27

ket-ball; a fourth, in the opinion of the same historian, was hastened
to his grave by continual bickerings with the House of Representa-
tives, and the remaining two, as well as their successors, till the
Revolution, were favored with few and brief intervals of peaceful
sway. The inferior members of the court party, in times of high political excitement, led scarcely a more desirable life. These remarks
may serve as a preface to the following adventures, which chanced
upon a summer night, not far from a hundred years ago. The reader,
in order to avoid a long and dry detail of colonial affairs, is requested
to dispense with an account of the train of circumstances that had
caused much temporary inflammation of the popular mind.

It was near nine o'clock of a moonlight evening, when a boat
crossed the ferry with a single passenger, who had obtained his
conveyance at that unusual hour by the promise of an extra fare.
While he stood on the landing-place, searching in either pocket for
the means of fulfilling his agreement, the ferryman lifted a lantern,
by the aid of which, and the newly risen moon, he took a very ac-
curate survey of the stranger's figure. He was a youth of barely
eighteen years, evidently country-bred, and now, as it should seem,
upon his first visit to town. He was clad in a coarse gray coat, well
worn, but in excellent repair; his under garments were durably constructed of leather, and fitted tight to a pair of serviceable and well-
shaped limbs; his stockings of blue yarn were the incontrovertible
work of a mother or a sister; and on his head was a three-cornered
hat, which in its better days had perhaps sheltered the graver brow
of the lad's father. Under the left arm was a heavy cudgel formed of
an oak sapling, and retaining a part of the hardened root; and his
equipment was completed by a wallet, not so abundantly stocked
as to incommode the vigorous shoulders on which it hung. Brown,
curly hair, well-shaped features, and bright, cheerful eyes were
nature's gifts, and worth all that art could have done for his adornment.

The youth, one of whose names was Robin, finally drew from his
pocket the half of a little province bill of five shillings which, in the
depreciation in that sort of currency, did but satisfy the ferryman's
demand, with the surplus of a sexanagular piece of parchment,
valued at three pence. He then walked forward into the town,
with as light a step as if his day's journey had not already exceeded

thirty miles, and with as eager an eye as if he were entering London city, instead of the little metropolis of a New England colony. Before Robin had proceeded far, however, it occurred to him that he knew not whither to direct his steps; so he paused, and looked up and down the narrow street, scrutinizing the small and mean wooden buildings that were scattered on either side.

"This low hovel cannot be my kinsman's dwelling," thought he, "nor yonder old house, where the moonlight enters at the broken casement; and truly I see none hereabouts that might be worthy of him. It would have been wise to inquire my way of the ferryman, and doubtless he would have gone with me, and earned a shilling from the Major for his pains. But the next man I meet will do as well."

He resumed his walk, and was glad to perceive that the street now became wider and the houses more respectable in their appearance. He soon discerned a figure moving on moderately in advance, and hastened his steps to overtake it. As Robin drew nigh, he saw that the passenger was a man in years, with a full periwig of gray hair, a wide-skirted coat of dark cloth, and silk stockings rolled above his knees. He carried a long and polished cane, which he struck down perpendicularly before him at every step; and at regular intervals he uttered two successive hems, of a peculiarly solemn and sepulchral intonation. Having made these observations, Robin laid hold of the skirt of the old man's coat, just when the light from the open door and windows of a barber's shop fell upon both their figures.

"Good evening to you, honored sir," said he, making a low bow, and still retaining his hold of the skirt. "I pray you tell me whereabouts is the dwelling of my kinsman, Major Molineux."

The youth's question was uttered very loudly; and one of the barbers, whose razor was descending on a well-soaped chin, and another who was dressing a Ramillies wig, left their occupations, and came to the door. The citizen, in the meantime, turned a long-favored countenance upon Robin, and answered him in a tone of excessive anger and annoyance. His two sepulchral hems, however, broke into the very center of his rebuke, with most singular effect, like a thought of the cold grave obtruding among wrathful passions.

"Let go my garment, fellow! I tell you, I know not the man you speak of. What! I have authority, I have—hem, hem—authority;

and if this be the respect you show for your betters, your feet shall be brought acquainted with the stocks by daylight, tomorrow morning!"

Robin released the old man's skirt, and hastened away, pursued by an ill-mannered roar of laughter from the barber's shop. He was at first considerably surprised by the result of the question, but, being a shrewd youth, soon thought himself able to account for the mystery.

"This is some country representative," was his conclusion, "who has never seen the inside of my kinsman's door, and lacks the breeding to answer a stranger civilly. The man is old, or verily—I might be tempted to turn back and smite him on the nose. Ah, Robin, Robin! even the barber's boys laugh at you for choosing such a guide! You will be wiser in time, friend Robin."

He now became entangled in a succession of crooked and narrow streets, which crossed each other, and meandered at no great distance from the water-side. The smell of tar was obvious to his nostrils, the masts of vessels pierced the moonlight above the tops of the buildings, and the numerous signs, which Robin paused to read, informed him that he was near the center of business. But the streets were empty, the shops were closed, and lights were visible only in the second stories of a few dwelling-houses. At length, on the corner of a narrow lane, through which he was passing, he beheld the broad countenance of a British hero swinging before the door of an inn, whence proceeded the voices of many guests. The casement of one of the lower windows was thrown back, and a very thin curtain permitted Robin to distinguish a party at supper, round a well-furnished table. The fragrance of the good cheer steamed forth into the outer air, and the youth could not fail to recollect that the last remnant of his travelling stock of provision had yielded to his morning appetite and that noon had found and left him dinnerless.

"Oh, that a parchment three-penny might give me a right to sit down at yonder table!" said Robin, with a sigh. "But the Major will make me welcome to the best of his victuals so I will even step boldly in, and inquire my way to his dwelling."

He entered the tavern, and was guided by the murmur of voices and the fumes of tobacco to the public-room. It was a long and low apartment, with oaken walls, grown dark in the continual smoke, and a floor which was thickly sanded, but of no immaculate purity. A number of persons—the larger part of whom appeared to be mariners, or in some way connected with the sea—occupied the wooden benches, or leather-bottomed chairs, conversing on various matters, and occasionally lending their attention to some topic of general interest. Three or four little groups were draining as many bowls of punch, which the West India trade had long since made a familiar drink in the colony. Others, who had the appearance of men who lived by regular and laborious handicraft, preferred the insulated bliss of an unshared potation, and became more taciturn under its influence. Nearly all, in short, evinced a predilection for the Good Creature in some of its various shapes, for this is a vice to which, as Fast Day sermons of a hundred years ago will testify, we have a long hereditary claim. The only guests to whom Robin's sympathies inclined him were two or three sheepish countrymen, who were using the inn somewhat after the fashion of a Turkish caravansary; they had gotten themselves into the darkest corner of the room, and heedless of the Nicotian atmosphere, were supping on the bread of their own ovens, and the bacon cured in their own chimney-smoke. But though Robin felt a sort of brotherhood with these strangers, his eyes were attracted from them to a person who stood near the door, holding whispered conversation with a group of ill-dressed associates. His features were separately striking almost to grotesqueness, and the whole face left a deep impression on the memory. The forehead bulged out into a double prominence, with a vale between; the nose came boldly forth in an irregular curve, and its bridge was of more than a finger's breadth; the eyebrows were deep and shaggy, and the eyes glowed beneath them like fire in a cave.

While Robin deliberated of whom to inquire respecting his kinsman's dwelling, he was accosted by the innkeeper, a little man in a stained white apron, who had come to pay his professional welcome to the stranger. Being in the second generation from a French Protestant, he seemed to have inherited the courtesy of his parent nation; but no variety of circumstances was ever known to change his voice from the one shrill note in which he now addressed Robin.

"From the country, I presume, sir?" said he, with a profound bow. "Beg leave to congratulate you on your arrival, and trust you intend a long stay with us. Fine town here, sir, beautiful buildings, and much that may interest a stranger. May I hope for the honor of your commands in respect to supper?"

"The man sees a family likeness! the rogue has guessed that I am related to the Major!" thought Robin, who had hitherto experienced little superfluous civility.

All eyes were now turned on the country lad, standing at the door, in his worn three-cornered hat, gray coat, leather breeches, and blue yarn stockings, leaning on an oaken cudgel, and bearing a wallet on his back.

Robin replied to the courteous innkeeper, with such an assumption of confidence as befitted the Major's relative. "My honest friend," he said, "I shall make it a point to patronize your house on some occasion, when"—here he could not help lowering his voice—"when I may have more than a parchment three-pence in my pocket. My present business," continued he, speaking with lofty confidence, "is merely to inquire my way to the dwelling of my kinsman, Major Molineux."

There was a sudden and general movement in the room, which Robin interpreted as expressing the eagerness of each individual to become his guide. But the innkeeper turned his eyes to a written paper on the wall, which he read, or seemed to read, with occasional recurrences to the young man's figure.

"What have we here?" said he, breaking his speech into little dry fragments. " 'Left the house of the subscriber, bounden servant, Hezekiah Mudge,—had on, when he went away, gray coat, leather breeches, master's third-best hat. One pound currency reward to whosoever shall lodge him in any jail of the providence.' Better trudge, boy; better trudge!"

Robin had begun to draw his hand towards the lighter end of the oak cudgel, but a strange hostility in every countenance induced him to relinquish his purpose of breaking the courteous innkeeper's head. As he turned to leave the room, he encountered a sneering glance from the bold-featured personage whom he had before noticed; and no sooner was he beyond the door, than he heard a general laugh, in which the innkeeper's voice might be distinguished, like the dropping of small stones into a kettle.

"Now, is it not strange," thought Robin, with his usual shrewdness,—"is it not strange that the confession of an empty pocket should outweigh the name of my kinsman, Major Molineux? Oh, if I had one of those grinning rascals in the woods, where I and my oak sapling grew together, I would teach him that my arm is heavy though my purse be light!"

On turning the corner of the narrow lane, Robin found himself in a spacious street, with an unbroken line of lofty houses on each side, and a steepled building at the upper end, whence the ringing of a bell announced the hour of nine. The light of the moon, and the lamps from the numerous shop-windows, discovered people promenading on the pavement, and amongst them Robin had hoped to recognize his hitherto inscrutable relative. The result of his former inquiries made him unwilling to hazard another, in a scene of such publicity, and he determined to walk slowly and silently up the street, thrusting his face close to that of every elderly gentleman, in search of the Major's lineaments. In his progress, Robin encountered many gay and gallant figures. Embroidered garments of showy colors, enormous periwigs, gold-laced hats, and silver-hilted swords glided past him and dazzled his optics. Travelled youths, imitators of the European fine gentlemen of the period, trod jauntily along, half dancing to the fashionable tunes which they hummed, and making poor Robin ashamed of his quiet and natural gait. At length, after many pauses to examine the gorgeous display of goods in the shop-windows, and after suffering some rebukes for the impertinence of his scrutiny into people's faces, the Major's kinsman found himself near the steepled building, still unsuccessful in his search. As yet, however, he had seen only one side of the thronged street; so Robin crossed, and continued the same sort of inquisition down the opposite pavement, with stronger hopes than the philosopher seeking an honest man, but with no better fortune. He had arrived about midway towards the lower end, from which his course began, when he overheard the approach of some one who struck down a cane on the flag-stones at every step, uttering at regular intervals, two sepulchral hems.

"Mercy on us!" quoth Robin, recognizing the sound.

Turning a corner, which chanced to be close at his right hand, he hastened to pursue his researches in some other part of the town. His patience now was wearing low, and he seemed to feel more fatigue from his rambles since he crossed the ferry, than from his journey of several days on the other side. Hunger also pleaded loudly within him, and Robin began to balance the propriety of demanding, violently, and with lifted cudgel, the necessary guidance from the first solitary passenger whom he should meet. While a resolution to this effect was gaining strength, he entered a street of mean appearance, on either side of which a row of ill-built houses was straggling towards the harbor. The moonlight fell upon no passenger along the whole extent, but in the third domicile which Robin passed there was a half-open door, and his keen glance detected a woman's garment within.

"My luck may be better here," said he to himself.

Accordingly, he approached the door, and beheld it shut closer as he did so; yet an open space remained, sufficing for the fair occupant to observe the stranger, without a corresponding displaying on her part. All that Robin could discern was a strip of scarlet petticoat, and the occasional sparkle of an eye, as if the moonbeams were trembling on some bright thing.

"Pretty mistress," for I may call her so with a good conscience, thought the shrewd youth, since I know nothing to the contrary,— "my sweet pretty mistress, will you be kind enough to tell me whereabouts I must seek the dwelling of my kinsman, Major Molineux?"

Robin's voice was plaintive and winning, and the female, seeing nothing to be shunned in the handsome country youth, thrust open the door, and came forth into the moonlight. She was a dainty little figure, with a white neck, round arms, and a tender waist, at the extremity of which her scarlet petticoat jutted out over a hoop, as if she were standing in a balloon. Moreover, her face was oval and pretty, her hair dark beneath the little cap, and her bright eyes possessed a sly freedom, which triumphed over those of Robin.

"Major Molineux dwells here," said this fair woman.

Now, her voice was the sweetest Robin had heard that night, yet he could not help doubting whether that sweet voice spoke Gospel truth. He looked up and down the mean street, and then surveyed the house before which they stood. It was a small dark edifice of two stories, the second of which projected over the lower floor, and the front apartment had the aspect of a shop for petty commodities.

"Now, truly, I am in luck," replied Robin cunningly, "and so indeed is my kinsman, the Major, in having so pretty a housekeeper.

But I prithee trouble him to step to the door; I will deliver him a message from his friends in the country, and then go back to my lodgings at the inn."

"Nay, the Major has been abed this hour or more," said the lady of the scarlet petticoat; "and it would be to little purpose to disturb him to-night, seeing his evening draught was of the strongest. But he is a kind-hearted man, and it would be as much as my life's worth to let a kinsman of his turn away from the door. You are the good old gentleman's very picture, and I could swear that was his rainy-weather hat. Also he has garments very much resembling those leather small-clothes. But come in, I pray, for I bid you hearty welcome in his name."

So saying, the fair and hospitable dame took our hero by the hand; and the touch was light, and the force was gentleness, and though Robin read in her eyes what he did not hear in her words, yet the slender-waisted woman in the scarlet petticoat proved stronger than the athletic country youth. She had drawn his half-willing footsteps nearly to the threshold, when the opening of a door in the neighborhood startled the Major's housekeeper, and, leaving the Major's kinsman, she vanished speedily into her own domicile. A heavy yawn preceded the appearance of a man, who, like the Moonshine of Pyramus and Thisbe, carried a lantern, needlessly aiding his sister luminary in the heavens. As he walked sleepily up the street, he turned his broad, dull face on Robin, and displayed a long staff, spiked at the end.

"Home, vagabond, home!" said the watchman, in accents that seemed to fall asleep as soon as they were uttered. "Home, or we'll set you in the stocks by peep of day!"

"This is the second hint of the kind," thought Robin. "I wish they would end my difficulties by setting me there to-night."

Nevertheless, the youth felt an instinctive antipathy towards the guardian of midnight order, which at first prevented him from asking his usual question. But just when the man was about to vanish behind the corner, Robin resolved not to lose the opportunity, and shouted lustily after him,—

"I say, friend! will you guide me to the house of my kinsman, Major Molineux?"

The watchman made no reply, but turned the corner and was gone; yet Robin seemed to hear the sound of drowsy laughter steal-

ing along the solitary street. At that moment, also, a pleasant titter saluted him from the open window above his head; he looked
up, and caught the sparkle of a saucy eye, a round arm beckoned
to him, and next he heard light footsteps descending the staircase
within. But Robin, being of the household of a New England clergyman, was a good youth, as well as a shrewd one; so he resisted
temptation, and fled away.

He now roamed desperately, and at random, through the town,
almost ready to believe that a spell was on him, like that by which
a wizard of his country had once kept three pursuers wandering, a
whole winter night, within twenty paces of the cottage which they
sought. The streets lay before him, strange and desolate, and the
lights were extinguished in almost every house. Twice, however,
little parties of men, among whom Robin distinguished individuals
in outlandish attire, came hurrying along; but though on both occasions, they paused to address him, such intercourse did not at all
enlighten his perplexity. They did but utter a few words in some
language of which Robin knew nothing, and perceiving his inability to answer, bestowed a curse upon him in plain English and hastened away. Finally, the lad determined to knock at the door of every mansion that might appear worthy to be occupied by his kinsman, trusting that perseverance would overcome the fatality that
had hitherto thwarted him. Firm in this resolve, he was passing beneath the walls of a church, which formed the corner of two streets,
when, as he turned into the shade of its steeple, he encountered a
bulky stranger, muffled in a cloak. The man was proceeding with
the speed of earnest business, but Robin planted himself full before
him, holding the oak cudgel with both hands across his body as a
bar to further passage.

"Halt, honest man, and answer me a question," said he, very resolutely. "Tell me, this instant, whereabouts is the dwelling of my
kinsman, Major Molineux!"

"Keep your tongue between your teeth, fool, and let me pass!"
said a deep, gruff voice, which Robin partly remembered. "Let me
pass, or I'll strike you to the earth!"

"No, no, neighbor!" cried Robin, flourishing his cudgel, and
then thrusting its larger end close to the man's muffled face. "No,
no, I'm not the fool you take me for, nor do you pass till I have an

answer to my question. Whereabouts is the dwelling of my kinsman, Major Molineux?"

The stranger, instead of attempting to force his passage, stepped back into the moonlight, unmuffled his face, and stared full into that of Robin.

"Watch here an hour, and Major Molineux will pass by," said he.

Robin gazed with dismay and astonishment on the unprecedented physiognomy of the speaker. The forehead with its double prominence, the broad hooked nose, the shaggy eyebrows, and fiery eyes were those which he had noticed at the inn, but the man's complexion had undergone a singular, or, more properly, a twofold change. One side of the face blazed in intense red, while the other was black as midnight, the division line being the broad bridge of the nose; and a mouth which seemed to extend from ear to ear was black or red, in contrast to the color of the cheek. The effect was as if two individual devils, a fiend of fire and a fiend of darkness, had united themselves to form this infernal visage. The stranger grinned in Robin's face, muffled his party-colored features, and was out of sight in a moment.

"Strange things we travellers see!" ejaculated Robin.

He seated himself, however, upon the steps of the church-door, resolving to wait the appointed time for his kinsman. A few moments were consumed in philosophical speculations upon the species of man who had just left him; but having settled this point shrewdly, rationally, and satisfactorily, he was compelled to look elsewhere for his amusement. And first he threw his eyes along the street. It was of more respectable appearance than most of those into which he had wandered; and the moon, creating, like the imaginative power, a beautiful strangeness in familiar objects, gave something of romance to a scene that might not have possessed it in the light of day. The irregular and often quaint architecture of the houses, some of whose roofs were broken into numerous little peaks, while others ascended, steep and narrow, into a single point, and others again were square; the pure snow-white of some of their complexions, the aged darkness of others, and the thousand sparklings, reflected from bright substances in the walls of many; these matters engaged Robin's attention for a while, and then began to grow wearisome. Next he endeavored to define the forms of distant objects, starting away, with almost ghostly indistinctness, just as his eye appeared to grasp them; and finally he took a minute survey of an edifice which stood on the opposite side of the street, directly in front of the church-door, where he was stationed. It was a large, square mansion, distinguished from its neighbors by a balcony which rested on tall pillars, and by an elaborate Gothic window, communicating therewith.

"Perhaps this is the very house I have been seeking," thought Robin.

Then he strove to speed away the time by listening to a murmur which swept continually along the street, yet was scarcely audible, except to an unaccustomed ear like his; it was a low, dull, dreamy sound, compounded of many noises, each of which was at too great a distance to be separately heard. Robin marvelled at this snore of a sleeping town, and marvelled more whenever its continuity was broken by now and then a distant shout, apparently loud where it originated. But altogether it was a sleep-inspiring sound, and, to shake off its drowsy influence, Robin arose, and climbed a window-frame, that he might view the interior of the church. There the moonbeams came trembling in, and fell down upon the deserted pews, and extended along the quiet aisles. A fainter yet more awful radiance was hovering around the pulpit, and the solitary ray had dared to rest upon the open page of the great Bible. Had nature, in that deep hour, become a worshipper in the house which man had builded? Or was that heavenly light the visible sanctity of the place,—visible because no earthly and impure feet were within the walls? The scene made Robin's heart shiver with a sensation of loneliness stronger than he had ever felt in the remotest depths of his native woods; so he turned away and sat down again before the door. There were graves around the church, and now an uneasy thought obtruded into Robin's breast. What if the object of his search, which had been so often and so strangely thwarted, were all the time mouldering in his shroud? What if his kinsman should glide through yonder gate, and nod and smile to him in dimly passing by?

"Oh, that any breathing thing were here with me!" said Robin.

Recalling his thoughts from this uncomfortable track, he sent them over forest, hill, and stream, and attempted to imagine how that evening of ambiguity and weariness had been spent by his father's household. He pictured them assembled at the door, beneath the tree, the great old tree, which had been spared for its huge twisted trunk and venerable shade, when a thousand leafy brethren fell. There, at the going down of the summer sun, it was his father's custom to perform domestic worship, that the neighbors might come and join with him like brothers of the family, and that the wayfaring man might pause to drink at that fountain, and keep his heart pure by freshening the memory of home. Robin distinguished the seat of every individual of the little audience; he saw the good man in the midst, holding the Scriptures in the golden light that fell from the western clouds; he beheld him close the book and all rise up to pray. He heard the old thanksgivings for daily mercies, the old supplications for their continuance, to which he had so often listened in weariness, but which were now among his dear remembrances. He perceived the slight inequality of his father's voice when he came to speak of the absent one; he noted how his mother turned her face to the broad and knotted trunk; how his elder brother scorned, because the beard was rough upon his upper lip, to permit his features to be moved; how the younger sister drew down a low hanging branch before her eyes; and how the little one of all, whose sports had hitherto broken the decorum of the scene, understood the prayer for her playmate, and burst into clamorous grief. Then he saw them go in at the door; and when Robin would have entered also, the latch tinkled into its place, and he was excluded from his home.

"Am I here, or there?" cried Robin, starting; for all at once, when his thoughts had become visible and audible in a dream, the long, wide, solitary street shone out before him.

He aroused himself, and endeavored to fix his attention steadily upon the large edifice which he had surveyed before. But still his mind kept vibrating between fancy and reality; by turns, the pillars of the balcony lengthened into the tall, bare stems of pines, dwindled down to human figures, settled again into their true shape and size, and then commenced a new succession of changes. For a single moment, when he deemed himself awake, he could have sworn that a visage—one which he seemed to remember, yet could not absolutely name as his kinsman's—was looking towards him from the Gothic window. A deeper sleep wrestled with and nearly overcame him, but fled at the sound of footsteps along the opposite pavement. Robin rubbed his eyes, discerned a man passing at the foot of the balcony, and addressed him in a loud, peevish, and lamentable cry.

"Hallo, friend! must I wait here all night for my kinsman, Major Molineux?"

The sleeping echoes awoke, and answered the voice; and the passenger, barely able to discern a figure sitting in the oblique shade of the steeple, traversed the street to obtain a nearer view. He was himself a gentleman in his prime, of open, intelligent, cheerful and altogether prepossessing countenance. Perceiving a country youth, apparently homeless and without friends, he accosted him in a tone of real kindness, which had become strange to Robin's ears.

"Well, my good lad, why are you sitting here?" inquired he. "Can I be of service to you in any way?"

"I am afraid not, sir," replied Robin, despondingly; "yet I shall take it kindly, if you'll answer me a single question. I've been searching, half the night, for one Major Molineux; now, sir, is there really such a person in these parts, or am I dreaming?"

"Major Molineux! The name is not altogether strange to me," said the gentleman, smiling. "Have you any objection to telling me the nature of your business with him?"

Then Robin briefly related that his father was a clergyman, settled on a small salary, at a long distance back in the country, and that he and Major Molineux were brothers' children. The Major, having inherited riches, and acquired civil and military rank, had visited his cousin, in great pomp, a year or two before; had manifested much interest in Robin and an elder brother, and, being childless himself, had thrown out hints respecting the future establishment of one of them in life. The elder brother was destined to succeed to the farm which his father cultivated in the interval of sacred duties; it was therefore determined that Robin should profit by his kinsman's generous intentions, especially as he seemed to be rather the favorite, and was thought to possess other necessary endowments.

"For I have the name of being a shrewd youth," observed Robin, in this part of his story.

"I doubt not you deserve it," replied his new friend, good-naturedly; "but pray proceed."

"Well, sir, being nearly eighteen years old, and well grown, as you see," continued Robin, drawing himself up to his full height, "I thought it high time to begin in the world. So my mother and sister put me in handsome trim, and my father gave me half the remnant of his last year's salary, and five days ago I started for this place, to pay the Major a visit. But, would you believe it, sir! I crossed the ferry a little after dark, and have yet found nobody that would show me the way to his dwelling; only, an hour or two since, I was told to wait here, and Major Molineux would pass by."

"Can you describe the man who told you this?" inquired the gentleman.

"Oh, he was a very ill-favored fellow, sir," replied Robin, "with two great bumps on his forehead, a hook nose, fiery eyes; and what struck me as the strangest, his face was of two different colors. Do you happen to know such a man, sir?"

"Not intimately," answered the stranger, "but I chanced to meet him a little time previous to your stopping me. I believe you may trust his word, and that the Major will very shortly pass through this street in the mean time, as I have a singular curiosity to witness your meeting, I will sit down here upon the steps and bear you company."

He seated himself accordingly, and soon engaged his companion in animated discourse. It was but of brief continuance, however, for a noise of shouting, which had long been remotely audible, drew so much nearer that Robin inquired its cause.

"What may be the meaning of this uproar?" asked he. "Truly, if your town be always as noisy, I shall find little sleep while I am an inhabitant."

"Why, indeed, friend Robin, there do appear to be three or four riotous fellows abroad to-night," replied the gentleman. "You must not expect all the stillness of your native woods here in our streets. But the watch will shortly be at the heels of these lads and"—

"Ay, and set them in the stocks by peep of day," interrupted Robin, recollecting his own encounter with the drowsy lantern-bearer. "But, dear sir, if I may trust my ears, an army of watchmen would never make head against such a multitude of rioters. There were at least a thousand voices went up to make that one shout."

"May not a man have several voices, Robin, as well as two complexions?" said his friend.

"Perhaps a man may; but Heaven forbid that a woman should!" responded the shrewd youth, thinking of the seductive tones of the Major's housekeeper.

The sounds of a trumpet in some neighboring street now became so evident and continual, that Robin's curiosity was strongly excited. In addition to the shouts, he heard frequent bursts from many instruments of discord, and a wild and confused laughter filled up the intervals. Robin rose from the steps, and looked wistfully towards a point whither people seemed to be hastening.

"Surely some prodigious merry-making is going on," exclaimed he. "I have laughed very little since I left home, sir, and should be sorry to lose an opportunity. Shall we step round the corner by that darkish house, and take our share of the fun?"

"Sit down again, sit down, good Robin," replied the gentleman, laying his hand on the skirt of the gray coat. "You forget that we must wait here for your kinsman; and there is reason to believe that he will pass by, in the course of a very few moments."

The near approach of the uproar had now disturbed the neighborhood; windows flew open on all sides; and many heads, in the attire of the pillow, and confused by sleep suddenly broken, were protruded to the gaze of whoever had leisure to observe them. Eager voices hailed each other from house to house, all demanding the explanation, which not a soul could give. Half-dressed men hurried towards the unknown commotion, stumbling as they went over the stone steps that thrust themselves into the narrow footwalk. The shouts, the laughter, and the tuneless bray, the antipodes of music, came onwards with increasing din, till scattered individuals, and then denser bodies began to appear round a corner at the distance of a hundred yards.

"Will you recognize your kinsman, if he passes in this crowd?" inquired the gentleman.

"Indeed, I can't warrant it, sir; but I'll take my stand here, and keep a bright look-out," answered Robin, descending to the outer edge of the pavement.

A mighty stream of people now emptied into the street and came rolling slowly towards the church. A single horseman wheeled the corner in the midst of them, and close behind him came a band of fearful wind-instruments, sending forth a fresher discord now that no intervening buildings kept it from the ear.

Then a redder light disturbed the moonbeams, and a dense multitude of torches shone along the street concealing, by their glare,
whatever object they illuminated. The single horseman, clad in a
military dress, and bearing a drawn sword, rode onward as the
leader, and, by his fierce and variegated countenance, appeared like
war personified; the red of one cheek was an emblem of fire and
sword; the blackness of the other betokened the mourning that at-
tends them. In his train were wild figures in the Indian dress, and
many fantastic shapes without a model, giving the whole march a
visionary air, as if a dream had broken forth from some feverish
brain and were sweeping visibly through the midnight streets. A
mass of people, inactive, except as applauding spectators, hemmed
the procession in; and several women ran along the sidewalk, piercing the confusion of heavier sounds with their shrill voices of mirth
or terror.

"The double-faced fellow has his eye upon me," muttered Robin,
with an indefinite but an uncomfortable idea that he was himself
to bear a part in the pageantry.

The leader turned himself in the saddle and fixed his glance full
upon the country youth, as the steed went slowly by. When Robin
had freed his eyes from those fiery ones, the musicians were passing before him, and the torches were close at hand; but the un-
steady brightness of the latter formed a veil which he could not
penetrate. The rattling of wheels over the stones sometimes found
its way to his ear, and confused traces of a human form appeared at
intervals, and then melted into the vivid light. A moment more,
and the leader thundered a command to halt: the trumpets vom-
ited a horrid breath, and then held their peace; the shouts and
laughter of the people died away, and there remained only a universal hum, allied to silence. Right before Robin's eyes was an un-
covered cart. There the torches blazed the brightest, there the
moon shone out like day, and there, in tar-and-feathery dignity, sat
his kinsman, Major Molineux.

He was an elderly man, of large and majestic person, and strong,
square features, betokening a steady soul; but steady as it was, his
enemies had found means to shake it. His face was pale as death,
and far more ghastly; the broad forehead was contracted in his
agony, so that his eyebrows formed one grizzled line; his eyes
were red and wild, and the foam hung white upon his quivering lip.

His whole frame was agitated by a quick and continual tremor, which his pride strove to quell, even in those circumstances of overwhelming humiliation. But perhaps the bitterest pang of all was when his eyes met those of Robin; for he evidently knew him on the instant, as the youth stood witnessing the foul disgrace of a head grown gray in honor. They stared at each other in silence, and Robin's knees shook, and his hair bristled, with a mixture of pity and terror. Soon, however, a bewildering excitement began to seize upon his mind; the preceding adventures of the night, the unexpected appearance of the crowd, the torches, the confused din and the hush that followed, the spectre of his kinsman reviled by that great multitude,—all this, and, more than all, a perception of tremendous ridicule in the whole scene, affected him with a sort of mental inebriety. At that moment a voice of sluggish merriment saluted Robin's ears; he turned instinctively, and just behind the corner of the church stood the lantern-bearer, rubbing his eyes, and drowsily enjoying the lad's amazement. Then he heard a peal of laughter like the ringing of silvery bells; a woman twitched his arm, a saucy eye met his, and he saw the lady of the scarlet petticoat. A sharp, dry cachinnation appealed to his memory, and standing on tiptoe in the crowd, with his white apron over his head, he beheld the courteous little innkeeper. And lastly, there sailed over the heads of the multitude a great, broad laugh, broken in the midst by two sepulchral hems; thus, "Haw, haw, haw,—hem, hem,—haw, haw, haw, haw!"

The sound proceeded from the balcony of the opposite edifice, and thither Robin turned his eyes. In front of the Gothic window stood the old citizen, wrapped in a wide gown, his gray periwig exchanged for a nightcap, which was thrust back from his forehead, and his silk stockings hanging about his legs. He supported himself on his polished cane in a fit of convulsive merriment, which manifested itself on his solemn old features like a funny inscription on a tombstone. Then Robin seemed to hear the voices of the barbers, of the guests of the inn, and of all who had made sport of him that night. The contagion was spreading among the multitude, when all at once, it seized upon Robin, and he sent forth a shout of laughter that echoed through the street—every man shook his sides, every man emptied his lungs, but Robin's shout was the loudest there. The cloud-spirits peeped from their silvery islands, as the congregated mirth went roaring up the sky. The Man in the Moon heard the far bellow. "Oho," quoth he, "the old earth is frolicsome tonight!"

When there was a momentary calm in that tempestuous sea of sound, the leader gave the sign, the procession resumed its march. On they went, like fiends that throng in mockery around some dead potentate, mighty no more, but majestic still in his agony. On they went, in counterfeit pomp, in senseless uproar, in frenzied merriment, trampling all on an old man's heart. On swept the tumult, and left a silent street behind.

"Well, Robin, are you dreaming?" inquired the gentleman, laying his hand on the youth's shoulder.

Robin started, and withdrew his arm from the stone post to which he had instinctively clung, as the living stream rolled by him. His cheek was somewhat pale, and his eye not quite as lively as in the earlier part of the evening.

"Will you be kind enough to show me the way to the ferry?" said he, after a moment's pause.

"You have, then, adopted a new subject of inquiry?" observed his companion, with a smile.

"Why, yes, sir," replied Robin, rather dryly. "Thanks to you, and to my other friends, I have at last met my kinsman, and he will scarce desire to see my face again. I begin to grow weary of a town life, sir. Will you show me the way to the ferry?"

"No, my good friend Robin,—not tonight, at least," said the gentleman. "Some few days hence, if you wish it, I will speed you on your journey. Or, if you prefer to remain with us, perhaps, as you are a shrewd youth, you may rise in the world without the help of your kinsman, Major Molineux."

HAWTHORNE: *My Kinsman, Major Molineaux*

1. *Q. D. Leavis calls this story a "prophetic forecast of . . . the rejection of England that was to occur in fact much later." Does this summary seem farfetched to you? How else would you account for the introductory material? Does the ending support this view?*

2. *This story is filled with Gothic trappings of hallucinations and grotesqueness. What do they contribute to the story?*

3. Who is the "Major's housekeeper" actually? What article of apparel gives away her identity?

4. What is the significance of the contagious laugh that spreads through the crowd, even to Robin? Why is his laugh the loudest? Why does he join the laughter at all?

5. What is the nature of Robin's quest? What does he find out about the world? about himself? Malcolm Cowley believes Robin is "searching for a spiritual father and finds that the object of his search is an impostor." Is there evidence in the story for either part of this proposition?

6. How does Hawthorne maintain the suspense of the narrative?

Ivan Turgenev:

THE DISTRICT DOCTOR

Among the Russian masters of realism, Ivan Turgenev contributed the most to shaping the raw material of life into the well-made story: a single subject, embodied in a dramatic situation worked out with economy of means, emphasizing character rather than plot. Born in 1818, the son of wealthy landowners in Orel, Turgenev attended the universities in Moscow and Berlin before making his mark with A Sportsman's Sketches *(1847-52), a collection of short stories highly praised by both Tolstoy and Dostoyevsky. In 1856, he took up residence in Paris, thereafter retaining his Russian roots (revealed in such novels as* Fathers and Sons *(1862);* Smoke *(1867); and* Virgin Soil *(1876) through periodic visits to his country estate, through contact with Russian emigrés like the young Tolstoy, and through a powerful memory capable of exact evocation. A regular visitor of his last years was Henry James, who admired and imitated Turgenev's art and brought it to the attention of the American public before his death in 1883.*

ᘓ

ONE day in autumn on my way back from a remote part of the country I caught cold and fell ill. Fortunately the fever attacked me in the district town at the inn; I sent for the doctor. In half-an-hour the district doctor appeared, a thin, dark-haired man of middle height. He prescribed me the usual sudorific, ordered a mustard plaster to be put on, very deftly slid a five-ruble note up his sleeve, coughing drily and looking away as he did so, and then was getting up to go home, but somehow fell into talk and remained. I was exhausted with feverishness; I foresaw a sleepless night, and was glad of a little chat with a pleasant companion. Tea was served. My doctor began to converse freely. He was a sensible fellow, and expressed himself with vigour and some humour. Queer things happen in the world: you may live a long while with some people, and be on friendly terms with them, and never once speak openly with them from your soul; with others you scarcely have time to get acquainted, and all at once you are pouring out to him or he to you—all your secrets, as though you were at confession. I don't know how I gained the confidence of my new friend—anyway, with nothing to lead up to it, he told me a rather curious incident; and here I will report his tale for the information of the indulgent reader. I will try to tell it in the doctor's own words.

"You don't happen to know," he began in a weak and quavering voice (the common result of the use of unmixed Berezov snuff); "you don't happen to know the judge here, Mylov, Pavel Lukich? . . . You don't know him? . . . Well, it's all the same." (He cleared his throat and rubbed his eyes.) "Well, you see, the thing happened, to tell you exactly without mistake, in Lent, at the very time of the thaws. I was sitting at his house—our judge's, you know—playing preference. Our judge is a good fellow, and fond of playing preference. Suddenly" (the doctor made frequent use of this word, suddenly) "they tell me, 'There's a servant asking for you.' I say 'What does he want?' They say 'He has brought a note—it must be from a patient.' 'Give me the note,' I say. So it is from a patient—well and good—you understand—it's our bread and butter. . . . But this is how it was: a lady, a widow, writes to me; she says, 'My daughter is dying. Come, for God's sake!' she says, 'and the horses have been sent for you!' . . . Well, that's all right. But she was twenty miles from town, and it was midnight out of doors, and the roads in such a state, my word! And as she was poor herself, one could not expect more than two silver rubles, and even that problematic; and perhaps it might only be a matter of a roll of linen and a sack of oatmeal in payment. However, duty, you know, before everything: a fellow-creature may be dying. I hand over my cards at once to Kalliopin, the member of the provincial commission, and return home. I look; a wretched little trap was standing at the steps, with peasant's horses, fat—too fat—and their coat as shaggy as felt; and the coachman sitting with his cap off out of respect. Well, I think to myself, 'It's clear, my friend, these patients aren't rolling in riches.' . . . You smile; but I tell you, a poor man like me has to take everything into consideration. . . . If the coachman sits like a prince, and doesn't touch his cap, and even sneers at you behind his beard, and flicks his whip—then you may bet on six rubles. But this case, I saw, had a very different air. However, I think there's no help for it; duty before everything. I snatch up the most necessary drugs, and set off. Will you believe it? I only just managed to get there at all. The road was infernal: streams, snow, watercourses, and the dyke had suddenly burst there—that was the worst of it! However, I arrived at last. It was a little thatched house. There was a light in the windows; that meant they expected me. I was met by an old lady, very venerable, in a cap. 'Save her!' she says; 'she is dying.' I say, 'Pray don't distress yourself— Where is the invalid?' 'Come this way.' I see a clean little room, a lamp in the corner; on the bed a girl of twenty, unconscious. She was in a burning heat, and breathing heavily—it was fever. There were two other girls, her sisters, scared and in tears. 'Yesterday,' they tell me, 'she was perfectly well and had a good appetite; this morning she complained of her head, and this evening, suddenly, you see, like this.' I say again: 'Pray don't be uneasy.' It's a doctor's duty, you know— and I went up to her and bled her, told them to put on a mustard plaster, and prescribed a mixture. Meantime I looked at her, you know—there, by God! I had never seen such a face!—she was a beauty, in a word! I felt quite shaken by pity. Such lovely features; such eyes! . . . But, thank God! she became easier; she fell into a perspiration, seemed to come to her senses, looked round, smiled, and passed her hand over her face. . . . Her sisters bent over her. They ask, 'How are you?' 'All right,' she says, and turns away. I looked at her; she had fallen asleep. 'Well,' I say, 'now the patient should be left alone.' So we all went out on tiptoe; only a maid remained, in case she was wanted. In the parlour there was a samovar standing on the table, and a bottle of rum; in our profession one can't get on without it. They gave me tea; asked me to stop the night. . . . I consented: where could I go, indeed, at that time of night? The old lady kept groaning. 'What is it?' I say; 'she will live; don't worry yourself; you had better take a little rest yourself; it is about two o'clock.' 'But will you send to wake me if anything happens?' 'Yes, yes.' The old lady went away, and the girls too went to their own room; they made up a bed for me in the parlour. Well, I went to bed—but I could not get to sleep, for a wonder! for in reality I was very tired. I could not get my patient out of my head. At last I could not put up with it any longer; I got up suddenly; I think to myself, 'I will go and see how the patient is getting on.' Her bedroom was next to the parlour. Well, I got up, and gently opened the door—how my heart beat! I looked in: the servant was asleep, her mouth wide open, and even snoring, the wretch! but the patient lay with her face towards me, and her arms flung wide apart, poor girl! I went up to her . . . when suddenly she opened her eyes and stared at me! 'Who is it? who is it?' I was in confusion. 'Don't be alarmed, madam,' I say; 'I am the doctor; I have come to see how you feel.' 'You the doctor?' 'Yes, the doctor; your mother sent for me from the town; we have bled you, madam; now pray go to sleep, and in a day or two, please God! we will set you on your feet again.' 'Ah, yes, yes, doctor, don't let me die . . . please, please.' 'Why do you talk like that? God bless you!' She is in a fever again, I think to myself; I felt her pulse; yes, she was feverish. She looked at me, and then took me by the hand. 'I will tell you why I don't want to die; I will tell you. . . . Now we are alone; and only, please don't you . . . not to anyone . . . Listen . . . !' I bent down; she moved her lips quite to my ear; she touched my cheek with her hair—I confess my head went round—and began to whisper. . . . I could make out nothing of it. . . . Ah, she was delirious! . . . She whispered and whispered, but so quickly, and as if it were not in Russian; at last she finished, and shivering dropped her head on the pillow, and threatened me with her finger: 'Remember, doctor, no one.' I calmed her somehow, gave her something to drink, waked the servant, and went away."

At this point the doctor again took snuff with exasperated energy, and for a moment seemed stupefied by its effects.

"However," he continued, "the next day, contrary to my expectations, the patient was no better. I thought and thought, and suddenly decided to remain there, even though my other patients were expecting me. . . . And you know one can't afford to disregard that; one's practice suffers if one does. But, in the first place, the patient was really in danger; and secondly to tell the truth, I felt strongly drawn to her. Besides, I liked the whole family. Though they were really badly off, they were singularly, I may say, cultivated people. . . . Their father had been a learned man, an author; he died, of course, in poverty, but he had managed before he died to give his children an excellent education; he left a lot of books too. Either because I looked after the invalid very carefully, or for some other reason; anyway, I can venture to say all the household loved me as one of the family. . . . Meantime the roads were in a worse state than ever; all communications, so to say, were cut off completely; even medicine could with difficulty be got from the town. . . . The sick girl was not getting better. . . . Day after day, and day after day . . . but . . . here. . . ." (The doctor made a brief pause.) "I declare I don't know how to tell you." . . . (He again took snuff, coughed, and swallowed a little tea.) "I will tell you without beating about the bush. My patient . . . how should I say? . . . Well she had fallen in love with me . . . or, no, it was not that she was in love . . . however . . . really, how should one say?" (The doctor looked down and grew red.) "No," he went on quickly, "in love, indeed! A man should not over-estimate himself. She was an educated girl, clever and well-read, and I had even forgotten my Latin, one may say, completely. As to appearance" (the doctor looked himself over with a smile) "I am nothing to boast of there either. But God Almighty did not make me a fool; I don't take black for white; I know a thing or two; I could see very clearly, for instance, that Aleksandra Andreyevna— that was her name—did not feel love for me, but had a friendly, so to say, inclination—a respect or something for me. Though she herself perhaps mistook this sentiment, anyway this was her attitude; you may form your own judgment of it. But," added the doctor, who had brought out all these disconnected sentences without taking breath, and with obvious embarrassment, "I seem to be wandering rather—you won't understand anything like this. . . . There with your leave, I will relate it all in order."

He drank a glass of tea, and began in a calmer voice.

"Well, then. My patient kept getting worse and worse. You are not a doctor, my good sir; you cannot understand what passes in a poor fellow's heart, especially at first, when he begins to suspect that the disease is getting the upper hand of him. What becomes of his belief in himself? You suddenly grow so timid; it's indescribable. You fancy then that you have forgotten everything you knew, and that the patient has no faith in you, and that other people begin to notice how distracted you are, and tell you the symptoms with reluctance; that they are looking at you suspiciously, whispering. . . . Ah! it's horrid! There must be a remedy, you think, for this disease, if one could find it. Isn't this it? You try—no, that's not it! You don't allow the medicine the necessary time to do good. . . . You clutch at one thing, then at another. Sometimes you take up a

book of medical prescriptions—here it is, you think! Sometimes, by
Jove, you pick one out by chance, thinking to leave it to fate. . . .
But meantime a fellow creature's dying, and another doctor would
have saved him. 'We must have a consultation,' you say; 'I will not
take the responsibility on myself.' And what a fool you look at such
times! Well, in time you learn to bear it; it's nothing to you. A man
has died—but it's not your fault; you treated him by the rules. But
what's still more torture to you is to see blind faith in you, and to
feel yourself that you are not able to be of use. Well, it was just this
blind faith that the whole of Aleksandra Andreyevna's family had
in me; they had forgotten to think that their daughter was in danger. I, too, on my side assure them that it is nothing, but meantime
my heart sinks into my boots. To add to our troubles, the roads were
in such a state that the coachman was gone for whole days together
to get medicine. And I never left the patient's room; I could not
tear myself away; I tell her amusing stories, you know, and play
cards with her. I watch by her side at night. The old mother thanks
me with tears in her eyes; but I think to myself, 'I don't deserve
your gratitude.' I frankly confess to you—there is no object in concealing it now—I was in love with my patient. And Aleksandra
Andreyevna had grown fond of me; she would not sometimes let
any one be in her room but me. She began to talk to me, to ask me
questions; where I had studied, how I lived, who are my people,
whom I go to see. I feel that she ought not to talk; but to forbid her
to—to forbid her resolutely, you know—I could not. Sometimes I
held my head in my hands, and asked myself, 'What are you doing,
villain?' . . . And she would take my hand and hold it, give me a
long, long look, and turn away, sigh, and say, 'How good you are!'
Her hands were so feverish, her eyes so large and languid. . . .
'Yes,' she says, 'you are a good, kind man; you are not like our
neighbours. . . . No, you are not like that. . . . Why did I not
know you till now!' 'Aleksandra Andreyevna, calm yourself,' I say.
. . . 'I feel, believe me, I don't know how I have gained . . . but
there, calm yourself. . . . All will be right; you will be well again.'
And meanwhile I must tell you," continued the doctor, bending forward and raising his eyebrows, "that they associated very little with
the neighbours, because the smaller people were not on their level,
and pride hindered them from being friendly with the rich. I tell
you, they were an exceptionally cultivated family, so you know it

was gratifying for me. She would only take her medicine from my
hands . . . she would lift herself up, poor girl, with my aid, take
it, and gaze at me. . . . My heart felt as if it were bursting. And
meanwhile she was growing worse and worse, worse and worse, all
the time; she will die, I think to myself; she must die. Believe me,
I would sooner have gone to the grave myself; and here were her
mother and sisters watching me, looking into my eyes . . . and
their faith in me was wearing away. 'Well, how is she?' 'Oh, all
right, all right!" All right, indeed! My mind was failing me. Well, I
was sitting one night alone again by my patient. The maid was sitting there too, and snoring away in full swing; I can't find fault with
the poor girl, though! she was worn out too. Aleksandra Andreyevna had felt very unwell all the evening; she was very feverish.
Until midnight she kept tossing about; at last she seemed to fall
asleep; at least, she lay still without stirring. The lamp was burning
in the corner before the holy image. I sat here, you know, with my
head bent; I even dozed a little. Suddenly it seemed as though
someone touched me in the side; I turned round. . . . Good God!
Aleksandra Andreyevna was gazing with intent eyes at me . . .
her lips parted, her cheeks seemed burning. 'What is it?' 'Doctor,
shall I die?' 'Merciful Heavens!' 'No, doctor, no; please don't tell
me I shall live . . . don't say so. . . . If you knew. . . . Listen!
For God's sake don't conceal my real position,' and her breath
came so fast. 'If I can know for certain that I must die . . . then I
will tell you all—all!' 'Aleksandra Andreyevna, I beg!' 'Listen; I
have not been asleep at all . . . I have been looking at you a long
while. . . . For God's sake! . . . I believe in you; you are a good
man, an honest man; I entreat you by all that is sacred in the world
—tell me the truth! If you knew how important it is for me. . . .
Doctor, for God's sake tell me. . . . Am I in danger?' 'What can I
tell you, Aleksandra Andreyevna pray?' 'For God's sake, I beseech
you!' 'I can't conceal from you,' I say, 'Aleksandra Andreyevna; you
are certainly in danger; but God is merciful.' 'I shall die, I shall die.'
And it seemed as though she were pleased; her face grew so bright;
I was alarmed. 'Don't be afraid, don't be afraid! I am not frightened
by death at all.' She suddenly sat up and leaned on her elbow.
'Now . . . yes, now I can tell you that I thank you with my whole
heart . . . that you are kind and good—that I love you!' I stared at
her, like one possessed; it was terrible for me, you know. 'Do you

hear, I love you!' 'Aleksandra Andreyevna, how have I deserved—'
'No, no, you don't—you don't understand me.' . . . And suddenly
she stretched out her arms, and taking my head in her hands, she
kissed it. . . . Believe me, I almost screamed aloud. . . . I threw
myself on my knees, and buried my head in the pillow. She did not
speak; her fingers trembled in my hair; I listen; she is weeping. I
began to soothe her, to assure her. . . . I really don't know what
I did say to her. 'You will wake up the girl,' I say to her; 'Aleksandra
Andreyevna, I thank you . . . believe me . . . calm yourself.'
'Enough, enough!' she persisted, 'never mind all of them; let them
wake, then; let them come in—it does not matter; I am dying, you
see. . . . And what do you fear? Why are you afraid? Lift up your
head. . . . Or, perhaps you don't love me; perhaps I am wrong.
. . . In that case, forgive me.' 'Aleksandra Andreyevna, what are
you saying! . . . I love you, Aleksandra Andreyevna.' She looked
straight into my eyes, and opened her arms wide. 'Then take me in
your arms.' I tell you frankly, I don't know how it was I did not go
mad that night. I feel that my patient is killing herself; I see that
she is not fully herself; I understand, too, that if she did not consider herself on the point of death she would never have thought of
me; and, indeed, say what you will, it's hard to die at twenty without having known love; this was what was torturing her; this was
why, in despair, she caught at me—do you understand now? But
she held me in her arms, and would not let me go. 'Have pity on
me, Aleksandra Andreyevna, and have pity on yourself,' I say.
'Why,' she says, 'what is there to think of? You know I must die.'
. . . This she repeated incessantly. . . . 'If I knew that I should return to life, and be a proper young lady again, I should be ashamed
. . . of course, ashamed . . . but why now?' 'But who has said
you will die?' 'Oh, no, leave off! you will not deceive me; you don't
know how to lie—look at your face.' . . . 'You shall live, Aleksandra Andreyevna; I will cure you; we will ask your mother's
blessing . . . we will be united—we will be happy.' 'No, no, I
have your word; I must die. . . . you have promised me . . . you
have told me.' . . . It was cruel for me—cruel for many reasons.
And see what trifling things can do sometimes; it seems nothing at
all, but it's painful. It occurred to her to ask me, what is my name;
not my surname, but my first name. I must needs be so unlucky as
to be called Trifon. Yes, indeed; Trifon Ivanich. Every one in the

house called me doctor. However, there's no help for it. I say,
'Trifon, madam.' She frowned, shook her head, and muttered something in French—ah, something unpleasant, of course!—and then
she laughed—disagreeably too. Well, I spent the whole night with
her in this way. Before morning I went away, feeling as though I
were mad. When I went again into her room it was daytime, after
morning tea. Good God! I could scarcely recognise her; people are
laid in their grave looking better than that. I swear to you, on my
honour, I don't understand—I absolutely don't understand—now,
how I lived through that experience. Three days and nights my patient still lingered on. And what nights! What things she said to
me! And on the last night—only imagine to yourself—I was sitting
near her, and kept praying to God for one thing only: 'Take her,'
I said, 'quickly, and me with her.' Suddenly the old mother comes
unexpectedly into the room. I had already the evening before told
her—the mother—there was little hope, and it would be well to
send for a priest. When the sick girl saw her mother she said: 'It's
very well you have come; look at us, we love one another—we have
given each other our word.' 'What does she say, doctor? what does
she say?' I turned livid. 'She is wandering,' I say; 'the fever.' But
she: 'Hush, hush; you told me something quite different just now,
and have taken my ring. Why do you pretend? My mother is good
—she will forgive—she will understand—and I am dying. . . . I
have no need to tell lies; give me your hand.' I jumped up and ran
out of the room. The old lady, of course, guessed how it was.

"I will not, however, weary you any longer, and to me, too, of
course, it's painful to recall all this. My patient passed away the
next day. God rest her soul!" the doctor added, speaking quickly
and with a sigh. "Before her death she asked her family to go out
and leave me alone with her."

" 'Forgive me,' she said; 'I am perhaps to blame towards you
. . . my illness . . . but believe me, I have loved no one more
than you . . . do not forget me . . . keep my ring.' "

The doctor turned away; I took his hand.

"Ah!" he said, "let us talk of something else, or would you care to
play preference for a small stake? It is not for people like me to
give way to exalted emotions. There's only one thing for me to
think of; how to keep the children from crying and the wife from
scolding. Since then, you know, I have had time to enter into lawful

wedlock, as they say. . . . Oh . . . I took a merchant's daughter—seven thousand for her dowry. Her name's Akulina; it goes well with Trifon. She is an ill-tempered woman, I must tell you, but luckily she's asleep all day. . . . Well, shall it be preference?"

We sat down to preference for halfpenny points. Trifon Ivanich won two rubles and a half from me, and went home late, well pleased with his success.

TURGENEV: *The District Doctor*

1. *What prompts the doctor to tell his story? Why is it told in retrospect and not reported directly by the author himself?*

2. *What kind of person is the doctor in the story he tells? What kind outside the story, particularly at the end? What is Turgenev's point in this subtle shift of character?*

3. *Avrahm Yarmolinsky, Turgenev's biographer, writes of A* Sportsman's Sketches, *in which this story appeared: "There is little overt drama . . . the author stands outside looking in, a position which allows him perspective but makes for a somewhat chilling detachment." Do you feel this opinion accurately describes "The District Doctor," or do you find the author is involved in a moving narrative? What details would you cite to support your answer?*

4. *The influence of Turgenev on Henry James has been fully studied. Do you find evidence of it in "The Death of the Lion"? Where, specifically?*

5. *Virginia Woolf writes: "Turgenev did not see his books as a succession of events; he saw them as a succession of emotions radiating from some character at the centre . . . the connection is not that of events, but of emotions. . . . Turgenev's ear for emotions was so fine that even if he uses an abrupt contrast, or passes from his people to the sky or to the forest, all is held together by the truth of his insight." Does this statement apply to this story? Does it apply equally well to other stories in this collection? Which in particular? What is the danger of this device?*

Feodor Dostoyevsky:

THE GRAND INQUISITOR

Feodor Dostoyevsky was born in Moscow in 1821, son of a stern and authoritarian doctor. Educated in military engineering, he left this occupation in order to write. His first story, Poor Folk (1846), *struck a new chord in Russian literature by its deep psychological study of poor, unhappy people, who—along with the insulted and the injured, the strange and abnormal sufferers who defy society— were to be the actors in his tremendously dramatic and intensely individual works. In 1849, he was arrested for alleged conspiracy against the government and sentenced to Siberia (see* The House of the Dead, *1861-62). After four more years there as a soldier, he returned to St. Petersburg to resume his career. Despite the bitter poverty and personal tragedies of the next years, he established his name through* Notes from Underground (1864) *and* Crime and Punishment (1866), *and found himself ranked with Tolstoy and Turgenev after* The Idiot (1869), The Possessed (1871) *and* The Brothers Karamazov (1880). *He died in 1881, practically revered as a Slavic saint.*

Dostoyevsky's sweeping genius did not accommodate itself to the short story, and the self-contained selection that best represents his work comes from The Brothers Karamazov. *Dostoyevsky himself regarded this chapter as the culmination of the book, and V. Rozanov, a critic and philosopher who wrote a remarkable book on the legend of the Grand Inquisitor, affirmed that without it Dostoyevsky would never have written his masterpiece.*

The scene is laid in a screened-off corner of a shabby tavern, where, amid "shouts for the waiters, the sound of popping corks, the click of billiard balls," Ivan Karamazov opens his heart to his younger brother, the saintly Alyosha. Ivan tells him that it is a marvel that "the idea of the necessity of God could enter the head of such a savage, vicious beast as man." For his own part, he is prepared to admit the actual existence of God, and even grant that all creation moves toward an ultimate harmony, but he cannot accept the ways of a Deity who includes in his scheme the suffering of the innocent. Therefore he rejects the world created by Him, and even though "the humiliating absurdity of human contradictions" may

[57

someday vanish, he prefers to stay outside, intransigent, unrecon-
ciled, unforgiving of a small-minded God. Is there a being in the
entire world, he asks, who has the right to forgive torturers of the
innocent, who can justify suffering? Alyosha points to Christ. There-
upon Ivan recites the following story.

"Do you know, Alyosha—don't laugh! I made a poem about a
year ago. If you can waste another ten minutes on me, I'll tell it to
you."

"You wrote a poem?"

"Oh, no, I didn't write it," laughed Ivan, "and I've never written
two lines of poetry in my life. But I made up this poem in prose
and I remembered it. I was carried away when I made it up. You
will be my first reader—that is, listener. Why should an author
forego even one listener?" smiled Ivan. "Shall I tell it to you?"

"I am all attention," said Alyosha.

"My poem is called 'The Grand Inquisitor'; it's a ridiculous thing,
but I want to tell it to you."

"Even this must have a preface—that is, a literary preface,"
laughed Ivan, "and I am a poor hand at making one. You see, my
action takes place in the sixteenth century, and at that time, as you
probably learnt at school, it was customary in poetry to bring down
heavenly powers on earth. Not to speak of Dante, in France, clerks,
as well as the monks in the monasteries, used to give regular per-
formances in which the Madonna, the saints, the angels, Christ, and
God Himself were brought on the stage. In those days it was done
in all simplicity. In Victor Hugo's 'Notre Dame de Paris' an edifying
and gratuitous spectacle was provided for the people in the Hotel
de Ville of Paris in the reign of Louis XI in honour of the birth of
the dauphin. It was called *Le bon jugement de la très sainte et
gracieuse Vierge Marie,* and she appears herself on the stage and
pronounces her *bon jugement.* Similar plays, chiefly from the Old
Testament, were occasionally performed in Moscow too, up to the
times of Peter the Great. But besides plays there were all sorts of
legends and ballads scattered about the world, in which the saints
and angels and all the powers of Heaven took part when required.
In our monasteries the monks busied themselves in translating,

copying, and even composing such poems—and even under the Tatars. There is, for instance, one such poem (of course, from the Greek), 'The Wanderings of Our Lady through Hell,' with descriptions as bold as Dante's. Our Lady visits Hell, and the Archangel Michael leads her through the torments. She sees the sinners and their punishment. There she seems among others one noteworthy set of sinners in a burning lake; some of them sink to the bottom of the lake so that they can't swim out, and 'these God forgets'—an expression of extraordinary depth and force. And so Our Lady, shocked and weeping, falls before the throne of God and begs for mercy for all in Hell—for all she has seen there, indiscriminately. Her conversation with God is immensely interesting. She beseeches Him, she will not desist, and when God points to the hands and feet of her Son, nailed to the Cross, and asks, 'How can I forgive His tormentors?' she bids all the saints, all the martyrs, all the angels and archangels to fall down with her and pray for mercy on all without distinction. It ends by her winning from God a respite of suffering every year from Good Friday till Trinity day, and the sinners at once raise a cry of thankfulness from Hell, chanting, 'Thou art just, O Lord, in this judgment.' Well, my poem would have been of that kind if it had appeared at that time. He comes on the scene in my poem, but He says nothing, only appears and passes on. Fifteen centuries have passed since He promised to come in His glory, fifteen centuries since His prophet wrote, 'Behold, I come quickly'; 'Of that day and that hour knoweth no man, neither the Son, but the Father,' as He Himself predicted on earth. But humanity awaits him with the same faith and with the same love. Oh, with greater faith, for it is fifteen centuries since man has ceased to see signs from Heaven.

> *No signs from Heaven come to-day*
> *To add to what the heart doth say.*

There was nothing left but faith in what the heart doth say. It is true there were many miracles in those days. There were saints who performed miraculous cures; some holy people, according to their biographies, were visited by the Queen of Heaven herself. But the devil did not slumber, and doubts were already arising among men of the truth of these miracles. And just then there appeared in the north of Germany a terrible new heresy. 'A huge

star like to a torch' (that is, to a church) 'fell on the sources of the
waters and they became bitter.' These heretics began, blasphe-
mously denying miracles. But those who remained faithful were
all the more ardent in their faith. The tears of humanity rose up to
Him as before, awaited His coming, loved Him, hoped for Him,
yearned to suffer and die for Him as before. And so many ages
mankind had prayed with faith and fervour, 'O Lord our God, hasten Thy coming,' so many ages called upon Him, that in His infinite
mercy He deigned to come down to His servants. Before that day
He had come down, He had visited some holy men, martyrs and
hermits, as is written in their 'Lives.' Among us, Tyutchev, with absolute faith in the truth of his words, bore witness that

> *Bearing the Cross, in slavish dress,*
> *Weary and worn, the Heavenly King*
> *Our mother, Russia, came to bless,*
> *And through our land went wandering.*

And that certainly was so, I assure you.

"And behold, He deigned to appear for a moment to the people,
to the tortured, suffering people, sunk in iniquity, but loving Him
like children. My story is laid in Spain, in Seville, in the most terrible time of the Inquisition, when fires were lighted every day to
the glory of God, and 'in the splendid *auto da fé* the wicked heretics
were burnt.' Oh, of course, this was not the coming in which He
will appear according to His promise at the end of time in all His
heavenly glory, and which will be sudden 'as lightning flashing
from east to west.' No, He visited His children only for a moment,
and there where the flames were crackling round the heretics. In
His infinite mercy He came once more among men in that human
shape in which He walked among men for three years fifteen centuries ago. He came down to the 'hot pavement' of the southern town
in which on the day before almost a hundred heretics had, *ad ma-
jorem gloriam Dei,* been burnt by the cardinal, the Grand Inquisitor, in a magnificent *auto da fé,* in the presence of the king, the
court, the knights, the cardinals, the most charming ladies of the
court, and the whole population of Seville.

"He came softly, unobserved, and yet, strange to say, every one
recognised Him. That might be one of the best passages in the
poem. I mean, why they recognised Him. The people are irresist-

ibly drawn to Him, they surround Him, they flock about Him, follow Him. He moves silently in their midst with a gentle smile of infinite compassion. The sun of love burns in His heart, light and power shine from His eyes, and their radiance, shed on the people, stirs their hearts with responsive love. He holds out His hands to them, blesses them, and a healing virtue comes from contact with Him, even with His garments. An old man in the crowd, blind from childhood, cries out, 'O Lord, heal me and I shall see Thee!' and, as it were, scales fall from his eyes and the blind man sees Him. The crowd weeps and kisses the earth under His feet. Children throw flowers before Him, sing, and cry hosannah. 'It is He—it is He!' all repeat. 'It must be He, it can be no one but Him!' He stops at the steps of the Seville cathedral at the moment when the weeping mourners are bringing in a little open white coffin. In it lies a child of seven, the only daughter of a prominent citizen. The dead child lies hidden in flowers. 'He will raise your child,' the crowd shouts to the weeping mother. The priest, coming to meet the coffin, looks perplexed, and frowns, but the mother of the dead child throws herself at His feet with a wail. 'If it is Thou, raise my child!' she cries, holding out her hands to Him. The procession halts, the coffin is laid on the steps at His feet. He looks with compassion, and His lips once more softly pronounce, 'Maiden, arise!' and the maiden arises. The little girl sits up in the coffin and looks round, smiling with wide-open wondering eyes, holding a bunch of white roses they had put in her hand.

"There are cries, sobs, confusion among the people, and at that moment the cardinal himself, the Grand Inquisitor, passes by the cathedral. He is an old man, almost ninety, tall and erect, with a withered face and sunken eyes, in which there is still a gleam of light. He is not dressed in his gorgeous cardinal's robes, as he was the day before, when he was burning the enemies of the Roman Church—at that moment he was wearing his coarse, old, monk's cassock. At a distance behind him come his gloomy assistants and slaves and the 'holy guard.' He stops at the sight of the crowd and watches it from a distance. He sees everything; he sees them set the coffin down at His feet, sees the child rise up, and his face darkens. He knits his thick grey brows and his eyes gleam with a sinister fire. He holds out his finger and bids the guards take Him. And such is his power, so completely are the people cowed into submission and trembling obedience to him, that the crowd immediately make way for the guards, and in the midst of deathlike silence they lay hands on Him and lead Him away. The crowd instantly bows down to the earth, like one man, before the old inquisitor. He blesses the people in silence and passes on. The guards lead their prisoner to the close, gloomy vaulted prison in the ancient palace of the Holy Inquisition and shut Him in it. The day passes and is followed by the dark, burning 'breathless' night of Seville. The air is 'fragrant with laurel and lemon.' In the pitch darkness the iron door of the prison is suddenly opened and the Grand Inquisitor himself comes in with a light in his hand. He is alone; the door is closed at once behind him. He stands in the doorway and for a minute or two gazes into His face. At last he goes up slowly, sets the light on the table and speaks.

" 'Is it Thou? Thou?' but receiving no answer, he adds at once, 'Don't answer, be silent. What canst Thou say, indeed? I know too well what Thou wouldst say. And Thou hast no right to add anything to what Thou hadst said of old. Why, then, art Thou come to hinder us? For Thou hast come to hinder us, and Thou knowest that. But dost Thou know what will be to-morrow? I know not who Thou art and care not to know whether it is Thou or only a semblance of Him, but to-morrow I shall condemn Thee and burn Thee at the stake as the worst of heretics. And the very people who have to-day kissed Thy feet, to-morrow at the faintest sign from me will rush to heap up the embers of Thy fire. Knowest Thou that? Yes, maybe Thou knowest it,' he added with thoughtful penetration, never for a moment taking his eyes off the Prisoner."

"I don't quite understand, Ivan. What does it mean?" Alyosha, who had been listening in silence, said with a smile, "Is it simply a wild fantasy, or a mistake on the part of the old man—some impossible *quiproquo?*"

"Take it as the last," said Ivan, laughing, "if you are so corrupted by modern realism and can't stand anything fantastic. If you like it to be a case of mistaken identity, let it be so. It is true," he went on, laughing, "the old man was ninety, and he might well be crazy over his set idea. He might have been struck by the appearance of the Prisoner. It might, in fact, be simply his ravings, the delusion of an old man of ninety, over-excited by the *auto da fé* of a hundred

heretics the day before. But does it matter to us after all whether it
was a mistake of identity or a wild fantasy? All that matters is that
the old man should speak out, should speak openly of what he has
thought in silence for ninety years."

"And the Prisoner too is silent? Does He look at him and not say
a word?"

"That's inevitable in any case," Ivan laughed again. "The old man
has told Him He hasn't the right to add anything to what He has
said of old. One may say it is the most fundamental feature of
Roman Catholicism, in my opinion at least. 'All has been given by
Thee to the Pope,' they say, 'and all, therefore, is still in the Pope's
hands, and there is no need for Thee to come now at all. Thou
must not meddle for the time, at least.' That's how they speak and
write too—the Jesuits, at any rate. I have read it myself in the
works of their theologians. 'Hast Thou the right to reveal to us one
of the mysteries of that world from which Thou hast come?' my old
man asks Him, and answers the question for Him. 'No, Thou hast
not; that Thou mayest not add to what has been said of old, and
mayest not take from men the freedom which Thou didst exalt
when Thou wast on earth. Whatsoever Thou revealest anew will
encroach on men's freedom of faith; for it will be manifest as a miracle, and the freedom of their faith was dearer to Thee than anything in those days fifteen hundred years ago. Didst Thou not often
say then, "I will make you free"? But now Thou hast seen these
"free" men,' the old man adds suddenly, with a pensive smile. 'Yes,
we've paid dearly for it,' he goes on, looking sternly at Him, 'but at
last we have completed that work in Thy name. For fifteen centuries we have been wrestling with Thy freedom, but now it is
ended and over for good. Dost Thou not believe that it's over for
good? Thou lookest meekly at me and deignest not even to be
wroth with me. But let me tell Thee that now, to-day, people are
more persuaded than ever that they have perfect freedom, yet they
have brought their freedom to us and laid it humbly at our feet.
But that has been our doing. Was this what Thou didst? Was this
Thy freedom?' "

"I don't understand again," Alyosha broke in. "Is he ironical, is
he jesting?"

"Not a bit of it! He claims it as a merit for himself and his Church
that at last they have vanquished freedom and have done so to

make men happy. 'For now' (he is speaking of the Inquisition, of course) 'for the first time it has become possible to think of the happiness of men. Man was created a rebel; and how can rebels be happy? Thou wast warned,' he says to Him. 'Thou hast had no lack of admonitions and warnings, but Thou didst not listen to those warnings; Thou didst reject the only way by which men might be made happy. But, fortunately, departing Thou didst hand on the work to us. Thou hast promised, Thou hast established by Thy word, Thou hast given to us the right to bind and to unbind, and now, of course, Thou canst not think of taking it away. Why, then, hast Thou come to hinder us?' "

"And what's the meaning of 'no lack of admonitions and warnings'?" asked Alyosha.

"Why, that's the chief part of what the old man must say."

" 'The wise and dread spirit, the spirit of self-destruction and non-existence,' the old man goes on, 'the great spirit talked with Thee in the wilderness, and we are told in the books that he "tempted" Thee. Is that so? And could anything truer be said than what he revealed to Thee in three questions and what Thou didst reject, and what in the books is called "the temptation"? And yet if there has ever been on earth a real stupendous miracle, it took place on that day, on the day of the three temptations. The statement of those three questions was itself the miracle. If it were possible to imagine simply for the sake of argument that those three questions of the dread spirit had perished utterly from the books, and that we had to restore them and to invent them anew, and to do so had gathered together all the wise men of the earth—rulers, chief priests, learned men, philosophers, poets—and had set them the task to invent three questions, such as would not only fit the occasion, but express in three words, three human phrases, the whole future history of the world and of humanity—dost Thou believe that all the wisdom of the earth united could have invented anything in depth and force equal to the three questions which were actually put to Thee then by the wise and mighty spirit in the wilderness? From those questions alone, from the miracle of their statement, we can see that we have here to do not with the fleeting human intelligence, but with the absolute and eternal. For in those three questions the whole subsequent history of mankind is, as it were, brought together into one whole, and foretold, and in them are united all the unsolved historical contradictions of human nature. At the time it could not be so clear, since the future was unknown; but now that fifteen hundred years have passed, we see that everything in those three questions was so justly divined and foretold, and has been so truly fulfilled, that nothing can be added to them or taken from them.

"'Judge Thyself who was right—Thou or he who questioned Thee then? Remember the first question; its meaning, in other words, was this: "Thou wouldst go into the world, and art going with empty hands, with some promise of freedom which men in their simplicity and their natural unruliness cannot even understand, which they fear and dread—for nothing has ever been more insupportable for a man and a human society than freedom. But seest Thou these stones in this parched and barren wilderness? Turn them into bread, and mankind will run after Thee like a flock of sheep, grateful and obedient, though for ever trembling, lest Thou withdraw Thy hand and deny them Thy bread." But Thou wouldst not deprive man of freedom and didst reject the offer, thinking, what is that freedom worth, if obedience is bought with bread? Thou didst reply that man lives not by bread alone. But dost Thou know that for the sake of that earthly bread the spirit of the earth will rise up against Thee and will strive with Thee and overcome Thee, and all will follow him, crying, "Who can compare with this beast? He has given us fire from heaven!" Dost Thou know that the ages will pass, and humanity will proclaim by the lips of their sages that there is no crime, and therefore no sin; there is only hunger? "Feed men, and then ask of them virtue!" that's what they'll write on the banner, which they will raise against Thee, and with which they will destroy Thy temple. Where Thy temple stood will rise a new building; the terrible tower of Babel will be built again, and though, like the one of old, it will not be finished, yet Thou mightest have prevented that new tower and have cut short the sufferings of men for a thousand years; for they will come back to us after a thousand years of agony with their tower. They will seek us again, hidden underground in the catacombs, for we shall be again persecuted and tortured. They will find us and cry to us, "Feed us, for those who have promised us fire from heaven haven't given it!" And then we shall finish building their tower, for he finishes the building who feeds them. And we

alone shall feed them in Thy name, declaring falsely that it is in
Thy name. Oh, never, never can they feed themselves without us!
no science will give them bread so long as they remain free. In the
end they will lay their freedom at our feet, and say to us, "Make us
your slaves, but feed us." They will understand themselves, at last,
that freedom and bread enough for all are inconceivable together,
for never, never will they be able to share between them! They
will be convinced, too, that they can never be free, for they are
weak, vicious, worthless and rebellious. Thou didst promise them
the bread of Heaven, but, I repeat again, can it compare with
earthly bread in the eyes of the weak, ever sinful and ignoble race
of man? And if for the sake of the bread of Heaven thousands and
tens of thousands shall follow Thee, what is to become of the millions and tens of thousands of millions of creatures who will not
have the strength to forego the earthly bread for the sake of the
heavenly? Or dost Thou care only for the tens of thousands of the
great and strong, while the millions, numerous as the sands of the
sea, who are weak but love Thee, must exist only for the sake of
the great and strong? No, we care for the weak too. They are sinful
and rebellious, but in the end they too will become obedient. They
will marvel at us and look on us as gods, because we are ready to
endure the freedom which they have found so dreadful and to rule
over them—so awful it will seem to them to be free. But we shall
tell them that we are Thy servants and rule them in Thy name. We
shall deceive them again, for we will not let Thee come to us
again. That deception will be our suffering, for we shall be forced
to lie.

" 'This is the significance of the first question in the wilderness,
and this is what Thou hast rejected for the sake of that freedom
which Thou hast exalted above everything. Yet in this question lies
hid the great secret of this world. Choosing "bread," Thou wouldst
have satisfied the universal and everlasting craving of humanity—
to find some one to worship. So long as man remains free he strives
for nothing so incessantly and so painfully as to find some one to
worship. But man seeks to worship what is established beyond dispute, so that all men would agree at once to worship it. For these
pitiful creatures are concerned not only to find what one or the
other can worship, but to find something that all would believe in
and worship; what is essential is that all may be *together* in it. This

craving for *community* of worship is the chief misery of every man individually and of all humanity from the beginning of time. For the sake of common worship they've slain each other with the sword. They have set up gods and challenged one another, "Put away your gods and come and worship ours, or we will kill you and your gods!" And so it will be to the end of the world, even when gods disappear from the earth; they will fall down before idols just the same. Thou didst know, Thou couldst not but have known, this fundamental secret of human nature, but Thou didst reject the one infallible banner which was offered Thee to make all men bow down to Thee alone—the banner of earthly bread; and Thou hast rejected it for the sake of freedom and the bread of Heaven. Behold what Thou didst further. And all again in the name of freedom! I tell Thee that man is tormented by no greater anxiety than to find some one quickly to whom he can hand over that gift of freedom with which the ill-fated creature is born. But only one who can appease their conscience can take over their freedom. In bread there was offered Thee an invincible banner; give bread, and man will worship Thee, for nothing is more certain than bread. But if some one else gains possession of his conscience—oh! then he will cast away Thy bread and follow after him who has ensnared his conscience. In that Thou wast right. For the secret of man's being is not only to live but to have something to live for. Without a stable conception of the object of life, man would not consent to go on living, and would rather destroy himself than remain on earth, though he had bread in abundance. That is true. But what happened? Instead of taking men's freedom from them, Thou didst make it greater than ever! Didst Thou forget that man prefers peace, and even death, to freedom of choice in the knowledge of good and evil? Nothing is more seductive for man than his freedom of conscience, but nothing is a greater cause of suffering. And behold, instead of giving a firm foundation for setting the conscience of man at rest for ever, Thou didst choose all that is exceptional, vague and enigmatic; Thou didst choose what was utterly beyond the strength of men, acting as though Thou didst not love them at all—Thou who didst come to give Thy life for them! Instead of taking possession of men's freedom, Thou didst increase it, and burdened the spiritual kingdom of mankind with its sufferings for ever. Thou didst desire man's free love, that he should follow Thee

freely, enticed and taken captive by Thee. In place of the rigid ancient law, man must hereafter with free heart decide for himself
what is good and what is evil, having only Thy image before him as
his guide. But didst Thou not know he would at last reject even
Thy image and Thy truth, if he is weighed down with the fearful
burden of free choice? They will cry aloud at last that the truth is
not in Thee, for they could not have been left in greater confusion
and suffering than Thou hast caused, laying upon them so many
cares and unanswerable problems.

" 'So that, in truth, Thou didst Thyself lay the foundation for the
destruction of Thy kingdom, and no one is more to blame for it. Yet
what was offered Thee? There are three powers, three powers
alone, able to conquer and to hold captive for ever the conscience
of these impotent rebels for their happiness—those forces are miracle, mystery and authority. Thou hast rejected all three and hast
set the example for doing so. When the wise and dread spirit set
Thee on the pinnacle of the temple and said to Thee, "If Thou
wouldst know whether Thou art the Son of God then cast Thyself
down, for it is written: the angels shall hold him up lest he fall and
bruise himself, and Thou shalt know then whether Thou art the
Son of God and shalt prove then how great is Thy faith in Thy
Father." But Thou didst refuse and wouldst not cast Thyself down.
Oh! of course, Thou didst proudly and well, like God; but the
weak, unruly race of men, are they gods? Oh, Thou didst know then
that in taking one step, in making one movement to cast Thyself
down, Thou wouldst be tempting God and have lost all Thy faith
in Him, and wouldst have been dashed to pieces against that earth
which Thou didst come to save. And the wise spirit that tempted
Thee would have rejoiced. But I ask again, are there many like
Thee? And couldst Thou believe for one moment that men, too,
could face such a temptation? Is the nature of men such, that they
can reject miracle, and at the great moments of their life, the moments of their deepest, most agonising spiritual difficulties, cling
only to the free verdict of the heart? Oh, Thou didst know that Thy
deed would be recorded in books, would be handed down to remote times and the utmost ends of the earth, and Thou didst hope
that man, following Thee, would cling to God and not ask for a
miracle. But Thou didst not know that when man rejects miracle
he rejects God too; for man seeks not so much God as the miracu-

lous. And as man cannot bear to be without the miraculous, he will create new miracles of his own for himself, and will worship deeds of sorcery and witchcraft, though he might be a hundred times over a rebel, heretic and infidel. Thou didst not come down from the Cross when they shouted to Thee, mocking and reviling Thee, "Come down from the cross and we will believe that Thou art He" Thou didst not come down, for again Thou wouldst not enslave man by a miracle, and didst crave faith given freely, not based on miracle, Thou didst crave for free love and not the base raptures of the slave before the might that has overawed him for ever. But Thou didst think too highly of men therein, for they are slaves, of course, though rebellious by nature. Look round and judge; fifteen centuries have passed, look upon them. Whom hast Thou raised up to Thyself? I swear, man is weaker and baser by nature than Thou hast believed him! Can he, can he do what Thou didst? By showing him so much respect, Thou didst, as it were, cease to feel for him, for Thou didst ask far too much from him— Thou who hast loved him more than Thyself! Respecting him less, Thou wouldst have asked less of him. That would have been more like love, for his burden would have been lighter. He is weak and vile. What though he is everywhere now rebelling against our power, and proud of his rebellion? It is the pride of a child and a schoolboy. They are little children rioting and barring out the teacher at school. But their childish delight will end; it will cost them dear. They will cast down temples and drench the earth with blood. But they will see at last, the foolish children, that, though they are rebels, they are impotent rebels, unable to keep up their own rebellion. Bathed in their foolish tears, they will recognise at last that He who created them rebels must have meant to mock at them. They will say this in despair, and their utterance will be a blasphemy which will make them more unhappy still, for man's nature cannot bear blasphemy, and in the end always avenges it on itself. And so unrest, confusion and unhappiness—that is the present lot of man after Thou didst bear so much for their freedom! Thy great prophet tells in vision and in image, that he saw all those who took part in the first resurrection and that there were of each tribe twelve thousand. But if there were so many of them, they must have been not men but gods. They had borne Thy cross, they had endured scores of years in the barren, hungry wilderness, liv-

ing upon locusts and roots—and Thou mayest indeed point with
pride at those children of freedom, of free love, of free and splendid
sacrifice for Thy name. But remember that they were only some
thousands; and what of the rest? And how are the other weak ones
to blame, because they could not endure what the strong have endured? How is the weak soul to blame that it is unable to receive
such terrible gifts? Canst Thou have simply come to the elect and
for the elect? But if so, it is a mystery and we cannot understand it.
And if it is a mystery, we too have a right to preach a mystery, and
to teach them that it's not the free judgment of their hearts, not
love that matters, but a mystery which they must follow blindly,
even against their conscience. So we have done. We have corrected
Thy work and have founded it upon *miracle, mystery* and *authority*. And men rejoiced that they were again led like sheep, and that
the terrible gift that had brought them such suffering, was, at last,
lifted from their hearts. Were we right teaching them this? Speak!
Did we not love mankind, so meekly acknowledging their feeble-
ness, lovingly lightening their burden, and permitting their weak
nature even sin with our sanction? Why hast Thou come now to
hinder us? And why dost Thou look silently and searchingly at me
with Thy mild eyes? Be angry. I don't want Thy love, for I love
Thee not. And what use is it for me to hide anything from Thee?
Don't I know to Whom I am speaking? All that I can say is known
to Thee already. And is it for me to conceal from Thee our mystery? Perhaps it is Thy will to hear it from my lips. Listen, then.
We are not working with Thee, but with *him*—that is our mystery.
It's long—eight centuries—since we have been on *his* side and not
on Thine. Just eight centuries ago, we took from him what Thou
didst reject with scorn, that last gift he offered Thee, showing Thee
all the kingdoms of the earth. We took from him Rome and the
sword of Cæsar, and proclaimed ourselves sole rulers of the earth,
though hitherto we have not been able to complete our work. But
whose fault is that? Oh, the work is only beginning, but it has begun. It has long to await completion and the earth has yet much to
suffer, but we shall triumph and shall be Cæsars, and then we shall
plan the universal happiness of man. But Thou mightest have taken
even then the sword of Cæsar. Why didst Thou reject that last gift?
Hadst Thou accepted that last counsel of the mighty spirit, Thou
wouldst have accomplished all that man seeks on earth—that is,

some one to worship, some one to keep his conscience, and some means of uniting all in one unanimous and harmonious ant-heap, for the craving for universal unity is the third and last anguish of men. Mankind as a whole has always striven to organize a universal state. There have been many great nations with great histories, but the more highly they were developed the more unhappy they were, for they felt more acutely than other people the craving for worldwide union. The great conquerors, Timours and Ghenghis-Khans, whirled like hurricanes over the face of the earth striving to subdue its people, and they too were but the unconscious expression of the same craving for universal unity. Hadst Thou taken the world and Cæsar's purple, Thou wouldst have founded the universal state and have given universal peace. For who can rule men if not he who holds their conscience and their bread in his hands? We have taken the sword of Cæsar, and in taking it, of course, have rejected Thee and followed *him*. Oh, ages are yet to come of the confusion of free thought, of their science and cannibalism. For having begun to build their tower of Babel without us, they will end, of course, with cannibalism. But then the beast will crawl to us and lick our feet and spatter them with tears of blood. And we shall sit upon the beast and raise the cup, and on it will be written, "Mystery." But then, and only then, the reign of peace and happiness will come for men. Thou art proud of Thine elect, but Thou hast only the elect, while we give rest to all. And besides, how many of those elect, those mighty ones who could become elect, have grown weary waiting for Thee, and have transferred and will transfer the powers of their spirit and the warmth of their heart to the other camp, and end by raising their *free* banner against Thee. Thou didst Thyself lift up that banner. But with us all will be happy and will no more rebel nor destroy one another as under Thy freedom. Oh, we shall persuade them that they will only become free when they renounce their freedom to us and submit to us. And shall we be right or shall we be lying? They will be convinced that we are right, for they will remember the horrors of slavery and confusion to which Thy freedom brought them. Freedom, free thought and science, will lead them into such straits and will bring them face to face with such marvels and insoluble mysteries, that some of them, the fierce and rebellious, will destroy themselves, others, rebellious but weak, will destroy one another,

while the rest, weak and unhappy, will crawl fawning to our feet
and whine to us: "Yes, you were right, you alone possess His mystery, and we come back to you, save us from ourselves!"

" 'Receiving bread from us, they will see clearly that we take the
bread made by their hands from them, to give it to them, without
any miracle. They will see that we do not change the stones to
bread, but in truth they will be more thankful for taking it from
our hands than for the bread itself! For they will remember only
too well that in old days, without our help, even the bread they
made turned to stones in their hands, while since they have come
back to us, the very stones have turned to bread in their hands. Too,
too well they know the value of complete submission! And until
men know that, they will be unhappy. Who is most to blame for
their not knowing it, speak? Who scattered the flock and sent it
astray on unknown paths? But the flock will come together again
and will submit once more, and then it will be once for all. Then
we shall give them the quiet humble happiness of weak creatures
such as they are by nature. Oh, we shall persuade them at last not
to be proud, for Thou didst lift them up and thereby taught them
to be proud. We shall show them that they are weak, that they are
only pitiful children, but that childlike happiness is the sweetest of
all. They will become timid and will look to us and huddle close to
us in fear, as chicks to the hen. They will marvel at us and will be
awe-stricken before us, and will be proud at our being so powerful
and clever, that we have been able to subdue such a turbulent flock
of thousands of millions. They will tremble impotently before our
wrath, their minds will grow fearful, they will be quick to shed
tears like women and children, but they will be just as ready at a
sign from us to pass to laughter and rejoicing, to happy mirth and
childish song. Yes, we shall set them to work, but in their leisure
hours we shall make their life like a child's game, with children's
songs and innocent dance. Oh, we shall allow them even sin, they
are weak and helpless, and they will love us like children because
we allow them to sin. We shall tell them that every sin will be ex-
piated, if it is done with our permission, that we allow them to sin
because we love them, and the punishment for these sins we take
upon ourselves. And we shall take it upon ourselves, and they will
adore us as their saviours who have taken on themselves their sins
before God. And they will have no secrets from us. We shall allow

or forbid them to live with their wives and mistresses, to have or not to have children—according to whether they have been obedient or disobedient—and they will submit to us gladly and cheerfully. The most painful secrets of their conscience, all, all they will bring to us, and we shall have an answer for all. And they will be glad to believe our answer, for it will save them from the great anxiety and terrible agony they endure at present in making a free decision for themselves. And all will be happy, all the millions of creatures except the hundred thousand who rule over them. For only we, we who guard the mystery, shall be unhappy. There will be thousands of millions of happy babes, and a hundred thousand sufferers who have taken upon themselves the curse of the knowledge of good and evil. Peacefully they will die, peacefully they will expire in Thy name, and beyond the grave they will find nothing but death. But we shall keep the secret, and for their happiness we shall allure them with the reward of heaven and eternity. Though if there were anything in the other world, it certainly would not be for such as they. It is prophesied that Thou wilt come again in victory, Thou wilt come with Thy chosen, the proud and strong, but we will say that they have only saved themselves, but we have saved all. We are told that the harlot who sits upon the beast, and holds in her hands the *mystery*, shall be put to shame, that the weak will rise up again, and will rend her royal purple and will strip naked her loathsome body. But then I will stand up and point out to Thee the thousand millions of happy children who have known no sin. And we who have taken their sins upon us for their happiness will stand up before Thee and say: "Judge us if Thou canst and darest." Know that I fear Thee not. Know that I too have been in the wilderness, I too have lived on roots and locusts, I too prized the freedom with which Thou hast blessed men, and I too was striving to stand among Thy elect, among the strong and powerful, thirsting "to make up the number." But I awakened and would not serve madness. I turned back and joined the ranks of those *who have corrected Thy work.* I left the proud and went back to the humble, for the happiness of the humble. What I say to Thee will come to pass, and our dominion will be built up. I repeat, to-morrow Thou shalt see that obedient flock who at a sign from me will hasten to heap up the hot cinders about the pile on which I shall burn Thee for coming to hinder us. For if any one has ever deserved our fires, it is Thou. To-morrow I shall burn Thee. Dixi.'"

. . . When the Inquisitor ceased speaking, he waited some time for his Prisoner to answer him. His silence weighed down upon him. He saw that the prisoner had listened intently all the time, looking gently in his face and evidently not wishing to reply. The old man longed for Him to say something, however bitter and terrible. But he suddenly approached the old man in silence and softly kissed him on his bloodless aged lips. That was all his answer. The old man shuddered. His lips moved. He went to the door, opened it, and said to Him: "Go, and come no more . . . come not at all, never, never!" And he let Him out into the dark alleys of the town. The Prisoner went away."

"And the old man?"

"The kiss glows in his heart, but the old man adheres to his idea."

"And you with him, you too?" cried Alyosha, mournfully.

Ivan laughed.

"Why, it's all nonsense, Alyosha. It's only the senseless poem of a senseless student, who could never write two lines of verse. Why do you take it so seriously? . . ."

Translated by Constance Garnett

DOSTOYEVSKY: *The Grand Inquisitor*

1. *Why does Ivan call this piece a poem in prose? Do you accept his further evaluation of it as "only the senseless poem of a senseless student"?*

2. *Why does the Inquisitor wish to contain Jesus' notion of freedom? What dangers does he discern in it?*

3. *What is the significance of the first temptation in the wilderness— to give man bread?*

4. *What does the Inquisitor mean by: "In bread there was offered Thee an invincible banner; give bread, and man will worship Thee, for nothing is more certain than bread"?*

5. *What is the Inquisitor's argument about man's free choice? What is his view of man?*

6. *Why will the church burn Jesus if necessary? What is His reaction to the threat? What does Ivan hope to convey by having Jesus react this way?*

7. *What are the political and social overtones of Ivan's fantasy? Do you think his fantasy has validity today?*

8. *Turgenev once described Dostoyevsky as "the most vicious Christian" he had ever known. Does this selection bear out that accusation?*

9. *For many years, Tolstoy dismissed Dostoyevsky as a "morbid mediocrity," but toward the end of his life,* The Brothers Karamazov *became Tolstoy's bedside book, the one he read and reread endlessly. William Barrett says that despite the tremendous differences in the literary and human atmospheres they create, both bring the same revelation to the philosophic mind. From the two stories representing these writers, can you say what that revelation is?*

Leo Tolstoy:

ALESHA THE POT

Honored as one of the world's greatest novelists, Leo Tolstoy was born on the family estate in the province of Tula, Russia, in 1828. In his early twenties when his attempt to establish a school for the peasants on his large estate failed, he turned to the carefree life available to a wealthy young nobleman in Moscow and St. Petersburg. While serving as an artillery officer in the Crimea, he began to write sketches and stories based upon his travels and military experiences. Encouraged by Ivan Turgenev, he settled down on his estate after his marriage and wrote the novels that gained him his fame, War and Peace *(1866) and* Anna Karenina *(1877). After 1876, he underwent a period of spiritual turmoil that lasted until his death in 1910. The Death of Ivan Ilyich (1886), Master and Man (1895), and stories like "Memoirs of a Lunatic" reflect his disenchantment with bourgeois, materialistic values and his discovery of a Christian way of life in the simple existence of the peasant. In the following story, a peasant boy who is everyone's drudge, is apotheosized as "the holy fool." D. S. Mirsky, the great Russian scholar, calls this story "one of the very few that make one forget the bedrock Luciferism and pride of the author."*

ß≥

ALESHA was a younger brother. They called him "the Pot" because once, when his mother sent him to bring a pot of milk to the deacon, he stumbled and smashed the pot. His mother beat him, and the children began calling him "the Pot" to tease him. Alesha the Pot—that became his nickname.

Alesha was a thin lop-eared boy (his ears stuck out like wings), and his nose was large. The children used to tease him: "Alesha has a nose like a pointing dog." There was a school in the village, but Alesha was not taught reading and writing, as he had no time to study. His older brother lived with a merchant in town, and from infancy on, Alesha helped his father. When he was six years old he was already watching the cow and the sheep in the pasture with his sister, and he was not full grown when he began watching over the horses day and night. From the age of twelve on, he was plowing and carting. He had no strength, but had a certain knack. He was always gay. When children laughed at him, he was silent or laughed. When his father cursed him, he was silent and listened. And as soon as the cursing stopped, he would smile and set about the task before him.

Alesha was nineteen when his brother was drafted into the army. And his father put Alesha in his brother's place with the merchant as an errand boy. Alesha was given his brother's old boots, his father's cap and coat, and was taken to the city. Alesha could not have been more delighted with his clothes, but the merchant remained dissatisfied with Alesha's appearance.

"I thought you were putting a real man in Semon's place," said the merchant, glancing at Alesha. "But you've brought me this runt instead. What's he good for?"

"He can do everything—harness the horses, go anywhere, and work ferociously. He just looks like a sapling. But he's wiry."

"Well, all right, I'll see."

"And most of all—he's dutiful. Eager to work."

"What can one do with you? Leave him."

So Alesha began living at the merchant's.

The merchant's family was not large: the master, his old mother, his elder married son, of elementary schooling, who was in business with his father; and another son, who was educated, having completed secondary school and attended a university from which he had been expelled and had returned to live at home; and there was also an unmarried daughter in secondary school.

At first Alesha was not much liked—he was still very peasant-like and badly dressed, he had no manners and addressed everyone familiarly, but they soon became accustomed to him. He was even more useful than his brother. He was truly dutiful; he was sent on every sort of errand, and he did everything willingly and quickly, going from one task to the next without a break. And at the merchant's just as at home, all the work was heaped on Alesha. The more he did, the more tasks were heaped on him. The master and the master's mother and the master's daughter and the master's son and the overseer and the cook—all constantly sent him here and there, and assigned him first this and then that to do. All you could hear was: "Run, lad" or: "Alesha, fix this." "Alesha, you forgot this, didn't you?" "Watch out, don't forget, Alesha." And Alesha ran, fixed, and watched out, and did not forget, and always managed everything and was always smiling.

He soon wore out his brother's boots, and the master scolded him thoroughly for walking in tattered boots with his bare toes showing, and ordered him to buy new boots at the bazaar. The boots were new, and Alesha, was delighted with them, but his feet were worn out and by evening they ached from running about, and he became angry with them. Alesha was afraid that when his father came to get the money he would be annoyed that the merchant had deducted the boots from his wages.

Alesha got up before dawn in winter, chopped firewood, swept out the house, and fed the cow and the horses and watered them. Then he lit the stove, cleaned the master's boots and clothes, put out the samovars and cleaned them; then the overseer would call him to fetch some goods, or the cook would order him to knead the dough, or to clean the pots. Then they sent him to town, either with a note, or to fetch the master's daughter at school, or for oil for the old woman. "Where've you been loitering, you wretch," first one, then the other said to him. "Why go yourself—Alesha will run over. Alesha! Oh Alesha!" And Alesha ran.

He had breakfast on the run, and rarely had time for dinner with the others. The cook cursed him for not being with the rest, but she was sorry for him all the same, and left him a hot dish for dinner and for supper. There was a particularly large amount of work before and during holidays. And Alesha was specially delighted with holidays because he was given a tip, although a small one, sixty kopecks in all; but, still, his own money, which he could spend as he wanted. He never set eyes on his salary. His father used to come, take it from the merchant, and give Alesha only reproaches for wearing out his boots so quickly. When Alesha had collected two rubles in tips, he purchased, on the advice of the cook, a red knitted jacket; and when he put it on, he was unable to keep his mouth closed, he was so contented.

Alesha said little, and when he said something, it was always disconnected and abrupt. When he was ordered to do something or asked whether he could do such and such, he always said, without the slightest hesitation: "Can do"—and immediately rushed out to do it, and did it.

He knew no prayers; he had forgotten those his mother had taught him; but he still prayed in the morning and at night—he prayed with his hands, crossing himself.

Thus Alesha lived for a year and a half; then, in the second half of the second year, a most unusual event happened in his life. This event consisted of his realizing, to his own amazement, that outside of those relationships between people which stem from their need for each other, there were other completely special relationships; that a person did not always clean boots, or fetch a parcel, or harness a horse because it was necessary to someone else, but that a person could, without there being any need of any kind on the part of the other, do things for him out of an urge to serve him, to be kind to him, and that he, Alesha, was the object of such an urge. It was the cook, Ustinya, who made him realize this. Ustinya was an orphan, young, and a hard worker, just like Alesha. She began feeling sorry for Alesha, and Alesha felt, for the first time, that he was not her servant, but was himself appreciated by another. When his mother used to feel sorry for him, he had paid no attention, and it had seemed to him just as when he felt sorry for himself. But suddenly he noticed that with Ustinya it was completely different: he saw how she took pity on him, and left *kasha* with butter for him in the pot; and how, when he ate, she leaned with her hand tucked under her chin and watched him. And he would glance at her, and she would laugh, and he would laugh.

This was so new and strange that at first it frightened Alesha. He felt it would prevent him from serving as well as he had before. But he was glad just the same, and when he looked at his trousers, patched by Ustinya, he nodded his head and smiled. Often after work or while on the run he would think of Ustinya and say: "Ah, yes, Ustinya!" She helped him whenever she could, and he helped her. She often told him the story of her life, how she was orphaned, how her aunt took her in, how she was sent away to town, how a cook's son had tried to seduce her, and how she cut him short. She loved to talk and he found it pleasant to listen to her. He heard that in towns peasants hired as laborers often married cooks. Once she asked him whether he would get married soon. He said he did not know, and that he was unwilling to take anyone in his village.

"What then, have you found someone?" she asked.

"Yes, you. You will, won't you?"

"Oh, my Pot, my Pot, how cleverly you put it," she said, slapping him on the back with her hand. "Why wouldn't I?"

At Shrovetide Alesha's father came to town for the money. The merchant's wife knew Alesha planned to marry Ustinya, and she did not like it. "She'll become pregnant, and what good will she be with a child?" she had told her husband.

The master gave Alesha's father the money.

"Well, is the boy behaving?" said the peasant. "I told you he was dutiful."

"He's dutiful all right, but he's planning something stupid. He's thought up marrying the cook. And I won't keep a married couple. It's not convenient for us."

"The fool, the fool, what a thing to think of," said the father. "Don't give it a thought. I'll order him to drop it."

The father went into the kitchen, sat down, and waited for his son on the bench. Alesha was running errands and returned, huffing and puffing.

"I thought you were lost. Now, what's this you're planning?" said the father.

"But nothing."

"What do you mean, nothing? You decided to get married. I'll marry you when the time comes, and to the wife you need, and not a city trollop."

The father spoke at length. Alesha stood and sighed. When his father had finished, Alesha smiled.

"Well, then, it can be put aside."

"All right."

When his father went away and he was left alone with Ustinya (who had been standing behind the door listening), he told her: "Our plans didn't work out; didn't work. You heard? He's furious; won't have it."

She cried silently in her apron.

Alesha clicked his tongue.

"How can I not obey? Naturally, we must drop it."

In the evening when the merchant's wife called him to close the shutters, she said to him:

"Well then, you've obeyed your father, dropped your foolishness?"

"Naturally I dropped it," Alesha said, then laughed, and immediately burst into tears.

From that time on Alesha never spoke of marriage to Ustinya again, and he lived as before.

During Lent, the overseer sent him to clean the snow off the roof. He climbed out on the roof, cleared everything away, and had begun tearing off the snow frozen on the gutters, when his feet slid and he fell, shovel and all. Unfortunately he fell, not onto the snow, but onto the iron roof over the porch. Ustinya ran up to him and so did the master's daughter.

"Did you hurt yourself, Alesha?"

"It looks like I did. It doesn't matter."

He tried to stand up, but could not, and started to smile. They took him to his room. A doctor came. He examined him and asked where it hurt.

"It hurts everywhere, but it doesn't matter. Except the master will be annoyed. Send word to papa."

Alesha lay in bed two days; on the third, the priest was sent for.

"What, you're not going to die, are you?" asked Ustinya.

"But, what of it? As if we lived forever? We have to die some time," Alesha said, speaking as rapidly as ever. "Thank you, Ustinya, for pitying me. You see, it's better he called off the marriage, it would have been for nothing. Now everything's fine."

He prayed with the priest only with his hands and his heart. And in his heart he believed that if you are good here, if you obey and don't give offense, then it will be good there, too.

He said little. Just asked for water and kept smiling at something.

Then he looked surprised at something, stretched himself, and died.

Translated by Arthur Mendel
and Barbara Makanowitzky

TOLSTOY: *Alesha the Pot*

1. *D. S. Mirsky calls this story "a masterpiece of rare perfection . . . concentrated into . . . six pages." Do you agree or disagree with this judgment? Since the story covers almost the entire career of Alesha, should it have been much longer?*

2. *What social and spiritual values does Tolstoy dramatize in this story? Are they valid today? Or are they unworkable in a society much more complex than Tolstoy imagined at the end of the nineteenth century?*

3. *Alesha obeys his father, remains celibate, and suffers from his fall for three days (in the spring). Do you think these details are deliberately suggestive? In what sense might this story be regarded as a parable?*

4. *Do you find Alesha's unquestioning submission admirable or contemptible? Is it necessary to the true religious spirit?*

5. *In many of the stories in this volume, the protagonist is a conscious, rational, restless soul who is seeking greater consciousness. In your estimation, would the purity of conscience and perfect peace that Alesha achieves be possible for such people? Is it this state of mind that they seek? Is there something wrong in the way they seek it, and does Tolstoy, in your judgment, have the key to the quest?*

Joaquim Maria Machado de Assis:

MIDNIGHT MASS

Machado de Assis was born in 1839 in Rio de Janeiro, the son of a mulatto house painter and a white woman from Portugal. Attracted to writing at an early age, he immersed himself in a literary atmosphere and turned out great quantities of stories and novels, poetry, drama, criticism, and journalistic commentary. Although he is regarded by Brazilians as their greatest writer, he was almost totally unknown in this country until his Epitaph of a Small Winner *was published here in 1952. Along with this "classic comedy of ideas," two other novels,* Dom Casmurro *and* Philosopher or Dog?, *form the basis of his reputation. Until his death in 1908, Machado was the president of the Brazilian Academy of Letters. With its light irony and characteristic understatement, "Midnight Mass" indicates his method, to suggest reality through light dabs and then to retreat to force the reader into drawing his own conclusions.*

I HAVE never quite understood a conversation that I had with a lady many years ago, when I was seventeen and she was thirty. It was Christmas Eve. I had arranged to go to Mass with a neighbor and was to rouse him at midnight for that purpose.

The two-story house in which I was staying belonged to the notary Menezes, whose first wife had been a cousin of mine. His second wife, Conceição [Conception], and her mother had received me hospitably upon my arrival a few months earlier. I had come to Rio from Mangaratiba to study for the college entrance examinations. I lived quietly with my books. Few contacts. Occasional walks. The family was small: the notary, his wife, his mother-in-law, and two female slaves. An old-fashioned household. By ten at night everyone was in his bedroom; by half-past ten the house was asleep.

I had never gone to a theater and, more than once, on hearing Menezes say that he was going, I asked him to take me along. On these occasions his mother-in-law frowned and the slaves tittered. Menezes did not reply; he dressed, went out, and returned the next morning. Later I learned that the theater was a euphemism. Menezes was having an affair with a married woman who was separated from her husband; he stayed out once a week. Conceição had grieved at the beginning, but after a time she had grown used to the situation. Custom led to resignation, and finally she came almost to accept the affair as proper.

Gentle Conceição! They called her the saint and she merited the title, so uncomplainingly did she suffer her husband's neglect. In truth, she possessed a temperament of great equanimity, with extremes neither of tears nor of laughter. Everything about her was passive and attenuated. Her very face was median, neither pretty nor ugly. She was what is called a kind person. She spoke ill of no one, she pardoned everything. She didn't know how to hate; quite possibly she didn't know how to love.

On that Christmas Eve (it was 1861 or 1862) the notary was at theater. I should have been back in Mangaratiba, but I had decided to remain till Christmas to see a Midnight Mass in the big city. The family retired at the usual hour. I sat in the front parlor, dressed and ready. From there I could leave through the entrance hall without waking anyone. There were three keys to the door: the notary had one, I had one, and one remained in the house.

"But Mr. Nogueira, what will you do all this while?" asked Conceição's mother.

"I'll read, Madame Ignacia."

I had a copy of an old translation of *The Three Musketeers,* published originally, I think, in serial form in *The Journal of Commerce*. I sat down at the table in the center of the room and, by the light of the kerosene lamp, while the house slept, mounted once more D'Artagnan's bony nag and set out upon adventure. In a short time I was completely absorbed. The minutes flew as they rarely do when one is waiting. I heard the clock strike eleven, but almost without noticing. After a time, however, a sound from the interior of the house roused me from my book. It was the sound of footsteps, in the hall that connected the parlor with the dining-room. I raised my head. Soon I saw the form of Conceição appear at the door.

"Haven't you gone?" she asked.

"No, I haven't. I don't think it's midnight yet."

"What patience!"

Conceição, wearing her bedroom slippers, came into the room. She was dressed in a white negligee, loosely bound at the waist. Her slenderness helped to suggest a romantic apparition quite in keeping with the spirit of my novel. I shut the book. She sat on the chair facing mine, near the sofa. To my question whether perchance I had awakened her by stirring about, she quickly replied:

"No, I woke up naturally."

I looked at her and doubted her statement. Her eyes were not those of a person who had just slept. However, I quickly put out of my mind the thought that she could be guilty of lying. The possibility that I might have kept her awake and that she might have lied in order not to make me unhappy, did not occur to me at the time. I have alreaady said that she was a good person, a kind person.

"I guess it won't be much longer now," I said.

"How patient you are to stay awake and wait while your friend sleeps! And to wait alone! Aren't you afraid of ghosts? I thought you'd be startled when you saw me."

"When I heard footsteps I was surprised. But then I soon saw it was you."

"What are you reading? Don't tell me, I think I know: it's *The Three Musketeers.*"

"Yes, that's right. It's very interesting."

"Do you like novels?"

"Yes."

"Have you ever read *The Little Sweetheart?*"

"By Mr. Macedo? I have it in Mangaratiba."

"I'm very fond of novels, but I don't have much time for them. Which ones have you read?"

I began to name some. Conceição listened, with her head resting on the back of her chair, looking at me past half-shut eyelids. From time to time she wet her lips with her tongue. When I stopped speaking she said nothing. Thus we remained for several seconds. Then she raised her head; she clasped her hands and rested her chin on them, with her elbows on the arms of her chair, all without taking from me her large, perceptive eyes.

"Maybe she's bored with me," I thought. And then, aloud: "Madame Conceição, I think it's getting late and I. . . ."

"No, it's still early. I just looked at the clock; it's half-past eleven. There's time yet. When you lose a night's sleep, can you stay awake the next day?"

"I did once."

"I can't. If I lose a night, the next day I just have to take a nap, if only for half an hour. But of course I'm getting on in years."

"Oh, no, nothing of the sort, Madame Conceição!"

I spoke so fervently that I made her smile. Usually her gestures were slow, her attitude calm. Now, however, she rose suddenly, moved to the other side of the room, and, in her chaste disarray, walked about between the window and the door of her husband's study. Although thin, she always walked with a certain rocking gait as if she carried her weight with difficulty. I had never before felt this impression so strongly. She paused several times, examining a curtain or correcting the position of some object on the sideboard. Finally she stopped directly in front of me, with the table between us. The circle of her ideas was narrow indeed: she returned to her surprise at seeing me awake and dressed. I repeated what she already knew, that I had never heard a Midnight Mass in the city and that I didn't want to miss the chance.

"It's the same as in the country. All Masses are alike."

"I guess so. But in the city there must be more elegance and more people. Holy Week here in Rio is much better than in the country. I don't know about St. John's Day or St. Anthony's. . . ."

Little by little she had leaned forward; she had rested her elbows on the marble top of the table and had placed her face between the palms of her hands. Her unbuttoned sleeves fell naturally, and I saw her forearms, very white and not so thin as one might have supposed. I had seen her arms before, although not frequently, but on this occasion sight of them impressed me greatly. The veins were so blue that, despite the dimness of the light, I could trace every one of them. Even more than the book, Conceição's presence had served to keep me wide awake. I went on talking about holy days in the country and in the city, and about whatever else came to my lips. I jumped from subject to subject, sometimes returning to an earlier one; and I laughed in order to make her laugh, so that I could see her white, shining, even teeth. Her eyes were not really black but were very dark; her nose, thin and slightly

curved, gave her face an air of interrogation. Whenever I raised
my voice a little, she hushed me.

"Softly! Mama may wake up."

And she did not move from that position, which filled me with
delight, so close were our faces. Really there was no need to speak
loudly in order to be heard. We both whispered, I more than she
because I had more to say. At times she became serious, very serious, with her brow a bit wrinkled. After a while she tired and
changed both position and place. She came around the table and
sat on the sofa. I turned my head and could see the tips of her slippers, but only for as long as it took her to sit down: her negligee
was long and quickly covered them. I remember that they were
black. Conceição said very softly:

"Mama's room is quite a distance away, but she sleeps so lightly.
If she wakes up now, poor thing, it will take her a long time to fall
asleep again."

"I'm like that, too."

"What?" she asked, leaning forward to hear better.

I moved to the chair immediately next to the sofa and repeated
what I had said. She laughed at the coincidence, for she, too, was a
light sleeper, we were all light sleepers.

"I'm just like mama: when I wake up I can't fall asleep again. I
roll all over the bed, I get up, I light the candle, I walk around,
I lie down again, and nothing happens."

"Like tonight."

"No, no," she hastened.

I didn't understand her denial; perhaps she didn't understand
it either. She took the ends of her belt and tapped them on her
knees, or rather on her right knee, for she had crossed her legs.
Then she began to talk about dreams. She said she had had only one
nightmare in her whole life, and that one during her childhood. She
wanted to know whether I ever had nightmares. Thus the conversation re-engaged itself and moved along slowly, continuously, and
I forgot about the hour and about Mass. Whenever I finished a bit
of narrative or an explanation she asked a question or brought up
some new point, and I started talking again. Now and then she had
to caution me.

"Softly, softly . . ."

Sometimes there were pauses. Twice I thought she was asleep. But her eyes, shut for a moment, quickly opened: they showed neither sleepiness nor fatigue, as though she had shut them merely so that she could see better. On one of these occasions I think she noticed that I was absorbed in her, and I remember that she shut her eyes again—whether hurried or slowly I do not remember. (Some of my recollections of that evening seem abortive or confused. I get mixed up, I contradict myself.) One thing I remember vividly is that at a certain moment she, who till then had been such engaging company (but nothing more), suddenly became beautiful, so very beautiful. She had stood up, with her arms crossed. I, out of respect for her, stirred myself to rise; she did not want me to, she put one of her hands on my shoulder, and I remained seated. I thought she was going to say something; but she trembled as if she had a chill, turned her back, and sat in the chair where she had found me reading. She glanced at the mirror above the sofa and began to talk about two engravings that were hanging on the wall.

"These pictures are getting old. I've asked Chiquinho to buy new ones."

Chiquinho was her husband's nickname. The pictures bespoke the man's principal interest. One was of Cleopatra; I no longer remember the subject of the other, but there were women in it. Both were banal. In those days I did not know they were ugly.

"They're pretty," I said.

"Yes, but they're stained. And besides, to tell the truth, I'd prefer pictures of saints. These are better for bachelors' quarters or a barber shop."

"A barber shop! I didn't think you'd ever been to. . . ."

"But I can imagine what the customers there talk about while they're waiting—girls and flirtations, and naturally the proprietor wants to please them with pictures they'll like. But I think pictures like that don't belong in the home. That's what I think, but I have a lot of queer ideas. Anyway, I don't like them. I have an Our Lady of the Immaculate Conception, my patron saint; it's very lovely. But it's a statue, it can't be hung on the wall, and I wouldn't want it here anyway. I keep it in my little oratory."

The oratory brought to mind the Mass. I thought it might be time to go and was about to say so. I think I even opened my mouth but shut it before I could speak, so that I could go on listening to what she was saying, so sweetly, so graciously, so gently that it drugged my soul. She spoke of her religious devotions as a child and as a young girl. Then she told about dances and walks and trips to the island of Paquetá, all mixed together, almost without interruption. When she tired of the past she spoke of the present, of household matters, of family cares, which, before her marriage, everyone said would be terrible, but really they were nothing. She didn't mention it, but I knew she had been twenty-seven when she married.

She no longer moved about, as at first, and hardly changed position. Her eyes seemed smaller, and she began to look idly about at the walls.

"We must change this wallpaper," she said, as if talking to herself.

I agreed, just to say something, to shake off my magnetic trance or whatever one may call the condition that thickened my tongue and benumbed my senses. I wished and I did not wish to end the conversation. I tried to take my eyes from her, and did so out of respect; but, afraid she would think I was tired of looking at her, when in truth I was not, I turned again towards her. The conversation was dying away. In the street, absolute stillness.

We stopped talking and for some time (I cannot say how long) sat there in silence. The only sound was the gnawing of a rat in the study; it stirred me from my somnolescence. I wanted to talk about it but didn't know how to begin. Conceição seemed to be abstracted. Suddenly I heard a beating on the window and a voice shouting:

"Midnight Mass! Midnight Mass!"

"There's your friend," she said, rising. "It's funny. You were to wake him, and here he comes to wake you. Hurry, it must be late. Goodbye."

"Is it time already?" I asked.

"Of course."

"Midnight Mass!" came the voice from outside, with more beating on the window.

"Hurry, hurry, don't make him wait. It was my fault. Goodbye until tomorrow."

And with her rocking gait Conceição walked softly down the

hall. I went out into the street and, with my friend, proceeded to the church. During Mass, Conceição kept appearing between me and the priest; charge this to my seventeen years. Next morning at breakfast I spoke of the Midnight Mass and of the people I had seen in church, without, however, exciting Conceição's interest. During the day I found her, as always, natural, benign, with nothing to suggest the conversation of the prior evening.

A few days later I went to Mangaratiba. When I returned to Rio in March, I learned that the notary had died of apoplexy. Conceição was living in the Engenho Novo district, but I neither visited nor met her. I learned later that she had married her husband's apprenticed clerk.

Translated by William Grossman

MACHADO: *Midnight Mass*

1. *Why is the scene set on Christmas Eve? Why is there such emphasis on the Midnight Mass?*

2. *What details about the narrator's mode of living contribute to the development of the episode?*

3. *Is the narrator's description of Conception reliable? Does she behave in a manner consistent with this description? What is the significance of her name and of the statue of Our Lady that she keeps in her oratory?*

4. *Why does the author choose to have the narrator reading* The Three Musketeers? *What is suggested by his absorption in books?*

5. *How does the sense of silence contribute to the story?*

6. *The narrator says: "Some of my recollections of that evening seem abortive or confused. I get mixed up. I contradict myself." Why should he be confused?*

7. *The narrator claims that he never quite understood the "conversation that I had with a lady many years ago." Can you explain what he failed to understand? Since he understands the meaning of the euphemism "the theater," do you believe he could be so naïve as not to understand the conversation? Why might he wish to pretend he didn't? Did anything happen that he failed to notice?*

8. *Machado gains his effects through understatement—can you cite some instances of it? Of what other writers in this volume does he remind you?*

Giovanni Verga:

THE ORPHANS

> Giovanni Verga was born in Catania, Sicily, in 1840 and died there
> in January, 1922. His best work—for example, The House by the
> Medlar Tree (1881), Little Novels of Sicily (1883), and Maestro
> Don Gesualdo (1888)—reflects life in the poverty-stricken areas of
> Sicily. With Manzoni, he is generally regarded as the greatest of
> Italian novelists, and among realistic writers anywhere he is of
> primary importance. His influence upon twentieth-century Italian
> literature is incalculable. With its emphasis upon poverty, suffering,
> and the need for the continuity of life despite continual setbacks,
> "The Orphans" is a typical Verga short story.

THE little girl appeared in the doorway twisting the corner of
her apron between her fingers, and said, "I've come."

Then as noboody took any notice of her, she began to look timidly
from one to the other of the village wives who were kneading up
the bread, and added: "They told me, 'You go to Neighbour Sidora's.'"

"Come on, come on," cried Goodwife Sidora, red as a tomato as
she turned from the oven-hole. "Wait and I'll make you a nice
bread-cake."

"That means they're bringing the extreme unction to Neighbour
Nunzia, if they've sent the child away," observed the Licodia goodwife.

One of the women who was helping to knead the bread turned
her head round, keeping on working with her fists in the kneading-
trough all the time, her arms bare to the elbows, and asked the
child:

"How is your step-mother?"

The child didn't know the woman, so she looked at her with wide eyes, and then lowering her head again, and rapidly, nervously twisting the corner of her apron, she mumbled in a low tone:

"She's in bed."

"Don't you hear there's the Host in the house?" replied the Licodia woman. "Now the neighbours have begun to lament round the door."

"When I've got the bread in the oven," said Neighbour Sidora, "I shall run across for a minute myself to see if they're not wanting anything. Master Meno will lose his right arm if this wife dies as well."

"There's some who have no luck with their wives, like others who are always unlucky with their cattle. As many as they get they are bound to lose. Look at Goodwife Angela!"

"Last night," added the Licodia woman, "I saw Neighbour Meno standing on his doorstep, come home from the vineyard before Ave Maria, and he was wiping his nose with his handkerchief."

"Yet you know," added the gossip who was kneading the bread, "he's a blessed good hand at killing off his wives. In less than three years this makes two daughters of Shepherd Nino that he's finished off, one after the other! Wait a bit, and he'll do for the third one, and then he'll get everything that belongs to Shepherd Nino."

"But is this child here Neighbour Nunzio's daughter, or is she by the first wife?"

"She's by the first wife. And the second one was as fond of her as if she was her own child, because the little orphan was her niece."

The child, hearing them speaking about her, began to cry quietly in a corner, to ease her aching heart, which she had kept still up till then by fidgeting with her apron.

"Come here then, come here," said Neighbour Sidora again. "The bread-cake is all nice and done. There, don't you cry, your mamma is in Paradise."

Then the child wiped her eyes with her fist the more readily because Neighbour Sidora was just setting about to open the oven.

"Poor Neighbour Nunzia!" a neighbour woman came saying in the doorway. "The grave-diggers have set off just now. They've just this minute gone past."

"Save us from it! I am a daughter of Holy Mary!" exclaimed the goodwives crossing themselves.

Goodwife Sidora took the bread-cake from the oven, dusted

the ashes off it, and gave it fiery hot to the child, who took it in her pinafore and went off with it very quietly, blowing on it.

"Where are you going?" Goodwife Sidora shouted after her. "You stop here. There's a bogey-man at home, with a black face, and he runs off with folks."

The orphan child listened very seriously, opening wide her eyes. Then she answered with the same obstinate little voice:

"I'm going to take it to mamma."

"Your mother's gone away. You stop here," repeated the neighbour. "You stop here and eat your bread-cake."

Then the child squatted on the doorstep, so unhappy, holding her bread-cake in her hands without thinking about it.

All at once, seeing her father approaching she got up quickly and ran to meet him. Neighbour Meno entered without saying anything, and sat in a corner with his hands hanging between his knees, long-faced, his lips white as paper, not having taken a mouthful of food since yesterday, he was so broken-hearted. He looked round at the women as if to say: I'm in a sad way!

The women, seeing him with his black kerchief round his neck, surrounded him in a circle, their hands still white with flour, sympathizing with him in chorus.

"Don't talk to me, Neighbour Sidora," he repeated, shaking his head and heaving his shoulders. "This is a thorn that'll never come out of my heart! A real saint that woman! I didn't deserve her, if I may say so. Even yesterday, bad as she was, she got up to see to the foal that is just weaned. And she wouldn't let me fetch the doctor so as not to spend money nor buy medicine. I shall never find another wife like her. You mark my word! Leave me alone and let me cry. I've reason to!"

And he kept shaking his head and swelling his shoulders, as if his trouble was heavy on him.

"As for finding another wife," added the Licodia woman to cheer him up, "you've only to look round for one."

"No! no!" Neighbour Meno kept repeating, with his head down like a mule. "I shall never find another wife like her. This time I'll stop a widower. I'm telling you."

Goodwife Sidora lifted up her voice: "Don't you talk rash, it doesn't do! You ought to look round for another wife, if for no other reason but out of regard for this poor little orphan, else who's going

to look after her, when you're away in the country! You don't want
to leave her in the middle of the road?"

"You find me another wife like her if you can! She didn't wash
herself so as not to dirty any water, and she waited on me in the
house better than a man-servant, loving and so faithful she
wouldn't have robbed me of a handful of beans from the shed, and
she never as much as opened her mouth to say, 'You give me this!'
And then a fine dowry with it all, stuff worth its weight in gold!
And now I've got to give it back, because there are no children! The
sexton told me just now he was coming with the holy water. And
how fond she was of that little thing there, because she reminded
her of her poor sister! Any other woman, who wasn't her aunt,
would have cast the evil eye on her, poor little orphan."

"If you take the third daughter of Shepherd Nino everything will
come all right, for the orphan and the dowry," said the Licodia
woman.

"That's what I say myself! But don't talk to me, for my mouth
is bitter as gall."

"That's not the way to be talking now," seconded Goodwife Sidora. "Better take a mouthful of something to eat, Neighbour
Meno, for you're at your last gasp."

"No! no!" Neighbour Meno kept repeating. "Don't talk to me
about eating, I've got a knot in my throat."

Neighbour Sidora put before him on a stool the hot bread with
black olives, a piece of sheep's cheese, and the flask of wine. And
the poor fellow began to munch slowly, slowly, keeping on mumbling with his long face.

"Such bread," he observed, becoming moved to tenderness. "Such
bread as she made, the poor departed soul, there wasn't her like
for it. It was as soft as meal, it was! And with a handful of wild
fennel she'd make you a soup that would make you lick your fingers after it. Now I shall have to buy my bread at the shop, from
that thief of a Master Puddo, and I shall get no more hot soup,
every time I come home wet through like a new hatched chicken.
And I shall have to go to bed on a cold stomach. Even the other
night, while I was sitting up with her, after I'd been hoeing all day
breaking up the lumps on the slope, and I heard myself snoring,
sitting beside the bed, I was so tired, the poor soul said to me: 'Go

and eat a spoonful. I've left the soup for you warm by the fire.' And she was always thoughtful for me, at home, mindful of whatever there was to be done, this, that and the other, so that she could never have done talking about it, telling me her last advice, like one who is setting off for a long journey, and I hearing her all the time murmuring when I was half asleep and half awake. And she went happy into the other world, with her crucifix on her breast, and her hands folded over it. She's got no need of rosaries and masses, saint that she is! The money for the priest would be money thrown away."

"It's a world of troubles!" exclaimed the neighbour woman. "And now Goodwife Angela's donkey, just close here, is going to die of indigestion."

"My troubles are worse than that!" wound up Neighbour Meno wiping his mouth with the back of his hand. "No, don't make me eat any more, for every mouthful goes down into my stomach like lead. Better you eat, poor innocent child who don't understand anything. Now you'll have nobody to wash you and comb your hair. Now you'll have no mother to keep you under her wing like a mother-hen, and you are lost as I am. I found you that one, but another step-mother like her you'll never have, my child!"

The little girl, all moved, pushed out her lips again and put her fists in her eyes.

"No, you can't do no less, I say," repeated Gossip Sidora. "You've got to look for another wife, out of regard for this poor little orphan who'd be left on the streets."

"And me, how am I left? And my young foal, and my house, and who's going to see to the fowls? Let me weep, Neighbour Sidora! I'd better have died myself, instead of that poor soul who's gone."

"Be quiet now, you don't know what you're saying, and you don't know what it means, a home without a master!"

"Ay, that's true enough!" agreed Neighbour Meno, somewhat comforted.

"Just think of poor Goodwife Angela, if you like! First she's lost her husband, then her big son, and now her donkey is dying as well!"

"If the donkey's got indigestion, he'd better be bled under the girth," said Neighbour Meno.

"You come and look at it, you understand about it," added the goodwife, "You'll be doing a work of charity for the soul of your wife."

Neighbour Meno got up to go to Goodwife Angela's, and the orphan ran after him like a chicken, now she had no one else in the world. Gossip Sidora, good housewife, reminded him:

"And what about the house? How are you leaving it, now there's nobody in it?"

"I've locked the door; and then Cousin Alfia lives just opposite, to keep an eye on it."

The ass of Neighbour Angela was stretched out in the middle of the courtyard, with his nose cold and his ears drooping, struggling from time to time with his four hoofs in the air, while the pains contracted his sides like a big pair of bellows. The widow, sitting before him on the stones, with her hands clutching her grey hair, and her eyes dry and despairing, watched him, pale as a dead woman.

Neighbour Meno began to walk round the animal, touching its ears, looking into its eyes, and as he saw that the blood was still flowing from the side, black, drop by drop, collecting at the ends of the bristly hairs, he asked:

"Then they have bled him?"

The widow fixed her gloomy eyes on his face without replying, and nodded her head.

"Then there's nothing more to be done," concluded Neighbour Meno, and he stood there watching the ass stretch itself out on the stones, rigid, with its hair all ruffled like a dead cat.

"It's the will of God, sister!" he said to comfort her. "We are both of us ruined, both of us."

He had seated himself on the stones beside the widow, with his little girl between his knees, and they were silent all of them watching the poor creature beating the air with its hoofs, from time to time, just like a dying man.

When Gossip Sidora had finished taking the bread from the oven she too came into the courtyard, along with Cousin Alfia, who had put on her new dress, and her silk kerchief on her head, to come for a minute's chat, and Gossip Sidora said to Neighbour Meno, drawing him aside: "Shepherd Nino won't be willing to give you the other daughter, seeing that they die like flies with you, and he loses the dowry if he does. And then Santa is too young, and there's the danger that she'd fill your house with children."

"If only they were boys, never mind! But what there is to fear is that they'd be girls. I'm a downright unfortunate man."

"There's always Cousin Alfia. She isn't so young as she was, and she's got her own bit, her house and a piece of vineyard."

Neighbour Meno turned his eyes on Cousin Alfia, who was pretending to look at the ass, with her hands on her hips, and he concluded:

"If that's how it is, we can talk about it after. But I'm a downright unlucky man."

Goodwife Sidora up and said:

"Think of those that are worse off than you, think of them."

"There aren't any, I tell you! I shall never find another wife like her! I shall never be able to forget her, not if I marry ten times more! Neither will this poor little orphan forget her."

"Be quiet, you'll forget her. And the child as well will forget her. Hasn't she forgotten her own true mother? You just look at Neighbour Angela, now her donkey is dying! And she's got nothing else! She, yes, she'll always remember it."

Cousin Alfia saw it was time for her to put in too, with a long face, and she began again the praising of the dead woman. She had arranged her in the coffin with her own hands, and put a handkerchief of fine linen on her face. Because she had plenty of linen and white things, though she said it herself. Then Neighbour Meno, touched, turned to Neighbour Angela, who never moved, no more than if she was made of stone, and said:

"Well, now what are you waiting for, why don't you have the ass skinned? At least get the money for the hide."

Translated by D. H. Lawrence

VERGA: *The Orphans*

1. *This story, like Pirandello's, concerns a man who is mourning his wife. How does Verga's treatment of the subject differ from Pirandello's? With what impression are you left at the end of the story? Is it hopeful, or hopeless?*

2. *The setting, poor people preparing bread, reminds us of Gorki's story. How does each writer suggest the theme through the setting? What does the short episode with the donkey signify?*

3. *Why is the title plural, when only one child seems to be orphaned?*

4. *Is this story of plot, or of character? How is it developed?*

5. *What attitude toward the lives of his rustic characters do you detect behind Verga's façade of naturalistic observation?*

6. *Do you find anything in this story that would have proved attractive to Lawrence (the translator) of "The Man Who Loved Islands"?*

Henry James

THE DEATH OF THE LION

*Born in 1843, Henry James, spent most of his adult life attempting
to make the novel into an art work, a devotion that extended until
the year of his death, in 1916. As a novelist and as a critic of the
novel, he has exerted great influence on the entire course of
twentieth-century American and English fiction, although he received little more than sporadic critical acclaim during his lifetime.
His most famous novels include* The American *(1876),* The Europe-
ans *(1878),* Daisy Miller *(1878),* The Portrait of a Lady *(1880),*
The Princess Casamassima *(1885),* The Wings of the Dove *(1902),*
The Ambassadors *(1903),* and The Golden Bowl *(1904). "The
Death of the Lion" is characteristically Jamesian, even though it
was written when the future course of his work was somewhat uncertain. In his portrait of Neil Paraday pursued by social harpies,
James has caught a situation in which his elegant irony can point
up the tragic role of the artist, or the man of integrity, in a society
unable to understand him.*

1

I HAD simply, I suppose, a change of heart, and it must have
begun when I received my manuscript back from Mr. Pinhorn. Mr.
Pinhorn was my "chief," as he was called in the office: he had accepted the high mission of bringing the paper up. This was a weekly
periodical, which had been supposed to be almost past redemption
when he took hold of it. It was Mr. Deedy who had let the thing
down so dreadfully: he was never mentioned in the office now save
in connection with that misdemeanour. Young as I was, I had been
in a manner taken over from Mr. Deedy, who had been owner as
well as editor; forming part of a promiscuous lot, mainly plant and
office-furniture, which poor Mrs. Deedy, in her bereavement and depression, parted with at a rough valuation. I could account for my
continuity but on the supposition that I had been cheap. I rather

resented the practice of fathering all flatness on my late protector, who was in his unhonoured grave; but as I had my way to make I found matter enough for complacency in being on a "staff." At the same time I was aware of my exposure to suspicion as a product of the old lowering system. This made me feel I was doubly bound to have ideas, and had doubtless been at the bottom of my proposing to Mr. Pinhorn that I should lay my lean hands on Neil Paraday. I remember how he looked at me—quite, to begin with, as if he had never heard of this celebrity, who indeed at that moment was by no means in the centre of the heavens; and even when I had knowingly explained he expressed but little confidence in the demand for any such stuff. When I had reminded him that the great principle on which we were supposed to work was just to create the demand we required, he considered a moment and then returned: "I see—you want to write him up."

"Call it that if you like."

"And what's your inducement?"

"Bless my soul—my admiration!"

Mr. Pinhorn pursed up his mouth. "Is there much to be done with him?"

"Whatever there is we should have it all to ourselves, for he hasn't been touched."

This argument was effective and Mr. Pinhorn responded. "Very well, touch him." Then he added: "But where can you do it?"

"Under the fifth rib!"

Mr. Pinhorn stared. "Where's that?"

"You want me to go down and see him?" I asked when I had enjoyed his visible search for the obscure suburb I seemed to have named.

"I don't 'want' anything—the proposal's your own. But you must remember that that's the way we do things *now*," said Mr. Pinhorn with another dig at Mr. Deedy.

Unregenerate as I was, I could read the queer implications of this speech. The present owner's superior virtue as well as his deeper craft spoke in his reference to the late editor as one of that baser sort who deal in false representations. Mr. Deedy would as soon have sent me to call on Neil Paraday as he would have published a "holiday-number"; but such scruples presented themselves as mere ignoble thrift to his successor, whose own sincerity

took the form of ringing doorbells and whose definition of genius
was the art of finding people at home. It was as if Mr. Deedy had
published reports without his young men's having, as Pinhorn
would have said, really been there. I was unregenerate, as I have
hinted, and couldn't be concerned to straighten out the journalistic
morals of my chief, feeling them indeed to be an abyss over the
edge of which it was better not to peer. Really to be there this time,
moreover, was a vision that made the idea of writing something
subtle about Neil Paraday only the more inspiring. I would be as
considerate as even Mr. Deedy could have wished, and yet I should
be as present as only Mr. Pinhorn could conceive. My allusion to
the sequestered manner in which Mr. Paraday lived—it had formed
part of my explanation, though I knew of it only by hearsay—was,
I could divine, very much what had made Mr. Pinhorn nibble. It
struck him as inconsistent with the success of his paper that any
one should be so sequestered as that. And then wasn't an immediate exposure of everything just what the public wanted? Mr. Pinhorn effectually called me to order by reminding me of the prompt-
ness with which I had met Miss Braby at Liverpool on her return
from her fiasco in the States. Hadn't we published, while its freshness and flavour were unimpaired, Miss Braby's own version of that
great international episode? I felt somewhat uneasy at this lump-
ing of the actress and the author, and I confess that after having
enlisted Mr. Pinhorn's sympathies I procrastinated a little. I had
succeeded better than I wished, and I had, as it happened, work
nearer at hand. A few days later I called on Lord Crouchley and
carried off in triumph the most unintelligible statement that had
yet appeared of his lordship's reasons for his change of front. I thus
set in motion in the daily papers columns of virtuous verbiage. The
following week I ran down to Brighton for a chat, as Mr. Pinhorn
called it, with Mrs. Bounder, who gave me, on the subject of her
divorce, many curious particulars that had not been articulated in
court. If ever an article flowed from the primal fount it was that
article on Mrs. Bounder. By this time, however, I became aware
that Neil Paraday's new book was on the point of appearing and
that its approach had been the ground of my original appeal to
Mr. Pinhorn, who was now annoyed with me for having lost so
many days. He bundled me off—we would at least not lose another.
I've always thought his sudden alertness a remarkable example of

the journalistic instinct. Nothing had occurred, since I first spoke
to him, to create a visible urgency, and no enlightenment could
possibly have reached him. It was a pure case of professional *flair*
—he had smelt the coming glory as an animal smells its distant
prey.

2

I may as well say at once that this little record pretends in no
degree to be a picture either of my introduction to Mr. Paraday or
of certain proximate steps and stages. The scheme of my narrative
allows no space for these things, and in any case a prohibitory
sentiment would hang about my recollection of so rare an hour.
These meagre notes are essentially private, so that if they see the
light the insidious forces that, as my story itself shows, make at
present for publicity will simply have overmastered my precautions. The curtain fell lately enough on the lamentable drama. My
memory of the day I alighted at Mr. Paraday's door is a fresh memory of kindness, hospitality, compassion, and of the wonderful illuminating talk in which the welcome was conveyed. Some voice
of the air had taught me the right moment, the moment of his
life at which an act of unexpected young allegiance might most
come home to him. He had recently recovered from a long grave
illness. I had gone to the neighbouring inn for the night, but I spent
the evening in his company, and he insisted the next day on my
sleeping under his roof. I hadn't an indefinite leave: Mr. Pinhorn
supposed us to put our victims through on the gallop. It was later,
in the office, that the rude motions of the jig were set to music.
I fortified myself, however, as my training had taught me to do, by
the conviction that nothing could be more advantageous for my
article than to be written in the very atmosphere. I said nothing to
Mr. Paraday about it, but in the morning, after my removal from
the inn, while he was occupied in his study, as he notified me he
should need to be, I committed to paper the main heads of my impression. Then thinking to commend myself to Mr. Pinhorn by my
celerity, I walked out and posted my little packet before luncheon.
Once my paper was written I was free to stay on, and if it was calculated to divert attention from my levity in so doing I could reflect
with satisfaction that I had never been so clever. I don't mean to

deny of course that I was aware it was much too good for Mr. Pinhorn; but I was equally conscious that Mr. Pinhorn had the supreme shrewdness of recognizing from time to time the cases in which an article was not too bad only because it was too good. There was nothing he loved so much as to print on the right occasion a thing he hated. I had begun my visit to the great man on a Monday, and on the Wednesday his book came out. A copy of it arrived by the first post, and he let me go out into the garden with it immediately after breakfast. I read it from beginning to end that day, and in the evening he asked me to remain with him the rest of the week and over the Sunday.

That night my manuscript came back from Mr. Pinhorn, accompanied with a letter the gist of which was the desire to know what I meant by trying to fob off on him such stuff. That was the meaning of the question, if not exactly its form, and it made my mistake immense to me. Such as this mistake was I could now only look it in the face and accept it. I knew where I had failed, but it was exactly where I couldn't have succeeded. I had been sent down to be personal and then in point of fact hadn't been personal at all: what I had despatched to London was just a little finicking feverish study of my author's talent. Anything less relevant to Mr. Pinhorn's purpose couldn't well be imagined, and he was visibly angry at my having (at his expense, with a second-class ticket) approached the subject of our enterprise only to stand off so helplessly. For myself, I knew but too well what had happened, and how a miracle—as pretty as some old miracle of legend—had been wrought on the spot to save me. There had been a big brush of wings, the flash of an opaline robe, and then, with a great cool stir of the air, the sense of an angel's having swooped down and caught me to his bosom. He held me only till the danger was over, and it all took place in a minute. With my manuscript back on my hands I understood the phenomenon better, and the reflexions I made on it are what I meant, at the beginning of this anecdote, by my change of heart. Mr. Pinhorn's note was not only a rebuke decidedly stern, but an invitation immediately to send him—it was the case to say so—the genuine article, the revealing and reverberating sketch to the promise of which, and of which alone, I owed my squandered privilege. A week or two later I recast my peccant paper, and giving it a particular application to Mr. Parady's new book, obtained for it the hospitality of another journal, where, I must admit, Mr. Pinhorn was so far vindicated as that it attracted not the least attention.

3

I was frankly, at the end of three days, a very prejudiced critic, so that one morning when, in the garden, my great man had offered to read me something I quite held my breath as I listened. It was the written scheme of another book—something put aside long ago, before his illness, but that he had lately taken out again to reconsider. He had been turning it round when I came down on him, and it had grown magnificently under this second hand. Loose liberal confident, it might have passed for a great gossiping eloquent letter—the overflow into talk of an artist's amorous plan. The theme I thought singularly rich, quite the strongest he had yet treated; and this familiar statement of it, full too of fine maturities, was really, in summarised splendour, a mine of gold, a precious independent work. I remember rather profanely wondering whether the ultimate production could possibly keep at the pitch. His reading of the fond epistle, at any rate, made me feel as if I were, for the advantage of posterity, in close correspondence with him— were the distinguished person to whom it had been affectionately addressed. It was a high distinction simply to be told such things. The idea he now communicated had all the freshness, the flushed fairness, of the conception untouched and untried: it was Venus rising from the sea and before the airs had blown upon her. I had never been so throbbingly present at such an unveiling. But when he had tossed the last bright word after the others, as I had seen cashiers in banks, weighing mounds of coin, drop a final sovereign into the tray, I knew a sudden prudent alarm.

"My dear master, how, after all, are you going to do it? It's infinitely noble, but what time it will take, what patience and independence, what assured, what perfect conditions! Oh for a lone isle in a tepid sea!"

"Isn't this practically a lone isle, and aren't you, as an encircling medium, tepid enough?" he asked, alluding with a laugh to the wonder of my young admiration and the narrow limits of his little provincial home. "Time isn't what I've lacked hitherto: the question hasn't been to find it, but to use it. Of course my illness made, while it lasted, a great hole—but I daresay there would have been a hole at any rate. The earth we tread has more pockets than a billiard-table. The great thing is now to keep on my feet."

"That's exactly what I mean."

Neil Paraday looked at me with eyes—such pleasant eyes as he had—in which, as I now recall their expression, I seem to have seen a dim imagination of his fate. He was fifty years old, and his illness had been cruel, his convalescence slow. "It isn't as if I weren't all right."

"Oh if you weren't all right I wouldn't look at you!" I tenderly said.

We had both got up, quickened as by this clearer air, and he had lighted a cigarette. I had taken a fresh one, which with an intense smile, by way of answer to my exclamation, he applied to the flame of his match. "If I weren't better I shouldn't have thought of *that!*" He flourished his script in his hand.

"I don't want to be discouraging, but that's not true," I returned. "I'm sure that during the months you lay here in pain you had visitations sublime. You thought of a thousand things. You think of more and more all the while. That's what makes you, if you'll pardon my familiarity, so respectable. At a time when so many people are spent you come into your second wind. But, thank God, all the same, you are better! Thank God too you're not, as you were telling me yesterday, 'successful.' If *you* weren't a failure what would be the use of trying? That's my one reserve on the subject of your recovery—that it makes you 'score,' as the newspapers say. It looks well in the newspapers, and almost anything that does that's horrible. 'We are happy to announce that Mr. Paraday, the celebrated author, is again in the enjoyment of excellent health.' Somehow I shouldn't like to see it."

"You won't see it; I'm not in the least celebrated—my obscurity protects me. But couldn't you bear even to see I was dying or dead?" my host inquired.

"Dead—*passe encore;* there's nothing so safe. One never knows what a living artist may do—one has mourned so many. However, one must make the worst of it. You must be as dead as you can."

"Don't I meet that condition in having just published a book?"

"Adequately, let us hope; for the book's verily a masterpiece."

At this moment the parlour-maid appeared in the door that opened from the garden: Paraday lived at no great cost, and the frisk of petticoats, with a timorous "Sherry, sir?" was about his modest mahogany. He allowed half his income to his wife, from whom he had succeeded in separating without redundancy of legend. I had a general faith in his having behaved well, and I had once, in London, taken Mrs. Paraday down to dinner. He now turned to speak to the maid, who offered him, on a try, some card or note, while, agitated, excited, I wandered to the end of the precinct. The idea of his security became supremely dear to me, and I asked myself if I were the same young man who had come down a few days before to scatter him to the four winds. When I retraced my steps he had gone into the house, and the woman—the second London post had come in—had placed my letters and a newspaper on a bench. I sat down there to the letters, which were a brief business, and then, without heeding the address, took the paper from its envelope. It was the journal of the highest renown, *The Empire* of that morning. It regularly came to Paraday, but I remembered that neither of us had yet looked at the copy already delivered. This one had a great mark on the "editorial" page, and, uncrumpling the wrapper, I saw it to be directed to my host and stamped with the name of his publishers. I instantly divined that *The Empire* had spoken of him, and I've not forgotten the odd little shock of the circumstance. It checked all eagerness and made me drop the paper a moment. As I sat there conscious of a palpitation I think I had a vision of what was to be. I had also a vision of the letter I would presently address to Mr. Pinhorn, breaking, as it were, with Mr. Pinhorn. Of course, however, the next minute the voice of *The Empire* was in my ears.

The article wasn't, I thanked heaven, a review; it was a "leader," the last of three, presenting Neil Paraday to the human race. His new book, the fifth from his hand, had been but a day or two out, and *The Empire*, already aware of it, fired, as if on the birth of a prince, a salute of a whole column. The guns had been booming these three hours in the house without our suspecting them. The big blundering newspaper had discovered him, and now he was proclaimed and anointed and crowned. His place was assigned him as publicly as if a fat usher with a wand had pointed to the topmost chair; he was to pass up and still up, higher and higher, between the watching faces and the envious sounds—away up to the dais and the throne. The article was "epoch-making," a landmark in his life; he had taken rank at a bound, waked up a national glory. A national glory was needed, and it was an immense convenience he was there. What all this meant rolled over me, and I fear I grew a little faint—it meant so much more than I could say "yea" to on the spot. In a flash, somehow, all was different; the tremendous wave I speak of had swept something away. It had knocked down, I suppose, my little customary altar, my twinkling tapers and my flowers, and had reared itself into the likeness of a temple vast and bare. When Neil Paraday should come out of the house he would come out a contemporary. That was what had happened: the poor man was to be squeezed into his horrible age. I felt as if he had been overtaken on the crest of the hill and brought back to the city. A little more and he would have dipped down the short cut to prosperity and escaped.

4

When he came out it was exactly as if he had been in custody, for beside him walked a stout man with a big black beard, who, save that he wore spectacles, might have been a policeman, and in whom at a second glance I recognised the highest contemporary enterprise.

"This is Mr. Morrow," said Paraday, looking, I thought, rather white: "he wants to publish heaven knows what about me."

I winced as I remembered that this was exactly what I myself had wanted. "Already?" I cried, with a sort of sense that my friend had fled to me for protection.

Mr. Morrow glared, agreeably, through his glasses: they suggested the electric headlights of some monstrous modern ship, and I felt as if Paraday and I were tossing terrified under his bows. I saw his momentum was irresistible. "I was confident that I should be the first in the field. A great interest is naturally felt in Mr. Paraday's surroundings," he heavily observed.

"I hadn't the least idea of it," said Paraday, as if he had been told he had been snoring.

"I find he hasn't read the article in *The Empire*," Mr. Morrow remarked to me. "That's so very interesting—it's something to start with," he smiled. He had begun to pull off his gloves, which were violently new, and to look encouragingly round the little garden. As a "surrounding" I felt how I myself had already been taken in; I was a little fish in the stomach of a bigger one. "I represent," our visitor continued, "a syndicate of influential journals, no less than thirty-seven, whose public—whose publics, I may say—are in peculiar sympathy with Mr. Paraday's line of thought. They would greatly appreciate any expression of his views on the subject of the art he so nobly exemplifies. In addition to my connexion with the syndicate just mentioned I hold a particular commission from *The Tatler*, whose most prominent department, 'Smatter and Chatter'— I daresay you've often enjoyed it—attracts such attention. I was honoured only last week, as a representative of *The Tatler*, with the confidence of Guy Walsingham, the brilliant author of 'Obsessions.' She pronounced herself thoroughly pleased with my sketch of her method; she went so far as to say that I had made her genius more comprehensible even to herself."

Neil Paraday had dropped on the garden-bench and sat there at once detached and confounded; he looked hard at a bare spot in the lawn, as if with an anxiety that had suddenly made him grave. His movement had been interpreted by his visitor as an invitation to sink sympathetically into a wicker chair that stood hard by, and while Mr. Morrow so settled himself I felt he had taken official possession and that there was no undoing it. One had heard of unfortunate people's having "a man in the house," and this was just what *we* had. There was a silence of a moment, during which we seemed to acknowledge in the only way that was possible the presence of universal fate; the sunny stillness took no pity, and my thought, as I was sure Paraday's was doing, performed within the minute a great distant revolution. I saw just how emphatic I should make my rejoinder to Mr. Pinhorn, and that having come, like Mr. Morrow, to betray, I must remain as long as possible to save. Not because I had brought my mind back, but because our visitor's last words were in my ear, I presently inquired with gloomy irrelevance if Guy Walsingham were a woman.

"Oh yes, a mere pseudonym—rather pretty isn't it?—and convenient, you know, for a lady who goes in for the larger latitude. ' "Obsessions," by Miss So-and so,' would look a little odd, but men

are more naturally indelicate. Have you peeped into 'Obsessions'?"
Mr. Morrow continued sociably to our companion.

Paraday, still absent, remote, made no answer, as if he hadn't
heard the question: a form of intercourse that appeared to suit the
cheerful Mr. Morrow as well as any other. Imperturbably bland, he
was a man of resources—he only needed to be on the spot. He had
pocketed the whole poor place while Paraday and I were wool-
gathering, and I could imagine that he had already got his "heads."
His system, at any rate, was justified by the inevitability with
which I replied, to save my friend the trouble: "Dear no—he hasn't
read it. He doesn't read such things!" I unwarily added.

"Things that are *too* far over the fence, eh?" I was indeed a godsend to Mr. Morrow. It was the psychological moment; it determined the appearance of his note-book, which, however, he at first
kept slightly behind him, even as the dentist approaching his victim keeps the horrible forceps. "Mr. Paraday holds with the good
old proprieties—I see!" And thinking of the thirty-seven influential
journals, I found myself, as I found poor Paraday, helplessly assist-
ing at the promulgation of this ineptitude. "There's no point on
which distinguished views are so acceptable as on this question—
raised perhaps more strikingly than ever by Guy Walsingham—of
the permissibility of the larger latitude. I've an appointment, precisely in connexion with it, next week, with Dora Forbes, author of
'The Other Way Round,' which everybody's talking about. Has Mr.
Paraday glanced at 'The Other Way Round'?" Mr. Morrow now
frankly appealed to me. I took on myself to repudiate the supposition, while our companion, still silent, got up nervously and walked
away. His visitor paid no heed to his withdrawal, but opened out
the note-book with a more fatherly pat. "Dora Forbes, I gather
takes the ground, the same as Guy Walsingham's, that the larger
latitude has simply got to come. He holds that it has got to be
squarely faced. Of course his sex makes him a less prejudiced
witness. But an authortative word from Mr. Paraday—from the
point of view of *his* sex, you know—would go right round the
globe. He takes the line that we *haven't* got to face it?"

I was bewildered: it sounded somehow as if there were three
sexes. My interlocutor's pencil was poised, my private responsibility great. I simply sat staring, none the less, and only found presence of mind to say: "Is this Miss Forbes a gentleman?"

Mr. Morrow had a subtle smile. "It wouldn't be 'Miss'—there's a wife!"

"I mean is she a man?"

"The wife?"—Mr. Morrow was for a moment as confused as myself. But when I explained that I alluded to Dora Forbes in person he informed me, with visible amusement at my being so out of it, that this was the "pen-name" of an indubitable male—he had a big red moustache. "He goes in for the slight mystification because the ladies are such popular favourites. A great deal of interest is felt in his acting on that idea—which *is* clever, isn't it?—and there's every prospect of its being widely imitated." Our host at this moment joined us again, and Mr. Morrow remarked invitingly that he should be happy to make a note of any observation the movement in question, the bid for success under a lady's name, might suggest to Mr. Paraday. But the poor man, without catching the allusion, excused himself, pleading that, though greatly honoured by his visitor's interest, he suddenly felt unwell and should have to take leave of him—have to go and lie down and keep quiet. His young friend might be trusted to answer for him, but he hoped Mr. Morrow didn't expect great things even of his young friend. His young friend, at this moment, looked at Neil Paraday with an anxious eye, greatly wondering if he were doomed to be ill again; but Paraday's own kind face met his question reassuringly, seemed to say in a glance intelligible enough: "Oh I'm not ill, but I'm scared; get him out of the house as quietly as possible." Getting newspapermen out of the house was odd business for an emissary of Mr. Pinhorn, and I was so exhilarated by the idea of it that I called after him as he left us: "Read the article in *The Empire* and you'll soon be all right!"

5

"Delicious my having come down to tell him of it!" Mr. Morrow ejaculated. "My cab was at the door twenty minutes after *The Empire* had been laid on my breakfast-table. Now what have you got for me?" he continued, dropping again into his chair, from which, however, he the next moment eagerly rose. "I was shown into the drawing-room, but there must be more to see—his study, his literary sanctum, the little things he has about, or other domestic objects and features. He wouldn't be lying down on his study-table? There's a great interest always felt in the scene of an author's labours. Sometimes we're favoured with very delightful peeps. Dora Forbes showed me all his table-drawers, and almost jammed my hand into one into which I made a dash! I don't ask that of you, but if we could talk things over right there where he sits I feel as if I should get the keynote."

I had no wish whatever to be rude to Mr. Morrow, I was much too initiated not to tend to more diplomacy; but I had a quick inspiration, and I entertained an insurmountable, an almost superstitious objection to his crossing the threshold of my friend's little lonely shabby consecrated workshop. "No, no—we shan't get at his life that way," I said. "The way to get at his life is to—— But wait a moment!" I broke off and went quickly into the house, whence I in three minutes reappeared before Mr. Morrow with the two volumes of Paraday's new book. "His life's here," I went on, "and I'm so full of this admirable thing that I can't talk of anything else. The artist's life's his work, and this is the place to observe him. What he has to tell us he tells us with *this* perfection. My dear sir, the best interviewer's the best reader."

Mr. Morrow good-humouredly protested. "Do you mean to say that no other source of information should be open to us?"

"None other till this particular one—by far the most copious— has been quite exhausted. Have you exhausted it, my dear sir? Had you exhausted it when you came down here? It seems to me in our time almost wholly neglected, and something should surely be done to restore its ruined credit. It's the course to which the artist himself at every step, and with such pathetic confidence, refers us. This last book of Mr. Paraday's is full of revelations."

"Revelations?" panted Mr. Morrow, whom I had forced again into his chair.

"The only kind that count. It tells you with a perfection that seems to me quite final all the author thinks, for instance, about the advent of the 'larger latitude.'"

"Where does it do that?" asked Mr. Morrow, who had picked up the second volume and was insincerely thumbing it.

"Everywhere—in the whole treatment of his case. Extract the opinion, disengage the answer—those are the real acts of homage."

Mr. Morrow, after a minute, tossed the book away. "Ah, but you mustn't take me for a reviewer."

"Heaven forbid I should take you for anything so dreadful! You came down to perform a little act of sympathy, and so, I may confide to you, did I. Let us perform our little act together. These pages overflow with the testimony we want: let us read them and taste them and interpret them. You'll of course have perceived for yourself that one scarcely does read Neil Paraday till one reads him aloud; he gives out to the ear an extraordinary full tone, and it's only when you expose it confidently to that test that you really get near his style. Take up your book again and let me listen, while you pay it out, to that wonderful fifteenth chapter. If you feel you can't do it justice, compose yourself to attention while I produce for you—I think I can!—this scarcely less admirable ninth."

Mr. Morrow gave me a straight look which was as hard as a blow between the eyes; he had turned rather red, and a question had formed itself in his mind which reached my sense as distinctly as if he had uttered it: "What sort of a damned fool are *you?*" Then he got up, gathering together his hat and gloves, buttoning his coat, projecting hungrily all over the place the big transparency of his mask. It seemed to flare over Fleet Street and somehow made the actual spot distressingly humble: there was so little for it to feed on unless he counted the blisters of our stucco or saw his way to do something with the roses. Even the poor roses were common kinds. Presently his eyes fell on the manuscript from which Paraday had been reading to me and which still lay on the bench. As my own followed them I saw it looked promising, looked pregnant, as if it gently throbbed with the life the reader had given it. Mr. Morrow indulged in a nod at it and a vague thrust of his umbrella. "What's that?"

"Oh it's a plan—a secret."

"A secret!" There was an instant's silence, and then Mr. Morrow made another movement. I may have been mistaken, but it affected me as the translated impulse of the desire to lay hands on the manuscript, and this led me to indulge in a quick anticipatory grab which may very well have seemed ungraceful, or even impertinent, and which at any rate left Mr. Paraday's two admirers very erect, glaring at each other while one of them held a bundle of papers well behind him. An instant later Mr. Morrow quitted me

abruptly, as if he had really carried something off with him. To reassure myself, watching his broad back recede, I only grasped my
manuscript the tighter. He went to the back door of the house, the
one he had come out from, but on trying the handle he appeared
to find it fastened. So he passed round into the front garden, and by
listening intently enough I could presently hear the outer gate
close behind him with a bang. I thought again of the thirty-seven
influential journals and wondered what would be his revenge. I
hasten to add that he was magnanimous: which was just the most
dreadful thing he could have been. *The Tatler* published a charming chatty familiar account of Mr. Paraday's "Home-life," and on
the wings of the thirty-seven influential journals it went, to use
Mr. Morrow's own expression, right round the globe.

6

A week later, early in May, my glorified friend came up to town,
where, it may be veraciously recorded, he was the king of the
beasts of the year. No advancement was ever more rapid, no exalta-
tion more complete, no bewilderment more teachable. His book
sold but moderately, though the article in *The Empire* had done
unwonted wonders for it; but he circulated in person to a measure
that the libraries might well have envied. His formula had been
found—he was a "revelation." His momentary terror had been real,
just as mine had been—the overclouding of his passionate desire
to be left to finish his work. He was far from unsociable, but he
had the finest conception of being let alone that I've ever met. For
the time, none the less, he took his profit where it seemed most to
crowd on him, having in his pocket the portable sophistries about
the nature of the artist's task. Observation too was a kind of work
and experience a kind of success; London dinners were all material
and London ladies were fruitful toil. "No one has the faintest conception of what I'm trying for," he said to me, "and not many have
read three pages that I've written; but I must dine with them first
—they'll find out why when they've time." It was rather rude justice perhaps; but the fatigue had the merit of being a new sort,
while the phantasmagoric town was probably after all less of a bat-
tlefield than the haunted study. He once told me that he had had
no personal life to speak of since his fortieth year, but had had

more than was good for him before. London closed the parenthesis and exhibited him in relations; one of the most inevitable of these being that in which he found himself to Mrs. Weeks Wimbush, wife of the boundless brewer and proprietress of the universal menagerie. In this establishment, as everybody knows, on occasions when the crush is great, the animals rub shoulders freely with the spectators and the lions sit down for whole evenings with the lambs.

It had been ominously clear to me from the first that in Neil Paraday this lady, who, as all the world agreed, was tremendous fun, considered that she had secured a prime attraction, a creature of almost heraldic oddity. Nothing could exceed her enthusiasm over her capture, and nothing could exceed the confused apprehensions it excited in me. I had an instinctive fear of her which I tried without effect to conceal from her victim, but which I let her notice with perfect impunity. Paraday heeded it, but she never did, for her conscience was that of a romping child. She was a blind violent force to which I could attach no more idea of responsibility than to the creaking of a sign in the wind. It was difficult to say what she conduced to but circulation. She was constructed of steel and leather, and all I asked of her for our tractable friend was not to do him to death. He had consented for a time to be of india-rubber, but my thoughts were fixed on the day he should resume his shape or at least get back into his box. It was evidently all right, but I should be glad when it was well over. I had a special fear—the impression was ineffaceable of the hour when, after Mr. Morrow's departure, I found him on the sofa in his study. That pretext of indisposition had not in the least been meant as a snub to the envoy of *The Tatler*—he had gone to lie down in very truth. He had felt a pang of his old pain, the result of the agitation wrought in him by this forcing open of a new period. His old programme, his old ideal even had to be changed. Say what one would, success was a complication and recognition had to be reciprocal. The monastic life, the pious illumination of the missal in the convent-cell were things of the gathered past. It didn't engender despair, but at least it required adjustment. Before I left him on that occasion we had passed a bargain, my part of which was that I should make it my business to take care of him. Let whoever would represent the interest in his presence (I must have had a mystical prevision of Mrs. Weeks Wimbush) I should represent the interest in his work—

or otherwise expressed in his absence. These two interests were in their essence opposed; and I doubt, as youth is fleeting, if I shall ever again know the intensity of joy with which I felt that in so good a cause I was willing to make myself odious.

One day in Sloane Street I found myself questioning Paraday's landlord, who had come to the door in answer to my knock. Two vehicles, a barouche and a smart hansom, were drawn up before the house.

"In the drawing-room, sir? Mrs. Weeks Wimbush."

"And in the dining-room?"

"A young lady, sir—waiting: I think a foreigner."

It was three o'clock, and on days when Paraday didn't lunch out he attached a value to these appropriated hours. On which days, however, didn't the dear man lunch out? Mrs. Wimbush, at such a crisis, would have rushed round immediately after her own repast. I went into the dining-room first, postponing the pleasure of seeing how, upstairs, the lady of the barouche would, on my arrival, point the moral of my sweet solicitude. No one took such an interest as herself in his doing only what was good for him, and she was always on the spot to see that he did it. She made appointments with him to discuss the best means of economising his time and protecting his privacy. She further made his health her special business, and had so much sympathy with my own zeal for it that she was the author of pleasing fictions on the subject of what my devotion had led me to give up. I gave up nothing (I don't count Mr. Pinhorn) because I had nothing, and all I had as yet achieved was to find myself also in the menagerie. I had dashed in to save my friend, but I had only got domesticated and wedged; so that I could do little more for him than exchange with him over people's heads looks of intense but futile intelligence.

7

The young lady in the dining-room had a brave face, black hair, blue eyes, and in her lap a big volume. "I've come for his autograph," she said when I had explained to her that I was under bonds to see people for him when he was occupied. "I've been waiting half an hour, but I'm prepared to wait all day." I don't know whether it was this that told me she was American, for the propen-

sity to wait all day is not in general characteristic of her race. I was
enlightened probably not so much by the spirit of the utterance as
by some quality of its sound. At any rate I saw she had an individual patience and a lovely frock, together with an expression that
played among her pretty features like a breeze among flowers.
Putting her book on the table she showed me a massive album,
showily bound and full of autographs of price. The collection of
faded notes, of still more faded "thoughts," of quotations, plati-
tudes, signatures, represented a formidable purpose.

I could only disclose my dread of it. "Most people apply to Mr.
Paraday by letter, you know."

"Yes, but he doesn't answer. I've written three times."

"Very true," I reflected; "the sort of letter you mean goes straight
into the fire."

"How do you know the sort I mean?" My interlocutress had
blushed and smiled, and in a moment she added: "I don't believe
he gets many like them!"

"I'm sure they're beautiful, but he burns without reading." I
didn't add that I had convinced him he ought to.

"Isn't he then in danger of burning things of importance?"

"He would perhaps be so if distinguished men hadn't an infallible nose for nonsense."

She looked at me a moment—her face was sweet and gay. "Do
you burn without reading too?"—in answer to which I assured
her that if she'd trust me with her repository I'd see that Mr. Paraday should write his name in it.

She considered a little. "That's very well, but it wouldn't make
me see him."

"Do you want very much to see him?" It seemed ungracious to
catechise so charming a creature, but somehow I had never yet
taken my duty to the great author so seriously.

"Enough to have come from America for the purpose."

I stared. "All alone?"

"I don't see that that's exactly your business, but if it will make
me more seductive I'll confess that I'm quite by myself. I had to
come alone or not come at all."

She was interesting; I could imagine she had lost parents, natural protectors—could conceive even she had inherited money. I
was at a pass of my own fortunes when keeping hansoms at doors

seemed to me pure swagger. As a trick of this bold and sensitive girl, however, it became romantic—a part of the general romance of her freedom her errand, her innocence. The confidence of young Americans was notorious, and I speedily arrived at a conviction that no impulse could have been more generous than the impulse that had operated here. I foresaw at that moment that it would make her my peculiar charge, just as circumstances had made Neil Paraday. She would be another person to look after, so that one's honour would be concerned in guiding her straight. These things became clearer to me later on; at the instant I had scepticism enough to observe to her, as I turned the pages of her volume, that her net had all the same caught many a big fish. She appeared to have had fruitful access to the great ones of the earth; there were people, moreover, whose signatures she had presumably secured without a personal interview. She couldn't have worried George Washington and Friedrich Schiller and Hannah More. She met this argument, to my surprise, by throwing up the album without a pang. It wasn't even her own; she was responsible for none of its treasures. It belonged to a girl-friend in America, a young lady in a western city. This young lady had insisted on her bringing it, to pick up more autographs: she thought they might like to see, in Europe, in what company they would be. The "girl-friend," the western city, the immortal names, the curious errand, the idyllic faith, all made a story as strange to me, and as beguiling, as some tale in the *Arabian Nights*. Thus it was that my informant had encumbered herself with the ponderous tome; but she hastened to assure me that this was the first time she had brought it out. For her visit to Mr. Paraday it had simply been a pretext. She didn't really care a straw that he should write his name; what she did want was to look straight into his face.

I demurred a little. "And why do you require to do that?"

"Because I just love him!" Before I could recover from the agitating effect of this crystal ring my companion had continued: "Hasn't there ever been any face that *you've* wanted to look into?"

How could I tell her so soon how much I appreciated the opportunity of looking into hers? I could only assent in general to the proposition that there were certainly for every one such yearnings, and even such faces: and I felt the crisis demand all my lucidity, all my wisdom. "Oh yes, I'm a student of physiognomy. Do you mean," I pursued, "that you've a passion for Mr. Paraday's books?"

"They've been everything to me and a little more besides—I know them by heart. They've completely taken hold of me. There's no author about whom I'm in such a state as I'm in about Neil Paraday."

"Permit me to remark, then," I presently returned, "that you're one of the right sort."

"One of the enthusiasts? Of course I am!"

"Oh there are enthusiasts who are quite of the wrong. I mean you're one of those to whom an appeal can be made."

"An appeal?" Her face lighted as if with the chance of some great sacrifice.

If she was ready for one it was only waiting for her, and in a moment I mentioned it. "Give up this crude purpose of seeing him. Go away without it. That will be far better."

She looked mystified, then turned visibly pale. "Why, hasn't he any personal charm?" The girl was terrible and laughable in her bright directness.

"Ah, that dreadful word 'personal'!" I wailed: "we're dying of it. For you women bring it out with murderous effect. When you meet with a genius as fine as this idol of ours, let him off the dreary duty of being a personality as well. Know him only by what's best in him and spare him for the same sweet sake."

My young lady continued to look at me in confusion and mistrust and the result of her reflexion on what I had just said was to make her suddenly break out. "Look here, sir, what's the matter with him?"

"The matter with him is that if he doesn't look out people will eat a great hole in his life."

She turned it over. "He hasn't any disfigurement?"

"Nothing to speak of!"

"Do you mean that social engagements interfere with his occupations?"

"That but feebly expresses it."

"So that he can't give himself up to his beautiful imagination?"

"He's beset, badgered, bothered—he's pulled to pieces on the pretext of being applauded. People expect him to give them his time, his golden time, who wouldn't themselves give five shillings for one of his books."

"Five? I'd give five thousand!"

"Give your sympathy—give your forbearance. Two-thirds of those who approach him only do it to advertise themselves."

"Why, it's too bad!" the girl exclaimed, with the face of an angel. "It's the first time I was ever called crude!" she laughed.

I followed up my advantage. "There's a lady with him now who's a terrible complication, and who yet hasn't read, I'm sure, ten pages he ever wrote."

My visitor's wide eyes grew tenderer. "Then how does she talk——?"

"Without ceasing. I only mention her as a single case. Do you want to know how to show a superlative consideration? Simply avoid him."

"Avoid him?" she despairingly breathed.

"Don't force him to have to take account of you; admire him in silence, cultivate him at a distance and secretly appropriate his message. Do you want to know," I continued, warming to my idea, "how to perform an act of homage really sublime?" Then as she hung on my words: "Succeed in never seeing him at all?"

"Never at all?"—she suppressed a shriek for it.

"The more you get into his writings the less you'll want to, and you'll be immensely sustained by the thought of the good you're doing him."

She looked at me without resentment or spite, and at the truth I had put before her with candour, credulity, pity. I was afterwards happy to remember that she must have gathered from my face the liveliness of my interest in herself. "I think I see what you mean."

"Oh I express it badly, but I should be delighted if you'd let me come to see you—to explain it better."

She made no response to this, and her thoughtful eyes fell on the big album, on which she presently laid her hands as if to take it away. "I did use to say out West that they might write little less for autographs—to all the great poets, you know—and study the thoughts and style a little more."

"What do they care for the thoughts and style? They didn't even understand you. I'm not sure," I added, "that I do myself, and I daresay that you by no means make me out."

She had got up to go, and though I wanted her to succeed in not seeing Neil Paraday I wanted her also, inconsequently, to remain

in the house. I was at any rate far from desiring to hustle her off. As
Mrs. Weeks Wimbush, upstairs, was still saving our friend in her
own way, I asked my young lady to let me briefly relate, in illustra-
tion of my point, the little incident of my having gone down into
the country for a profane purpose and been converted on the spot
to holiness. Sinking again into her chair to listen she showed a deep
interest in the anecdote. Then thinking it over gravely she returned
with her odd intonation: "Yes, but you do see him!" I had to admit
that this was the case; and I wasn't so prepared with an effective
attenuation as I could have wished. She eased the situation off,
however, by the charming quaintness with which she finally said:
"Well, I wouldn't want him to be lonely!" This time she rose in earnest, but I persuaded her to let me keep the album to show Mr.
Paraday. I assured her I'd bring it back to her myself. "Well,' you'll
find my address somewhere in it on a paper!" she sighed all resignedly at the door.

8

I blush to confess it, but I invited Mr. Paraday that very day to
transcribe into the album one of his most characteristic passages. I
told him how I had got rid of the strange girl who had brought it—
her ominous name was Miss Hurter and she lived at an hotel; quite
agreeing with him, moreover, as to the wisdom of getting rid with
equal promptitude of the book itself. This was why I carried it to
Albemarle Street no later than on the morrow. I failed to find her
at home, but she wrote to me and I went again: she wanted so
much to hear more about Neil Paraday. I returned repeatedly, I
may briefly declare, to supply her with this information. She had
been immensely taken, the more she thought of it, with that idea
of mine about the act of homage: it had ended by filling her with a
generous rapture. She positively desired to do something sublime
for him, though indeed I could see that, as this particular flight was
difficult, she appreciated the fact that my visits kept her up. I had
it on my conscience to keep her up; I neglected nothing that would
contribute to it, and her conception of our cherished author's independence became at last as fine as his very own. "Read him, read
him—*that* will be an education in decency." I constantly repeated;
while, seeking him in his works even as God in nature, she repre-

sented herself as convinced that, according to my assurance, this
was the system that had, as she expressed it, weaned her. We read
him together when I could find time, and the generous creature's
sacrifice was fed by our communion. There were twenty selfish
women about whom I told her and who stirred her to a beautiful
rage. Immediately after my first visit her sister, Mrs. Milsom,
came over from Paris, and the two ladies began to present, as they
called it, their letters. I thanked our stars that none had been presented to Mr. Paraday. They received invitations and dined out,
and some of these occasions enabled Fanny Hurter to perform, for
consistency's sake, touching feats of submission. Nothing indeed
would now have induced her even to look at the object of her admiration. Once, hearing his name announced at a party, she instantly left the room by another door and then straightway quitted
the house. At another time when I was at the opera with them—
Mrs. Milsom had invited me to their box—I attempted to point
Mr. Paraday out to her in the stalls. On this she asked her sister to
change places with her and, while that lady devoured the great
man through a powerful glass, presented, all the rest of the evening, her inspired back to the house. To torment her tenderly I
pressed the glass upon her, telling her how wonderfully near it
brought out our friend's handsome head. By way of answer she simply looked at me in charged silence, letting me see that tears had
gathered in her eyes. These tears, I may remark, produced an effect
on me of which the end is not yet. There was a moment when I felt
it my duty to mention them to Neil Paraday, but I was deterred by
the reflexion that there were questions more relevant to his happiness.

These questions indeed, by the end of the season, were reduced
to a single one—the question of reconstituting so far as might be
possible the conditions under which he had produced his best
work. Such conditions could never all come back, for there was a
new one that took up too much place; but some perhaps were not
beyond recall. I wanted above all things to see him sit down to
the subject he had, on my making his acquaintance, read me that
admirable sketch of. Something told me there was no security but
in his doing so before the new factor, as we used to say at Mr. Pinhorn's, should render the problem incalculable. It only half-reas-
sured me that the sketch itself was so copious and so eloquent that

even at the worst there would be the making of a small but complete book, a tiny volume which, for the faithful, might well become an object of adoration. There would even not be wanting critics to declare, I foresaw, that the plan was a thing to be more thankful for than the structure to have been read on it. My impatience for the structure, none the less, grew and grew with the interruptions. He had on coming up to town begun to sit for his portrait to a young painter, Mr. Rumble, whose little game, as we also used to say at Mr. Pinhorn's, was to be the first to perch on the shoulders of renown. Mr. Rumble's studio was a circus in which the man of the hour, and still more the woman, leaped through the hoops of his showy frames almost as electrically as they burst into telegrams and "specials." He pranced into the exhibitions on their back; he was the reporter on canvas, the Vandyke up to date, and there was one roaring year in which Mrs. Bounder and Miss Braby, Guy Walsingham and Dora Forbes proclaimed in chorus from the same pictured walls that no one had yet got ahead of him.

Paraday had been promptly caught and saddled, accepting with characteristic good humour his confidential hint that to figure in his show was not so much a consequence as a cause of immortality. From Mrs. Wimbush to the last "representative" who called to ascertain his twelve favourite dishes, it was the same ingenuous assumption that he would rejoice in the repercussion. There were moments when I fancied I might have had more patience with them if they hadn't been so fatally benevolent. I hated at all events Mr. Rumble's picture, and had my bottled resentment ready when, later on, I found my distracted friend had been stuffed by Mrs. Wimbush into the mouth of another cannon. A young artist in whom she was intensely interested, and who had no connexion with Mr. Rumble, was to show how far *he* could make him go. Poor Paraday, in return, was naturally to write something somewhere about the young artist. She played her victims against each other with admirable ingenuity, and her establishment was a huge machine in which the tiniest and the biggest wheels went round to the same treadle. I had a scene with her in which I tried to express that the function of such a man was to exercise his genius—not to serve as a hoarding for pictorial posters. The people I was perhaps angriest with were the editors of magazines who had introduced what they called new features, so aware were they that the newest feature of all would be to make him grind their axes by contributing his views on vital topics and taking part in the periodical prattle about the future of fiction. I made sure that before I should have done with him there would scarcely be a current form of words left me to be sick of; but meanwhile I could make surer still of my animosity to bustling ladies for whom he drew the water that irrigated their social flowerbeds.

I had a battle with Mrs. Wimbush over the artist she protected, and another over the question of a certain week, at the end of July, that Mr. Paraday appeared to have contracted to spend with her in the country. I protested against this visit; I intimated that he was too unwell for hospitality without a *nuance,* for caresses without imagination; I begged he might rather take the time in some restorative way. A sultry air of promises, of ponderous parties, hung over his August, and he would greatly profit by the interval of rest. He had not told me he was ill again—that he had had a warning; but I had not needed this, and I found his reticence his worst symptom. The only thing he said to me was that he believed a comfortable attack of something or other would set him up: it would put out of the question everything but the exemptions he prized. I am afraid I shall have presented him as a martyr in a very small cause if I fail to explain that he surrendered himself much more liberally than I surrendered him. He filled his lungs, for the most part, with the comedy of his queer fate: the tragedy was in the spectacles through which I chose to look. He was conscious of inconvenience, and above all of a great renouncement; but how could he have heard a mere dirge in the bells of his accession? The sagacity and the jealousy were mine, and his the impressions and the anecdotes. Of course, as regards Mrs. Wimbush, I was worsted in my encounters, for was not the state of his health the very reason for his coming to her at Prestidge? Wasn't it precisely at Prestidge that he was to be coddled, and wasn't the dear Princess coming to help her to coddle him? The dear Princess, now on a visit to England, was of a famous foreign house, and, in her gilded cage, with her retinue of keepers and feeders, was the most expensive specimen in the good lady's collection. I don't think her august presence had had to do with Paraday's consenting to go, but it is not impossible that he had operated as bait to the illustrious stranger. The party had been made up for him, Mrs. Wimbush averred, and every one was counting on it, the dear Princess most of all. If he was well enough he was to read them something absolutely fresh, and it was on that particular prospect the Princess had set her heart. She was so fond of genius, in *any* walk of life, and was so used to it and understood it so well: she was the greatest of Mr. Paraday's admirers, she devoured everything he wrote. And then he read like an angel. Mrs. Wimbush reminded me that he had again and again given her, Mrs. Wimbush, the privilege of listening to him.

I looked at her a moment. "What has he read to you?" I crudely inquired.

For a moment too she met my eyes, and for the fraction of a moment she hesitated and coloured. "Oh all sorts of things!"

I wondered if this were an imperfect recollection or only a perfect fib, and she quite understood my unuttered comment on her measure of such things. But if she could forget Neil Paraday's beauties she could of course forget my rudeness, and three days later she invited me, by telegraph, to join the party at Prestidge. This time she might indeed have had a story about what I had given up to be near the master. I addressed from that fine residence several communications to a young lady in London, a young lady whom, I confess, I quitted with reluctance and whom the reminder of what she herself could give up was required to make me quit at all. It adds to the gratitude I owe her on other grounds that she kindly allows me to transcribe from my letters a few of the passages in which that hateful sojourn is candidly commemorated.

9

"I suppose I ought to enjoy the joke of what's going on here," I wrote, "but somehow it doesn't amuse me. Pessimism on the contrary possesses me and cynicism deeply engages. I positively feel my own flesh sore from the brass nails in Neil Paraday's social harness. The house is full of people who like him, as they mention, awfully, and with whom his talent for talking nonsense has prodigious success. I delight in his nonsense myself; why is it therefore that I grudge these happy folk their artless satisfaction? Mystery of the human heart—abyss of the critical spirit! Mrs. Wimbush thinks she can answer that question, and as my want of gaiety has at last worn out her patience she has given me a glimpse of her shrewd guess. I'm made restless by the selfishness of the insincere friend— I want to monopolise Paraday in order that he may push me on. To be intimate with him's a feather in my cap; it gives me an importance that I couldn't naturally pretend to, and I seek to deprive him of social refreshment because I fear that meeting more disinterested people may enlighten him as to my real motive. All the disinterested people here are his particular admirers and have been carefully selected as such. There's supposed to be a copy of his last book in the house, and in the hall I come upon ladies, in attitudes, bending gracefully over the first volume. I discreetly avert my eyes, and when I next look round the precarious joy has been superseded by the book of life. There's a sociable circle or a confidential couple, and the relinquished volume lies open on its face and as dropped under extreme coercion. Somebody else presently finds it and transfers it, with its air of momentary desolation, to another piece of furniture. Every one's asking every one about it all day, and everyone's telling every one where they put it last. I'm sure it's rather smudgy about the twentieth page. I've a strong impression too that the second volume is lost—has been packed in the bag for some departing guest; and yet everybody has the impression that somebody else has read to the end. You see therefore that the beautiful book plays a great part in our existence. Why should I take the occasion of such distinguished honours to say that I begin to see deeper into Gustave Flaubert's doleful refrain about the hatred of literature? I refer you again to the perverse constitution of man.

"The Princess is a massive lady with the organisation of an athlete and the confusion of tongues of a *valet de place*. She contrives to commit herself extraordinarily little in a great many languages, and is entertained and conversed with in detachments and relays like an institution which goes on from generation to generation or a big building contracted for under a forfeit. She can't have a personal taste any more than, when her husband succeeds, she can have a personal crown, and her opinion on any matter is rusty and heavy and plain—made, in the night of ages, to last and be transmitted. I feel as if I ought to 'tip' some *custode* for my glimpse of it. She had been told everything in the world and has never perceived anything, and the echoes of her education respond awfully to the rash footfall—I mean the casual remark—in the cold Valhalla of

her memory. Mrs. Wimbush delights in her wit and says there's
nothing so charming as to hear Mr. Paraday draw it out. He's perpetually detailed for this job, and he tells me it has a peculiarly ex-
hausting effect. Every one's beginning—at the end of two days—
to sidle obsequiously away from her, and Mrs. Wimbush pushes
him again into the breach. None of the uses I have yet seen him
put to infuriate me quite so much. He looks very fagged and has
at last confessed to me that his condition makes him uneasy—has
even promised me he'll go straight home instead of returning to his
final engagement in town. Last night I had some talk with him
about going to-day, cutting his visit short, so sure am I that he'll be
better as soon as he's shut up in his lighthouse. He told me that this
is what he would like to do; reminding me, however, that the first
lesson of his greatness has been precisely that he can't do what he
likes. Mrs. Wimbush would never forgive him if he should leave
her before the Princess has received the last hand. When I hint that
a violent rupture with our hostess would be the best thing in the
world for him he gives me to understand that if his reason assents
to the proposition his courage hangs woefully back. He makes no
secret of being mortally afraid of her, and when I ask what harm
she can do him that she hasn't already done he simply repeats: 'I'm
afraid, I'm afraid! Don't inquire too closely,' he said last night;
'only believe that I feel a sort of terror. It's strange, when she's so
kind! At any rate, I'd as soon overturn that piece of priceless Sèvres
as tell her I must go before my date.' It sounds dreadfully weak,
but he has some reason, and he pays for his imagination, which
puts him (I should hate it) in the place of others and makes him
feel, even against himself, their feelings, their appetites, their motives. It's indeed inveterately against himself that he makes his
imagination act. What a pity he has such a lot of it! He's too
beastly intelligent. Besides, the famous reading's still to come off,
and it has been postponed a day to allow Guy Walsingham to arrive. It appears this eminent lady's staying at a house a few miles
off, which means of course that Mrs. Wimbush has forcibly an-
nexed her. She's to come over in a day or two—Mrs. Wimbush
wants her to hear Mr. Paraday.

"To-day's wet and cold, and several of the company, at the invitation of the Duke, have driven over to luncheon at Bigwood. I saw
poor Paraday wedge himself, by command, into the little supple-

mentary seat of a brougham in which the Princess and our hostess
were already ensconced. If the front glass isn't open on his dear old
back perhaps he'll survive. Bigwood, I believe, is very grand and
frigid, all marble and precedence, and I wish him well out of the
adventure. I can't tell you how much more and more *your* attitude
to him, in the midst of all this, shines out by contrast. I never willingly talk to these people about him, but see what a comfort I find
it to scribble to you! I appreciate it—it keeps me warm; there are
no fires in the house. Mrs. Wimbush goes by the calendar, the
temperature goes by the weather, the weather goes by God knows
what, and the Princess is easily heated. I've nothing but my acri-
mony to warm me, and have been out under an umbrella to restore
my circulation. Coming in an hour ago I found Lady Augusta
Minch rummaging about the hall. When I asked her what she was
looking for she said she had mislaid something that Mr. Paraday
had lent her. I ascertained in a moment that the article in question
is a manuscript, and I've a foreboding that it's the noble morsel he
read me six weeks go. When I expressed my surprise that he should
have bandied about anything so precious (I happen to know it's
his only copy—in the most beautiful hand in all the world) Lady
Augusta confessed to me that she hadn't had it from himself, but
from Mrs. Wimbush, who had wished to give her a glimpse of it
as a salve for her not being able to stay and hear it read.

" 'Is that the piece he's to read,' I asked, 'when Guy Walsingham
arrives?'

" 'It's not for Guy Walsingham they're waiting now, it's for Dora
Forbes,' Lady Augusta said. 'She's coming, I believe, early to-morrow. Meanwhile Mrs. Wimbush has found out about *him*, and is
actively wiring to him. She says he also must hear him.'

" 'You bewilder me a little,' I replied; 'in the age we live in one
gets lost among the genders and the pronouns. The clear thing is
that Mrs. Wimbush doesn't guard such a treasure so jealously as
she might.'

" 'Poor dear, she has the Princess to guard! Mr. Paraday lent her
the manuscript to look over.'

" 'She spoke, you mean, as if it were the morning paper?'

"Lady Augusta stared—my irony was lost on her. 'She didn't have
time, so she gave me a chance first; because unfortunately I go to-
morrow to Bigwood.'

" 'And your chance has only proved a chance to lose it?'

" 'I haven't lost it. I remember now—it was very stupid of me to have forgotten. I told my maid to give it to Lord Dorimont—or at least to his man.'

" 'And Lord Dorimont went away directly after luncheon.'

" 'Of course he gave it back to my maid—or else his man did,' said Lady Augusta. 'I daresay it's all right.'

"The conscience of these people is like a summer sea. They haven't time to 'look over' a priceless composition; they've only time to kick it about the house. I suggested that the 'man,' fired with a noble emulation, had perhaps kept the work for his own perusal; and her ladyship wanted to know whether, if the thing shouldn't reappear for the grand occasion appointed by our hostess, the author wouldn't have something else to read that would do just as well. Their questions are too delightful! I declared to Lady Augusta briefly that nothing in the world can ever do so well as the thing that does best; and at this she looked a little disconcerted. But I added that if the manuscript had gone astray our little circle would have the less of an effort of attention to make. The piece in question was very long—it would keep them three hours.

" 'Three hours! Oh the Princess will get up!' said Lady Augusta.

" 'I thought she was Mr. Paraday's greatest admirer.'

" 'I daresay she is—she's so awfully clever. But what's the use of being a Princess——'

" 'If you can't dissemble your love?' I asked as Lady Augusta was vague. She said at any rate that she'd question her maid; and I'm hoping that when I go down to dinner I shall find the manuscript has been recovered."

10

"It has *not* been recovered," I wrote early the next day, "and I'm moreover much troubled about our friend. He came back from Bigwood with a chill and, being allowed to have a fire in his room, lay down a while before dinner. I tried to send him to bed and indeed thought I had put him in the way of it; but after I had gone to dress Mrs. Wimbush came up to see him, with the inevitable result that when I returned I found him under arms and flushed and feverish, though decorated with the rare flower she had brought him for his button-hole. He came down to dinner, but Lady Augusta Minch was very shy of him. To-day he's in great pain, and the advent of *ces dames*—I mean of Guy Walsingham and Dora Forbes—doesn't at all console me. It does Mrs. Wimbush, however, for she has consented to his remaining in bed so that he may be all right to-morrow for the listening circle. Guy Walsingham's already on the scene, and the doctor for Paraday also arrived early. I haven't yet seen the author of 'Obsessions,' but of course I've had a moment by myself with the Doctor. I tried to get him to say that our invalid must go straight home—I mean to-morrow or next day; but he quite refuses to talk about the future. Absolute quiet and warmth and the regular administration of an important remedy are the points he mainly insists on. He returns this afternoon, and I'm to go back to see the patient at one o'clock, when he next takes his medicine. It consoles me a little that he certainly won't be able to read—an exertion he was already more than unfit for. Lady Augusta went off after breakfast, assuring me her first care would be to follow up the lost manuscript. I can see she thinks me a shocking busybody and doesn't understand my alarm, but she'll do what she can, for she's a good-natured woman. "So are they all honourable men.' That was precisely what made her give the thing to Lord Dorimont and made Lord Dorimont bag it. What use *he* has for it God only knows. I've the worst forebodings, but somehow I'm strangely without passion—desperately calm. As I consider the unconscious, the well-meaning ravages of our appreciative circle, I bow my head in submission to some great natural, some universal accident; I'm rendered almost indifferent, in fact quite gay (ha-ha!) by the sense of immitigable fate. Lady Augusta promises me to trace the precious object and let me have it through the post by the time Paraday's well enough to play his part with it. The last evidence is that her maid did give it to his lordship's valet. One would suppose it some thrilling number of *The Family Budget*. Mrs. Wimbush, who's aware of the accident, is much less agitated by it than she would doubtless be were she not for the hour inevitably engrossed with Guy Walsingham."

Later in the day I informed my correspondent, for whom indeed I kept a loose diary of the situation, that I had made the acquaintance of this celebrity and that she was a pretty little girl who wore her hair in what used to be called a crop. She looked so juvenile

and so innocent that if, as Mr. Morrow had announced, she was resigned to the larger latitude, her superiority to prejudice must have
come to her early. I spent most of the day hovering about Neil Paraday's room, but it was communicated to me from below that Guy
Walsingham, at Prestidge, was a success. Toward evening I became
conscious somehow that her superiority was contagious, and by the
time the company separated for the night I was sure the larger latitude had been generally accepted. I thought of Dora Forbes and
felt that he had no time to lose. Before dinner I received a telegram
from Lady Augusta Minch. "Lord Dorimont thinks he must have
left bundle in train—inquire." How could I inquire—if I was to
take the word as a command? I was too worried and now too
alarmed about Neil Paraday. The Doctor came back, and it was an
immense satisfaction to me to be sure he was wise and interested.
He was proud of being called to so distinguished a patient, but he
admitted to me that night that my friend was gravely ill. It was
really a relapse, a recrudescence of his old malady. There could
be no question of moving him: we must at any rate see first, on the
spot, what turn his condition would take. Meanwhile, on the morrow, he was to have a nurse. On the morrow the dear man was easier, and my spirits rose to such cheerfulness that I could almost
laugh over Lady Augusta's second telegram: "Lord Dorimont's
servant been to station—nothing found. Push inquiries." I did
laugh, I'm sure, as I remember this to be the mystic scroll I had
scarcely allowed poor Mr. Morrow to point his umbrella at. Fool
that I had been; the thirty-seven influential journals wouldn't have
destroyed it, they'd only have printed it. Of course I said nothing to
Paraday.

When the nurse arrived she turned me out of the room, on which
I went downstairs. I should premise that at breakfast the news that
our brilliant friend was doing well excited universal complacency,
and the Princess graciously remarked that he was only to be commiserated for missing the society of Miss Collop. Mrs. Wimbush,
whose social gift never shone brighter than in the dry decorum with
which she accepted this fizzle in her fireworks, mentioned to me
that Guy Walsingham had made a very favourable impression on
her Imperial Highness. Indeed I think every one did so, and that,
like the money-market or the national honour, her Imperial Highness was constitutionally sensitive. There was a certain gladness,

a perceptible bustle in the air, however, which I thought slightly anomalous in a house where a great author lay critically ill. "*Le roy est mort—vive le roy*": I was reminded that another great author had already stepped into his shoes. When I came down again after the nurse had taken possession I found a strange gentleman hanging about the hall and pacing to and fro by the closed door of the drawing-room. This personage was florid and bald; he had a big red moustache and wore showy knickerbockers—characteristics all that fitted to my conception of the identity of Dora Forbes. In a moment I saw what had happened: the author of "The Other Way Round" had just alighted at the portals of Prestidge, but had suffered a scruple to restrain him from penetrating further. I recognised his scruple when, pausing to listen at his gesture of caution, I heard a shrill voice lifted in a sort of rhythmic uncanny chant. The famous reading had begun, only it was the author of "Obsessions" who now furnished the sacrifice. The new visitor whispered to me that he judged something was going on he oughtn't to interrupt.

"Miss Collop arrived last night," I smiled, "and the Princess has a thirst for the *inédit*."

Dora Forbes raised his bushy brows. "Miss Collop?"

"Guy Walsingham, your distinguished *confrére*—or shall I say your formidable rival?"

"Oh!" growled Dora Forbes. Then he added: "Shall I spoil it if I go in?"

"I should think nothing could spoil it!" I ambiguously laughed.

Dora Forbes evidently felt the dilemma; he gave an irritated crook to his moustache. "*Shall* I go in?" he presently asked.

We looked at each other hard a moment; then I expressed something bitter that was in me, expressed it in an infernal "Do!" After this I got out into the air, but not so fast as not to hear, when the door of the drawing-room opened, the disconcerted drop of Miss Collop's public manner: she must have been in the midst of the larger latitude. Producing with extreme rapidity, Guy Walsingham has just published a work in which amiable people who are not initiated have been pained to see the genius of a sister-novelist held up to unmistakable ridicule; so fresh an exhibition does it seem to them of the dreadful way men have always treated women. Dora Forbes, it's true, at the present hour, is immensely pushed by Mrs.

Wimbush and has sat for his portrait to the young artists she protects, sat for it not only in oils but in monumental alabaster.

What happened at Prestidge later in the day is of course contemporary history. If the interruption I had whimsically sanctioned
was almost a scandal, what is to be said of that general scatter of
the company which, under the Doctor's rule, began to take place
in the evening? His rule was soothing to behold, small comfort as I
was to have at the end. He decreed in the interest of his patient
an absolutely soundless house and a consequent break-up of the
party. Little country practitioner as he was, he literally packed off
the Princess. She departed as promptly as if a revolution had
broken out, and Guy Walsingham emigrated with her. I was kindly
permitted to remain, and this was not denied even to Mrs. Wimbush. The privilege was withheld indeed from Dora Forbes; so
Mrs. Wimbush kept her latest capture temporarily concealed. This
was so little, however, her usual way of dealing with her eminent
friends that a couple of days of it exhausted her patience and she
went up to town with him in great publicity. The sudden turn for
the worse her afflicted guest had, after a brief improvement, taken
on the third night raised an obstacle to her seeing him before her
retreat; a fortunate circumstance doubtless, for she was fundamentally disappointed in him. This was not the kind of performance
for which she had invited him to Prestidge, let alone invited the
Princess. I must add that none of the generous acts marking her
patronage of intellectual and other merit have done so much for
her reputation as her lending Neil Paraday the most beautiful
of her numerous homes to die in. He took advantage to the utmost
of the singular favour. Day by day I saw him sink, and I roamed
alone about the empty terraces and gardens. His wife never came
near him, but I scarcely noticed it: as I paced there with rage in my
heart I was too full of another wrong. In the event of his death it
would fall to me perhaps to bring out in some charming form, with
notes, with the tenderest editorial care, that precious heritage of
his written project. But where *was* that precious heritage, and were
both the author and the book to have been snatched from us? Lady
Augusta wrote me she had done all she could and that poor Lord
Dorimont, who had really been worried to death, was extremely
sorry. I couldn't have the matter out with Mrs. Wimbush, for I
didn't want to be taunted by her with desiring to aggrandise my-

self by a public connexion with Mr. Paraday's sweepings. She had signified her willingness to meet the expense of all advertising, as indeed she was already ready to do. The last night of the horrible series, the night before he died, I put my ear closer to his pillow.

"That thing I read you that morning, you know."

"In your garden that dreadful day? Yes!"

"Won't it do as it is?"

"It would have been a glorious book."

"It *is* a glorious book," Neil Paraday murmured. "Print it as it stands—beautifully."

"Beautifully!" I passionately promised.

It may be imagined whether, now that he's gone, the promise seems to me less sacred. I'm convinced that if such pages had appeared in his lifetime the Abbey would hold him to-day. I've kept the advertising in my own hands, but the manuscript has not been recovered. It's impossible, and at any rate intolerable, to suppose it can have been wantonly destroyed. Perhaps some hazard of a blind hand, some brutal fatal ignorance has lighted kitchen-fires with it. Every stupid and hideous accident haunts my meditations. My undiscourageable search for the lost treasure would make a long chapter. Fortunately I've a devoted associate in the person of a young lady who has every day a fresh indignation and a fresh idea, and who maintains with intensity that the prize will still turn up. Sometimes I believe her, but I've quite ceased to believe myself. The only thing for us at all events is to go on seeking and hoping together, and we should be closely united by this firm tie even were we not at present by another.

JAMES: *The Death of the Lion*

1. *What is the relevance of the title?*

2. *Other images of animals (what kinds?) recur throughout the story. How, through these images and the one in the title, does James suggest the theme of his story?*

3. *Why is the story divided into ten sections? Would eight or twelve do as well?*

4. *Does the narrator speak for the author? (cf. the technique of Turgenev's "The District Doctor"). What is the author's attitude toward the*

narrator? Would the story lose in force if it were told in the third person? Or by James himself in the first person?

5. What is James's attitude toward Neil Paraday? Toward Mrs. Wimbush? Toward Fanny Hurter?

6. There is often a "turn of the screw" in the typical James story. Where does it come in this one? Is there more than one "turn"?

7. Why does James name a female novelist Guy and a male novelist Dora? Can you cite some other instances of wit (take a second look at place names and proper names)?

8. Alongside the subtle comedy there is also deep pathos. Do the two conflict here?

9. What view of people does James suggest in this story?

10. How would you characterize the style? Oblique, circuitous, straightforward, elegant? Does it seem appropriate to the character of the narrator?

Guy de Maupassant

LITTLE LOUISE ROQUE

Born in Normandy in 1850, Maupassant was fortunate in having for a neighbor the novelist Flaubert, who introduced him to many of his literary friends. Under Flaubert's tutelage, Maupassant learned to write the kind of short story which became his stock in trade: the controlled precise work that drives to an inevitable climax and conclusion. By the time of his death in 1893, Maupassant had written sixteen volumes of stories whose quality remained high despite his prodigious output. Although less known than some of his other stories, "Little Louise Roque" is typical of Maupassant's mature work, with its sensuality, its sense of human tragedy, its recognition of forces which man cannot control.

MEDERIC ROMPEL, the postman, familiarly called by the country people "Mederi," started at his usual hour from the post-house at Rouy-le-Tors. Having passed through the little town, striding like an old trooper, he cut across the meadows of Villaumes in order to reach the bank of the Brindelle, which led him along the water's edge to the village of Carvelin, where his distribution commenced. He traveled quickly, following the course of the narrow river, which frothed, murmured, and boiled along its bed of grass under the arching willow trees. The big stones, impeding the flow of water, created around them a sort of aqueous necktie ending in a knot of foam. In some places, there were cascades a foot wide, often invisible, which made under the leaves, under the tendrils, under a roof of verdure, a noise at once angry and gentle. Further on, the banks widened out, and you saw a small, placid lake where trout were swimming in the midst of all that green vegetation which keeps undulating in the depths of tranquil streams.

Mederic went on without a halt, seeing nothing and with only one thought in his mind: "My first letter is for the Poivron family; then I have one for M. Renardet; so I must cross the wood."

His blue blouse, fastened round his waist by a black leathern belt, moved in quick, regular fashion above the green hedge of willow-trees; and his stick of stout holly kept time with the steady march of his feet.

He crossed the Brindelle over a bridge formed of a single tree thrown lengthwise, with a rope attached to two stakes driven into the river banks as its only balustrade.

The wood, which belonged to M. Renardet, the mayor of Carvelin, and the largest landowner in the district, consisted of a number of huge old trees, straight as pillars, and extended for about half a league along the left bank of the stream which served as a boundary for this immense arch of foliage. Alongside the water there were large shrubs warmed by the sun: but under the trees you found nothing but moss, thick, soft, plastic moss, which exhaled into the stagnant air a light odor of loam and withered branches.

Mederic slackened his pace, took off his black cap trimmed with red lace, and wiped his forehead, for it was by this time hot in the meadows, though not yet eight o'clock in the morning.

He had just recovered from the effects of the heat, and had accelerated his pace when he noticed at the foot of a tree a knife, a child's small knife. As he picked it up, he discovered a thimble, and then a needlecase, not far away.

Having found these objects, he thought: "I'll intrust them to the mayor," and resumed this journey. But now he kept his eyes open, expecting to find something else.

All of a sudden, he drew up stiffly as if he had run up against a wooden bar. Ten paces in front of him on the moss, lay stretched on her back a little girl, quite naked. She was about twelve years old. Her arms were hanging down, her legs parted, and her face covered with a handkerchief. There were little spots of blood on her thighs.

Mederic now advanced on tiptoe, as if afraid to make a noise; he apprehended some danger, and glanced toward the spot uneasily.

What was this? No doubt, she was asleep. Then, he reflected that a person does not go to sleep thus, naked, at half past seven in the morning under cool trees. Then she must be dead; and he must be face to face with a crime. At this thought, a cold shiver ran through his frame, although he was an old soldier. And then a murder was such a rare thing in the country—and above all the murder of a child—that he could not believe his eyes. But she had no wound—nothing save these blood drops on her legs. How, then, had she been killed?

He stopped when quite near her and stared at her, while leaning on his stick. Certainly, he knew her, as he knew all the inhabitants of the district; but, not being able to get a look at her face, he could not guess her name. He stooped forward in order to take off the handkerchief which covered her face; then paused with outstretched hand, restrained by an idea that occurred to him.

Had he the right to disarrange anything in the condition of the corpse before the magisterial investigation? He pictured justice to himself as a general whom nothing escapes, who attaches as much importance to a lost button as to a stag of a knife in the stomach. Perhaps under this handkerchief evidence to support a capital charge could be found; in fact if there were sufficient proof there to secure a conviction, it might lose its value if touched by an awkward hand.

Then he straightened up with the intention of hastening toward the mayor's residence, but again another thought held him back. If the little girl was still alive, by any chance—he could not leave her lying there in this way. He sank on his knees very gently, a yard away from her, through precaution, and stretched his hand toward her feet. The flesh was icy cold, with that terrible coldness which makes dead flesh frightful, and leaves us no longer in doubt. The letter-carrier, as he touched her, felt his heart leap to his mouth, as he said himself afterward, and his lips were parched with dry saliva. Rising up abruptly he rushed off through the trees to M. Renardet's house.

He hurried on in double-quick time, with his stick under his arm, his hands clenched, and his head thrust forward, and his leathern bag, filled with letters and newspapers, flapping regularly at his side.

The mayor's residence was at the end of the wood, which he used as a park, and one side of it was washed by a little lagoon formed at this spot by the Brindelle.

It was a big, square house of gray stone, very old. It had stood many a siege in former days, and at the end of it was a huge tower, twenty meters high, built in the water. From the top of this fortress the entire country around could be seen in olden times. It was called the Fox's Tower, without anyone knowing exactly why; and from the appellation, no doubt, had come the name Renardet, borne by the owners of this fief, which had remained in the same family, it was said, for more than two hundred years. For the Renardets formed part of that upper middle class which is all but noble and was met with so often in the provinces before the Revolution.

The postman dashed into the kitchen where the servants were taking breakfast, and exclaimed:

"Is the mayor up? I want to speak to him at once."

Mederic was recognized as a man of weight and authority, and it was soon understood that something serious had happened.

As soon as word was brought to M. Renardet, he ordered the postman to be sent up to him. Pale and out of breath, with his cap in his hand, Mederic found the mayor seated in front of a long table covered with scattered papers.

He was a big, tall man, heavy and red-faced, strong as an ox, and greatly liked in the district, though of an excessively violent disposition. Very nearly forty years old, and a widower for the past six months, he lived on his estate like a country gentleman. His choleric temperament had often brought him into trouble, from which the magistrates of Rouy-le-Tors, like indulgent and prudent friends, had extricated him. Had he not one day thrown the conductor of the diligence from the top of his seat because the letter had nearly crushed his retriever, Micmac? Had he not broken the ribs of a gamekeeper, who had abused him for having passed through a neighbor's property with a gun in his hand? Had he not even caught by the collar the sub-prefect, who stopped in the village in the course of an administrative round described by M. Renardet as an electioneering tour; for he was against the government, according to his family tradition?

The mayor asked:

"What's the matter now, Mederic?"

"I have found a little girl dead in your wood."

Renardet rose up, with his face the color of brick.

"A little girl, do you say?"

"Yes, M'sieu', a little girl, quite naked, on her back, with blood on her, dead—quite dead!"

The mayor gave vent to an oath:

"By God, I'd make a bet 'tis little Louise Roque! *I* have just learned that she did not go home to her mother last night. Where did you find her?"

The postman pointed out where the place was, gave full details, and offered to conduct the mayor to the spot.

But Renardet became brusque:

"No. I don't need you. Send the steward, the mayor's secretary, and the doctor immediately to me, and resume your rounds. Quick, go quick, and tell them to meet me in the wood."

The letter-carrier, a man used to discipline, obeyed and withdrew, angry and grieved at not being able to be present at the investigation.

The mayor, in his turn, prepared to go out. He took his hat, a big soft hat, and paused for a few seconds on the threshold of his abode. In front of him stretched a wide lawn in which three large patches were conspicuous—three large beds of flowers in full bloom, one facing the house and the others at either side of it. Further on, rose skyward the principal trees in the wood, while at the left, above the spot where the Brindelle widened into a pool, could be seen long meadows, an entirely flat green sweep of country, cut by dykes and monster-like willows, twisted drawf-trees, always cut short, having on their thick squat trunks a quivering tuft of branches.

To the right, behind the stables, the outhouses, and the buildings connected with the property, might be seen the village, which was prosperous, being mainly inhabited by raisers of oxen.

Renardet slowly descended the steps in front of his house, and, turning to the left, gained the water's edge, which he followed at a slow pace, his hands behind his back. He went on, with bent head, and from time to time he glanced round in search of the persons for whom he had sent.

When he stood beneath the trees, he stopped, took off his hat, and wiped his forehead as Mederic had done; for the burning sun was shedding its fiery rain upon the ground. Then the mayor resumed his journey, stopped once more, and retraced his steps. Suddenly stooping down, he steeped his handkerchief in the stream that glided at his feet and stretched it round his head, under his hat. Drops of water flowed along his temples, over his purple ears, over his strong red neck, and trickled one after the other, under his white shirt-collar.

As yet nobody had appeared; he began tapping with his foot, then he called out: "Hallo! Hallo!"

A voice at his right answered: "Hallo! Hallo!" and the doctor appeared under the trees. He was a thin little man, an ex-military surgeon, who passed in the neighborhood for a very skillful practitioner. He limped, having been wounded while in the service, and had to use a stick to assist him in walking.

Next came the steward and the mayor's secretary, who, having been sent for at the same time, arrived together. They seemed scared, as they hurried forward, out of breath, walking and trotting in turn in order to hasten, and moving their arms up and down so vigorously that they seemed to do more work with them than with their legs.

Renardet said to the doctor:

"You know what the trouble is about?"

"Yes, a child found dead in the wood by Mederic."

"That's quite correct. Come on."

They walked on side by side, followed by the two men.

Their steps made no noise on the moss, their eyes were gazing downward right in front of them.

The doctor hastened his steps, interested by the discovery. As soon as they were near the corpse, he bent down to examine it without touching it. He had put on a pair of glasses, as you do when you are looking at some curious object; then he turned round very quietly and said, without rising up:

"Violated and murdered, as we shall prove presently. The little girl, moreover, is almost a woman—look at her throat."

Her two breasts, already nearly full-developed, fell over her chest, relaxed by death. The doctor lightly drew away the handkerchief which covered her face. It was almost black, frightful to look at, the tongue protruding, the eyes bloodshot. He went on:

"Faith, she was strangled the moment the deed was done."

He felt her neck:

"Strangled with the hands without leaving any special trace, neither the mark of the nails nor the imprint of the fingers. Quite right. It is little Louise Roque, sure enough!"

He delicately replaced the handkerchief:

"There's nothing for me to do. She's been dead for the last hour at least. We must give notice of the matter to the authorities."

Renardet, standing up, with his hands behind his back, kept staring with a stony look at the little body exposed to view on the grass. He murmured:

"What a wretch! We must find the clothes."

The doctor felt the hands, the arms, the legs. He said:

"She must have been bathing, no doubt. They ought to be at the water's edge."

The mayor thereupon gave directions:

"Princèpe [this was his secretary], go and look for those clothes for me along the river. Maxime [this was the steward], hurry on towards Rouy-le-Tors, and bring on here to me the examining magistrate with the gendarmes. They must be here within an hour. You understand."

The two men quickly departed, and Renardet said to the doctor:

"What miscreant has been able to do such a deed in this part of the country?"

The doctor murmured:

"Who knows? Everyone is capable of that! Everyone in particular and nobody in general. However, it must be some prowler, some workman out of employment. As we live under a Republic, we must expect to meet this sort of miscreant along the roads."

Both of them were Bonapartists. The mayor went on:

"Yes, it could only be a stranger, a passer-by, a vagabond without heart or home."

The doctor added with the shadow of a smile on his face:

"And without a wife. Having neither a good supper nor a good bed, he procured the rest for himself. You can't tell how many men there may be in the world capable of a crime at a given moment. Did you know that this little girl had disappeared?"

And with the end of his stick he touched one after the other the stiffened fingers of the corpse, resting on them as on the keys of a piano.

"Yes, the mother came last night to look for me about nine o'clock, the child not having come home for supper up to seven. We went to try and find her along the roads up to midnight, but we did not think of the wood. However, we needed daylight to carry out a search with a practical result."

"Will you have a cigar?" said the doctor.

"Thanks, I don't care to smoke. It gives me a turn to look at this."

They remained standing in front of the young girl's body, pale and still, on the dark background of moss. A big fly was walking along one of the thighs, it stopped at the blood-stains, went on again, always rising higher, ran along the side with his lively, jerky movements, climbed up one of the breasts, then came back again to explore the other. The two men silently watched this wandering black speck. The doctor said:

"How tantalizing it is, a fly on the skin! The ladies of the last century had good reason to paste them on their faces. Why has the fashion gone out?"

But the mayor seemed not to hear, plunged as he was in deep thought.

All of a sudden he turned around, surprised by a shrill noise. A woman in a cap and a blue apron rushed up through the trees. It was the mother, La Roque. As soon as she saw Renardet she began to shriek:

"My little girl, where's my little girl?" in such a distracted manner that she did not glance down at the ground. Suddenly, she saw the corpse, stopped short, clasped her hands, and raised both her arms while she uttered a sharp, heartrending cry—the cry of a mutilated animal. Then, she rushed toward the body, fell on her knees, and snatched the handkerchief that covered the face. When she saw that frightful countenance, black and convulsed, she recoiled with a shudder, then pressed her face against the ground, giving vent to terrible and continuous choking screams, her mouth close to the thick moss.

Her tall, thin frame, to which her clothes clung tightly, was palpitating, shaken with convulsions. They could see her bony ankles and withered limbs covered with thick blue stockings, shivering horribly. Unconsciously she dug at the soil with her crooked fingers as if to make a grave in which to hide herself.

The doctor pityingly said in a low tone:

"Poor old woman!"

Renardet felt a strange rumbling in his stomach; then he gave vent to a sort of loud sneeze that issued at the same time through nose and mouth; and, drawing his handkerchief from his pocket, began to weep copiously, coughing, sobbing noisily, wiping his face, and stammering:

"Damn—damn—damned pig to do this! I would like to see him guillotined!"

But Princèpe reappeared, with his hands empty. He murmured:

"I have found nothing, M'sieu', le Maire, nothing at all anywhere."

The mayor, scared, replied in a thick voice, drowned in tears:

"What is it you could not find?"

"The little girl's clothes."

"Well—well—look again, and find them—or you'll have to answer to me."

The man, knowing that the mayor would not brook opposition, set forth again with hesitating steps, casting on the corpse horrified and timid glances.

Distant voices arose under the trees, confused sound, the noise of an approaching crowd; for Mederic had, in the course of his rounds, carried the news from door to door. The people of the neighborhood, stupefied at first, had gone gossiping from their own firesides into the street, and from one threshold to another. Then they gathered together. They talked over, discussed, and commented on the event for some minutes, and they had now come to see it for themselves.

They arrived in groups, a little faltering and uneasy through fear of the first impression of such a scene on their minds. When they saw the body they stopped, not daring to advance, and speaking low. Then they grew bold, went on a few steps, stopped again, advanced once more, and soon formed around the dead girl, her mother, the doctor, and Renardet, a thick circle, agitated and noisy, which swayed forward under the sudden pushes of the last comers. And now they touched the corpse. Some of them even bent down to feel it with their fingers. The doctor kept them back. But the mayor, waking abruptly out of his torpor, broke into a rage, and, seizing Dr. Labarbe's stick, flung himself on his townspeople, stammering:

"Clear out—clear out—you pack of brutes—clear out!"

And in a second the crowd of sightseers had fallen back two hundred metres.

La Roque was lifted up, turned round, and placed in a sitting posture; she remained weeping with her hands clasped over her face.

The occurrence was discussed among the crowd; and young lads, with eager eyes, curiously scrutinized the nude body of the girl. Renardet perceived this, and, abruptly taking off his vest, flung it over the little girl, who was entirely lost to view under the wide garment.

The spectators drew quietly nearer. The wood was filled with people, and a continuous hum of voices rose up under the tangled foliage of the tall trees.

The mayor, in his shirt-sleeves, remained standing, with his stick in his hands, in a fighting attitude. He seemed exasperated by this curiosity on the part of the people, and kept repeating:

"If one of you comes nearer, I'll break his head just as I would a dog's."

The peasants were greatly afraid of him. They held back. Dr. La-barbe, who was smoking, sat down beside La Roque, and spoke to her in order to distract her attention. The old woman soon removed her hands from her face, and replied with a flood of tearful words, pouring forth her grief in rapid sentences. She told the whole story of her life, her marriage, the death of her man—a bull-sticker, who had been gored to death—the infancy of her daughter, her wretched existence as a widow without resources and with a child to support. She had only this one, her little Louise, and the child had been killed—killed in this wood. All of a sudden, she felt anxious to see it again, and dragging herself on her knees toward the corpse, she raised up one corner of the garment that covered it; then she let it fall again, and began wailing once more. The crowd remained silent, eagerly watching the mother's gestures.

But all of a sudden there was a swaying of the crowd, and a cry of "The gendarmes! The gendarmes!"

Two gendarmes appeared in the distance, coming on at a rapid trot, escorting their captain and a little gentleman with red whiskers, who was bobbing up and down like a monkey on a big white mare.

The steward had found M. Putoin, the examining magistrate, just at the moment when he was mounting to take his daily ride, for he posed as a good horseman, to the great amusement of the officers.

He dismounted along with the captain, and pressed the hands of the mayor and the doctor, casting a ferret-like glance on the linen vest which swelled above the body lying underneath.

When he was thoroughly acquainted with the facts, he first gave orders to get rid of the public, whom the gendarmes drove out of the wood, but who soon reappeared in the meadow, and formed a line, a long line of excited and moving heads all along the Brindelle, on the other side of the stream.

The doctor in his turn gave explanations of which Renardet took a note in his memorandum book. All the evidence was given, taken down, and commented on without leading to any discovery. Maxime, too, came back without having found any trace of the clothes.

This surprised everybody; no one could explain it on the theory of theft, since these rags were not worth twenty sous; so this theory was inadmissible.

The examining magistrate, the mayor, the captain, and the doctor set to work by searching in pairs, putting aside the smallest branches along the water.

Renardet said to the judge:

"How does it happen that this wretch should conceal or carry away the clothes, and should then leave the body exposed in the open air and visible to everyone?"

The other, sly and knowing, answered:

"Perhaps a dodge. This crime has been committed either by a brute or by a crafty blackguard. In any case, we'll easily succeed in finding him."

The rolling of a vehicle made them turn their heads. It was the deputy magistrate, another doctor, and the registrar of the court who had arrived in their turn. They resumed their searches, all chatting in an animated fashion.

Renardet said suddenly:

"Do you know that I am expecting you to lunch with me?"

Everyone smilingly accepted the invitation, and the examining magistrate, finding that the case of little Louise Roque was quite enough to bother about for one day, turned toward the mayor:

"I can have the body brought to your house, can I not? You have a room in which you can keep it for me till this evening."

The other got confused, and stammered:

"Yes—no—no. To tell the truth, I prefer that it should not come into my house on account of—on account of my servants who are already talking about ghosts in—in my tower, in the Fox's Tower. You know—I could no longer keep a single one. No—I prefer not to have it in my house."

The magistrate began to smile:

"Good! I am going to get it carried off at once to Rouy, for the legal examination."

Turning toward the doctor:

"I can make use of your trap, can I not?"

"Yes, certainly."

Everybody came back to the place where the corpse lay. La Roque, now seated beside her daughter, had caught hold of her hand, and was staring right before her, with a wandering listless eye.

The two doctors endeavored to lead her away, so that she might not witness the dead girl's removal; but she understood at once what they wanted to do, and, flinging herself on the body, she seized it in both arms. Lying on top of the corpse, she exclaimed:

"You shall not have it—'tis mine—'tis mine now. They have killed her for me, and I want to keep her—you shall not have her——!"

All the men, affected and not knowing how to act, remained standing around her. Renardet fell on his knees, and said to her:

"Listen, La Roque, it is necessary—in order to find out who killed her. Without this it could not be found out. We must make a search for him in order to punish him. When we have found him, we'll give her up to you. I promise you this."

This explanation shook the woman's mind, and a feeling of hatred manifested in her distracted glance.

"So then they'll take him?"

"Yes, I promise you that."

She rose up, deciding to let them do as they liked; but when the captain remarked: " 'Tis surprising that her clothes cannot be found," a new idea, which she had not previously thought of, abruptly found an entrance into her brain, and she asked:

"Where are her clothes? They're mine. I want them. Where have they been put?"

They explained to her that they had not been found, then she called out for them with desperate obstinacy and with repeated moans:

"They're mine—I want them. Where are they? I want them!"

The more they tried to calm her, the more she sobbed, and persisted in her demands. She no longer wanted the body, she insisted on having the clothes, as much perhaps through the unconscious cupidity of a wretched being to whom a piece of silver represents a fortune, as through maternal tenderness.

And when the little body, rolled up in blankets which had been brought out from Renardet's house, had disappeared in the vehicle, the old woman, standing under the trees, held up by the mayor and the captain, exclaimed:

"I have nothing, nothing, nothing in the world, not even her little cap—her little cap."

The curé had just arrived, a young priest already growing stout. He took it on himself to carry off La Roque, and they went away together toward the village. The mother's grief was modified under the sugary words of the clergyman who promised her a thousand compensations. But she incessantly kept repeating: "If I had only her little cap."

This idea now dominated every other.

Before they were out of hearing Renardet exclaimed:

"You will lunch with us, Monsieur l'Abbé—in an hour's time?"

The priest turned his head round, and replied:

"With pleasure, Monsieur le Maire. I'll be with you at twelve."

And they all directed their steps toward the house, whose gray front and large tower, built on the edge of the Brindelle, could be seen through the branches.

The meal lasted a long time. They talked about the crime and everybody was of the same opinion. It had been committed by some tramp passing there by chance while the little girl was bathing.

Then the magistrates returned to Rouy, announcing that they would return next day at an early hour. The doctor and the curé went to their respective homes, while Renardet, after a long walk through the meadows, returned to the wood, where he remained walking till nightfall with slow steps, his hands behind his back.

He went to bed early, and was still asleep next morning when the examining magistrate entered his room. He rubbed his hands together with a self-satisfied air. He said:

"Ha! ha! Still sleeping? Well, my dear fellow, we have news this morning."

The mayor sat up on his bed.

"What pray?"

"Oh! Something strange. You remember well how the mother yesterday clamored for some memento of her daughter, especially her little cap? Well, on opening her door this morning, she found on the threshold her child's two little wooden shoes. This proves that the crime was perpetrated by some one from the district, some one who felt pity for her. Besides, the postman Mederic found and brought me the thimble, the scissors, and the needlecase of the dead girl. So then the man in carrying off the clothes in order to hide them, must have let fall the articles which were in the pocket. As for me, I attach special importance to the wooden shoes, as they indicate a certain moral culture and a faculty for tenderness on the part of the murderer. We will therefore, if you have no objection, pass in review together the principal inhabitants of your district."

The mayor got up. He rang for hot water to shave with, and said:

"With pleasure, but it will take rather a long time, so let us begin at once."

M. Putoin sat astride on a chair, thus pursuing even in a room, his mania for horsemanship. Renardet now covered his chin with a white lather while he looked at himself in the glass; then he sharpened his razor on the strop and went on:

"The principal inhabitant of Carvelin bears the name of Joseph Renardet, mayor, a rich landowner, a rough man who beats guards and coachmen—"

The examining magistrate burst out laughing:

"That's enough; let us pass on to the next."

"The second in importance is ill. Pelledent, his deputy, a rearer of oxen, an equally rich landowner, a crafty peasant, very sly, very close-fisted on every question of money, but incapable in my opinion of having perpetrated such a crime."

M. Putoin said:

"Let us pass on."

Then, while continuing to shave and wash himself, Renardet

went on with the moral inspection of all the inhabitants of Carvelin. After two hours' discussion, their suspicions were fixed on three individuals who had hitherto borne a shady reputation—a poacher named Cavalle, a fisher for club and cray-fish named Paquet, and a bull-sticker named Clovis.

2

The search for the perpetrator of the crime lasted all the summer, but he was not discovered. Those who were suspected and those who were arrested easily proved their innocence, and the authorities were compelled to abandon the attempt to capture the criminal.

But the murder seemed to have moved the entire country in a singular fashion. It left a disquietude, a vague fear, a sensation of mysterious terror, springing not merely from the impossibility of discovering any trace of the assassin, but above all from that strange finding of the wooden shoes in front of La Roque's door on the day after the crime. The certainty that the murderer had assisted at the investigation and that he was doubtless still living in the village, left a gloomy impression on every mind, and hung over the neighborhood like a constant menace.

The wood, besides, had become a dreaded spot, a place to be avoided, and supposed to be haunted.

Formerly, the inhabitants used to come and lounge there every Sunday afternoon. They used to sit down on the moss at the foot of the huge trees, or walk along the water's edge watching the trout gliding under the green undergrowth. The boys used to play bowls, hide-and-seek, and other games in certain places where they had up-turned, smoothed out, and leveled the soil, and the girls, in rows of four or five, used to trip along holding one another by the arms, and screaming out with their shrill voices ballads which grated on the ear, disturbed the tranquil air with discord and set the teeth on edge like vinegar. Now nobody ventured into and under the towering trees, as if afraid of finding there some corpse lying on the ground.

Autumn arrived; the leaves began to fall. They fell day and night from the tall trees, whirling round and round to the ground; and the sky could be seen through the bare branches. Sometimes when a gust of wind swept over the tree-tops, the slow, continuous rain suddenly grew heavier, and became a hoarsely growling storm, which drenched the moss with thick yellow water that made the ground swampy and yielding. And the almost imperceptible murmur, the floating, ceaseless whisper, gentle and sad, of this rainfall seemed like a low wail, and the continually falling leaves, like tears, big tears shed by the tall mournful trees, which were weeping, as it were, day and night over the close of the year, over the ending of warm dawns and soft twilights, over the ending of hot breezes and bright suns, and also perhaps over the crime which they had seen committed under the shade of their branches, over the girl violated and killed at their feet. They wept in the silence of the desolate empty wood, the abandoned, dreaded wood, where the soul, the childish soul of the dead little girl must have been wandering all alone.

The Brindelle, swollen by the storms, rushed on more quickly, yellow and angry, between its dry banks, lined with thin, bare willow-hedges.

Renardet suddenly resumed his walks under the trees. Every day, at sunset, he came out of his house, descended the front steps slowly, and entered the wood, in a dreamy fashion with his hands in his pockets. For a long time he would pace over the damp, soft moss, while a legion of rooks, rushing to the spot from all the neighboring haunts in order to rest in the tall summits, spread themselves through space, like an immense mourning veil floating in the wind, uttering violent and sinister screams. Sometimes they would perch on the tangled branches dotting with black spots the red sky, the sky crimsoned with autumn twilight. Then, all of a sudden, they would set off again, croaking frightfully and trailing once more above the wood the long darkness of their flight. Then they would swoop down, at last, on the highest tree-tops, and gradually their cawings would die away, while advancing night merged their black plumes into the blackness of space.

Renardet was still strolling slowly under the trees; then, when the darkness prevented him from walking any longer, he went back to the house, sank all of a heap into his armchair in front of the glowing hearth and dried his feet at the fire.

Now, one morning, an important bit of news was circulated around the district: the mayor was getting his wood cut down.

Twenty woodcutters were already at work. They had commenced at the corner nearest to the house, and they worked rapidly in the master's presence.

At first the loppers climbed up the trunk. Tied to it by a rope collar, they clung round it in the beginning with both arms, then, lifting one leg, struck the tree hard with the edge of a steel instrument attached to each foot. The edge penetrated the wood and remained stuck in it; and the man rose up as if on a step in order to strike with the steel attached to the other foot, and then once more supported himself till he could lift his first foot again.

With every upward movement was slipped higher the rope collar which fastened him to the tree. Over his loins hung and glittered the steel hatchet. He kept continually climbing in easy fashion like some parasite attacking a giant, mounting slowly up the immense trunk, embracing it and spurring it in order to decapitate it.

As soon as he reached the lowest branches, he stopped, detached from his side the sharp ax, and struck. Slowly, methodically, he chopped at the limb close to the trunk. Suddenly the branch cracked, gave way, bent, tore itself off, and fell, grazing the neighboring trees in its fall. Then it crashed down on the ground with a great sound of broken wood, and its lighter branches quivered for a long time.

The soil was covered with fragments which other men cut in their turn, bound in bundles, and piled in heaps, while the trees which were still left standing looked like enormous posts, gigantic forms amputated and shorn by the keen steel axes of the cutters.

When the lopper had finished his task, he left at the top of the straight slender shaft of the tree the rope collar which he had brought up with him, descending again with spur-like prods along the discrowned trunk, which the woodcutters below attacked at the base, striking it with heavy blows which resounded through all the rest of the wood.

When the base of the tree seemed pierced deeply enough, some men commenced dragging, to the accompaniment of a signal cry in which all joined harmoniously, at the rope attached to the top. All of a sudden, the immense column cracked and tumbled to the earth with the dull sound and shock of a distant cannon-shot. Each day the wood grew thinner, losing its trees one by one as an army loses its soldiers.

Renardet no longer walked up and down. He remained from morning till night, contemplating, motionless, with his hands behind his back, the slow death of his wood. When a tree fell, he placed his foot on it as if it were a corpse. Then he raised his eyes to the next with a kind of secret, calm impatience, as if he expected or hoped for something at the end of this massacre.

Meanwhile, they were approaching the place where little Louise Roque had been found. At length, they came to it—one evening, at the hour of twilight.

As it was dark, the sky being overcast, the woodcutters wanted to stop their work, putting off till next day the fall of an enormous beech-tree. But Renardet objected to this, insisting that even at this late hour they should lop and cut down this giant, which had overshadowed and seen the crime.

When the lopper had laid it bare, had finished its toilet for the guillotine, and the woodcutters had sapped its base, five men commenced hauling at the rope attached to the top.

The tree resisted; its powerful trunk, although cut half-way through, was as rigid as iron. The workmen, altogether, with a sort of regular jump, strained at the rope, stooping down to the ground, and they gave vent to a cry with lungs out of breath, so as to indicate and direct their efforts.

Two woodcutters stood close to the giant, with axes in their grip, like two executioners ready to strike once more, and Renardet, motionless, with his hand on the bark, awaited the fall with an uneasy, nervous feeling.

One of the men said to him:

"You're too near, Monsieur le Maire. When it falls, it may hurt you."

He did not reply and did not recoil. He seemed ready to catch the beech-tree in his open arms in order to cast it on the ground like a wrestler.

All at once, at the foot of the tall column of wood there was a shudder which seemed to run to the top, like a painful shiver; it bent slightly, ready to fall, but still resisted. The men, in a state of excitement, stiffened their arms, renewed their efforts with greater vigor, and, just as the tree, breaking, came crashing down, Renardet suddenly made a forward step, then stopped, his shoulders raised to receive the irresistible shock, the mortal blow which would crush him to the earth.

But the beech-tree, having deviated a little, only grazed against his loins, throwing him on his face five metres away.

The workmen rushed forward to lift him up. He had already risen to his knees, stupefied, with wandering eyes, and passing his hand across his forehead, as if he were awaking out of an attack of madness.

When he had got to his feet once more, the men, astonished, questioned him, not being able to understand what he had done. He replied, in faltering tones, that he had had for a moment a fit of abstraction, or rather a return to the days of his childhood, that he imagined he had to pass under that tree, just as street-boys rush in front of vehicles driving rapidly past, that he had played at danger, that, for the past eight days, he felt this desire growing stronger within him, asking himself whether, every time a tree was cracking, was on the point of falling, he could pass beneath it without being touched. It was a piece of stupidity, he confessed; but everyone has these moments of insanity, these temptations to boyish folly.

He made this explanation in a slow tone, searching for his words and speaking in a stupefied fashion.

Then he went off saying:

"Till to-morrow, my friends—till to-morrow."

As soon as he had reached his study, he sat down before his table, which his lamp, covered with a shade, lighted up brightly, and, clasping his hands over his forehead, began to cry.

He remained crying for a long time, then wiped his eyes, raised his head, and looked at the clock. It was not yet six o'clock.

"I have time before dinner."

And he went to the door and locked it. He then came back, and sat down before his table. He pulled out a drawer in the middle of it, and taking from it a revolver, laid it down over his papers, under the glare of the lamp. The barrel of the firearm glittered, and cast reflections which resembled flames.

Renardet gazed at it for some time with the uneasy glance of a drunken man; then he rose and began to pace up and down the room.

He walked from one end of the apartment to the other, stopped from time to time and started to pace up and down again a moment afterward. Suddenly, he opened the door of his dressing-room, steeped a towel in the water-jug and moistened his forehead, as he had done on the morning of the crime.

Then he began to walk up and down once more. Each time he passed the table the gleaming revolver attracted his glance, and tempted his hand; but he kept watching the clock, thinking:

"I still have time."

It struck half past six. Then he took up the revolver, opened his mouth wide with a frightful grimace, and stuck the barrel into it, as if he wanted to swallow it. He remained in this position for some seconds without moving, his finger on the lock; then, suddenly, seized with a shudder of horror, he dropped the pistol on the carpet, and fell back on his armchair, sobbing:

"I can't. I dare not! My God! My God! My God! How can I have the courage to kill myself?"

There was a knock at the door. He rose up in a stupefied condition. A servant said:

"Monsieur's dinner is ready."

He replied: "All right. I'm going down."

He picked up the revolver, locked it up again in the drawer, then looked at himself in the glass over the mantelpiece to see whether his face did not look too much troubled. It was as red as usual, a little redder perhaps. That was all. He went down, and seated himself before the table.

He ate slowly, like a man who wants to drag on the meal, who does not want to be alone with himself.

Then he smoked several pipes in the dining-room while the plates were being removed. After that, he went back to his room.

As soon as he was alone, he looked under his bed, opened all his cupboards, explored every corner, rummaged through all the furniture. Then he lighted the tapers over the mantelpiece, and, turning round several times, ran his eye all over the apartment in an anguish of terror that made his face lose its color, for he knew well that he was going to see her, as he did every night—little Louise Roque, the little girl he had violated and afterward strangled.

Every night the odious vision came back again. First, it sounded in his ears like the snorting that is made by a thrashing machine or the distant passage of a train over a bridge. Then he commenced to pant, to feel suffocated, and had to unbutton his shirt-collar and loosen his belt. He moved about to make his blood circulate, he tried to read, he attempted to sing. It was in vain. His thoughts, in spite of himself, went back to the day of the murder, made him go through it again in all its most secret details, with all the violent emotions he had experienced from first to last.

He had felt on rising up that morning, the morning of the horrible day, a little vertigo and dizziness which he attributed to the heat, so that he remained in his room till the time came for lunch.

After the meal he had taken a siesta, then, toward the close of the afternoon, he had gone out to breathe the fresh, soothing breeze under the trees in the wood.

But, as soon as he was outside, the heavy scorching air of the plain oppressed him more. The sun, still high in the heavens, poured out on the parched, dry, and thirsty soil, floods of ardent light. Not a breath of wind stirred the leaves. Beasts and birds, even the grasshoppers, were silent. Renardet reached the tall trees, and began to walk over the moss where the Brindelle sent forth a slight, cool vapor under the immense roof of trees. But he felt ill at ease. It seemed to him that an unknown, invisible hand was squeezing his neck, and he could scarcely think rationally, having usually few ideas in his head. For the last three months, only one thought haunted him, the thought of marrying again. He suffered from living alone, suffered from it morally and physically. Accustomed for ten years past to feeling a woman near him, habituated to her presence every moment, to her embrace each successive day, he had need, an imperious and perplexing need, of incessant contact with her and the regular touch of her lips. Since Madame Renardet's death, he had suffered continually without knowing why, had suffered from not feeling her dress brush against his legs every day, and, above all, from no longer being able to grow calm and languid in her arms. He had been scarcely six months a widower, and he had already been looking out through the district for some young girl or some widow he might marry when his period of mourning was at an end.

He had a chaste soul, but it was lodged in a vigorous Herculean body, and carnal images began to disturb his sleep and his vigils. He drove them away; they came back again; and he murmured from time to time, smiling at himself:

"Here I am, like St. Antony."

Having had this morning several besetting visions, the desire suddenly came into his breast to bathe in the Brindelle in order to refresh himself and reduce his feverishness.

He knew, a little further on, of a large deep spot where the people of the neighborhood came sometimes to take a dip in the summer. He went there.

Thick willow-trees hid this clear pool of water where the current rested and went to sleep for a little while before starting on its way again. Renardet, as he appeared, thought he heard a light sound, a faint plash which was not that of the stream or the banks. He softly put aside the leaves and looked. A little girl, quite naked in the transparent water, was beating the waves with both hands, dancing about in them a little, and dipping herself with pretty movements. She was not a child nor was she yet a woman. She was plump and well formed, yet had an air of youthful precocity, as of one who had grown rapidly, and who was now almost ripe. He no longer moved, overcome with surprise, with a pang of desire, holding his breath with a strange, poignant emotion. He remained there, his heart beating as if one of his sensual dreams had just been realized; as if an impure fairy had conjured up before him this young creature, this little rustic Venus born of the river foam, who was making his heart beat faster.

Suddenly the little girl came out of the water, and without seeing him came over to where he stood, looking for her clothes in order to dress herself. While she was gradually approaching him with little hesitating steps, through fear of the sharp pointed stones, he felt himself pushed toward her by an irresistible force, by a bestial transport of passion, which stirred up all his carnality, stupefied his soul, and made him tremble from head to foot.

She remained standing some seconds behind the willow-tree which concealed him from view. Then, losing his reason entirely, he opened the branches, rushed on her, and seized her in his arms. She fell, too scared to offer any resistance, too much terror-stricken to cry out, and he possessed her without understanding what he was doing.

He woke up from his crime, as one wakes out of a nightmare. The child burst out weeping.

He said:

"Hold your tongue! Hold your tongue! I'll give you money."

But she did not hear him, she went on sobbing.

He went on:

"Come now, hold your tongue! Do hold your tongue. Keep quiet."

She still kept shrieking, writhing in the effort to get away from him. He suddenly realized that he was ruined, and he caught her by the neck to stop her from uttering these heartrending, dreadful screams. As she continued to struggle with the desperate strength of a being who is flying from death, he pressed his enormous hands on that little throat swollen with cries. In a few seconds he had strangled her, so furiously did he grip her, yet not intending to kill but only to silence her.

Then he rose up overwhelmed with horror.

She lay before him with her face bleeding and blackened. He was going to rush away when there sprang up in his agitated soul the mysterious and undefined instinct that guides all beings in the hour of danger.

It was necessary to throw the body into the water; but he did not; another impulse drove him toward the clothes, of which he made a thin parcel. Then, as he had a piece of twine, he tied it up and hid it in a deep portion of the stream, under the trunk of a tree, the foot of which was immersed in the Brindelle.

Then he went off at a rapid pace, reached the meadows, took a wide turn in order to show himself to peasants who dwelt some distance away on the opposite side of the district, and came back to dine at the usual hour, telling his servants all that was supposed to have happened during his walk.

He slept, however, that night—slept with a heavy, brutish sleep, such as the sleep of persons condemned to death must occasionally be. He opened his eyes at the first glimmer of dawn, and waited, tortured by the fear of having his crime discovered, for his usual waking hour.

Then he would have to be present at all the stages of the inquiry as to the cause of death. He did so after the fashion of a somnambulist, in a hallucination which showed him things and human beings in a sort of dream, in a cloud of intoxication, with that dubious sense of unreality which perplexes the mind at times of the greatest catastrophes.

The only thing that pierced his heart was La Roque's cry of anguish. At that moment he felt inclined to cast himself at the old woman's feet, and to exclaim: "It is I."

But he restrained himself. He went back, however, during the night, to fish up the dead girl's wooden shoes, in order to carry them to her mother's threshold.

As long as the inquiry lasted, so long as it was necessary to guide and aid justice, he was calm, master of himself, sly and smiling. He discussed quietly with the magistrates all the suppositions that passed through their minds, combated their opinions, and demolished their arguments. He even took a keen and mournful pleasure in disturbing their investigations, in confuting their ideas, in showing the innocence of those whom they suspected.

But from the day when the investigation came to a close, he became gradually nervous, more excitable than he had been before, although he mastered his irritability. Sudden noises made him jump up with fear; he shuddered at the slightest thing, trembled sometimes from head to foot when a fly alighted on his forehead. Then he was seized with an imperious desire for motion, which compelled him to keep continually on foot, and made him remain up whole nights walking to and fro in his own room.

It was not that he was goaded by remorse. His brutal mind did not lend itself to any shade of sentiment or of moral terror. A man of energy and even of violence, born to make war, to ravage conquered countries, and to massacre the vanquished, full of the savage instincts of the hunter and the fighter, he scarcely took count of human life. Though he respected the Church through policy, he believed neither in God nor in the devil, expecting consequently in another life neither chastisement nor recompense for his acts. As his sole creed, he retained a vague philosophy composed of all the ideas of the encyclopedists of the last century. He regarded religion as a moral sanction of the law, both one and the other having been invented by men to regulate social relations.

To kill anyone in a duel, or in a battle, or in a quarrel, or by accident, or for the sake of revenge, or even through bravado, would have seemed to him an amusing and clever thing, and would not have left more impression on his mind than a shot fired at a hare; but he had experienced a profound emotion at the murder of this child. He had, in the first place, perpetrated it in the distraction of an irresistible gust of passion, in a sort of sensual tempest that had overpowered his reason. And he had cherished in his heart, cherished in his flesh, cherished on his lips, cherished even to the very tips of his murderous fingers, a kind of bestial love, as well as a feeling of horror and grief, toward this little girl he had surprised and basely killed. Every moment his thoughts returned to that horrible scene, and, though he endeavored to drive away the picture from his mind, though he put it aside with terror, with disgust, he felt it surging through his soul, moving about in him, waiting incessantly for the moment to reappear.

Then, in the night, he was afraid, afraid of the shadows falling around him. He did not yet know why the darkness seemed frightful to him; but he instinctively feared it, felt that it was peopled with terrors. The bright daylight did not lend itself to fears. Things and beings were seen there; there only natural things and beings which could exhibit themselves in the light of day could be met. But the night, the impenetrable night, thicker than walls, and empty, the infinite night, so black, so vast, in which one might brush against frightful things, the night when one feels that mysterious terror is wandering, prowling about, appeared to him to conceal an unknown danger, close and menacing.

What was it?

He knew it before long. As he sat in his armchair, rather late, one evening when he could not sleep, he thought he saw the curtain of his window move. He waited, in an uneasy state of mind, with beating heart. The drapery did not stir, then, all of a sudden it moved once more. He did not venture to rise up; he no longer ventured to breathe, and yet he was brave. He had often fought, and he would have liked to catch thieves in his house.

Was it true that this curtain did move? he asked himself, fearing that his eyes had deceived him. It was, moreover, such a slight thing, a gentle flutter of lace, a kind of trembling in its folds, less than such an undulation as is caused by the wind.

Renardet sat still, with staring eyes, and outstretched neck. Then he sprang to his feet abruptly, ashamed of his fear, took four steps, seized the drapery with both hands, and pulled it wide apart. At first, he saw nothing but darkened glass, resembling plates of glittering ink. The night, the vast, impenetrable night stretched out before him as far as the invisible horizon. He remained standing in front of the illimitable shadow, and suddenly perceived a light, a moving light, which seemed some distance away.

Then he put his face close to the windowpane, thinking that a person looking for crayfish might be poaching in the Brindelle, for it was past midnight. The light rose up at the edge of the stream, under the trees. As he was not yet able to see clearly, Renardet placed his hands over his eyes. Suddenly this light became an illumination, and he beheld little Louise Roque naked and bleeding on the moss. He recoiled frozen with horror, sank into his chair and fell backward. He remained there some minutes, his soul in distress; then he sat up and began to reflect. He had had a hallucination—that was all: a hallucination due to the fact that a marauder of the night was walking with a lantern in his hand near the water's edge. What was there astonishing, besides, in the circumstance that the recollection of his crime should sometimes bring before him the vision of the dead girl?

He rose up, swallowed a glass of wine and sat down again. He thought:

"What am I to do if this came back?"

And it did come back; he felt it; he was sure of it. Already his glance was drawn toward the window; it called him; it attracted him. In order to avoid looking at it, he turned aside his chair. Then, he took a book and tried to read; but it seemed to him that he presently heard something stirring behind him, and he swung round his armchair on one foot.

The curtain still moved—unquestionably, it did move this time; he could no longer have any doubt about it.

He rushed forward and seized it in his grasp so violently that he knocked it down with its fastener. Then, he eagerly pressed his face against the glass. He saw nothing. All was black without; and he breathed with the delight of a man whose life has just been saved.

Then he went back to his chair, and sat down again; but almost immediately he felt a longing to look out through the window once more. Since the curtain had fallen, the space in front of him made a sort of dark patch, fascinating and terrible, on the obscure landscape. In order not to yield to this dangerous temptation, he took off his clothes, extinguished the lamp, and lay down, shutting his eyes.

Lying on his back motionless, his skin hot and moist, he awaited sleep. Suddenly a great gleam of light flashed across his eyelids. He opened them believing that his dwelling was on fire. All was black as before, and he leaned on his elbow in order to try to distinguish his window, which had still for him an unconquerable attraction. By dint of straining his eyes, he could perceive some stars, and he arose, groped his way across the room, discovered the panes with his outstretched hands, and placed his forehead close to them. There below, under the trees, the body of the little girl glittered like phosphorus, lighting up the surrounding darkness.

Renardet uttered a cry and rushed toward his bed, where he lay till morning, his head hidden under the pillow.

From that moment, his life became intolerable. He passed his days in apprehension of each succeeding night; and each night the vision came back again. As soon as he had locked himself up in his room, he strove to struggle; but in vain. An irresistible force lifted him up and pushed him against the glass, as if to call the phantom, and before long he saw it lying in the spot where the crime was committed, lying with arms and legs outspread, just in the way the body had been found.

Then the dead girl rose up and came toward him with little steps just as the child had done when she came out of the river. She advanced quietly, passing straight across the grass, and over the border of withered flowers. Then she rose up into the air toward Renardet's window. She came toward him, as she had come on the day of the crime. And the man recoiled before the apparition—he retreated to his bed, and sank down upon it, knowing well that the little one had entered the room, and that she now was standing behind the curtain, which presently moved. And until daybreak, he kept staring at this curtain, with a fixed glance, ever waiting to see his victim depart.

But she did not show herself any more; she remained there behind the curtain which quivered tremulously now and then.

And Renardet, his fingers clinging to the bedclothes, squeezed them as he had squeezed the throat of little Louise Roque.

He heard the clock striking the hours; and in the stillness the pendulum kept time with the loud beating of his heart. And he suffered, the wretched man, more than any man had ever suffered before.

Then, as soon as a white streak of light on the ceiling announced the approaching day, he felt himself free, alone at last, alone in his room; and then he went to sleep. He slept some hours—a restless, feverish sleep in which he retraced in dreams the horrible vision of the night just past.

When, later on, he went down to breakfast, he felt exhausted as if after prodigious fatigue; and he scarcely ate anything, haunted as he was by the fear of what he had seen the night before.

He knew, however, that it was not an apparition—that the dead do not come back, and that his sick soul, possessed by one thought alone, by an indelible remembrance, was the only cause of his punishment, was the only evoker of that awful image, brought back by it to life, called up by it and raised by it before his eyes, in which the ineffaceable resemblance remained imprinted. But he knew, too, that he could not cure it, that he could never escape from the savage persecution of his memory; and he resolved to die, rather than endure these tortures any longer.

Then, he pondered how he would kill himself. He wished for some simple and natural death which would preclude the idea of suicide. For he clung to his reputation, to the name bequeathed to him by his ancestors; and if there was any suspicion as to the cause of his death, people's thoughts might be perhaps directed toward the mysterious crime, toward the murderer who could not be found, and they would not hesitate to accuse him.

A strange idea came into his head, that of letting himself be crushed by the tree at the foot of which he had murdered little Louise Roque. So he determined to have the wood cut down and to simulate an accident. But the beech-tree refused to smash his ribs.

Returning to his house, a prey to utter despair, he had snatched up his revolver, and then he did not dare to fire it.

The dinner bell summoned him. He could eat nothing, and went upstairs again. But he did not know what he was going to do. Now that he had escaped the first time, he felt himself a coward. Presently, he would be ready, fortified, decided, master of his courage and of his resolution; just now, he was weak, and feared death as much as he did the dead girl.

He faltered out to himself:

"I will not venture it again—I will not venture it."

Then he glanced with terror, first at the revolver on the table, and next at the curtain which hid his window. It seemed to him, moreover, that something horrible would occur as soon as his life was ended. Something? What? A meeting with her, perhaps! She was watching for him; she was waiting for him; she was calling him; and her object was to seize him in her turn, to exhibit herself to him every night so that she might draw him toward the doom that would avenge her, and lead him to death.

He began to cry like a child, repeating:

"I will not venture it again—I will not venture it."

Then he fell on his knees, and murmured: "My God! my God!" without believing, nevertheless, in God. He no longer dared, in fact, to look out through his window where he knew the apparition was visible, nor at the table where his revolver gleamed.

When he had risen up, he said:

"This cannot last; there must be an end of it."

The sound of his voice in the silent room made a shiver of fear pass through his limbs, but, as he could not come to a decision, as he felt certain that his finger would always refuse to pull the trigger of his revolver, he turned round to hide his head under the bed-clothes, and to plunge into reflection.

He would have to find some way in which he could force himself to die, to invent some device against himself, which would not permit of any hesitation on his part, any delay, any possible regrets. He began to envy condemned criminals who are led to the scaffold surrounded by soldiers. Oh! if he could only beg of some one to shoot him; if he could, confessing the state of his soul, confessing his crime to a sure friend who would never divulge it, obtain from him death.

But from whom could he ask this terrible service? From whom? He cast about for one among his friends whom he knew intimately. The doctor? No, he would talk about it afterward, most certainly. And suddenly a fantastic idea entered his mind. He would write to the examining magistrate, who was on terms of close friendship with him and would denounce himself as the perpetrator of the crime. He would in this letter confess everything, revealing how his soul had been tortured, how he had resolved to die, how he had hesitated about carrying out his resolution, and what means he had employed to strengthen his failing courage. And in the name of their old friendship he would implore of the other to destroy the letter as soon as he had ascertained that the culprit had inflicted justice on himself. Renardet could rely on this magistrate; he knew him to be sure, discreet, incapable of even an idle word. He was one of those men who have an inflexible conscience, governed, directed, regulated by their reason alone.

Scarcely had he formed this project when a strange feeling of joy took possession of his heart. He was calm now. He would write his letter slowly, then at daybreak he would deposit it in the box nailed to the wall in his office, then he would ascend his tower to watch for the postman's arrival, and when the man in the blue blouse came in sight, he would cast himself headlong on to the rocks on which the foundations rested. First he would take care to be seen by the workmen who were cutting down his wood. He would then climb to the parapet some distance up which bore the flagstaff displayed on *fête* days. He would smash this pole with a shake and precipitate it along with him.

Who would suspect that it was not an accident? And he would be dashed to pieces, having regard to his weight and the height of the tower.

Presently he got out of bed, went over to the table, and began to write. He omitted nothing, not a single detail of the crime, not a single detail of the torments of his heart, and he ended by announcing that he had passed sentence on himself—that he was going to execute the criminal—and begged of his friend, his old friend, to be careful that there should never be any stain on his memory.

When he had finished his letter, he saw that the day had dawned.

He closed it, sealed it, and wrote the address; then he descended with light steps, hurried toward the little white box fastened to the wall in the corner of the farmhouse, and when he had thrown into it the fatal paper which made his hand tremble, he came back quickly, shot the bolts of the great door, and climbed up to his tower to wait for the passing of the postman, who would convey his death sentence.

He felt self-possessed, now. Liberated! Saved!

A cold dry wind, an icy wind, passed across his face. He inhaled it eagerly, with open mouth, drinking in its chilling kiss. The sky was red, with a burning red, the red of winter, and all the plain whitened with frost glistened under the first rays of the sun, as if it had been powdered with bruised glass.

Renardet, standing up, with his head bare, gazed at the vast tract of country before him, the meadow to the left, and to the right the village whose chimneys were beginning to smoke with the preparations for the morning meal. At his feet he saw the Brindelle flowing toward the rocks, where he would soon be crushed to death. He felt himself reborn on that beautiful frosty morning, full of strength, full of life. The light bathed him and penetrated him like a new-born hope. A thousand recollections assailed him, recollections of similar mornings, of rapid walks, the hard earth which rang under his footsteps, of happy chases on the edges of pools where wild ducks sleep. At the good things that he loved, the good things of existence rushed into memory, penetrated him with fresh desires, awakened all the vigorous appetites of his active, powerful body.

And he was about to die? Why? He was going to kill himself stupidly, because he was afraid of a shadow—afraid of nothing. He was still rich and in the prime of life! What folly! All he wanted was distraction, absence, a voyage in order to forget.

This night even he had not seen the little girl because his mind was preoccupied, and so had wandered toward some other subject. Perhaps he would not see her any more? And even if she still haunted him in his house, certainly she would not follow him elsewhere! The earth was wide, the future was long.

Why die?

His glance traveled across the meadows, and he perceived a blue spot in the path which wound along-side of the Brindelle. It was Mederic coming to bring letters from the town and to carry away those of the village.

Renardet got a start, a sensation of pain shot through his breast, and he rushed toward the winding staircase to get back his letter, to demand it back from the postman. Little did it matter to him now whether he was seen. He hurried across the grass moistened by the light frost of the previous night, and he arrived in front of the box in the corner of the farmhouse exactly at the same time as the letter-carrier.

The latter had opened the little wooden door, and drew forth the papers deposited there by the inhabitants of the locality.

Renardet said to him:

"Good morrow, Mederic."

"Good morrow, M'sieu' le Maire."

"I say, Mederic, I threw a letter into the box that I want back again. I came to ask you to give it back to me."

"That's all right, M'sieu' le Maire—you'll get it."

And the postman raised his eyes. He stood petrified at the sight of Renardet's face. The mayor's cheeks were purple, his eyes were glaring with black circles round them as if they were sunk in his head, his hair was all tangled, his beard untrimmed, his necktie unfastened. It was evident that he had not gone to bed.

The postman asked:

"Are you ill, M'sieu' le Maire?"

The other suddenly comprehending that his appearance must be unusual, lost countenance and faltered:

"Oh! no—oh! no. Only I jumped out of bed to ask you for this letter. I was asleep. You understand?"

Said Mederic: "What letter?"

"The one you are going to give back to me."

Mederic now began to hesitate. The mayor's attitude did not strike him as natural. There was perhaps a secret in that letter, a political secret. He knew Renardet was not a Republican and he knew all the tricks and chicaneries employed at elections.

He asked:

"To whom is it addressed, this letter of yours?"

"To M. Putoin, the examining magistrate—you know my friend, M. Putoin, well!"

The postman searched through the papers, and found the one asked for. Then he began looking at it, turning it round and round between his fingers, much perplexed, much troubled by the fear of committing a grave offense or of making an enemy for himself of the mayor.

Seeing his hesitation, Renardet made a movement for the purpose of seizing the letter and snatching it away from him. This abrupt action convinced Mederic that some important secret was at stake and made him resolve to do his duty, cost what it might.

So he flung the letter into his bag and fastened it up, with the reply:

"No, I can't, M'sieu' le Maire. From the moment it is addressed and sent to the magistrate, I can't."

A dreadful pang wrung Renardet's heart, and he murmured:

"Why, you know me well. You are even able to recognize my handwriting. I tell you I want that paper."

"I can't."

"Look here, Mederic, you know that I'm incapable of deceiving you—I tell you I want it."

"No, I can't."

A tremor of rage passed through Renardet's soul.

"Damn it all, take care! You know that I don't go in for chaffing, and that I could get you out of your job, my good fellow, and without much delay either. And then, I am the mayor of the district after all; and I now order you to give me back that paper."

The postman answered firmly:

"No, I can't, M'sieu' le Maire."

Thereupon Renardet, losing his head, caught hold of the postman's arms in order to take away his bag; but, freeing himself by a strong effort, and springing backward, the letter-carrier raised his holly stick. Without losing his temper, he said emphatically:

"Don't touch me, M'sieu' le Maire, or I'll strike. Take care, I'm only doing my duty!"

Feeling that he was lost, Renardet suddenly became humble, gentle, appealing to him like a crying child:

"Look here, look here, my friend, give me back that letter, and I'll give you money. Stop! Stop! I'll give you a hundred francs, you understand—a hundred francs!"

The postman turned on his heel and started on his journey.

Renardet followed him, out of breath, faltering:

"Mederic, Mederic, listen! I'll give you a thousand francs, you understand—a thousand francs."

The postman still went on without giving any answer.

Renardet went on:

"I'll make your fortune, you understand—whatever you wish— fifty thousand francs—fifty thousand francs—fifty thousand francs for that letter! What does it matter to you? You won't? Well, a hundred thousand—I say—a hundred thousand francs—a hundred thousand francs."

The postman turned back, his face hard, his eyes severe:

"Enough of this, or else I'll repeat to the magistrate everything you have just said to me."

Renardet stopped abruptly. It was all over. He turned back and rushed toward his house, running like a hunted animal.

Then, in his turn, Mederic stopped, and watched this flight with stupefaction. He saw the mayor re-entering his own house and he waited still as if something astonishing was about to happen.

Presently the tall form of Renardet appeared on the summit of the Fox's Tower. He ran round the platform like a madman. Then he seized the flagstaff and shook it furiously without succeeding in breaking it; then, all of a sudden, like a swimmer taking a plunge, he dived into the air with his two hands in front of him.

Mederic rushed forward to give succor. As he crossed the park, he saw the woodcutters going to work. He called out to them, telling them an accident had occurred, and at the foot of the walls they found a bleeding body the head of which was crushed on a rock. The Brindelle surrounded this rock, and over its clear, calm waters, swollen at this point, could be seen a long, thin, red stream of mingled brains and blood.

MAUPASSANT: *Little Louise Roque*

1. *At what specific point in the story did you suspect the mayor of the crime? Why, at an early point, does the author reveal the identity of the slayer?*

2. *Why is the character of the postman, who seems to be little more than the counterpart of the messenger in the Greek plays, developed in some detail at the beginning of the story?*

3. *What is the significance of the river Brindelle in the story?*

4. *What is the purpose of the tree-cutting episode? What is the significance of the images that Maupassant creates? Do they work? Why does the mayor place himself before a falling tree?*

5. *Why does the murder of the child so upset the mayor when killing itself is not repugnant to him?*

6. *Has Maupassant succeeded in transforming a grisly episode into a moving tale? If you think he succeeds, how does he do it? Where does the story fail? Can any subject be suitable for fiction if it is sensitively and effectively handled?*

7. *Is Maupassant suggesting that respectability may cloak the worst of criminals? That many criminals escape notice because of their social position? Or that the ordinary person may have moments of criminal passion without having a criminal temperament? In Unamuno's story, Dr. Montarco makes a simple distinction between the sane and the insane. Does it have any relevance to this story?*

Joseph Conrad

IL CONDE

Joseph Conrad was born in Berdiczew, Poland, on December 3, 1857, and died in England on August 3, 1924. Trained as a seaman, he turned to fiction under the encouragement of Edward Garnett, then a publisher's reader. Once he gave up thoughts of returning to the sea, Conrad rapidly published a large number of novels and stories which brought him critical acclaim, although popular success was not to come until later with the publication of Chance (1914) and Victory (1915). The turning point in his career came with the writing of The Nigger of the "Narcissus" (1897), which indicated a marked development in his fiction. In the next ten or so years, he wrote most of his major works: "Heart of Darkness" (1899), Lord Jim (1900), Nostromo (1904), The Secret Agent (1907) and Under Western Eyes (1911). Conceived and written during this period, "Il Conde" contains in miniature several of his most important themes.

"Vedi Napoli e poi mori."

ᘓᕽ

THE first time we got into conversation was in the National Museum in Naples, in the rooms on the ground floor containing the famous collection of bronzes from Herculaneum and Pompeii: that marvelous legacy of antique art whose delicate perfection has been preserved for us by the catastrophic fury of a volcano.

He addressed me first, over the celebrated Resting Hermes which we had been looking at side by side. He said the right things about that wholly admirable piece. Nothing profound. His taste was natural rather than cultivated. He had obviously seen many fine things in his life and appreciated them; but he had no jargon of a dilettante or the connoisseur. A hateful tribe. He spoke like a fairly intelligent man of the world, a perfectly unaffected gentleman.

We had known each other by sight for some few days past. Staying in the same hotel—good, but not extravagantly up to date—I had noticed him in the vestibule going in and out. I judged he was an old and valued client. The bow of the hotelkeeper was cordial in its deference, and he acknowledged it with familiar courtesy. For the servants he was *Il Conde.* There was some squabble over a man's parasol—yellow silk with white lining sort of thing—the waiter had discovered abandoned outside the dining-room door. Our gold-laced doorkeeper recognized it and I heard him directing one of the lift boys to run after *Il Conde* with it. Perhaps he was the only count staying in the hotel, or perhaps he had the distinction of being *the* Count *par excellence,* conferred upon him because of his tried fidelity to the house.

Having conversed at the Museo—(and by the by he had expressed his dislike of the busts and statues of Roman emperors in the gallery of marbles: their faces were too vigorous, too pronounced for him)—having conversed already in the morning I did not think I was intruding when in the evening, finding the dining room very full, I proposed to share his little table. Judging by the quiet urbanity of his consent he did not think so either. His smile was very attractive.

He dined in an evening waistcoat and a "smoking" (he called it so) with a black tie. All this of very good cut, not new—just as these things should be. He was, morning or evening, very correct in his dress. I have no doubt that his whole existence had been correct, well ordered and conventional, undisturbed by startling events. His white hair brushed upwards off a lofty forehead gave him the air of an idealist, of an imaginative man. His white mustache, heavy but carefully trimmed and arranged, was not unpleasantly tinted a golden yellow in the middle. The faint scent of some very good perfume, and of good cigars (that last an odor quite remarkable to come upon in Italy) reached me across the table. It was in his eyes that his age showed most. They were a little weary with creased eyelids. He must have been sixty or a couple of years more. And he was communicative. I would not go so far as to call it garrulous—but distinctly communicative.

He had tried various climates, of Abbazia, of the Riviera, of other places, too, he told me, but the only one which suited him was the climate of the Gulf of Naples. The ancient Romans, who, he pointed out to me were men expert in the art of living, knew very well what they were doing when they built their villas on these shores, in Baiæ, in Vico, in Capri. They came down to this seaside in search of health, bringing with them their trains of mimes and flute-players to amuse their leisure. He thought it extremely probable that the Romans of the higher classes were specially predisposed to painful rheumatic affections.

This was the only personal opinion I heard him express. It was based on no special erudition. He knew no more of the Romans than an average informed man of the world is expected to know. He argued from personal experience. He had suffered himself from a painful and dangerous rheumatic affection till he found relief in this particular spot of Southern Europe.

This was three years ago, and ever since he had taken up his quarters on the shores of the gulf, either in one of the hotels in Sorrento or hiring a small villa in Capri. He had a piano, a few books; picked up transient acquaintances of a day, week, or month in the stream of travelers from all Europe. One can imagine him going out for his walks in the streets and lanes, becoming known to beggars, shopkeepers, children, country people; talking amiably over the walls to the *contadini*—and coming back to his rooms or his villa to sit before the piano, with his white hair brushed up and his thick orderly mustache, "to make a little music for myself." And, of course, for a change there was Naples near by—life, movement, animation, opera. A little amusement, as he said, is necessary for health. Mines and flute-players, in fact. Only unlike the magnates of ancient Rome, he had no affairs of the city to call him away from these moderate delights. He had no affairs at all. Probably he had never had any grave affairs to attend to in his life. It was a kindly existence, with its joys and sorrows regulated by the course of Nature—marriages, births, deaths—ruled by the prescribed usages of good society and protected by the State.

He was a widower; but in the months of July and August he ventured to cross the Alps for six weeks on a visit to his married daughter. He told me her name. It was that of a very aristocratic family. She had a castle—in Bohemia, I think. This is as near as I ever came to ascertaining his nationality. His own name, strangely enough, he never mentioned. Perhaps he thought I had seen in to the published list. Truth to say, I never looked. At any rate, he was a good European—he spoke four languages to my certain knowledge—and a man of fortune. Not of great fortune evidently and appropriately. I imagine that to be extremely rich would have appeared to him improper, *outré*—too blatant altogether. And obviously, too, the fortune was not of his making. The making of a fortune cannot be achieved without some roughness. It is a matter of temperament. His nature was too kindly for strife. In the course of conversation he mentioned his estate quite by the way, in reference to that painful and alarming rheumatic affection. One year, staying incautiously beyond the Alps as late as the middle of September, he had been laid up for three months in that lonely country house with no one but his valet and the caretaking couple to attend to him. Because, as he expressed it, he "kept no establishment there." He had only gone for a couple of days to confer with his land agent. He promised himself never to be so imprudent in the future. The first weeks of September would find him on the shores of his beloved gulf.

Sometimes in traveling one comes upon such lonely men, whose only business is to wait for the unavoidable. Deaths and marriages have made a solitude round them, and one really cannot blame their endeavors to make the waiting as easy as possible. As he remarked to me, "At my time of life freedom from physical pain is a very important matter."

It must not be imagined that he was a wearisome hypochondriac. He was really much too well bred to be a nuisance. He had an eye for the small weaknesses of humanity. But it was a good-natured eye. He made a restful, easy, pleasant companion for the hours between dinner and bedtime. We spent three evenings together, and then I had to leave Naples in a hurry to look after a friend who had fallen seriously ill in Taormina. Having nothing to do, *Il Conde* came to see me off at the station. I was somewhat upset, and his idleness was always ready to take a kindly form. He was by no means an indolent man.

He went along the train peering into the carriages for a good seat for me, and then remained talking cheerily from below. He declared he would miss me that evening very much and announced his intention of going after dinner to listen to the band in the public garden, the Villa Nazionale. He would amuse himself by hearing excellent music and looking at the best society. There would be a lot of people, as usual.

I seem to see him yet—his raised face with a friendly smile under the thick mustaches, and his kind, fatigued eyes. As the train began to move, he addressed me in two languages: first in French, saying, *"Bon voyage"*; then in his very good, somewhat emphatic English, encouragingly, because he could see my concern: "All will—be—well—yet!"

My friend's illness having taken a decidedly favorable turn, I returned to Naples on the tenth day. I cannot say I had given much thought to *Il Conde* during my absence, but entering the dining room I looked for him in his habitual place. I had an idea he might have gone back to Sorrento to his piano and his books and his fishing. He was great friends with all the boatmen, and fished a good deal with lines from a boat. But I made out his white head in the crowd of heads, and even from a distance noticed something unusual in his attitude. Instead of sitting erect, gazing all round with alert urbanity, he drooped over his plate. I stood opposite him for some time before he looked up, a little wildly, if such a strong word can be used in connection with his correct appearance.

"Ah, my dear sir! Is it you?" he greeted me. "I hope all is well."

He was very nice about my friend. Indeed, he was always nice, with the niceness of people whose hearts are genuinely humane. But this time it cost him an effort. His attempts at general conversation broke down into dullness. It occurred to me he might have been indisposed. But before I could frame the inquiry he muttered:

"You find me here very sad."

"I am sorry for that," I said. "You haven't had bad news, I hope?"

It was very kind of me to take an interest. No. It was not that. No bad news, thank God. And he became very still as if holding his breath. Then, leaning forward a little, and in an odd tone of awed embarrassment, he took me into his confidence.

"The truth is that I have had a very—a very—how shall I say?— abominable adventure happen to me."

The energy of the epithet was sufficiently startling in that man of moderate feelings and toned-down vocabulary. The word unpleasant I should have thought would have fitted amply the worst experience likely to befall a man of his stamp. And an adventure, too. Incredible! But it is in human nature to believe the worst; and I confess I eyed him stealthily, wondering what he had been up to. In a moment, however, my unworthy suspicions vanished. There was a fundamental refinement of nature about the man which made me dismiss all idea of some more or less disreputable scrape.

"It is very serious. Very serious." He went on, nervously. "I will tell you after dinner, if you will allow me."

I expressed my perfect acquiescence by a little bow, nothing more. I wished him to understand that I was not likely to hold him to that offer, if he thought better of it later on. We talked of indifferent things, but with a sense of difficulty quite unlike our former easy, gossipy intercourse. The hand raising a piece of bread to his lips, I noticed, trembled slightly. This symptom, in regard to my reading of the man, was no less than startling.

In the smoking room he did not hang back at all. Directly we had taken our usual seats he leaned sideways over the arm of his chair and looked straight into my eyes earnestly.

"You remember," he began, "that day you went away? I told you then I would go to the Villa Nazionale to hear some music in the evening."

I remembered. His handsome old face, so fresh for his age, unmarked by any trying experience, appeared haggard for an instant. It was like the passing of a shadow. Returning his steadfast gaze, I took a sip of my black coffee. He was systematically minute in his narrative, simply in order, I think, not to let his excitement get the better of him.

After leaving the railway station, he had an ice, and read the paper in a café. Then he went back to the hotel, dressed for dinner, and dined with a good appetite. After dinner he lingered in the hall (there were chairs and tables there) smoking his cigar; talked to the little girl of the Primo Tenore of the San Carlo Theater, and exchanged a few words with that "amiable lady," the wife of the Primo Tenore. There was no performance that evening, and these people were going to the Villa also. They went out of the hotel. Very well.

At the moment of following their example—it was half-past nine already—he remembered he had a rather large sum of money in his pocketbook. He entered, therefore, the office and deposited the greater part of it with the bookkeeper of the hotel. This done, he took a *carozzella* and drove to the seashore. He got out of the cab and entered the Villa on foot from the Largo di Vittoria end.

He stared at me very hard. And I understood then how really

impressionable he was. Every small fact and event of that evening stood out in his memory as if endowed with mystic significance. If he did not mention to me the color of the pony which drew the *carozella,* and the aspect of the man who drove, it was a mere oversight arising from his agitation, which he repressed manfully.

He had then entered the Villa Nazionale from the Largo di Vittoria end. The Villa Nazionale is a public pleasure-ground laid out in grass plots, bushes, and flowerbeds between the houses of the Riviera di Chiaja and the waters of the bay. Alleys of trees, more or less parallel, stretch its whole length—which is considerable. On the Riviera di Chiaja side the electric tramcars run close to the railings. Between the garden and the sea is the fashionable drive, a broad road bordered by a low wall, beyond which the Mediterranean splashes with gentle murmurs when the weather is fine.

As life goes on late at night in Naples, the broad drive was all astir with a brilliant swarm of carriage lamps moving in pairs, some creeping slowly, others running rapidly under the thin, motionless line of electric lamps defining the shore. And a brilliant swarm of stars hung above the land humming with voices, piled up with houses, glittering with lights—and over the silent flat shadows of the sea.

The gardens themselves are not very well lit. Our friend went forward in the warm gloom, his eyes fixed upon a distant luminous region extending nearly across the whole width of the Villa, as if the air had glowed there with its own cold, bluish, and dazzling light. This magic spot, behind the black trunks of trees and masses of inky foliage, breathed out sweet sounds mingled with bursts of brassy roar, sudden clashes of metal, and grave, vibrating thuds.

As he walked on, all these noises combined together into a piece of elaborate music whose harmonious phrases came persuasively through a great disorderly murmur of voices and shuffling of feet on the gravel of that open space. An enormous crowd immersed in the electric light, as if in a bath of some radiant and tenuous fluid shed upon their heads by luminous globes, drifted in hundreds round the band. Hundreds more sat on chairs in more or less concentric circles, receiving unflinchingly the great waves of sonority that ebbed out into the darkness. The Count penetrated the throng, drifted with it in tranquil enjoyment, listening and looking at the faces. All people of good society: mothers with their daughters, parents and children, young men and young women all talking, smiling, nodding to each other. Very many pretty faces, and very many pretty toilettes. There was, of course, a quantity of diverse types: showy old fellows with white mustaches, fat men, thin men, officers in uniform; but what predominated, he told me, was the South Italian type of young man, with a colorless, clear complexion, red lips, jet-black little mustache and liquid black eyes so wonderfully effective in leering or scowling.

Withdrawing from the throng, the Count shared a little table in front of the café with a young man of just such a type. Our friend had some lemonade. The young man was sitting moodily before an empty glass. He looked up once, and then looked down again. He also tilted his hat forward. Like this—

The Count made the gesture of a man pulling his hat down over his brow, and went on:

"I think to myself: he is sad; something is wrong with him; young men have their troubles. I take no notice of him, of course. I pay for my lemonade, and go away."

Strolling about in the neighborhood of the band, the Count thinks he saw twice that young man wandering alone in the crowd. Once their eyes met. It must have been the same young man, but there were so many there of that type that he could not be certain. Moreover, he was not very much concerned except in so far that he had been struck by the marked, peevish discontent of that face.

Presently, tired of the feeling of confinement one experiences in a crowd, the Count edged away from the band. An alley, very somber by contrast, presented itself invitingly with its promise of solitude and coolness. He entered it, walking slowly on till the sound of the orchestra became distinctly deadened. Then he walked back and turned about once more. He did this several times before he noticed that there was somebody occupying one of the benches.

The spot being midway between two lampposts the light was faint.

The man lolled back in the corner of the seat, his legs stretched out, his arms folded and his head drooping on his breast. He never stirred, as though he had fallen asleep there, but when the Count passed by next time he had changed his attitude. He sat leaning forward. His elbows were propped on his knees, and his hands were rolling a cigarette. He never looked up from that occupation.

The Count continued his stroll away from the band. He returned slowly, he said. I can imagine him enjoying to the full, but with his usual tranquility, the balminess of this southern night and the sounds of music softened delightfully by the distance.

Presently, he approached for the third time the man on the garden seat, still leaning forward with his elbows on his knees. It was a dejected pose. In the semiobscurity of the alley his high shirt collar and his cuffs made small patches of vivid whiteness. The Count said that he had noticed him getting up brusquely as if to walk away, but almost before he was aware of it the man stood before him asking in a low, gentle tone whether the signore would have the kindness to oblige him with a light.

The Count answered this request by a polite "Certainly," and dropped his hands with the intention of exploring both pockets of his trousers for the matches.

"I dropped my hands," he said, "but I never put them in my pockets. I felt a pressure there—"

He put the tip of his finger on a spot close under his breastbone, the very spot of the human body where a Japanese gentleman begins the operations of the hara-kiri, which is a form of suicide following upon dishonor, upon an intolerable outrage to the delicacy of one's feelings.

"I glance down," the Count continued in an awe-struck voice, "and what do I see? A knife! A long knife—"

"You don't mean to say," I exclaimed, amazed, "that you have been held up like this in the Villa at half-past ten o'clock, within a stone's throw of a thousand people!"

He nodded several times, staring at me with all his might.

"The clarinet," he declared, solemnly, "was finishing its solo, and I assure you I could hear every note. Then the band crashed *fortissimo,* and that creature rolled its eyes and gnashed its teeth hissing at me with the greatest ferocity, 'Be silent! No noise or—' "

I could not get over my astonishment.

"What sort of knife was it?" I asked, stupidly.

"A long blade. A stiletto—perhaps a kitchen knife. A long narrow blade. It gleamed. And his eyes gleamed. His white teeth, too. I could see them. He was very ferocious. I thought to myself: 'If I hit him he will kill me.' How could I fight with him? He had the knife and I had nothing. I am nearly seventy, you know, and that was a young man. I seemed even to recognize him. The moody young man of the café. The young man I met in the crowd. But I could not tell. There are so many like him in this country."

The distress of that moment was reflected in his face. I should think that physically he must have been paralyzed by surprise. His thoughts, however, remained extremely active. They ranged over every alarming possibility. The idea of setting up a vigorous shouting for help occurred to him, too. But he did nothing of the kind, and the reason why he refrained gave me a good opinion of his mental self-possession. He saw in a flash that nothing prevented the other from shouting, too.

"That young man might in an instant have thrown away his knife and pretended I was the aggressor. Why not? He might have said I attacked him. Why not? It was one incredible story against another! He might have said anything—bring some dishonoring charge against me—what do I know? By his dress he was no common robber. He seemed to belong to the better classes. What could I say? He was an Italian—I am a foreigner. Of course, I have my passport, and there is our consul—but to be arrested, dragged at night to the police office like a criminal!"

He shuddered. It was in his character to shrink from scandal much more than from mere death. And certainly for many people this would have always remained—considering certain peculiarities of Neapolitan manners—a deucedly queer story. The Count was no fool. His belief in the respectable placidity of life having received this rude shock, he thought that now anything might happen. But also a notion came into his head that this young man was perhaps merely an infuriated lunatic.

This was for me the first hint of his attitude towards this adventure. In his exaggerated delicacy of sentiment he felt that nobody's self esteem need be affected by what a madman may choose to do to one. It became apparent, however, that the Count was to be denied that consolation. He enlarged upon the abominably savage way in which that young man rolled his glistening eyes and gnashed his white teeth. The band was going now through a slow movement of solemn braying by all the trombones, with deliberately repeated bangs of the big drum.

"But what did you do?" I asked, greatly excited.

"Nothing," answered the Count. "I let my hands hang down very still. I told him quietly I did not intend making a noise. He snarled like a dog, then said in an ordinary voice:

"*Vostro portofolio.*"

"So I naturally," continued the Count—and from this point acted the whole thing in pantomime. Holding me with his eyes, he went through all the motions of reaching into his inside breast pocket, taking out a pocketbook, and handing it over. But that young man, still bearing steadily on the knife, refused to touch it.

He directed the Count to take the money out himself, received it into his left hand, motioned the pocketbook to be returned to the pocket, all this being done to the sweet trilling of flutes and clarinets sustained by the emotional drone of the hautboys. And the "young man," as the Count called him, said: "This seems very little."

"It was, indeed, only 340 or 360 lire," the Count pursued. "I had left my money in the hotel, as you know. I told him this was all I had on me. He shook his head impatiently and said:

"*Vostro orologio.*"

The Count gave me the dumb show of pulling out his watch, detaching it. But, as it happened, the valuable gold half-chronometer he possessed had been left at a watchmaker's for cleaning. He wore that evening (on a leather guard) the Waterbury fifty-franc thing he used to take with him on his fishing expeditions. Perceiving the nature of this booty, the well-dressed robber made a contemptuous clicking sound with his tongue like this, "Tse-Ah!" and waved it away hastily. Then, as the Count was returning the disdained object to his pocket, he demanded with a threateningly increased pressure of the knife on the epigastrium, by way of reminder:

"*Vostri anelli.*"

"One of the rings," went on the Count, "was given me many years ago by my wife; the other is the signet ring of my father. I said, 'No. *That* you shall not have!'"

Here the Count reproduced the gesture corresponding to that declaration by clapping one hand upon the other, and pressing both thus against his chest. It was touching in its resignation. "That you shall not have," he repeated, firmly, and closed his eyes, fully expecting—I don't know whether I am right in recording that such an unpleasant word had passed his lips—fully expecting to feel himself being—I really hesitate to say—being disemboweled by the push of the long, sharp blade resting murderously against the pit of his stomach—the very seat, in all human beings, of anguishing sensations.

Great waves of harmony went on flowing from the band.

Suddenly the Count felt the nightmarish pressure removed from the sensitive spot. He opened his eyes. He was alone. He had heard nothing. It is probable that "the young man" had departed, with light steps, some time before, but the sense of the horrid pressure had lingered even after the knife had gone. A feeling of weakness came over him. He had just time to stagger to the garden seat. He felt as though he had held his breath for a long time. He sat all in a heap, panting with the shock of the reaction.

The band was executing, with immense bravura, the complicated finale. It ended with a tremendous crash. He heard it, unreal and remote, as if his ears had been stopped, and then the hard clapping of a thousand, more or less, pairs of hands, like a sudden hail shower passing away. The profound silence which succeeded recalled him to himself.

A tramcar resembling a long glass box wherein people sat with their heads strongly lighted, ran along swiftly within sixty yards of the spot where he had been robbed. Then another rustled by, and yet another going the other way. The audience about the band had broken up, and were entering the alley in small conversing groups. The Count sat up straight and tried to think calmly of what had happened to him. The vileness of it took his breath away again. As far as I can make it out he was disgusted with himself. I do not mean to say with his behavior. Indeed, if his pantomimic rendering of it for my information was to be trusted, it was simply perfect. No, it was not that. He was not ashamed. He was shocked at being the selected victim, not of robbery so much as of contempt. His tranquillity had been wantonly desecrated. His lifelong, kindly nicety of outlook had been defaced.

Nevertheless, at that stage, before the iron had time to sink deep, he was able to argue himself into comparative equanimity. As his agitation calmed down somewhat, he became aware that he was frightfully hungry. Yes, hungry. The sheer emotion had made him simply ravenous. He left the seat and, after walking for some time, found himself outside the gardens and before an arrested tramcar, without knowing very well how he came there. He got in as if in a dream, by a sort of instinct. Fortunately he found in his trouser pocket a copper to satisfy the conductor. Then the car stopped, and as everybody was getting out he got out, too. He recognized the Piazza San Ferdinando, but apparently it did not occur to him to take a cab and drive to the hotel. He remained in distress on the Piazza like a lost dog, thinking vaguely of the best way of getting something to eat at once.

Suddenly he remembered his twenty-franc piece. He explained to me that he had that piece of French gold for something like three years. He used to carry it about with him as a sort of reserve in case of accident. Anybody is liable to have his pocket picked—a quite different thing from a brazen and insulting robbery.

The monumental arch of the Galleria Umberto faced him at the top of a noble flight of stairs. He climbed these without loss of time, and directed his steps towards the Café Umberto. All the tables outside were occupied by a lot of people who were drinking. But as he wantd something to eat, he went inside into the café, which is divided into aisles by square pillars set all round with long looking glasses. The Count sat down on a red plush bench against one of these pillars, waiting for his *risotto*. And his mind reverted to his abominable adventure.

He thought of the moody, well-dressed young man, with whom he had exchanged glances in the crowd around the bandstand, and who, he felt confident, was the robber. Would he recognize him again? Doubtless. But he did not want ever to see him again. The best thing was to forget this humiliating episode.

The Count looked round anxiously for the coming of his *risotto*, and, behold! to the left against the wall—there sat the young man. He was alone at a table, with a bottle of some sort of wine or syrup and a carafe of iced water before him. The smooth olive cheeks, the red lips, the little jet-black mustache turned up gallantly, the fine black eyes a little heavy and shaded by long eyelashes, that peculiar expression of cruel discontent to be seen only in the busts of some Roman emperors—it was he, no doubt at all. But that was a type. The Count looked away hastily. The young officer over there reading a paper was like that, too. Same type. Two young men farther away playing checkers also resembled—

The Count lowered his head with the fear in his heart of being everlastingly haunted by the vision of that young man. He began to eat his *risotto*. Presently he heard the young man on his left call the waiter in a bad-tempered tone.

At the call, not only his own waiter, but two other idle waiters belonging to a quite different row of tables, rushed towards him with obsequious alacrity, which is not the general characteristic of the waiters in the Café Umberto. The young man muttered something and one of the waiters walking rapidly to the nearest door called out into the Galleria: "Pasquale! O! Pasquale!"

Everybody knows Pasquale, the shabby old fellow who, shuffling between the tables, offers for sale cigars, cigarettes, picture postcards, and matches to the clients of the café. He is in many respects an engaging scoundrel. The Count saw the gray-haired, unshaven ruffian enter the café, the glass case hanging from his neck by a leather strap, and, at a word from the waiter, make his shuffling way with a sudden spurt to the young man's table. The young man was in need of a cigar with which Pasquale served him fawningly. The old peddler was going out, when the Count, on a sudden impulse, beckoned to him.

Pasquale approached, the smile of deferential recognition combining oddly with the cynical searching expression of his eyes. Leaning his case on the table, he lifted the glass lid without a word. The Count took a box of cigarettes and urged by a fearful curiosity, asked as casually as he could—

"Tell me, Pasquale, who is that young signore sitting over there?"

The other bent over his box confidentially.

"That, *Signor Conde*," he said, beginning to rearrange his wares busily and without looking up, "that is a young *Cavaliere* of a very good family from Bari. He studies in the University here, and is the chief, *capo*, of an association of young men—of very nice young men."

He paused, and then, with mingled discretion and pride of knowledge, murmured the explanatory word "*Camorra*" and shut down the lid. "A very powerful *Camorra*," he breathed out. "The professors themselves respect it greatly . . . *una lira e cinquanti centesimi, Signor Conde*."

Our friend paid with the gold piece. While Pasquale was making up the change, he observed that the young man, of whom he had heard so much in a few words, was watching the transaction covertly. After the old vagabond had withdrawn with a bow, the Count settled with the waiter and sat still. A numbness, he told me, had come over him.

The young man paid, too, got up, and crossed over, apparently for the purpose of looking at himself in the mirror set in the pillar nearest to the Count's seat. He was dressed all in black with a dark green bow tie. The count looked round, and was startled by meeting a vicious glance out of the corners of the other's eyes. The young *Cavaliere* from Bari (according to Pasquale; but Pasquale is, of course, an accomplished liar) went on arranging his tie, settling his hat before the glass, and meantime he spoke just loud enough to be heard by the Count. He spoke through his teeth with the most insulting venom of contempt and gazing straight into the mirror.

"Ah! So you had some gold on you—you old liar—you old *birba* —you *furfante!* But you are not done with me yet."

The fiendishness of his expression vanished like lightning, and he lounged out of the café with a moody impassive face.

The poor Count, after telling me this last episode fell back trembling in his chair. His forehead broke into perspiration. There was a wanton insolence in the spirit of this outrage which appalled even me. What it was to the Count's delicacy I won't attempt to guess. I am sure that if he had been not too refined to do such a blatantly vulgar thing as dying from apoplexy in a café, he would have had a fatal stroke there and then. All irony apart, my difficulty was to keep him from seeing the full extent of my commiseration. He shrank from every excessive sentiment, and my commiseration was practically unbounded. It did not surprise me to hear that he had been in bed a week. He had got up to make his arrangements for leaving Southern Italy for good and all.

And the man was convinced that he could not live through a whole year in any other climate!

No argument of mine had any effect. It was not timidity, though he did say to me once: "You do not know what a *Camorra* is, my dear sir. I am a marked man." He was not afraid of what could be done to him. His delicate conception of his dignity was defiled by a degrading experience. He couldn't stand that. No Japanese gentleman, outraged in his exaggerated sense of honor, could have gone about his preparations for hara-kiri with greater resolution. To go home really amounted to suicide for the poor Count.

There is a saying of Neapolitan patriotism, intended for the information of foreigners, I presume: "See Naples and then die." *Vedi Napoli e poi mori*. It is a saying of excessive vanity, and everything excessive was abhorrent to the nice moderation of the poor Count. Yet, as I was seeing him off at the railway station, I thought he was behaving with singular fidelity to its conceited spirit. *Vedi Napoli!* . . . He had seen it! He had seen it with startling thoroughness—and now he was going to his grave. He was going to it by the *train de luxe* of the International Sleeping Car Company, via Trieste and Vienna. As the four long, somber coaches pulled out of the station I raised my hat with the solemn feeling of paying the last tribute of respect to a funeral cortège. *Il Conde's* profile, much aged already, glided away from me in stony immobility, behind the lighted pane of glass—*Vedi Napoli e poi mori!*

CONRAD: *Il Conde*

1. *What is the significance of the first paragraph, with its description of the collection of bronzes in the National Museum in Naples?*

2. *What does the old Count represent?*

3. *What does the young man with the knife represent? Why does Conrad make him well-born?*

4. *Why does Conrad have the confrontation take place in gardens, against the backdrop of a beautiful Italian night?*

5. *What is the importance of the concert in this scene? Compare Conrad's use of music in the background with Mann's in "Little Lizzie."*

6. *Why does the experience in the garden so upset the Count, beyond the usual fear that such a meeting would cause?*

7. *What relevance does the epigraph, "See Naples and then die," have to the story?*

8. *Can you see any political and social significance to the events in the story?*

9. *Does the pace of this story seem too slow? What justification is there for such a leisurely pace? Does Conrad extract the full drama from the situation? Would the Hemingway style be more effective for this episode?*

Sholom Aleichem

TIT FOR TAT

Sholom Aleichem (b. Solomon Rabinowitz) was born in Pereyaslav, Russia, in 1859. Educated in traditional Hebrew lore, he was supporting himself at seventeen by tutoring the children of the wealthy. He served as a government rabbi in the town of Yuben for several years, gained and lost a family fortune by 1900, and retired from business to devote himself to writing. The pogrom of 1905 forced him to flee Russia with his family, and he lived quietly in western Europe until the outbreak of World War I, when he came to this country. He died in New York in 1916. He is generally regarded as the greatest of the modern Yiddish writers for his tragicomic presentation of Jewish life, and his novels such as Tevia der Milchiger *and* Der Blutiger Shpass *have been translated into many languages. "Tit for Tat" is a typical Aleichem story, with its undertones of humor, its realistic representation of his people, and its great warmth and feeling for erring human beings.*

ℬ☙

ONCE I was a rabbiner. A rabbiner, not a rabbi. That is, I was called rabbi—but a rabbi of the crown.

To old-country Jews I don't have to explain what a rabbi of the crown is. They know the breed. What are his great responsibilities? He fills out birth certificates, officiates at circumcisions, performs marriages, grants divorces. He gets his share from the living and the dead. In the synagogue he has a place of honor, and when the congregation rises, he is the first to stand. On legal holidays he appears in a stovepipe hat and holds forth in his best Russian: *"Gospoda Prihozhane!"* To take it for granted that among our people a rabbiner is well loved—let's not say any more. Say rather that we put up with him, as we do a government inspector or a deputy sheriff. And yet he is chosen from among the people, that is, every three years a proclamation is sent us: *"Na Osnavania Predpisania . . ."* Or, as we would say: "Your Lord, the Governor, orders you to come together in the synagogue, poor little Jews, and pick out a rabbiner for yourselves . . ."

Then the campaign begins. Candidates, hot discussions, brandy, and maybe even a bribe or two. After which come charges and countercharges, the elections are annulled, and we are ordered to hold new elections. Again the proclamations: "*Na Osnavania Predpisania* . . ." Again candidates, discussions, party organizations, brandy, a bribe or two . . . That was the life!

Well, there I was—a rabbiner in a small town in the province of Poltava. But I was anxious to be a modern one. I wanted to serve the public. So I dropped the formalities of my position and began to mingle with the people—as we say: to stick my head into the community pot. I got busy with the *Talmud Torah*, the charity fund; interpreted a law, settled disputes or just gave plain advice.

The love of settling disputes, helping people out, or advising them, I inherited from my father and my uncles. They—may they rest in peace—also enjoyed being bothered all the time with other people's business. There are two kinds of people in the world: those that you can't bother at all, and others whom you can bother all the time. You can climb right on their heads—naturally not in one jump, but gradually. First you climb into their laps, then onto their shoulders, then their heads—and after that you can jump up and down on their heads and stamp on their hearts with your heavy boots—as long as you want to.

I was that kind, and without boasting I can tell you that I had plenty of ardent followers and plain hangers-on who weren't ashamed to come every day and fill my head with their clamoring and sit around till late at night. They never refused a glass of tea, or cigarettes. Newspapers and books they took without asking. In short, I was a regular fellow.

Well, there came a day . . . The door opened, and in walked the very foremost men of the town, the sparkling best, the very cream of the city. Four householders—men of affairs—you could almost say: real men of substance. And who were these men? Three of them were the *Troika*—that was what we called them in our town because they were together all the time—partners in whatever business any one of them was in. They always fought, they were always suspicious of each other, and watched everything the others did, and still they never separated—working always in this principle: if the business is a good one and there is profit to be made, why shouldn't I have a lick at the bone too? And on the other hand, if it should end in disaster—you'll be buried along with me, and lie with me deep in the earth. And what does God do? He brings together the three partners with a fourth one. They operate together a little less than a year and end up in a brawl. That is why they're here.

What had happened? "Since God created thieves, swindlers and crooks, you never saw a thief, swindler or crook like this one." That is the way the three old partners described the fourth one to me. And he, the fourth, said the same about them. Exactly the same, word for word. And who was this fourth one? He was a quiet little man, a little innocent-looking fellow, with thick, dark eyebrows under which a pair of shrewd, ironic, little eyes watched everything you did. Everyone called him Nachman Lekach.

His real name was Nachman Noss'n, but everybody called him Nachman Lekach, because as you know, *Noss'n* is the Hebrew for "he gave," and *Lekach* means "he took," and in all the time we knew him, no one had ever seen him give anything to anyone—while at taking no one was better.

Where were we? Oh, yes . . . So they came to the rabbiner with the complaints, to see if he could find a way of straightening out their tangled accounts. "Whatever you decide, Rabbi, and whatever you decree, and whatever you say, will be final."

That is how the three old partners said it, and the fourth, Reb Nachman, nodded with that innocent look on his face to indicate that he too left it all up to me: "For the reason," his eyes said, "that I know that I have done no wrong." And he sat down in a corner, folded his arms across his chest like an old woman, fixed his shrewd, ironic, little eyes on me, and waited to see what his partners would have to say. And when they had all laid out their complaints and charges, presented all their evidence, said all they had to say, he got up, patted down his thick eyebrows, and not looking at the others at all, only at me, with those deep, deep, shrewd little eyes of his, he proceeded to demolish their claims and charges—so completely, that it looked as if they were the thieves, swindlers and crooks—the three partners of his—and he, Nachman Lekach, was a man of virtue and piety, the little chicken that is slaughtered before *Yom Kippur* to atone for our sins—a sacrificial lamb. "And every word that you heard them say is a complete lie, it never was and never could be. It's simply out of the question." And he proved with evidence, arguments and supporting data that everything he said was true and holy, as if Moses himself had said it.

All the time he was talking, the others, the *Troika*, could hardly sit in their chairs. Every moment one or another of them jumped up, clutched his head—or his heart: "Of all things! How can a man talk like that! Such lies and falsehoods!" It was almost impossible to calm them down, to keep them from tearing at the fourth one's beard. As for me—the rabbiner—it was hard, very hard to crawl out from this horrible tangle, because by now it was clear that I had a fine band to deal with, all four of them swindlers, thieves and crooks, and informers to boot, and all four of them deserving a severe punishment. But what? At last this idea occurred to me, and I said to them:

"Are you ready, my friends? I am prepared to hand down my decision. My mind is made up. But I won't disclose what I have to say until each of you has deposited twenty-five *rubles*—to prove that you will act upon the decision I am about to hand down."

"With the greatest of pleasure," the three spoke out at once, and Nachman Lekach nodded his head, and all four reached into their pockets, and each one counted out his twenty-five on the table. I gathered up the money, locked it up in a drawer, and then I gave them my decision in these words:

"Having heard the complaints and the arguments of both parties, and having examined your accounts and studied your evidence, I find according to my understanding and deep conviction, that all four of you are in the wrong, and not only in the wrong, but that it is a shame and a scandal for Jewish people to conduct themselves in such a manner—to falsify accounts, perjure yourselves and even act as informers. Therefore I have decided that since we have a *Talmud Torah* in our town with many children who have neither clothes nor shoes, and whose parents have nothing with which to pay their tuition, and since there has been no help at all from you gentlemen (to get a few pennies from you one has to reach down into your very gizzards) therefore it is my decision that this hundred *rubles* of yours shall go to the *Talmud Torah*, and as for you, gentlemen, you can go home, in good health, and thanks for your contribution. The poor children will now have some shoes and socks and shirts and pants, and I'm sure they'll pray to God for you and your children. Amen."

Having heard the sentence, the three old partners—the *Troika* —looked from one to the other—flushed, unable to speak. A decision like this they had not anticipated. The only one who could say a word was Reb Nachman Lekach. He got up, patted down his thick eyebrows, held out a hand, and looking at me with his ironic little eyes, said this:

"I thank you, Rabbi Rabbiner, in behalf of all four of us, for the wise decision which you have just made known. Such a judgment could have been made by no one since King Solomon himself. There is only one thing that you forgot to say, Rabbi Rabbiner, and that is: what is your fee for this wise and just decision?"

"I beg your pardon," I tell him. "You've come to the wrong address. I am not one of those rabbiners who tax the living and the dead." That is the way I answered him, like a real gentleman. And this was his reply:

"If that's the case, then you are not only a sage and a rabbi among men, you're an honest man besides. So, if you would care to listen, I'd like to tell you a story. Say that we will pay you for your pains at least with a story."

"Good enough. Even with two stories."

"In that case, sit down, Rabbi Rabbiner, and let us have your cigarette case. I'll tell you an interesting story, a true one, too, something that happened to me. What happened to others I don't like to talk about."

And we lit our cigarettes, sat down around the table, and Reb Nachman spread out his thick eyebrows, and looking at me with his shrewd, smiling, little eyes, he slowly began to tell his true story of what had once happened to him himself.

All this happened to me a long time ago. I was still a young man and I was living not far from here, in a village near the railroad. I traded in this and that, I had a small tavern, made a living. A Rothschild I didn't become, but bread we had, and in time there were about ten Jewish families living close by—because, as you know, if one of us makes a living, others come around. They think you're shoveling up gold . . . But that isn't the point. What I was getting at was that right in the midst of the busy season one year, when things were moving and traffic was heavy, my wife had to go and have a baby—our boy—our first son. What do you say to that? "Congratulations! Congratulations everybody!" But that isn't all. You have to have a *bris,* the circumcision. I dropped everything, went into town, bought all the good things I could find, and came back with the *Mohel* with all his instruments, and for good measure I also brought the *shammes* of the synagogue. I thought that with these two holy men and myself and the neighbors we'd have the ten men that we needed, with one to spare. But what does God do? He has one of my neighbors get sick—he is sick in bed and can't come to the *bris,* you can't carry him. And another has to pack up and go off to the city. He can't wait another day! And here I am without the ten men. Go do something. Here it is—Friday! Of all days, my wife has to pick Friday to have the *bris*—the day before the Sabbath. The *Mohel* is frantic—he has to go back right away. The *shammes* is actually in tears. "What did you ever drag us off here for?" they both want to know. And what can I do?

All I can think of is to run off to the railroad station. Who knows —so many people come through every day—maybe God will send some one. And that's just what happened. I come running up to the station—the agent has just called out that a train is about to leave. I look around—a little roly-poly man carrying a huge traveling bag comes flying by, all sweating and out of breath, straight toward the lunch counter. He looks over the dishes—what is there a good Jew can take in a country railroad station? A piece of herring—an egg. Poor fellow—you could see his mouth was watering. I grab him by the sleeve. "Uncle, are you looking for something to eat?" I ask him, and the look he gives me says: "How did you know that?" I keep on talking: "May you live to be a hundred —God himself must have sent you." He still doesn't understand, so I proceed: "Do you want to earn the blessings of eternity—and at the same time eat a beef roast that will melt in your mouth, with a fresh, white loaf right out of the oven?" He still looks at me as if I'm crazy. "Who are you? What do you want?"

So I tell him the whole story—what a misfortune had overtaken us: here we are, all ready for the *bris,* the *Mohel* is waiting, the food is ready—and such food!—and we need a tenth man! "What's that got to do with me?" he asks, and I tell him: "What's that got to do with you? Why—everything depends on you—you're the tenth man! I beg you—come with me. You will earn all the rewards of heaven—and have a delicious dinner in the bargain!" "Are you crazy," he asks me, "or are you just out of your head? My train is leaving in a few minutes, and it's Friday afternoon—almost sundown. Do you know what that means? In a few more hours the Sabbath will catch up with me, and I'll be stranded." "So what!" I tell him. "So you'll take the next train. And in the meantime you'll earn eternal life—and taste a soup, with fresh dumplings, that only my wife can make . . ."

Well, why make the story long? I had my way. The roast and the hot soup with fresh dumplings did their work. You could see my customer licking his lips. So I grab the traveling bag and I lead him home, and we go through with the *bris*. It was a real pleasure! You could smell the roast all over the house, it had so much garlic in it. A roast like that, with fresh warm twist, is a delicacy from heaven. And when you consider that we had some fresh dill pickles, and a bottle of beer, and some cognac before the meal and cherry cider after the meal—you can imagine the state our guest was in! His cheeks shone and his forehead glistened. But what then? Before we knew it the afternoon was gone. My guest jumps up, he looks around, sees what time it is, and almost has a stroke! He reaches for his traveling bag: "Where is it?" I say to him, "What's your hurry? In the first place, do you think we'll let you run off like that—before the Sabbath? And in the second place —who are you to leave on a journey an hour or two before the Sabbath? And if you're going to get caught out in the country somewhere, you might just as well stay here with us."

He groans and he sighs. How could I do a thing like that to him —keep him so late? What did I have against him? Why hadn't I reminded him earlier? He doesn't stop bothering me. So I say to him: "In the first place, did I have to tell you that it was Friday afternoon? Didn't you know it yourself? And in the second place, how do you know—maybe it's the way God wanted it? Maybe He wanted you to stay here for the Sabbath so you could taste some of my wife's fish? I can guarantee you, that as long as you've eaten fish, you haven't eaten fish like my wife's fish—not even in a dream!" Well, that ended the argument. We said our evening prayers, had a glass of wine, and my wife brings the fish to the table.

My guest's nostrils swell out, a new light shines in his eyes and he goes after that fish as if he hadn't eaten a thing all day. He can't get over it. He praises it to the skies. He fills a glass with brandy and drinks a toast to the fish. And then comes the soup, a specially rich Sabbath soup with noodles. And he likes that, too, and the *tzimmes* also, and the meat that goes with the *tzimmes*, a nice, fat piece of brisket. I'm telling you, he just sat there licking his fingers! When we're finishing the last course he turns to me: "Do you know what I'll tell you? Now that it's all over, I'm really glad that I stayed over for *Shabbes*. It's been a long time since I've enjoyed a Sabbath as I've enjoyed this one." "If that's how you feel, I'm happy," I tell him. "But wait. This is only a sample. Wait till to-morrow. Then you'll see what my wife can do."

And so it was. The next day, after services, we sit down at the table. Well, you should have seen the spread. First the appetizers: crisp wafers and chopped herring, and onions and chicken fat, with radishes and chopped liver and eggs and *gribbenes*. And after that the cold fish and the meat from yesterday's *tzimmes*, and then the jellied neat's foot, or *fisnoga* as you call it, with thin slices of garlic, and after that the potato *cholent* with the *kugel* that had been in the oven all night—and you know what that smells like when you take it out of the oven and take the cover off the pot. And what it tastes like. Our visitor could not find words to praise it. So I tell him: "This is still nothing. Wait until you have tasted our borsht tonight, then you'll know what good food is." At that he laughs out loud—a friendly laugh, it is true—and says to me: "Yes, but how far do you think I'll be from here by the time your borsht is ready?" So I laugh even louder than he does, and say: "You can forget that right now! Do you think you'll be going off tonight?"

And so it was. As soon as the lights were lit and we had a glass of wine to start off the new week, my friend begins to pack his things again. So I call out to him: "Are you crazy? Do you think we'll let you go off, the Lord knows where, at night? And besides, where's your train?" "What?" he yells at me. "No train? Why, you're murdering me! You know I have to leave!" But I say, "May this be the greatest misfortune in your life. Your train will come, if all is well, around dawn tomorrow. In the meantime I hope your appetite and digestion are good, because I can smell the borsht already!

All I ask," I say, "is just tell me the truth. Tell me if you've ever touched a borsht like this before. But I want the absolute truth!" What's the use of talking—he had to admit it: never before in all his life had he tasted a borsht like this. Never. He even started to ask how you made the borsht, what you put into it, and how long you cooked it. Everything. And I say: "Don't worry about that! Here, taste this wine and tell me what you think of *it*. After all, you're an expert. But the truth! Remember—nothing but the truth! Because if there is anything I hate, it's flattery . . ."

So we took a glass, and then another glass, and we went to bed. And what do you think happened? My traveler overslept, and missed the early morning train. When he wakes up he boils over! He jumps on me like a murderer. Wasn't it up to me, out of fairness and decency, to wake him up in time? Because of me he's going to have to take a loss, a heavy loss—he doesn't even know himself how heavy. It was all my fault. I ruined him. I! . . . So I let him talk. I listen, quietly, and when he's all through, I say: "Tell me yourself, aren't you a queer sort of person? In the first place, what's your hurry? What are you rushing for? How long is a person's life altogether? Does he have to spoil that little with rushing and hurrying? And in the second place, have you forgotten that today is the third day since the *bris?* Doesn't that mean a thing to you? Where we come from, on the third day we're in the habit of putting on a feast better than the one at the *bris* itself. The third day—it's something to celebrate! You're not going to spoil the celebration, are you?"

What can he do? He can't control himself any more, and he starts laughing—a hysterical laugh. "What good does it do to talk?" he says. "You're a real leech!" "Just as you say," I tell him, "but after all, you're a visitor, aren't you?"

At the dinner table, after we've had a drink or two, I call out to him: "Look," I say, "it may not be proper—after all, we're Jews—to talk about milk and such things while we're eating meat, but I'd like to know your honest opinion: what do you think of *kreplach* with cheese?" He looks at me with distrust. "How did we get around to that?" he asks. "Just like this," I explain to him. "I'd like to have you try the cheese *kreplach* that my wife makes—because tonight, you see, we're going to have a dairy supper . . ." This is too much for him, and he comes right back at me with, "Not this time! You're trying to keep me here another day, I can see that. But you can't do it. It isn't right! It isn't right!" And from the way he fusses and fumes it's easy to see that I won't have to coax him too long, or fight with him either, because what is he but a man with an appetite, who has only one philosophy, which he practices at the table? So I say this to him: "I give you my word of honor, and if that isn't enough, I'll give you my hand as well—here, shake—that tomorrow I'll wake you up in time for the earliest train. I promise it, even if the world turns upside down. If I don't, may I—you know what!" At this he softens and says to me: "Remember, we're shaking hands on that!" And I: "A promise is a promise." And my wife makes a dairy supper—how can I describe it to you? With such *kreplach* that my traveler has to admit that it was all true: he has a wife too, and she makes *kreplach* too, but how can you compare hers with these? It's like night to day!

And I kept my word, because a promise is a promise. I woke him when it was still dark, and started the samovar. He finished packing and began to say goodbye to me and the rest of the household in a very handsome, friendly style. You could see he was a gentleman. But I interrupt him: "We'll say goodbye a little later. First, we have to settle up." "What do you mean—settle up?" "Settle up," I say, "means to add up the figures. That's what I'm going to do now. I'll add them up, let you know what it comes to, and you will be so kind as to pay me."

His face flames red. "Pay you?" he shouts. "Pay you for what?" "For what?" I repeat. "You want to know for what? For everything. The food, the drink, the lodging." This time he becomes white—not red—and he says to me: "I don't understand you at all. You came and invited me to the *bris*. You stopped me at the train. You took my bag away from me. You promised me eternal life." "That's right," I interrupt him. "That's right. But what's one thing got to do with the other? When you came to the *bris* you earned your reward in heaven. But food and drink and lodging—do I have to give you these things for nothing? After all, you're a businessman, aren't you? You should understand that fish costs money, and that the wine you drank was the very best, and the beer, too, and the cherry cider. And you remember how you praised the *tzimmes* and the puddings and the borsht. You remember how you licked your fingers. And the cheese *kreplach* smelled pretty good to you, too. Now, I'm glad you enjoyed these things; I don't begrudge you that in the least. But certainly you wouldn't expect that just because you earned a reward in heaven, and enjoyed yourself in the bargain, that *I* should pay for it?" My traveling friend was really sweating; he looked as if he'd have a stroke. He began to throw himself around, yell, scream, call for help. "This is Sodom!" he cried. "Worse than Sodom! It's the worst outrage the world has ever heard of! How much do you want?" Calmly I took a piece of paper and a pencil and began to add it up. I itemized everything, I gave him an inventory of everything he ate, of every hour he spent in my place. All in all it added up to something like thirty-odd *rubles* and some *kopeks*—I don't remember it exactly.

When he saw the total, my good man went green and yellow, his hands shook, and his eyes almost popped out, and again he let out a yell, louder than before. "What did I fall into—a nest of thieves? Isn't there a single human being here? Is there a God anywhere?" So I say to him, "Look, sir, do you know what? Do you know what you're yelling about? Do you have to eat your heart out? Here is my suggestion: let's ride into town together—it's not far from here—and we'll find some people—there's a rabbiner there—let's ask the rabbi. And we'll abide by what he says." When he heard me talk like that, he quieted down a little. And—don't worry—we hired a horse and wagon, climbed in, and rode off to town, the two of us, and went straight to the rabbi.

When we got to the rabbi's house, we found him just finishing his morning prayers. He folded up his prayer shawl and put his philacteries away. "Good morning," we said to him, and he: "What's the news today?" The news? My friend tears loose and lets him have the whole story—everything from A to Z. He doesn't leave a word out. He tells how he stopped at the station, and so on and so on, and when he's through he whips out the bill I had given him and hands it to the rabbi. And when the rabbi had heard everything, he says: "Having heard one side I should now like to hear the other." And turning to me, he asks, "What do you have to say to all that?" I answer: "Everything he says is true. There's not a word I can add. Only one thing I'd like to have him tell you—on his word of honor: did he eat the fish, and did he drink the beer and cognac and the cider, and did he smack his lips over the borsht that my wife made?" At this the man becomes almost frantic, he jumps and he thrashes about like an apoplectic. The rabbi begs him not to boil like that, not to be so angry, because anger is a grave sin. And he asks him again about the fish and the borsht and the *kreplach,* and if it was true that he had drunk not only the wine, but beer and cognac and cider as well. Then the rabbi puts on his spectacles, looks the bill over from top to bottom, checks every line, and finds it correct! Thirty-odd *rubles* and some *kopeks,* and he makes his judgment brief: he tells the man to pay the whole thing, and for the wagon back and forth, and a judgment fee for the rabbi himself . . .

The man stumbles out of the rabbi's house looking as if he'd been in a steam bath too long, takes out his purse, pulls out two twenty-fives and snaps at me: "Give me the change." "What change?" I ask, and he says: "For the thirty you charged me—for that bill you gave me." "Bill? What bill? What thirty are you talking about? What do you think I am, a highwayman? Do you expect me to take money from you? I see a man at the railroad station, a total stranger; I take his bag away from him, and drag him off almost by force to our own *bris,* and spend a wonderful *Shabbes* with him. So am I going to charge him for the favor he did me, and for the pleasure I had?" Now he looks at me as if I really am crazy, and says: "Then why did you carry on like this? Why did you drag me to the rabbi?" "Why this? Why that?" I say to him. "You're a queer sort of person, you are! I wanted to show you what kind of man our rabbi was, that's all . . ."

When he finished the story, my litigant, Reb Nachman Lekach, got up with a flourish, and the other three partners followed him. They buttoned their coats and prepared to leave. But I held them off. I passed the cigarettes around again, and said to the story-teller:

"So you told me a story about a rabbi. Now maybe you'll be so kind as to let me tell you a story—also about a rabbi, but a much shorter story than the one you told."

And without waiting for a yes or no, I started right in, and made it brief:

This happened, I began, not so long ago, and in a large city, on Yom Kippur eve. A stranger falls into the town—a businessman, a traveler, who goes here and there, everywhere, sells merchandise, collects money . . . On this day he comes into the city, walks up and down in front of the synagogue, holding his sides with both hands, asks everybody he sees where he can find the rabbi. "What do you want the rabbi for?" people ask. "What business is that of yours?" he wants to know. So they don't tell him. And he asks one man, he asks another: "Can you tell where the rabbi lives?" "What do you want the rabbi for?" "What do you care?" This one and that one, till finally he gets the answer, finds the rabbi's house, goes in, still holding his sides with both hands. He calls the rabbi aside, shuts the door, and says, "Rabbi, this is my story. I am a traveling man, and I have money with me, quite a pile. It's not my money. It belongs to my clients—first to God and then to my clients. It's *Yom Kippur* eve. I can't carry money with me on *Yom Kippur,* and I'm afraid to leave it at my lodgings. A sum like that! So do me a favor—take it, put it away in your strong box till tomorrow night, after *Yom Kippur.*"

And without waiting, the man unbuttons his vest and draws out one pack after another, crisp and clean, the real red, crackling, hundred *ruble* notes!

Seeing how much there was, the rabbi said to him: "I beg your pardon. You don't know me, you don't know who I am." "What do you mean, I don't know who you are? You're a rabbi, aren't you?" "Yes, I'm a rabbi. But I don't know *you*—who you are or what you are." They bargain back and forth. The traveler: "You're a rabbi." The rabbi: "I don't know who you are." And time does not stand still. It's almost *Yom Kippur!* Finally the rabbi agrees to take the money. The only thing is, who should be the witnesses? You can't trust just anyone in a matter like that.

So the rabbi sends for the leading townspeople, the very cream, rich and respectable citizens, and says to them: "This is what I called you for. This man has money with him, a tidy sum, not his own, but first God's and then his clients'. He wants me to keep it for him till after *Yom Kippur.* Therefore I want you to be witnesses, to see how much he leaves with me, so that later—you understand?" And the rabbi took the trouble to count it all over three times before the eyes of the townspeople, wrapped the notes in a kerchief, sealed the kerchief with wax, and stamped his initials on the seal. He passed this from one man to the other, saying, "Now

look. Here is my signature, and remember, you're the witnesses."
The kerchief with the money in it he handed over to his wife, had
her lock it in a chest, and hide the keys where no one could find
them. And he himself, the rabbi, went to *shul,* and prayed and
fasted as it was ordained, lived through *Yom Kippur,* came home,
had a bite to eat, looked up, and there was the traveler. "Good evening, Rabbi." "Good evening. Sit down. What can I do for you?"
"Nothing. I came for my package." "What package?" "The money."
"What money?" "The money I left with you to keep for me." "You
gave *me* money to keep for you? When was that?"

The traveler laughs out loud. He thinks the rabbi is joking with
him. The rabbi asks: "What are you laughing at?" And the man
says: "It's the first time I met a rabbi who liked to play tricks." At
this the rabbi is insulted. No one, he pointed out, had ever called
him a trickster before. "Tell me, my good man, what do you want
here?"

When he heard these words, the stranger felt his heart stop.
"Why, Rabbi, in the name of all that's holy, do you want to kill
me? Didn't I give you all my money? That is, not mine, but first
God's and then my clients'? I'll remind you, you wrapped it in a
kerchief, sealed it with wax, locked it in your wife's chest, hid the
key where no one could find it. And here is better proof: there were
witnesses, the leading citizens of the city!" And he goes ahead and
calls them all off by name. In the midst of it a cold sweat breaks
out on his forehead, he feels faint, and asks for a glass of water.

The rabbi sends the *shammes* off to the men the traveler had
named—the leading citizens, the flower of the community. They
come running from all directions. "What's the matter? What's
happened?" "A misfortune. A plot! A millstone around our necks!
He insists that he brought a pile of money to me yesterday, to
keep over *Yom Kippur,* and that you were witnesses to the act."

The householders look at each other, as if to say: "Here is where
we get a nice bone to lick!" And they fall on the traveler: how
could he do a thing like that? He ought to be ashamed of himself!
Thinking up an ugly plot like that against their rabbi!

When he saw what was happening, his arms and legs went limp,
he just about fainted. But the rabbi got up, went to the chest, took
out the kerchief and handed it to him.

"What's the matter with you! Here! Here is your money! Take it

and count it, see if it's right, here in front of your witnesses. The
seal, as you see, is untouched. The wax is whole, just as it ought to
be."

The traveler felt as if a new soul had been installed in his body.
His hands trembled and tears stood in his eyes.

"Why did you have to do it, Rabbi? Why did you have to play
this trick on me? A trick like this."

"I just wanted to show you—the kind—of—leading citizens—
we have in our town."

> *Translated by Julius*
> *and Frances Butwin*

ALEICHEM: *Tit for Tat*

1. *How does Sholom Aleichem achieve his humorous effects? How does
his technique differ from that of Henry James in "The Death of a Lion"
or Samuel Beckett in "Yellow"?*

2. *What is the point of Reb Nachman Lekach's story?*

3. *What is the point of the rabbiner's story?*

4. *Is the rabbiner's decision to "tax" Troika and Lekach a wise one?
Or is it mainly an act of vengeance? Why does Lekach, who is victimized,
compare the rabbiner to Solomon?*

5. *Is there much difference between this story and the ordinary humorous anecdote or "shaggy dog" story? What are the essential differences?
In answering this question, you will come to a clearer understanding of
the writer's purpose in a short story.*

6. *What sense of life do you obtain from the rabbiner's community?
Compare Aleichem's "feeling for life" with that of two other Jewish writers
represented in this volume, Franz Kafka and Isaac Babel.*

Anton Chekhov

THE BET

*Born in Taganrog, Russia, in 1860, Anton Chekhov first took up
writing to support himself while studying to be a doctor. From these
beginnings—Chekhov was the son of a shopkeeper and the grand-
son of a serf—there developed the greatest of Russian short-story
writers and one of the greatest of playwrights. His principal dramas,
most of which were written during the last six years of his life,
include* The Sea Gull *(1896),* Uncle Vanya *(1899),* The Three
Sisters *(1901), and* The Cherry Orchard *(1904), while before his
death in 1904 he had written hundreds of short stories and novellas.
His influence on future generations of short-story writers both in
Europe and in the United States has been immense. In "The Bet,"
Chekhov begins typically with a light scene only to proceed into a
tragic situation in which life is itself too much for his characters.*

ह্ৰ

IT was a dark autumn night. The old banker was pacing from
corner to corner of his study, recalling to his mind the party he gave
in the autumn fifteen years before. There were many clever people
at the party and much interesting conversation. They talked among
other things of capital punishment. The guests, among them not a
few scholars and journalists, for the most part disapproved of capital
punishment, found it obsolete as a means of punishment, unfitted to
a Christian State, and immoral. Some of them thought that capital
punishment should be replaced universally by life-imprisonment.

"I don't agree with you," said the host. "I myself have experienced neither capital punishment nor life-imprisonment, but if one
may judge *a priori,* then in my opinion capital punishment is more
moral and more humane than imprisonment. Execution kills instantly, life-imprisonment kills by degrees. Who is the more humane executioner, one who kills you in a few seconds or one who
draws the life out of you incessantly, for years?"

"They're both equally immoral," remarked one of the guests,

"because their purpose is the same, to take away life. The State is not God. It has no right to take away that which it cannot give back, if it should so desire."

Among the company was a lawyer, a young man about twenty-five. On being asked his opinion, he said:

"Capital punishment and life-imprisonment are equally immoral; but if I were offered the choice between them, I would certainly choose the second. It's better to live somehow than not to live at all."

There ensued a lively discussion. The banker who was then younger and more nervous suddenly lost his temper, banged his fist on the table, and turning to the young lawyer, cried out:

"It's a lie. I bet you two millions you wouldn't stick in a cell even for five years."

"If you mean it seriously," replied the lawyer, "then I bet I'll stay not five but fifteen."

"Fifteen! Done!" cried the banker. "Gentlemen, I stake two millions."

"Agreed. You stake two millions, I my freedom," said the lawyer.

So this wild, ridiculous bet came to pass. The banker, who at that time had too many millions to count, spoiled and capricious, was beside himself with rapture. During supper he said to the lawyer jokingly:

"Come to your senses, young man, before it's too late. Two millions are nothing to me, but you stand to lose three or four of the best years of your life. I say three or four, because you'll never stick it out any longer. Don't forget either, you unhappy man, that voluntary is much heavier than enforced imprisonment. The idea that you have the right to free yourself at any moment will poison the whole of your life in the cell. I pity you."

And now the banker, pacing from corner to corner, recalled all this and asked himself:

"Why did I make this bet? What's the good? The lawyer loses fifteen years of his life and I throw away two millions. Will it convince people that capital punishment is worse or better than imprisonment for life? No, no! all stuff and rubbish. On my part, it was the caprice of a well-fed man; on the lawyer's, pure greed of gold."

He recollected further what happened after the evening party.

It was decided that the lawyer must undergo his imprisonment under the strictest observation, in a garden wing of the banker's house. It was agreed that during the period he would be deprived of the right to cross the threshold, to see living people, to hear human voices, and to receive letters and newspapers. He was permitted to have a musical instrument, to read books, to write letters, to drink wine and smoke tobacco. By the agreement he could communicate, but only in silence, with the outside world through a little window specially constructed for this purpose. Everything necessary, books, music, wine, he could receive in any quantity by sending a note through the window. The agreement provided for all the minutest details, which made the confinement strictly solitary, and it obliged the lawyer to remain exactly fifteen years from twelve o'clock of November 14th, 1870, to twelve o'clock of November 14th, 1885. The least attempt on his part to violate the conditions, to escape if only for two minutes before the time, freed the banker from the obligation to pay him the two millions.

During the first year of imprisonment, the lawyer, as far as it was possible to judge from his short notes, suffered terribly from loneliness and boredom. From his wing day and night came the sound of the piano. He rejected wine and tobacco. "Wine," he wrote, "excites desires, and desires are the chief foes of a prisoner; besides, nothing is more boring than to drink good wine alone," and tobacco spoiled the air in his room. During the first year the lawyer was sent books of a light character; novels with a complicated love interest, stories of crime and fantasy, comedies, and so on.

In the second year the piano was heard no longer and the lawyer asked only for classics. In the fifth year, music was heard again, and the prisoner asked for wine. Those who watched him said that during the whole of that year he was only eating, drinking, and lying on his bed. He yawned often and talked angrily to himself. Books he did not read. Sometimes at night he would sit down to write. He would write for a long time and tear it all up in the morning. More than once he was heard to weep.

In the second half of the sixth year, the prisoner began zealously to study languages, philosophy, and history. He fell on these subjects so hungrily that the banker hardly had time to get books enough for him. In the space of four years about six hundred volumes were bought at his request. It was while that passion

lasted that the banker received the following letter from the prisoner: "My dear jailer, I am writing these lines in six languages.
Show them to experts. Let them read them. If they do not find one
single mistake, I beg you to give orders to have a gun fired off in
the garden. By the noise I shall know that my efforts have not been
in vain. The geniuses of all ages and countries speak in different
languages; but in them all burns the same flame. Oh, if you knew
my heavenly happiness now that I can understand them!" The
prisoner's desire was fulfilled. Two shots were fired in the garden
by the banker's order.

Later on, after the tenth year, the lawyer sat immovable before
his table and read only the New Testament. The banker found it
strange that a man who in four years had mastered six hundred eru-
dite volumes, should have spent nearly a year in reading one book,
easy to understand and by no means thick. The New Testament
was then replaced by the history of religions and theology.

During the last two years of his confinement the prisoner read an
extraordinary amount, quite haphazard. Now he would apply
himself to the natural sciences, then he would read Byron or Shake-
speare. Notes used to come from him in which he asked to be sent
at the same time a book on chemistry, a text-book of medicine, a
novel, and some treatise on philosophy or theology. He read as
though he were swimming in the sea among broken pieces of
wreckage, and in his desire to save his life was eagerly grasping
one piece after another.

The banker recalled all this, and thought:

"To-morrow at twelve o'clock he receives his freedom. Under the
agreement, I shall have to pay him two millions. If I pay, it's all
over with me. I am ruined forever . . ."

Fifteen years before he had too many millions to count, but now
he was afraid to ask himself which he had more of, money or
debts. Gambling on the Stock-Exchange, risky speculation, and
the recklessness of which he could not rid himself even in old age,
had gradually brought his business to decay; and the fearless, self-
confident, proud man of business had become an ordinary banker,
trembling at every rise and fall in the market.

"That cursed bet," murmured the old man clutching his head in despair. . . . "Why didn't the man die? He's only forty years old. He will take away my last farthing, marry, enjoy life, gamble on the Exchange, and I will look on like an envious beggar and hear the same words from him every day: 'I'm obliged to you for the happiness of my life. Let me help you.' No, it's too much! The only escape from bankruptcy and disgrace—is that the man should die."

The clock had just struck three. The banker was listening. In the house every one was asleep, and one could hear only the frozen trees whining outside the windows. Trying to make no sound, he took out of his safe the key of the door which had not been opened for fifteen years, put on his overcoat, and went out of the house. The garden was dark and cold. It was raining. A damp, penetrating wind howled in the garden and gave the trees no rest. Though he strained his eyes, the banker could see neither the ground, nor the white statues, nor the garden wing, nor the trees. Approaching the garden wing, he called the watchman twice. There was no answer. Evidently the watchman had taken shelter from the bad weather and was now asleep somewhere in the kitchen or the greenhouse.

"If I have the courage to fulfil my intention," thought the old man, "the suspicion will fall on the watchman first of all."

In the darkness he groped for the steps and the door and entered the hall of the garden-wing, then poked his way into a narrow passage and struck a match. Not a soul was there. Some one's bed, with no bedclothes on it, stood there, and an iron stove loomed dark in the corner. The seals on the door that led into the prisoner's room were unbroken.

When the match went out, the old man, trembling from agitation peeped into the little window.

In the prisoner's room a candle was burning dimly. The prisoner himself sat by the table. Only his back, the hair on his head and his hand were visible. Open books were strewn about on the table, the two chairs and on the carpet near the table.

Five minutes passed and the prisoner never once stirred. Fifteen years' confinement had taught him to sit motionless. The banker tapped on the window with his finger, but the prisoner made no movement in reply. Then the banker cautiously tore the seals from the door and put the key into the lock. The rusty lock gave a hoarse groan and the door creaked. The banker expected instantly to hear a cry of surprise and the sound of steps. Three minutes passed and it was as quiet inside as it had been before. He made up his mind to enter.

Before the table sat a man, unlike an ordinary human being. It was a skeleton, with tight-drawn skin, with long curly hair like a woman's, and a shaggy beard. The color of his face was yellow, of an earthy shade; the cheeks were sunken, the back long and narrow, and the hand upon which he leaned his hairy head was so lean and skinny that it was painful to look upon. His hair was already silvering with gray, and no one who glanced at the senile emaciation of the face would have believed that he was only forty years old. On the table, before his bended head, lay a sheet of paper on which something was written in a tiny hand.

"Poor devil," thought the banker, "he's asleep and probably seeing millions in his dreams. I have only to take and throw this half-dead thing on the bed, smother him a moment with the pillow, and the most careful examination will find no trace of unnatural death. But, first, let us read what he has written here."

The banker took the sheet from the table and read:

"Tomorrow at twelve o'clock midnight, I shall obtain my freedom and the right to mix with people. But before I leave this room and see the sun I think it necessary to say a few words to you. On my own clear conscience and before God who sees me I declare to you that I despise freedom, life, health, and all that your books call the blessings of the world.

"For fifteen years I have diligently studied earthly life. True, I saw neither the earth nor the people, but in your books I drank fragrant wine, sang songs, hunted deer and wild boar in the forests, loved women. . . . And beautiful women, like clouds ethereal, created by the magic of your poets' genius, visited me by night and whispered to me wonderful tales, which made my head drunken. In your books I climbed the summits of Elbruz and Mont Blanc and saw from there how the sun rose in the morning, and in the evening suffused the sky, the ocean and the mountain ridges with a purple gold. I saw from there how above the lightnings glimmered, cleaving the clouds; I saw green forests, fields, rivers, lakes, cities; I heard sirens singing, and the playing of the pipes of Pan; I touched the wings of beautiful devils who came flying to me to speak of God. . . . In your books I cast myself into bottomless abysses, worked miracles, burned cities to the ground, preached new religions, conquered whole countries. . . .

"Your books gave me wisdom. All that unwearying human thought created in the centuries is compressed to a little lump in my skull. I know that I am cleverer than you all.

"And I despise your books, despise all worldly blessings and wisdom. Everything is void, frail, visionary and delusive as a mirage. Though you be proud and wise and beautiful, yet will death wipe you from the face of the earth like the mice underground; and your posterity, your history, and the immortality of your men of genius will be as frozen slag, burnt down together with the terrestrial globe.

"You are mad, and gone the wrong way. You take falsehood for truth and ugliness for beauty. You would marvel if suddenly apple and orange trees should bear frogs and lizards instead of fruit, and if roses should begin to breathe the odor of a sweating horse. So do I marvel at you, who have bartered heaven for earth. I do not want to understand you.

That I may show you in deed my contempt for that by which you live, I waive the two millions of which I once dreamed as of paradise, and which I now despise. That I may deprive myself of my right to them, I shall come out from here five minutes before the stipulated term, and thus shall violate the agreement."

When he had read, the banker put the sheet on the table, kissed the head of the strange man, and began to weep. He went out of the wing. Never at any other time, not even after his terrible losses on the Exchange, had he felt such contempt for himself as now. Coming home, he lay down on his bed, but agitation and tears kept him a long time from sleeping. . . .

The next morning the poor watchman came running to him and told him that they had seen the man who lived in the wing climb through the window into the garden. He had gone to the gate and disappeared. The banker instantly went with his servants to the wing and established the escape of his prisoner. To avoid unnecessary rumors he took the paper with the renunciation from the table and, on his return, locked it in his safe.

CHEKHOV: *The Bet*

1. Does the title suggest a view of life? What is at stake here?

2. Why does Chekhov rush right into the bet without much preparation?

3. Does the bet prove that life imprisonment is preferable to capital punishment? What does it prove? Is it better to live somehow than not to live at all? Compare Sartre's view in "The Wall."

4. Why is knowledge by itself insufficient for the prisoner's satisfaction?

5. Fifteen years of contemplation might lead to saintliness, but here what does it lead to?

6. Can you understand why the prisoner would willfully wish to break the pact for which he suffered so greatly? What is involved here in terms of attitudes toward life? If the prisoner had honored the pact up to the end, what would he have gained?

7. Has the prisoner been ennobled or degraded? What point is Chekhov making?

8. Does Chekhov seem closer to his fellow countrymen like Tolstoy and Dostoyevsky or to later authors like Moravia, Sartre, Lagerkvist?

9. Can you find any scenic elements in the story, qualities that would indicate that the author was also a great playwright?

10. Chekhov himself provided an alternative ending to this story. Can you devise one that would be more satisfactory to you, or do you find the present conclusion right?

Miguel de Unamuno y Jugo

THE MADNESS OF DR. MONTARCO

A figure of dissent in his homeland, Miguel de Unamuno y Jugo spent his life attempting to resolve the tragic conflicts that split man into fragments. Born in the Basque seaport of Bilbao in 1864, Unamuno earned a doctorate at the University of Madrid and at 27 received a chair in Greek at the University of Salamanca. His growing reputation as a writer and scholar was enhanced by the publication of The Life of Don Quixote *(1905) and* The Tragic Sense of Life *(1912). In his short novel* Abel Sanchez *(1917), he created in the opposing selves of Abel Sanchez, the calm man of the world, and Joaquín Monegro, the obsessed man who would be God, the same dualism that appears in "The Madness of Dr. Montarco." As Unamuno saw his characters, so he saw himself; as he saw Spain, so he saw the world, torn by its quixotic nature, unable to reconcile its desire for mortality with its longing for immortality. In 1936, Unamuno died, true to his quixotic nature, having first supported Franco's rebels in the Spanish Civil War and then later denouncing them.*

ᗌᕲ

I FIRST met Dr. Montarco just after his arrival in the city. A secret attraction drew me to him. His appearance was obviously in his favor, and his face had an open and guileless look about it. He was tall, blond, robust, yet quick in movement. He immediately made a friend of everyone he knew, because if he was not to make a person his friend, he restrained from making him his acquaintance. It was difficult to know which of his gestures were natural and which were studied, so subtly had he combined naturalness and art. From this proceeded the fact that while there were some who criticized him for affectation and found his simplicity studied, others of us thought that whatever he did was natural and spontaneous. He himself told me later: "There are gestures which, natural enough to begin with, later become artificial after they have been repeatedly

[209

praised. And then there are other gestures which, though we have acquired them after hard work and even against our very nature, end by becoming completely natural and seemingly native to us."

This observation should be enough to show that Dr. Montarco was not, while he was still of sound mind, the extravagant personality which many claimed. Far from it. He was, on the contrary, a man who in conversation expressed discreet and judicious opinions. Only on rare occasions, and even then only with persons completely in his confidence (as I came to be), did he unbridle his feelings and let himself go; it was then he would indulge in vehement invective against the people who surrounded him and from whom he had to gain his livelihood. And thus was prefigured the abyss into which his spirit was finally to fall.

He was one of the most orderly and simple men I have ever known. He was not a "connoisseur" or collector of anything, not even of books, nor did I ever detect in him any monomania whatever. His practice, his home, and his literary work: these were his only preoccupations. He had a wife and two daughters, aged eight and ten, when he arrived in the city. He was preceded by a very good reputation as a doctor; nevertheless, it was no secret that he had been forced by his peculiar conduct to leave his native town. His greatest peculiarity, in the eyes of his medical colleagues, lay in the fact that although he was an excellent practitioner and very well versed in medical science and biology, and that although he was a voluminous writer, it never seemed to occur to him to write about medicine. As he told me once, in his characteristically violent manner: "Why must these idiots insist that I write of professional matters? I studied medicine simply to cure sick people and earn my living doing so. Do I cure them? I do; and therefore let them leave me in peace and spare me their nonsense, and let them keep out of my business. I earn my living as conscientiously as I can, and, once my living is made, I do with my life what I want, and not what these louts want me to do. You can't imagine what profound misery of a moral sort there is in the attempt, which so many people make, to confine everybody to a specialty. For my part, I find a tremendous advantage in living *from* one activity and *for* another. . . . You probably don't need to be reminded of Schopenhauer's justified denunciation of professional philosophers and busybodies."

A little while after arriving in the city, and after he had built up
a better than average practice and had acquired the reputation of a
serious, careful, painstaking and well-endowed doctor, a local journal published his first story, a story half-way between fantasy and
humor, without descriptive writing and without a moral. Two
days later I found him very upset; when I asked the reason, he
burst forth: "Do you think I'm going to be able to resist the overwhelming pressure of the idiocy prevailing here? Tell me, do you
think so? It's the same thing all over again, exactly the same as in
my town, the very same! And just as happened there, I'll end by
becoming known as a madman. I, who am a marvel of calm. And
my patients will gradually drop away, and I'll lose my practice.
Then the dismal days will come again, days filled with despair,
disgust, and bad temper, and I will have to leave here just as I had
to leave my own town."

"But what has happened?" I was finally able to ask.

"What has happened? Simply that five people have already approached me to ask what I meant by writing the piece of fiction I
just published, what I intended to say, and what bearing did it
have. Idiots, idiots, and thrice idiots! They're worse than children
who break dolls to find out what's inside. This town has no hope of
salvation, my friend; it's simply condemned to seriousness and sil-
liness, two blood sisters. People here have the souls of school
teachers. They believe no one could write except to prove something, or defend or attack some proposition, or from an ulterior motive. One of these blockheads asked me the meaning of my story
and by way of reply I asked *him:* 'Did it amuse you?' And he answered: 'As far as that goes, it certainly did; as a matter of fact, I
found it quite amusing; but . . .' I left the last word in his mouth,
because as soon as he reached this point in the conversation, I
turned my back on him and walked away. That a piece of writing
is amusing wasn't enough for this monster. They have the souls of
school teachers, the souls of school teachers!"

"But, now . . ." I ventured to take up the argument.

"Listen," he interrupted, "don't you come at me with any more
'buts.' Don't bother. The infectious disease, the itch of our Spanish
literature is the urge to preach. Everywhere a sermon, and a bad
sermon at that. Every little Christ sets himself up to dispense advice, and does it with a poker-face. I remember picking up the

Moral Epistle to Fabian and being unable to get beyond the first three verses; I simply couldn't stomach it. This breed of men is totally devoid of imagination, and so all their madness is merely silly. An oyster-like breed—there's no use of your denying it—; oysters, that's what they are, nothing but oysters. Everything here savors of oyster beds, or ground-muck. I feel like I'm living among human tubers. And they don't even break through the ground, or lift their heads up, like regular tubers."

In any case, Dr. Montarco did not take heed, and he went and published another story, more satirical and fantastic than the first. I recall Servando Fernández Gómez, a patient of Dr. Montarco, discussing it with me.

"Well sir," said the good Fernández Gómez, "I really don't know what to do now that my doctor has published his stories."

"How is that?" I asked him with some surprise.

"Frankly, it seems rather risky, putting oneself in the hands of a man who writes things like that."

"Come, now, he gives you good care as a doctor, doesn't he?"

"There's no question of that. I've no complaint on that score. Ever since putting myself in his hands, consulting with him and following his regimen, I'm much better and every day I notice a further improvement. Still, those pieces of his . . . he must not be well himself. He sounds as if he had a head full of crickets."

"Don't be alarmed, Don Servando. I have many dealings with him, as you know, and I've observed nothing at all wrong with him. He is a very sensible man."

"When one talks to him he answers appropriately enough and what he says is very sensible, but . . ."

"Listen, I'd rather have a man operate on me who had a steady hand and eye even if he did speak wildly (though Montarco doesn't do that either), than a man who was exquisitely proper, full of sententious wisdom and every kind of platitude and then went ahead and threw my whole body out of joint."

"That may be. Still . . ."

The next day I asked Dr. Montarco about Fernández Gómez, and he responded dryly: "A constitutional fool!"

"What's that?"

"A fool by physiological constitution, *a nativitate,* congenital, irremediable."

"Sounds like the absolute and eternal fool."

"No doubt . . . for, in this area an Absolute fool and a Constitutional one are the same thing; it's not as in politics, where the Absolutists and the Constitutionalists are at opposite poles."

"He says your head must be full of crickets. . . ."

"And his head, and those of his kind, are full of cockroaches. And cockroaches are merely mute crickets. At least mine can sing, or chirrup, or creak out something."

A short time later the doctor published his third tale; and this time the narrative was more pointed, full of ironies, mockery and ill-concealed invective.

"I don't know whether you're doing the wisest thing by publishing these stories," I told him.

"By heaven, I have to. I simply have to express myself and work off my feelings. If I didn't write out these atrocities I'd end by committing them. I know well enough what I'm doing."

"There are some people who say that all this doesn't suit a man of your age, position, and profession. . . ." I said by way of drawing him out.

At this, he jumped to his feet and exclaimed:

"Just as I told you, exactly what I've said a thousand times: I'll have to go away from here, or I shall die of hunger, or they'll drive me crazy, or all of these things together. Yes, that's it, all three at once: I shall have to leave, a madman, to die of hunger. And they talk about my position, do they? What do those blockheads mean by position? Listen, believe me, we shall never emerge from barbarism in Spain, never be more than fancy Moroccans, fancy and false, for we'd be better off being our simple African selves, until we stop insisting that our chief of state be illiterate, that he write not a word, not even a volume of epigrams, or some children's tales, or a farce, while he is in office. He risks his prestige by literacy, they say. Meanwhile, we risk our history and our evolution with the opposite. How stupid and heavy-handed we are!"

Thus impelled by a fatal insight did Dr. Montarco set himself to combat the public sentiment of the city in which he lived and worked. At the same time he strove to be more and more conscientious and meticulous in his professional duties and in his civic and domestic obligations. He took extreme care to attend to his patients in every way, and to study their ills. He greeted everyone with extreme affability; he was rude to no one. In speaking to a person he would choose the topic he thought most likely to interest them, seeking thus to please them. In his private life he continued to be the ideal, the exemplary, husband and father. Still, his tales continued to grow more fanciful and extravagant: such was the opinion of the multitude, who also thought he was straying further and further from the "normal", the "usual". And his patients were beginning to abandon him, creating a void around him. Whereupon his ill-concealed animosity became evident once more.

And this was not the worst of it, for a malicious rumor began to take form and to spread: he was said to be arrogant. Without foundation of any sort, it began to be whispered that the doctor was a haughty spirit, a man concerned only with himself, who gave himself airs and considered himself a genius, while he thought other people poor devils incapable of understanding him. I told him about this consensus and this time, instead of breaking out into one of his customary diatribes, as I had expected, he answered me calmly:

"Haughty and proud am I? No! Only ignorant people, fools, are ever really haughty; and frankly, I don't consider myself a fool; my type of foolishness doesn't qualify me. If we actually could peer into the depths of each other's conscience like that! I know they think I am disdainful of others, but they are wrong. The truth is merely that I don't have the same opinion of them that they have of themselves. And besides—I might as well tell you what I'm really thinking—what is all this talk about pride and striving for superiority worth anyway? For the truth is, my friend, that when a man tries to get ahead of others he is simply trying to save himself. When a man tries to drown out the names of other men he is merely trying to insure that his own be preserved in the memory of living men, because he knows that posterity is a close-meshed sieve which allows few names to get through to other ages. For instance, have you ever noticed the way a fly-trap works?"

"What do you mean? What kind of a . . . ?"

"One of those bottles filled with water, which in the country are set around to catch flies. The poor flies try to save themselves and, since there is no way out but to climb on the backs of others, and thus navigate on cadavers in those enclosed waters of death, a ferocious struggle takes place to see which one can win out. They do not in the least mean to drown each other; all they are trying to do is to stay afloat. Just so in the struggle for fame, which is a thousand times more terrible than the struggle for bread."

"And the struggle for life," I added, "is the same, too. Darwin . . ."

"Darwin?" he cut me off. "Do you know the book *Biological Problems* by William Henry Rolph?"

"No."

"Well, read it. Read it and you will see that it is not the growth and multiplication of a species which necessitates more food and which leads to such struggle, but rather that it is a tendency toward needing more and more food, an impulse to go beyond the purely necessary, to exceed it, which causes a species to grow and multiply. It is not an instinct toward self-preservation which impels us to action, but rather an instinct toward expansion, toward invasion and encroachment. We don't strive to maintain ourselves only, but to be more than we are already, to be everything. In the strong words of Father Alonso Rodriguez, that great man, we are driven by an 'appetite for the divine.' Yes, an appetite for the divine. 'You will be as gods!': thus it was the Devil tempted our first parents, they say. Whoever doesn't aspire to be more than he is, will not be anything. All or nothing! There is profound meaning in that. Whatever Reason may tell us—that great liar who has invented, for the consolation of failures, the doctrine of the golden mean, the *aurea mediocritas,* the 'neither envied nor envying' and other such nonsense—whatever Reason may tell us—and she is not only a liar but a great whore—in our innermost soul, which we now call the Unconscious, with a capital U, in the depths of our spirit, we know that in order to avoid becoming, sooner or later, nothing, the best course to follow is to attempt to become all.

"The struggle for life, for the more-than-life, rather, is an offensive and not a defensive struggle. . . . In this Rolph is quite right. And I, my friend, do not defend myself; I am never on the defensive, instead I believe in the attack. I don't want a shield, which would only weigh me down and hinder me. I don't want anything but a sword. I would rather deliver fifty blows, and receive ten back, than deliver only ten and not receive any. Attack, attack, and no defense. Let them say what they want about me; I won't hear them, I'll take no notice, I will stop my ears, and if in spite of my precautions, word of what they say reaches me, I will not answer them. If we had centuries of time to spare, I would sooner be able to convince them that they are fools—and you may imagine the difficulty in doing that—than they would convince me I am mad or over-proud."

"But this purely offensive system of yours, Montarco, my friend . . ." I began.

"Yes, yes," he interrupted me again, "it has its flaws. And even one great danger, and that is that on the day my arm weakens or my sword is blunted they will trample me under their feet, drag me about, and make dust of me. But before that happens they will have already accomplished their purpose: they will have driven me mad."

And so it was to be. I began to suspect it when I heard him talk repeatedly about the character of madness, and to inveigh against reason. In the end, they would succeed in driving him mad.

He persisted in issuing his stories, fictions totally different from anything current at this time and place; and he persisted, simultaneously, in not departing one whit from the reasonable sort of life he outwardly led. His patients continued to leave him. Eventually, dire want made itself felt in his household. Finally, as a culmination to his troubles, he could no longer find a journal or paper to print his contributions, nor did his name make any headway or gain any ground in the republic of letters. It all came to an end when a few of us who were his friends took over responsibility for his wife and daughters, and arranged for him to go into an asylum. His verbal aggression had been growing steadily more pronounced.

I remember as if it were yesterday the first day I visited him in the asylum where he was confined. The director, Dr. Atienza, had been a fellow student of Dr. Montarco and manifested an affection and sympathy for him.

"Well, he is quieter these days, more tranquil than at the beginning," the director told me. "He reads a little, very little; I think it would be unwise to deprive him of reading matter absolutely. Mostly, he reads the *Quixote*, and, if you were to pick up his copy of the book and open it at random, it would almost certainly open to Chapter 32, of the Second Part, where is to be found the reply made by Don Quixote to his critic, the ponderous ecclesiastic who at the table of the duke and duchess severely reprimanded the knight-errant for his mad fancies. If you want, we will go and see him now."

And we did so.

"I am very glad that you've come to call," he exclaimed as soon as he saw me, raising his eyes from the *Quixote*, "I'm glad. I was just thinking and wondering if, despite what Christ tells us in the twenty-second verse of the fifth chapter of St. Matthew, we are ever permitted to make use of the forbidden weapon."

"And what is the forbidden weapon?" I asked him.

" 'Whoever shall call his brother "Fool!" shall be liable to the fires of Gehenna.' You see what a terrible sentence that is. It doesn't say whoever calls him assassin, or thief, or bandit, or swindler, or coward, or whoreson, or cuckold, or liberal; no, it says, whosoever shall call him a 'fool.' That, then, is the forbidden weapon. Everything can be questioned except the intelligence, wit and judgment of other people. When a man takes it into his head to have aspirations, to presume to some special knowledge or talent, it's even more complicated. There have been popes who, because they considered themselves great Latinists, would rather have been condemned as heretics than as poor Latinists guilty of solecisms. And there are weighty cardinals who take greater pride in the purity of their literary style than in being good Christians, and for them orthodoxy is no more than a consequence of literary purity. The forbidden weapon! Just consider the comedy of politics: the participants accuse one another of the ugliest crimes, they charge each other covertly with grave offenses, but they are always careful to call each other eloquent, clever, well-intentioned, talented. . . . For, 'Whosoever shall call his brother a fool, shall be liable to the fires of Gehenna.' Nevertheless, do you know why we make no real progress?"

"Perhaps because we must carry tradition on our backs," I ventured to say.

"No, no. It's simply because it is impossible to convince the fools that they *are* fools. On the day on which fools, that is to say, mankind, become truly convinced that they are just that, fools, on that day progress will have reached its goal. Man is born foolish. . . . And yet whosoever calls his brother a fool shall expose himself to the fires of Gehenna. And expose himself to hellfire he did, that grave clergyman, 'one of those who presume to govern great men's houses, and who, not being nobly born themselves, don't know how to instruct those that are, but would have the liberality of the great measured by the narrowness of their own souls, making those whom they govern stingy, when they pretend to teach them frugality. . . .' "

"Do you see," Dr. Atienza whispered to me, "he knows chapters 31 and 32 of the second part of our book by heart."

"He exposed himself to hellfire, I say," the poor madman went on, "this grave ecclesiastic who came out with the duke and duchess to receive Don Quixote, and who sat down at table with him, face to face while they ate. For, a little while later, furious, stupidly envious, and animated by low passions decked out as high wisdom, this boor charged the duke with responsibility before Our Lord for the actions of this 'good man'. . . . *This good man,* the ridiculous and pompous cleric called Don Quixote, and then went on to call him Mister Fool. Mister Fool!, and he the greatest madman of all time! But he condemned himself to hellfire for calling him that. And in hell he lies."

"Perhaps he is only in purgatory, for the mercy of God is infinite," I dared to say.

"But the guilt of the grave ecclesiastic—who clearly stands for our country in the book, and nothing else—is an enormous one, really enormous," he continued, ignoring my qualifying suggestion. "That ponderous idiot, a genuine incarnation and representative, if there ever was one, of that section of our population which considers itself cultured, that insufferable pedant, after rising peevishly from table and questioning the good sense of his lord, who was feeding him—though it is doubtful if he did anything to earn his keep,—said: 'Well may fools be mad, when wise men celebrate their madness. Your Grace may remain with this pair, if you please, but for my part, as long as they are in this house, I shall keep to my quarters, and thus save myself the labor of reprehending what I can't mend.' And with that, 'leaving the rest of his dinner behind him, away he flung.' He went away; but not entirely, for he and his like still prowl about, classifying people as sane or mad, and deciding which persons are which. . . . It's scandalous and hypocritical, but these great judges call Don Quixote 'the sublime madman' in public—and another packet of phrases they have heard somewhere—and in private, alone with themselves, they call him Mister Fool. Don Quixote, who, in order to go off in pursuit of an empire, the empire of fame, left Sancho Panza the government of an Island! And what office did Mister Fool keep for himself? Not even a ministry! And after all, why did God create the world? For His greater glory, they say, to make it manifest. And should we do less? . . . Pride! Pride! Diabolic pride! That's the cry of the weak and impotent. Bring them here, all those grave and ponderous gentlemen infected with common sense. . . ."

"Let's leave," Dr. Atienza whispered, "he is getting excited."

We cut short the visit with some excuse or other, and I took leave of my poor friend.

"He has been driven mad," Dr. Atienza said as soon as we were alone. "One of the wisest and sanest men I ever knew, and he has been driven mad."

"Why do you say that?" I asked, "Why 'driven'?"

"The greatest difference between the sane and the insane," he answered me, "is that the sane, even though they may occasionally have mad thoughts, neither express them nor carry them out, while the insane—unless they are hopeless, in which case they do not think mad thoughts at all—have no power of inhibition, no ability to contain themselves. Who has not thought of carrying out some piece of madness—unless he is a person whose lack of imagination borders on imbecility? But he has known how to control himself. And if he doesn't know, he evolves into a madman or a genius, to a greater or lesser extent of one or the other depending on his form of madness. It is very convenient to speak of 'delusions' in this connection, but any delusion which proves itself to be practical, or which impels us to maintain, advance or intensify life, is just as real an emotion and makes as valid an impression as any which can be registered, in a more precise manner, by the scientific instruments so far invented for the purpose. That necessary store of madness —to give it its plainest name—which is indispensable for any progress, the lack of balance which propels the world of the spirit and without which there would be absolute repose—that is, death— this madness, this imbalance, must be made use of in some way or other. Dr. Montarco used it to create his fantastic narratives, and in doing so he freed himself from it and was able to carry on the very orderly and sensible life which he led. And really, those stories. . . ."

"Ah!" I interrupted, "they are profoundly suggestive, they are rich in surprising points of view. I can read and re-read them because of their freshness, for I find nothing more tedious than to be told something in writing which I have already ruminated. I can always read stories like these, without a moral and without description. I have been thinking of writing a critical study of his work, and I entertain the hope that once the public is put on the right track they will finally see in them what they don't today. The public isn't as slow-witted or disdainful as we sometimes think; their limitation is that they want everything given them already masticated, predigested, and made up into capsules ready to be swallowed. Everyone has enough to do simply making a living and can't take the time to chew on a cud which tastes bitter when it is first put in the mouth. But a worthwhile commentary can bring out the virtues of a writer like Dr. Montarco, in whose work only the letter and not the spirit has so far been apperceived."

"Well, his stories certainly fell on rocky ground," Dr. Atienza resumed. "His very strangeness, which in another country would have attracted readers, scared people away here. At every step of the way and confronted with the simplest things, people surfeited with the most didactic and pedantic junk asked insistently: 'Now what does he mean here, what is this man trying to say in this passage?' And then, you know how his patients all deserted him, despite the fact that he gave them perfect care. People began to call him mad, despite his exemplary life. He was accused of passions which, in spite of appearances, did not really dominate him. His writings were all rejected. And then, when he and his family found themselves in actual need, he gave way to mad talk and acts; and it was this madness which he had previously vented in his writings."

"Madness?" I interrupted.

"No, you're right. It wasn't madness. But, now they have succeeded in making it turn into madness. I have been reading his work since he has been here and I realize now that one of their mistakes was to take him for a man of ideas, a writer of ideas, when fundamentally he is no such thing. His ideas were a point of departure, mere raw material, and had as much importance in his writing as earth used by Velásquez in making the pigments had to do with his painting, or as the type of stone Michelangelo used had to do with his *Moses*. And what would we say of a man who, equipped with a microscope and reagent, went to make an analysis of the marble by way of arriving at a judgment of the *Venus de Milo?* At best, ideas are no more than raw material, as I've already said, for works of art, or philosophy, or for polemics."

"I have always thought so," I said, "but I have found this to be one of the doctrines which meets with the most resistance on the part of the public. I remember that once, in the course of watching a game of chess, I witnessed the most intense drama of which I have ever been spectator. It was a truly terrible spectacle. The players did no more than move the chessmen, and they were limited by the canons of the game and by the chessboard; nevertheless, you can not imagine what intensity of passion there was, what tension of a truly spiritual nature, what flow of vital energy! Those who only followed the progress of the game thought they were attending an everyday match, for the two players certainly played without great skill. For my part I was watching the way they picked out the chessmen and played them; I was attentive to the solemn silence, the frowns on the players' brows. There was one move, one of the most ordinary and undistinguished no doubt, a check which did not eventuate in a checkmate, which was nevertheless most extraordinary. You should have seen how the one player grasped his knight with his whole hand and placed him on the board with a rap, and how he exclaimed 'Check!' And those two passed for two commonplace players! Commonplace? I'm certain that Morphy or Philidor were more so. . . . Poor Montarco!"

"Yes, poor Montarco! And today you have heard him speak more or less reasonably. . . . Rarely, only rarely, does he talk complete extravagance. When he does, he imagines he is a grotesque character whom he calls the Privy Counsellor Herr Schmarotzender; he puts on a wig which he has found somewhere, gets up on a chair, and makes a wild speech,—full of spirit, however, and in words which somehow echo all the longing and eternal seeking of humanity. At the end, he gets down and asks me: 'Don't you think, Atienza, my friend, that there is a good deal of truth, basically, in the ravings of the poor Privy Counsellor Herr Schmarotzender?' And, in fact, it often strikes me that the feeling of veneration accorded madmen in certain countries is quite justified."

"You know, it seems to me that you should give up the management of this place."

"Don't concern yourself, my friend. It's not that I believe that the veil of a superior world, a world hidden from us, is lifted for these unfortunates; it's simply that I think they say things we all think but don't dare express because of timidity or shame. Reason, which we have acquired in the struggle for life and which is a conservative force, tolerates only what serves to conserve or affirm this life. We don't understand anything but what we must understand in order to live. But who can say that the inextinguishable longing to survive, the thirst for immortality, is not the proof, the revelation of another world, a world which envelops, and also makes possible, our world? And who can say that when reason and its chains have been broken, such dreams and delirium, such frenzied outbursts as Dr. Montarco's, are not desperate leaps by the spirit to reach this other world?"

"It seems to me, and you will forgive my bluntness in saying so, that instead of your treating Dr. Montarco, Dr. Montarco is treating you. The speeches of the Privy Counsellor are beginning to affect you adversely."

"It may be. The only thing I am sure of is that every day I immure myself deeper in this asylum; for I would rather watch over madmen, than have to put up with fools. The only trouble, really, is that there are many madmen who are also fools. But now I have Dr. Montarco to devote myself to. Poor Montarco!"

"Poor Spain!" I said. I extended my hand and we parted.

Dr. Montarco did not last long in the asylum. He was gradually overcome by a profound melancholy, a crushing depression, and finally sank into an obstinate state of muteness. He emerged from his silence only to murmur: "All or nothing. . . . All or nothing. . . . All or nothing. . . ." His illness deepened and ended in death.

After his death, the drawer to his desk yielded a bulky manuscript whose title page read:

ALL OR NOTHING

I request that on my death this manuscript be burned without being read.

I don't know whether Dr. Atienza resisted the temptation to read it; or whether, in compliance with the madman's last wish, he burned it.

Poor Dr. Montarco! May he rest in peace, for he deserved both peace and final rest.

Translated by Anthony Kerrigan

UNAMUNO: *The Madness of Dr. Montarco*

1. *Are the townspeople justified in suspecting Dr. Montarco's motives for writing stories?*

2. *Why does he persist in publishing in the face of public sentiment?*

3. *What does the image of the "fly-trap" signify? Do you agree with Dr. Montarco's point?*

4. *Dr. Montarco explains his philosophy thus: "I would rather deliver fifty blows, and receive ten back, than deliver only ten and not receive any." What does he mean? Does the metaphor mask nothing more than a belligerent nature which, when frustrated, takes an extreme course?*

5. *Did you think Dr. Montarco is right in attacking the statement of Jesus Christ: "Whoever shall call his brother 'Fool!' shall be liable to the fires of Gehenna [Hell]"?*

6. *What is the relevance of Don Quixote to this story? One critic calls Unamuno a descendant of Don Quixote rather than of Cervantes. Do you agree?*

7. *What does the narrator mean by "Poor Spain" after Dr. Atienza comments "Poor Montarco!"?*

8. *Is Dr. Montarco, after all, a madman?*

9. *Sartre, Hemingway, and Unamuno set their stories in Spain. How does the setting enter into each of these stories?*

10. *Is there any similarity between the stories of Unamuno and James? What are the chief differences in style and structure?*

11. *Arturo Barea writes of Unamuno: "With passionate, self-centered energy Unamuno pursued a few basic problems through everything he wrote, through repetition, interpetation, exaggeration and contradiction. . . . Those problems were his own, but he conceived them also as the problems of other Spaniards, of his country as a whole, and of humanity." Does this statement apply to "The Madness of Dr. Montarco"? How?*

Luigi Pirandello

THE SOFT TOUCH OF GRASS

Luigi Pirandello was born (in 1867) and raised in Sicily, whose bitter landscape dominates the spirit of his early work. After taking a doctorate at Bonn, he began to teach literature at a Roman school, writing poetry and short stories as an avocation before he turned to the theater. Though his fiction develops out of the naturalistic style of his friend Giovanni Verga, it is distinguished by an attitude of benevolent pity and irony toward people pinioned uncomfortably, sometimes grotesquely or terrifyingly, to an alien time or place. Often his compassionate bitterness worked to best advantage in his plays, in, for example, Six Characters in Search of an Author *(1921),* Henry IV *(1922), and* As You Desire Me *(1931). After 1918, Pirandello devoted himself fully to his last love, the theater, and achieved an international reputation through his satirical and symbolic dramas. He died in Rome in 1936, two years after receiving the Nobel Prize.*

ξ∾

THEY went into the next room, where he was sleeping in a big chair, to ask if he wanted to look at her for the last time before the lid was put on the coffin.

"It's dark. What time is it?" he asked.

It was nine-thirty in the morning, but the day was overcast and the light dim. The funeral had been set for ten o'clock.

Signor Pardi stared up at them with dull eyes. It hardly seemed possible that he could have slept so long and well all night. He was still numb with sleep and the sorrow of these last days. He would have liked to cover his face with his hands to shut out the faces of his neighbors grouped about his chair in the thin light; but sleep had weighted his body like lead, and although there was a tingling in his toes urging him to rise, it quickly went away. Should he still give way to his grief? He happened to say aloud, "Al-ways . . ." but he said it like someone settling himself under the

224]

covers to go back to sleep. They all looked at him questioningly. Always what?

Always dark, even in the daytime, he had wanted to say, but it made no sense. The day after her death, the day of her funeral, he would always remember this wan light and his deep sleep, too, with her lying dead in the next room. Perhaps the windows . . .

"The windows?"

Yes, they were still closed. They had not been opened during the night, and the warm glow of those big dripping candles lingered. The bed had been taken away and she was there in her padded casket, rigid and ashen against the creamy satin.

No. Enough. He had seen her.

He closed his eyes, for they burned from all the crying he had done these past few days. Enough. He had slept and everything had been washed away with that sleep. Now he was relaxed, with a sense of sorrowful emptiness. Let the casket be closed and carried away with all it held of his past life.

But since she was still there . . .

He jumped to his feet and tottered. They caught him and, with eyes still closed, he allowed himself to be led to the open casket. When he opened his eyes and saw her, he called her by name, her name that lived for him alone, the name in which he saw her and knew her in all the fullness of the life they had shared together. He glared resentfully at the others daring to stare at her lying still in death. What did they know about her? They could not even imagine what it meant to him to be deprived of her. He felt like screaming, and it must have been apparent, for his son hurried over to take him away. He was quick to see the meaning of this and felt a chill as though he were stripped bare. For shame—those foolish ideas up to the very last, even after his night-long sleep. Now they must hurry so as not to keep the friends waiting who had come to follow the coffin to the church.

"Come on, Papa. Be reasonable."

With angry, piteous eyes, the bereaved man turned back to his big chair.

Reasonable, yes; it was useless to cry out the anguish that welled within him and that could never be expressed by words or deeds. For a husband who is left a widower at a certain age, a man still yearning for his wife, can the loss be the same as that of a son for whom—at a certain point—it is almost timely to be left an orphan? Timely, since he was on the point of getting married and would, as soon as the three months' mourning were passed, now that he had the added excuse that it was better for both of them to have a woman to look after the house.

"Pardi! Pardi!" they shouted from the entrance hall.

His chill became more intense when he understood clearly for the first time that they were not calling him but his son. From now on their surname would belong more to his son than to him. And he, like a fool, had gone in there to cry out the living name of his mate, like a profanation. For shame! Yes, useless, foolish ideas, he now realized, after that long sleep which had washed him clean of everything.

Now the one vital thing to keep him going was his curiosity as to how their new home would be arranged. Where, for example, were they going to have him sleep? The big double bed had been removed. Would he have a small bed? he wondered. Yes, probably his son's single bed. Now he would have the small bed. And his son would soon be lying in a big bed, his wife beside him within arm's reach. He, alone, in his little bed, would stretch out his arms into thin air.

He felt torpid, perplexed, with a sensation of emptiness inside and all around him. His body was numb from sitting so long. If he tried now to get up he felt sure that he would rise light as a feather in all that emptiness, now that his life was reduced to nothing. There was hardly any difference between himself and the big chair. Yet that chair appeared secure on its four legs, whereas he no longer knew where his feet and legs belonged nor what to do with his hands. What did he care about his life? He did not care particularly about the lives of others, either. Yet as he was still alive he must go on. Begin again—some sort of life which he could not yet conceive and which he certainly would never have contemplated if things had not changed in his own world. Now, deposed like this all of a sudden, not old and yet no longer young . . .

He smiled and shrugged his shoulders. For his son, all at once, he had become a child. But after all, as everyone knows, fathers are children to their grown sons who are full of worldly ambition and have successfully outdistanced them in positions of importance. They keep their fathers in idleness to repay all they have

received when they themselves were small, and their fathers in
turn become young again.

The single bed . . .

But they did not even give him the little room where his son had
slept. Instead, they said, he would feel more independent in another, almost hidden on the courtyard; he would feel free there to
do as he liked. They refurnished it with all the best pieces, so it
would not occur to anyone that it had once been a servant's room.
After the marriage, all the front rooms were pretentiously decorated and newly furnished, even to the luxury of carpets. Not a
trace remained of the way the old house had looked. Even with his
own furniture relegated to that little dark room, out of the main-
stream of the young people's existence, he did not feel at home. Yet,
oddly enough, he did not resent the disregard he seemed to have
reaped along with the old furniture, because he admired the new
rooms and was satisfied with his son's success.

But there was another deeper reason, not too clear as yet, a
promise of another life, all shining and colorful, which was eras-
ing the memory of the old one. He even drew a secret hope from
it that a new life might begin for him too. Unconsciously, he sensed
the luminous opening of a door at his back whence he might escape
at the right moment, easy enough now that no one bothered about
him, leaving him as if on holiday in the sanctuary of his little room
"to do as he pleased." He felt lighter than air. His eyes had a gleam
in them that colored everything, leading him from marvel to marvel, as though he really were a child again. He had the eyes of a
child—lively and open wide on a world which was still new.

He took the habit of going out early in the morning to begin
his holiday which was to last as long as his life lasted. Relieved
of all responsibilities, he agreed to pay his son so much every
month out of his pension for his maintenance. It was very little.
Though he needed nothing, his son thought he should keep some
money for himself to satisfy any need he might have. But need for
what? He was satisfied now just to look on at life.

Having shaken off the weight of experience, he no longer knew
how to get along with oldsters. He avoided them. And the younger
people considered him too old, so he went to the park where the
children played.

That was how he started his new life—in the meadow among the children in the grass. What an exhilarating scent the grass had, and so fresh where it grew thick and high. The children played hide-and-seek there. The constant trickle of some hidden stream outpurled the rustle of the leaves. Forgetting their game, the children pulled off their shoes and stockings. What a delicious feeling to sink into all that freshness of soft new grass with bare feet!

He took off one shoe and was stealthily removing the other when a young girl appeared before him, her face flaming. "You pig!" she cried, her eyes flashing.

Her dress was caught up in front on a bush, and she quickly pulled it down over her legs, because he was looking up at her from where he sat on the ground.

He was stunned. What had she imagined? Already she had disappeared. He had wanted to enjoy the children's innocent fun. Bending down, he put his two hands over his hard, bare feet. What had she seen wrong? Was he too old to share a child's delight in going barefoot in the grass? Must one immediately think evil because he was old? Ah, he knew that he could change in a flash from being a child to becoming a man again, if he must. He was still a man, after all, but he didn't want to think about it. He refused to think about it. It was really as a child that he had taken off his shoes. How wrong it was of that wretched girl to insult him like that! He threw himself face down on the grass. All his grief, his loss, his daily loneliness had brought about this gesture, interpreted now in the light of vulgar malice. His gorge rose in disgust and bitterness. Stupid girl! If he had wanted that—even his son admitted he might have "some desires"—he had plenty of money in his pocket for such needs.

Indignant, he pulled himself upright. Shamefacedly, with trembling hands, he put on his shoes again. All the blood had gone to his head and the pulse now beat hot behind his eyes. Yes, he knew where to go for that. He knew.

Calmer now, he got up and went back to the house. In the welter of furniture which seemed to have been placed there on purpose to drive him mad, he threw himself on the bed and turned his face to the wall.

Translated by Lily Duplaix

PIRANDELLO: *The Soft Touch of Grass*

1. *On one level, both this story and Kafka's are concerned with the relationship between parents and their children. Compare and contrast the situations.*

2. *On another level, this story, like Turgenev's and Verga's, dramatizes a man's reaction to the death of a dear person. Again, compare and contrast the handling of this theme in each story. Does Hawthorne approach this theme in "My Kinsman"? In which of the four stories is irony used consistently? What is the effect of it?*

3. *Why are we never told the name of the deceased?*

4. *Why does Pirandello juxtapose Pardi and the chair? His single bed and the coffin?*

5. *Why does Pardi turn to the children of the park for solace? Why not to his own child?*

6. *What does the rejection in the park mean to him?*

7. *Though he denies it, does Pardi unconsciously nurse a motive similar to that of the mayor in "Little Louise Roque"? Or is the child's accusation entirely unjust? Are you reminded of Akutagawa's view of a shifting reality?*

8. *Discuss the final paragraph of the story. Does Pirandello reach a level of tragedy? If you have the chance, read Katherine Mansfield's "Miss Brill" and compare it to this story.*

Maxim Gorki

TWENTY-SIX MEN AND A GIRL

The life of Maxim Gorki (b. Aleksey Maximovich Pyeshkov) spans the later years of Czarist rule in Russia as well as the first two decades of Communist government. Born in 1868, Gorki took to the road as a young man and began to turn out artistically success-ful short stories when he was little more than twenty. From the beginning, Gorki showed interest in those whom society had made marginal. His best-known long prose works are the novel Foma Gordeyev *(1899) and the long autobiography,* My Childhood *(1913), while his play,* The Lower Depths, *has been performed throughout the world. "Twenty-Six Men and a Girl," or "Twenty-Six and One," as it is sometimes called, demonstrates Gorki's con-cern with the rejected ones, the outcasts who have little from which to construct their lives and feed their hopes. Returning to Russia from exile in 1928, Gorki was lionized by the Soviet Government. He died in 1936.*

ॐ

THERE were twenty-six of us—twenty-six living robots shut up in a damp cellar, where from morning to evening we kneaded dough to make cakes and rolls. The windows of our cellar looked upon a ditch yawning open before them and crammed full of bricks, green with damp mould; the window-frames were partly covered from the outside by an iron grating, and the light of the sun could not reach us through the window-panes covered with flour dust. Our master had closed up the windows with iron in order that we might not give away a morsel of his bread to the poor, or to those of our comrades who were living without work, and therefore starving; our master called us galley-slaves, and gave us rotten entrails for dinner instead of butcher's meat.

It was a narrow, stuffy life we lived in that stone cage beneath the low and heavy rafters covered with soot and cobwebs. It was a grievous evil life we lived within those thick walls, plastered over with patches of dirt and mould. . . . We rose at five o'clock in the morning, without having had our sleep out, and—stupid and indifferent—at six o'clock we were sitting behind the table to make biscuits from dough already prepared for us by our comrades while we were still sleeping. And the whole day, from early morning to ten o'clock at night, some of us sat at the table kneading the yeasty dough and rocking to and fro so as not to get benumbed, while the others mixed the flour with water. And all day long, dreamily and wearily, the boiling water hummed in the cauldron where the biscuits were steamed, and the shovel of the baker rasped swiftly and evilly upon our ears from beneath the oven as often as it flung down baked bits of dough on the burning bricks. From morning to evening, in one corner of the stove, they burned wood, and the red reflection of the flames flickered on the wall of the workshop as if silently laughing at us. The huge stove was like the misshapen head of some fairy-tale monster—it seemed to stick out from under the ground, opening its wide throat full of bright fire, breathing hotly upon us, and regarding our endless labour with its two black vent-holes just over its forehead. Those two deep cavities were like eyes—the passionless and pitiless eyes of a monster; they always regarded us with one and the same sort of dark look, as if they were weary of looking at their slaves and, not expecting anything human from us, despised us with the cold contempt of worldly wisdom.

From day to day in tormenting dust, in dirt brought in by our feet from the yard, in a dense malodorous steaming vapour, we kneaded dough and made biscuits, moistening them with our sweat, and we hated our work with a bitter hatred; we never ate of that which came forth from our hands, preferring black bread to the biscuits. Sitting behind the long table face to face with each other, nine over against nine, we mechanically used our arms and fingers during the long hours, and were so accustomed to our work that we no longer noticed our own movements. And we had examined one another so thoroughly that everyone of us knew all the wrinkles in the faces of his comrades. We had nothing to talk about, so we got accustomed to talking about nothing, and were silent the whole time unless we quarrelled—there is always a way to make a man quarrel, especially if he be a comrade. But it was rarely that we even quarrelled—how can a man be up to much if he is half dead, if he is like a figure-head, if his feelings are blunted by grievous labour? But silence is only a terror and a torture to those who have said everything and can have nothing more to say; but for people who have not begun to find their voices, silence is simple and easy. . . . Sometimes, however, we sang; it came about in this way. One of us in the midst of his work would suddenly whinny like a tired horse and begin to croon very softly one of those protracted ditties, the sadly caressing *motif* of which always lightens the heaviness of the singer's soul. One of us would begin singing, I say, and the rest would, at first, merely listen to his lonely song, and beneath the heavy roof of the cellar his song would flicker and die out like a tiny camp-fire in the steppe on a grey autumn night when the grey sky hangs over the earth like a leaden roof. Presently the first singer would be joined by another, and then two voices, softly and sadly, would float upwards from the stifling heat of our narrow ditch. And then, suddenly, several voices together would lay hold of the song, and the song would swell forth like a wave, and become stronger and more sonorous, and seem to amplify the heavy grey walls of our stony prison.

And so it came about that the whole six-and-twenty of us would find ourselves singing—our sustained, sonorous concert would fill the work-room, and the song would seem not to have room enough therein. It would beat against the stone wall, wail, weep, stir within the benumbed heart the sensation of a gentle tickling ache, reopen old wounds in it, and awake it to anguish. The singers would sigh deeply and heavily; one of them would unexpectedly break off his own song and listen to the singing of his comrades, and then his voice would blend once more with the common billow of sound. Another of us, perhaps, would utter an anguished "Ah!" and then continue singing with fast-closed eyes. No doubt the broad, dense wave of sound presented itself to his mind as a road stretching far, far away—a broad road lit up by the bright sun, with he himself walking along that road. . . .

And all the time the flame of the furnace was flickering and the baker's shovel was harshly scraping the brick floor, and the boiling water was humming in the cauldron, and the reflection of the fire was quivering on the wall and laughing at us noiselessly. . . . And we were wailing forth in the words of others our dull misery, the heavy anguish of living beings deprived of the sun, the anguish of slaves. Thus we lived, twenty-six of us, in the cellar of a large stone house, and life was as grievous to us as if all the three upper stories of this house had been built right upon our very shoulders.

But, besides the singing, we had one other good thing—a thing we set great store by and which, possibly, stood to us in the place of sunshine. In the second story of our house was a gold-embroidery factory, and among the numerous factory girls employed there was a damsel sixteen years old, Tanya by name. Every morning she would come to the little window pierced through the door in the wall of our workshop, and pressing against it her tiny rosy face, with its merry blue eyes, would cry to us with a musical, friendly voice: "Poor little prisoners! give me some little biscuits!"

All of us would instantly turn round at the familiar sound of that bright voice, and gaze good-naturedly and joyously at the pure virginal little face smiling upon us so gloriously. It became a usual and very pleasant thing for us to see the little nose pressed against the window-pane, to see the tiny white teeth gleaming from under the rosy lips parted by a smile. There would then be a general rush to open the door, each one trampling upon his fellows in his haste, and then in she would come, always so bright and pleasant, and stand before us, her head perched a little on one side, holding up her apron and smiling all the time. The long thick locks of her chestnut hair, falling across her shoulders, lay upon her breast. We dirty, grimy, misshapen wretches stood there looking up at her— the threshold of the door was four steps above the level of the floor—we had to raise our heads to look at her, we would wish her good-morning, and would address her in especial language—the words seemed to come to us expressly for her and for her alone. When we conversed with her our voices were gentler than usual, and our jests were less rough. We had quite peculiar and different manners—and all for her. The baker would take out of the oven a shovelful of the ruddiest, best-toasted biscuits, and skilfully fling them into Tanya's apron.

"Take care you don't fall into the clutches of the master!" we would always caution her. And she, roguishly laughing, would call to us: "Good-bye, little prisoners," and vanish as quickly as a little mouse.

Only—long after her departure, we would talk pleasantly about her among ourselves; we always said the same thing, and we said

it late and early, because she and we and everything around
us was always the same early and late. It is a heavy torment for a
man to live where everything around him is unchanging, and if this
does not kill the soul within him, the longer he lives the more tormenting will the immobility of his environment become. We always spoke of women in such a way that sometimes it went against
the grain with us to listen to our own coarse, shameful speeches,
and it will be understood that the sort of women we knew were
unworthy to be alluded to in any other way. But we never spoke
ill of Tanya. None of us ever permitted himself to lay so much as
a finger upon her; nay, more, she never heard a loose jest from any
of us. Possibly this was because she never remained very long with
us: she twinkled before our eyes like a star falling from heaven and
vanished; but, possibly also, it was because she was so tiny and so
very pretty, and everything beautiful awakens respect for it even
in coarse people. And there was something else. Although our
prison-like labour had made dull brutes of us, for all that we were
still human beings, and, like all human beings, we could not live
without worshipping something or other. We had nothing better
than she, and nobody but she took any notice of us who lived in
that vault; nobody, though scores of people lived in that house.
And finally—and that, after all, was the chief thing—we all of us
accounted her as in some sort our own, as, in some sort, only exist-
ing thanks to our biscuits; we looked upon it as our duty to give
her biscuits piping hot, and this became to us a daily sacrifice to
our idol; it became almost a sacred office, and every day bound us
to her more and more. Besides the biscuits we gave to Tanya a
good deal of advice—she was to put on warmer clothes, not run
rapidly upstairs, not to carry heavy loads of wood. She listened
to our advice with a smile, responded to it with laughter, and
never followed it at all; but we were not offended with her on that
account, we only wanted to show her that we were taking care of
her.

Sometimes she asked us to do different things for her; such, for
instance, as to open the heavy cellar door, to chop up wood and
so on, and we joyfully, nay, with a sort of pride, did for her all that
she asked us to do.

But once, when one of us asked her to mend his only shirt, she sniffed contemptuously and said: "What next! do you think I've nothing better to do?"

We laughed heartily at the silly fellow—and never asked her to do anything more. We loved her—and when that is said all is said. A man always wants to lay his love upon someone, although sometimes he may crush her beneath the weight of it, and sometimes he may soil her; he may poison the life of his neighbour with his love, because in loving he does not revere the beloved. We were obliged to love Tanya because we had none else to love.

At times one or other of us would begin to reason about it like this: "Why are we spoiling the wench like this? What is there in her after all? Eh? We are making a great deal of fuss about her!"

The fellow who ventured to use such language was pretty roughly snubbed, I can tell you. We wanted something to love, we had found what we wanted, and we loved it; and what we six-and-twenty loved was bound to be inviolate, because it was our holy shrine, and everyone who ran contrary to us in this matter was our enemy. No doubt people often love what is not really good—but here we were, all twenty-six of us, in the same boat, and therefore what we considered dear we would have others regard as sacred.

Besides the biscuit factory our master had a fancy-bakery; it was located in the same house, and only separated from our hole by a wall; but the fancy-bakers—there were four of them—kept us at arm's length, considering their work as cleaner than ours, and for that reason considering themselves as better than we. So they did not come into our workshop, and laughed contemptuously at us when they met us in the yard. We, too, did not go to them; our master had forbidden us to do so for fear we should steal the milk scones. We did not like the fancy-bakers because we envied them. Their work was lighter than ours; they got more than we did and were better fed; they had a spacious, well-lighted workshop, and they were all so clean and healthy—quite the opposite to us. We indeed, the whole lot of us, looked greyish or yellowish; three of us were suffering from disease, others from consumption, one of us was absolutely crippled by rheumatism. They, on feast-days and in their spare time, put on pea-jackets and boots that creaked; two of them had concertinas, and all of them went strolling in the Park

—we went about in little better than dirty rags, with down-at-heel slippers or bast shoes on our feet, and the police would not admit us into the Park—how could we possibly love the fancy-bakers?

Presently we heard that their overseer had taken to drink, that the master had dismissed him and hired another, and that this other was a soldier who went about in a rich satin waistcoat, and on great occasions wore a gold chain. We were curious to see such a toff, and, in the hope of seeing him, took it in turns to run out into the yard one after the other.

But he himself appeared in our workshop. He kicked at the door, it flew open, and, keeping it open, he stood on the threshold, smiled, and said to us: "God be with you! I greet you, my children!"

The frosty air, rushing through the door in thick smoky clouds, whirled round his feet, and there he stood on the threshold looking down upon us from his eminence, and from beneath his blond, skilfully twisted moustaches gleamed his strong yellow teeth. His vest really was something quite out of the common—it was blue, embroidered with flowers, and had a sort of sparkle all over it, and its buttons were made of pretty little pearls. And the gold chain *was* there. . . .

He was handsome, that soldier was, quite tall, robust, with ruddy cheeks, and his large bright eyes looked good and friendly and clear. On his head was a white stiffly starched cap, and from beneath his clean spotless spats appeared the bright tops of his modish, brilliantly polished boots.

Our baker asked him, respectfully, to shut the door. He did so, quite deliberately, and began asking us questions about our master. We outdid each other in telling him that our master was a blood-sucker, a slave-driver, a malefactor, and a tormentor; everything in short that we could and felt bound to say about our master, but it is impossible to write it down here. The soldier listened, twirled his moustache, and regarded us with a gentle, radiant look.

"And I suppose now you've a lot of little wenches about here?" he suddenly said.

Some of us laughed respectfully, other made languishing grimaces; one of us made it quite clear to the soldier that there *were* wenches here—a round dozen of them.

"Do you amuse yourselves?" asked the soldier, blinking his eyes.

Again we laughed, not very loudly, and with some confusion of face. . . . Many of us would have liked to show the soldier that they were as dashing fellows as himself, but none dared to do so; no, not one. One of us indeed hinted as much by murmuring: "Situated as we are . . ."

"Yes, of course, it would be hard for you!" observed the soldier confidentially, continuing to stare at us. "You ought to be—well, not what you are. You're down on your luck—there's a way of holding one's self—there's the look of the thing—you know what I mean! And women, you know, like a man with style about him. He must be a fine figure of a man—everything neat and natty, you know. And then, too, a woman respects strength. Now what do you think of that for an arm, eh?"

The soldier drew his right arm from his pocket, with the shirt-sleeve stripped back, bare to the elbow, and showed it to us. It was a strong, white arm, bristling with shiny, gold-like hair.

"Legs and breast the same—plenty of grit there, eh? And then, too, a man must be stylishly dressed, and must have nice things. Now look at me—all the women love me! I neither call to them nor wink at them—they come falling on my neck by the dozen."

He sat down on a flour-basket and discoursed to us for a long time about how the women loved him, and how valiantly he comported himself with them. After he had gone, and when the creaking door had closed behind him, we were silent for a long time, thinking of him and of his yarns. And after a bit we suddenly all fell a-talking at once, and agreed unanimously that he was a very pleasant fellow. He was so straightforward and jolly—he came and sat down and talked to us just as if he were one of us. No one had ever come and talked to us in such a friendly way before. And we talked of him and of his future successes with the factory girls at the gold-embroiderer's, who, whenever they met us in the yard, either curled their lips contemptuously, or gave us a wide berth, or walked straight up to us as if we were not in their path at all. And as for us, we only feasted our eyes upon them when we met them in the yard, or when they passed by our window, dressed in winter in peculiar little fur caps and fur pelisses, and in summer in hats covered with flowers, and with sunshades of various colours in their hands. But, on the other hand, among ourselves, we talked of these girls in such a way that, had they heard it, they would have gone mad with rage and shame. . . .

"But how about little Tanya—I hope he won't spoil her!" said our chief baker suddenly with a gloomy voice.

We were all silent, so greatly had these words impressed us. We had almost forgotten about Tanya: the soldier had shut her out from us, as it were, with his fine burly figure. Presently a noisy dispute began. Some said that Tanya would not demean herself by any such thing; others maintained that she would be unable to stand against the soldier; finally, a third party proposed that if the soldier showed any inclination to attach himself to Tanya, we should break his ribs. And, at last, we all resolved to keep a watch upon the soldier and Tanya, and warn the girl to beware of him. . . . And so the dispute came to an end.

A month passed by. The soldier baked his fancy-rolls, walked out with the factory girls, and frequently paid us a visit in our workshop, but of his victories over the wenches he said never a word, but only twirled his moustache and noisily smacked his lips.

Tanya came to us every morning for her "little biscuits," and was always merry, gentle and friendly with us. We tried to talk to her about the soldier—she called him "the goggle-eyed bull-calf," and other ridiculous names, and that reassured us. We were proud of our little girl when we saw how the factory girls clung to the soldier. Tanya's dignified attitude towards him seemed to raise the whole lot of us, and we, as the directors of her conduct, even began to treat the soldier himself contemptuously. But her we loved more than ever, her we encountered each morning more and more joyfully and good-humouredly.

But one day the soldier came to us a little the worse for liquor, he sat him down, began laughing, and when we asked him what he was laughing about, he explained:

"Two of the wenches have been quarrelling about me, Liddy and Gerty," said he. "How they did blackguard each other! Ha, ha, ha! They caught each other by the hair, and were down on the floor in a twinkling, one on the top of the other; ha, ha, ha! And they tore and scratched like anything, and I was nearly bursting with laughter. Why can't women fight fair? Why do they always scratch, eh?"

He was sitting on the bench; there he sat so healthy, clean, and light-hearted, and roared with laughter. We were silent. Somehow, or other, he was disagreeable to us at that moment.

"No, I can't make it out. What luck I do have with women, it is ridiculous. I've but to wink, and—she is ready. The d-deuce is in it."

His white arms, covered with shining gold down, rose in the air and fell down again on his knees with a loud bang. And he regarded us with such a friendly look of amazement, just as if he himself were frankly puzzled by the felicity of his dealings with women. His plump, ruddy face regularly shone with happiness and self-complacency, and he kept on noisily smacking his lips.

Our chief baker scraped his shovel along the hearth violently and angrily, and suddenly remarked, with a sneer:

"It is no great feat of strength to fell little fir trees, but to fell a full-grown pine is a very different matter. . . ."

"Is that meant for me, now?" queried the soldier.

"It *is* meant for you."

"What do you mean?"

"Nothing. . . . Never mind."

"Nay, stop a bit! What's your little game? What pine tree do you mean?"

Our master-baker didn't answer, he was busily working with his shovel at the stove, shovelled out the well-baked biscuits, sifted those that were ready, and flung them boisterously on to the floor to the lads who were arranging them in rows on the bast wrappings. He seemed to have forgotten the soldier and his talk with him. But the soldier suddenly became uneasy. He rose to his feet and approached the stove, running the risk of a blow in the chest from the handle of the shovel which was whirling convulsively in the air.

"Come, speak—what *she* did you mean? You have insulted me. Not a chance she shall ever get the better of me, n-no—I say. And then, too, you used such offensive words to me. . . ."

He really seemed to be seriously offended. No doubt he had but a poor opinion of himself except on this one point: his ability to win women. Possibly, except this one quality, there was nothing really vital in the man at all, and only this single quality allowed him to feel himself a living man.

There are people who look upon some disease, either of the body or of the soul, as the best and most precious thing in life. They nurse it all their lives, and only in it do they live at all. Though they suffer by it, yet they live upon it. They complain of it to other people, and by means of it attract to themselves the attention of their neighbours. They use it as a means of obtaining sympathy, and without it—they are nothing at all. Take away from them this disease, cure them, and they will be unhappy because they are deprived of the only means of living—there they stand empty. Sometimes the life of a man is poor to such a degree that he is involuntarily obliged to put a high value on some vice, and live thereby; indeed, we may say straight out that very often people become vicious from sheer ennui.

The soldier was offended, rushed upon our master-baker, and bellowed: "Come, I say—speak out! Who was it?"

"Speak out, eh?" and the master-baker suddenly turned round upon him.

"Yes! Well?"

"Do you know Tanya?"

"Well!"

"Well, there you are!—try her!"

"I?"

"You."

"Pooh! That's nothing."

"Let us see!"

"You shall see. Ha-ha-ha!"

"She look at you!"

"Give me a month!"

"What a braggart you are, soldier!"

"A fortnight! I'll show you. Who's she? Little Tanya! Pooh!"

"And now be off!—you're in the way."

"A fortnight, I say—and the thing's done. Poor you, I say!"

"Be off, I say."

Our baker suddenly grew savage, and flourished his shovel. The soldier backed away from him in astonishment, and observed us in silence. "Good!" he said at last with ominous calmness—and departed.

During the dispute we all remained silent, we were too deeply interested in it to speak. But when the soldier departed, there arose from among us a loud and lively babble of voices.

Someone shrieked at the baker: "A pretty business you've set a-going, Paul!"

"Go on working, d'ye hear?" replied the master-baker fiercely.

We felt that the soldier would make the assault, and that Tanya was in danger. We felt this, and yet at the same time we were all seized by a burning curiosity that was not unpleasant—what would happen? Would Tanya stand firm against the soldier? And almost all of us cried, full of confidence:

"Little Tanya? She'll stand firm enough!"

We had all of us a frightful longing to put the fortitude of our little idol to the test. We excitedly proved to each other that our little idol was a strong little idol, and would emerge victorious from this encounter. It seemed to us, at last, that we had not egged on our soldier enough, that he was forgetting the contest, and that we ought to spur his vanity just a little bit. From that day forth we began to live a peculiar life, at high nervous tension, such as we had never lived before. We quarrelled with each other for days together, just as if we had all grown wiser, and were able to talk more and better. It seemed to us as if we were playing a sort of game with the devil, and the stake on our part was—Tanya. And when we heard from the fancy-bread-bakers that the soldier had begun "to run after our little Tanya," it was painfully well with us, and so curious were we to live it out, that we did not even observe that our master, taking advantage of our excitement, had added 14 poods[1] of paste to our daily task. We practically never left off working at all. The name of Tanya never left our tongues all day. And every morning we awaited her with a peculiar sort of impatience.

Nevertheless we said not a word to her of the contest actually proceeding. We put no questions to her, and were kind and affectionate to her as before. Yet in our treatment of her there had already crept in something new and strangely different to our former feeling for Tanya—and this new thing was a keen curiosity, keen and cold as a steel knife.

[1] 560 lbs.

"My friends, the time's up to-day," said the master-baker one morning as he set about beginning his work.

We knew that well enough without any reminder from him but we trembled all the same.

"Look at her well, she'll be here immediately," continued the baker.

Someone exclaimed compassionately:

"As if eyes could see anything!"

And again a lively, stormy debate arose among us. To-day we were to know at last how clean and inviolable was the vessel in which we had placed our best. That morning, all at once and as if for the first time, we began to feel that we were really playing a great game, and that this test of the purity of our divinity might annihilate it altogether so far as we were concerned. We had all heard during the last few days that the soldier was obstinately and persistently persecuting Tanya, yet how was it that none of us asked her what her relations with him were? And she used to come to us regularly, every morning, for her little biscuits, and was the same as ever.

And this day also we very soon heard her voice.

"Little prisoners, I have come. . . ."

We crowded forward to meet her, and when she came in, contrary to our usual custom, we met her in silence. Looking at her with all our eyes, we knew not what to say to her, what to ask her. We stood before her a gloomy, silent crowd. She was visibly surprised at this unusual reception—and all at once we saw her grow pale, uneasy, fidget in her place, and inquire in a subdued voice:

"What's the matter with you?"

"And how about yourself?" the master-baker sullenly said, never taking his eyes off her.

"Myself? What do you mean?"

"Oh, nothing, nothing."

"Come, give me the biscuits!—quick!"

Never before had she been so sharp with us.

"You're in a hurry," said the baker, not moving and never taking his eyes from her face.

Then she suddenly turned round and disappeared through the door.

The baker caught up his shovel and, turning towards the stove, remarked quietly:

"It means—she's all ready for him. Ah, that soldier . . . the scoundrel . . . the skunk!"

We, like a flock of sheep, rubbing shoulders with each other, went to our table, sat down in silence, and wearily began to work. Presently, someone said: "Yet it is possible . . . ?"

"Well, well, what's the good of talking?" screeched the baker.

We all knew that he was a wise man, far wiser than we. And we understood his exclamation as a conviction of the victory of the soldier. . . . We felt miserable and uneasy.

At twelve o'clock—dinner-time—the soldier arrived. He was, as usual, spruce and genteel and—as he always did—looked us straight in the eyes. But we found it awkward to look at *him*.

"Well, my worthy gentlemen, if you like, I'll show you a bit of martial prowess," said he, laughing proudly. "Just you come out into the outhouse and look through the crevices—do you understand?"

Out we went, elbowing each other on the way, and glued our faces to the crevices in the boarded-up wall of the outhouse looking upon the courtyard. We had not long to wait. Very soon, at a rapid pace, and with a face full of anxiety, Tanya came tearing through the yard, springing over the puddles of stale snow and mud. Shortly afterwards, in not the least hurry and whistling as he went, appeared the soldier, making his way in the same direction as Tanya, evidently they had arranged a rendezvous. His arms were thrust deep down in his pockets, and his moustaches were moving up and down. . . . He also disappeared. . . . Then the rain came and we watched the raindrops falling into the puddles, and the puddles wrinkle beneath their impact. The day was damp and grey—a very wearying day. Snow still lay upon the roofs, and on the earth dark patches of mud were already appearing. And the snow on the roofs also got covered with dirty dark-brown smuts. The rain descended slowly with a melancholy sound. We found it cold and unpleasant to stand waiting there, but we were furious with Tanya for having deserted us, her worshippers, for the sake of a common soldier, and we waited for her with the grim delight of executioners.

After a while—we saw Tanya returning. Her eyes—yes, *her* eyes, actually sparkled with joy and happiness, and her lips—were smiling. And she was walking as if in a dream, rocking a little to and fro, with uncertain footsteps. . . .

We could not endure this calmly. The whole lot of us suddenly burst through the door, rushed into the yard, and hissed and yelled at her with evil, bestial violence.

On perceiving us she trembled—and stood as if rooted in the mud beneath her feet. We surrounded her and, maliciously, without any circumlocution, we reviled her to our hearts' content, and called her the most shameful things.

We did not raise our voices, we took our time about it. We saw that she had nowhere to go, that she was in the midst of us, and we might vent our rage upon her as much as we liked. I don't know why, but we did not beat her. She stood in the midst of us, and kept turning her head now hither now thither, as she listened to our insults. And we—bespattered her, more and more violently, with the mud and the venom of our words.

The colour quitted her face, her blue eyes, a minute before so radiant with happiness, opened widely, her bosom heaved heavily, and her lips trembled.

And we, surrounding her, revenged ourselves upon her, for she had robbed us. She had belonged to us, we had expended our best upon her, and although that best was but a beggar's crumb, yet we were six-and-twenty and she was but one, therefore we could not devise torments worthy of her fault. How we did abuse her! She was silent all along—all along she looked at us with the wild eyes of a hunted beast, she was all of a tremble.

We ridiculed, we reviled, we baited her. . . . Other people came running up to us. . . . One of us pulled Tanya by the sleeve.

Suddenly her eyes gleamed, she leisurely raised her hands to her head and, tidying her hair, looked straight into our faces, and ejaculated loudly but calmly:

"Ugh! you miserable jail-birds!"

And she walked straight up to us, unhesitatingly as if we were not standing there in front of her at all, as if we were not obstructing her way. And for that very reason not one of us was actually standing in her way when she came up to us.

And as she passed by, without so much as turning her face towards us, she added as loudly and as haughtily:

"Oh you riff-raff! you . . . you filth!"

And—away she went, erect, beautiful, haughty.

We remained standing in the yard, in the midst of the mud, beneath the pouring rain and the grey, sunless sky.

Presently we returned in silence to our grey, stony dungeon. As before, the sun never looked through our window to us, and—Tanya did not come again.

Translated by Emily Jakovlev
and Dora B. Montefiore

GORKI: *Twenty-Six Men and a Girl*

1. *No reader can afford to disregard the importance of setting, which, along with plot and characterization, serves to indicate the theme. A careful study of the setting in this story (as well as in several other stories in this volume) will reveal that setting is not merely an embellishment or ornamentation, but an integral part of the total experience which is the story. As T. S. Eliot said of Henry James, the writer must "make a place real not descriptively but by something happening there." What is the importance of setting in Gorki?*

2. *Why does Gorki stress the monotony of the men's work? What does he mean by ". . . often men are vicious out of boredom"? Does this statement have any bearing on Conrad's "Il Conde"?*

3. *How do the men at first regard Tanya? Do they overrate her? Why? So regarded, is she bound to fail them?*

4. *Why do the men put Tanya on the block when she is the sole joy in their lives? What is their relationship to the soldier? Do they really like him or not?*

5. *Gorki, who greatly admired Chekhov, also turns his story on the device of a wager. What significance does the bet assume in the larger view of events?*

6. *At the end, what have the prisoners gained? What have they lost? What kind of future do they face? Have they brought their situation upon themselves?*

Marcel Proust

THE MELANCHOLY SUMMER
OF MADAME DE BREYVES

Marcel Proust's name is of course best known for his long series of interconnected novels which brilliantly bring to life a generation of French society, Remembrance of Things Past. *Born in a Paris suburb in 1871, Proust suffered from ill-health for nearly his entire life, virtually isolating himself except for late-evening forays into high society.* "The Melancholy Summer of Madame de Breyves" *was written long before Proust began his great work in 1906, but like so many other works of short fiction by major writers, it sets out in small what was later to be developed at length. Until his death in 1922, Proust worked on* Remembrance, *what has since become a monument in twentieth-century fiction.*

"Ariadne, O my Sister, by what a love wounded
Have you died, on those same shores abandoned!"

ც➤

1

FRANÇOISE DE BREYVES that evening could not make up her mind whether to go to the reception of the Princess Elizabeth A—, to the opera, or to see the Livrays' plays.

At the house where she had dined they had left the table more than an hour ago. She really must decide.

Her friend Genevieve, who was to leave with her, wanted to go to the reception, while Madame de Breyves would have preferred either of the other alternatives, or even a third, going home to bed. The carriage was announced. She was still undecided.

"Really," said Genevieve, "you're being horrid—Reszke is probably going to sing and that would amuse me. One would think something dreadful was going to happen to you if you went to

Elizabeth's. Besides, you know, you haven't been to one of her big affairs this season, and, being such a close friend, it's really not nice of you."

Françoise, since the death of her husband, who had left her a widow at twenty—that was four years ago—rarely went anywhere without Genevieve and always tried to please her. She could resist no longer, and after taking leave of her hosts and of the guests, disappointed at the departure of one of the most popular women of Paris, said to the footman, "To the Princess A—'s."

2

The evening at the Princess A—'s was very boring. Once Madame de Breyves asked Genevieve, "Who is the young man who escorted you to the buffet?"

"He is a Monsieur de Laléande whom I never heard of. Would you like me to introduce him? In fact, he asked me to, but I was evasive because he is so insignificant and boring, and as he thinks you very pretty you'd never get rid of him."

"Then decidedly no!" said Françoise. "Besides, he's rather ugly and vulgar-looking in spite of his beautiful eyes."

"You are right," said Genevieve. "And as you would be meeting him often it might be embarrassing if you knew him."

Then she added, laughing, "Unless, of course, you'd like a more intimate acquaintance—in that case you're missing a fine opportunity."

"Yes, a fine opportunity," said Françoise, already thinking of something else.

"But after all," Genevieve added, probably seized with remorse at having been such an unfaithful emissary, gratuitously depriving the young man of a pleasure, "this is one of the last affairs of the season, so it wouldn't really matter and might be more civil."

"So be it, if he comes over this way."

He was on the other side of the drawing room facing them, and did not come over.

"We should be going," Genevieve said a moment later.

"Oh, just a second," said Françoise.

And out of caprice, above all impelled by an urge to flirt with a young man who must indeed find her pretty, she began to look at

him a little lingeringly, quickly dropping her eyes and then staring at him again. She made her expression as caressing as possible,
she hardly knew why, for no reason, for the pleasure of it, the
pleasure of being charitable, the pleasure of vanity, too, and of
futility, the pleasure of those who write their names on trees for a
passer-by they will never see, of those who throw bottles into the
ocean. It was getting late. Monsieur de Laléande was going toward the door. As it remained open after he had left, Madame de
Breyves could see him at the other end of the entrance-hall, holding out his number to the cloakroom attendant.

"You're right. We really must be going," she said to Genevieve.

They both rose. But by chance Genevieve being detained by
one of her friends for a moment, Françoise was left alone near the
cloakroom. There was no one there at the moment but Monsieur
de Laléande, who could not find his cane. To amuse herself, Françoise gave him one last lingering look. He passed close to her,
lightly rubbing his elbow against hers, and, while still touching
her, his eyes very bright, and still pretending to be looking for his
cane, said, "Come to my place, 5 Rue Royale."

This was something she had so little anticipated, and Monsieur
de Laléande was so seriously searching for his cane again, that she
was never able to decide later whether it was only an hallucination
or not. Above all she was horribly frightened and, Prince A— passing just then, she called to him and began talking volubly, arranging for an outing the next day. During this conversation Monsieur
de Laléande had left. In another moment Genevieve arrived and
the two women took their departure. Madame de Breyves said
nothing. She was still shocked and flattered and, at bottom, indifferent. Two days later, recalling the incident by chance, she began
to wonder if Monsieur de Laléande had really spoken those words.
Trying in vain to remember, she decided she must have heard them
as in a dream, and that the movement of his elbow had been involuntary. Then she thought no more of Monsieur de Laléande
and when by chance she heard his name mentioned, she vaguely
recalled his face but had entirely forgotten what must have been
an hallucination outside the cloakroom.

She saw him again at the last reception of the season (June was
nearly over), dared not ask to have him presented and yet, in spite

of the fact that she thought him almost ugly, knew he was not intelligent, felt a desire to meet him. She went up to Genevieve and said, "After all, you might introduce Monsieur de Laléande. I don't like to be impolite. But don't say I suggested it, for I don't want to get myself involved."

"All right, later if we see him. He isn't around just now."

"But can't you look for him?"

"He may have left."

"Oh, no," Françoise said quickly, "he couldn't have left, it's too early. Oh, twelve o'clock already! Darling, please, it isn't so difficult. The other evening you were keen on it. It has a special interest for me."

Genevieve looked at her, a little surprised, and went in search of Monsieur de Laléande. He had left.

"You see, I was right," said Genevieve, coming back to Françoise.

"I'm too bored for words," said Françoise, "and I have a headache. Let's go home. Do you mind?"

3

Françoise never missed an evening at the opera now and, with vague hope, accepted all the dinner invitations she received. Two weeks went by without her seeing Monsieur de Laléande again, and she would wake up in the night trying to devise some scheme for meeting him. While all the time repeating to herself that he was boring and not even handsome, she thought of him more than of all the witty and charming men she knew. The season being over, there would be no chance of seeing him again, and she decided to create an opportunity, thought of nothing else.

One evening she said to Genevieve, "Didn't you tell me that you knew a Monsieur de Laléande?"

"Jacques de Laléande? Yes and no; he was introduced to me, but he never left cards and I don't see him."

"Well, you know, I have a certain interest, a considerable interest, I might say—oh, nothing to do with me, and I can't say anything about it for a month" (before then she would have devised with him some plausible story, and the thought of a secret shared with him alone gave her a delicious thrill) "in seeing and talking to him. Do try to manage it, because now that the season is over there won't be any more parties where I might meet him."

The practice of close friendship, so purifying when it is sincere, saved Genevieve, as well as Françoise, from that curiosity which is the shameful amusement of most people in society. So it was that Genevieve with all her heart and without for an instant entertaining the intention or the desire or even an idea of questioning her friend, began her search for Monsieur de Laléande, distressed only because she was unable to find him.

"It is unfortunate that Elizabeth A— has left. Of course there is Monsieur de Grumello, but that doesn't help us very much, for what are we to say to him? Oh! I have an idea. Monsieur de Laléande plays the cello—badly, but that doesn't matter. Monsieur de Grumello admires him and is so stupid and besides, he would be overjoyed to please you. The only thing is—you've always avoided him and, as you hate dropping people after making use of them, you would be obliged to invite him next season."

But Françoise was already flushed with joy. "That doesn't matter, I don't care; I'd invite all the upstarts and adventurers of Paris if necessary. Oh! Please, darling, don't waste a second!"

And Genevieve wrote:

Monsieur,
    You know that I would do anything in the world to please my friend, Madame de Breyves, whom you must have met. I have heard her say several times, when the cello was mentioned, how much she regretted never having heard your good friend Monsieur de Laléande play. I wonder if you could get him to play for her and for me. Now that we all have more time, perhaps this will not inconvenience you too much, and it would be very good of you. With kindest regards,
                                        Alériouvre Buivres

"Take this letter to Monsieur de Grumello," Françoise said to a servant. "Do not wait for an answer, but make sure that he receives it at once."

The next day Genevieve had Monsieur de Grumello's reply taken by hand to Madame de Breyves:

Madame,

I should have been more delighted than you can imagine to have been able to satisfy your desire and that of Madame de Breyves, whom I know slightly but for whom I feel the most respectful and the keenest sympathy. And I am utterly disconsolate that by a most unhappy chance Monsieur de Laléande left for Biarritz two days ago, where, alas! he will remain for several months.

Please accept, madame, etc.
Grumello

Françoise, as white as a sheet, rushed to her room to lock herself in. She had hardly time to reach it before she was shaken by sobs, and tears were flowing. Until then, preoccupied as she had been in imagining all sorts of romantic ways of meeting and knowing him, believing that she could realize them when she wished, she had been, perhaps unconsciously, living on this desire and this hope. Deeply implanted in her, they had sent down a thousand little imperceptible roots and started a new mysterious sap coursing through her. And now, all at once, they were uprooted and thrown into the discard. She suffered the agonizing laceration of that hidden self suddenly torn up by the roots. Now she saw clearly through all the lies that hope and desire had held out to her and, at last, from the depths of her grief came suddenly face to face with the reality of her love.

4

Every day Françoise seemed to grow more and more indifferent to all her habitual pleasures. Even from her most intense and intimate joys, those shared with her mother and with Genevieve, even from the hours she gave to music, from her reading, from her walks, her heart was absent, devoured by a jealous sorrow that never left her. And she felt that there was no end to this pain, since it was impossible for her to go to Biarritz and, even had that been possible, she was determined not to compromise by any desperate action the prestige she might enjoy in the eyes of Monsieur de Laléande. Poor little victim, tortured without knowing why, she was terrified to think that this suffering might last for months without relief, drive away sleep, trouble her dreams. She worried, too, thinking that, without her knowing it, he might pass through Paris again. And her fear of letting happiness so near at hand once more escape her gave her the courage to send a servant to make inquiries of Monsieur de Laléande's concierge. He knew nothing. Then, realizing that there was now no hope of a sail appearing on the horizon of this sea of sorrow which spread out infinitely and beyond which it seemed there was nothing, and that earth had ended, she felt she was being driven to some folly, what, she did not know—writing to him, perhaps—and to calm herself a little, becoming her own doctor, she decided on a scheme for letting him know that she had deliberately tried to see him. To that end she wrote to Monsieur de Grumello:

Monsieur,
   Madame de Buivres has told me of your kind thought. How touched I was, how grateful to you! But there is something that worries me. Did Monsieur de Laléande think me indiscreet? In case you do not know, would you ask him, and when you have found out let me know and promise to tell me the exact truth. I am curious, and you would be doing me a kindness. Again thank you, monsieur, etc.

                                        Voragines Breyves

One hour later a servant brought this letter:

   You have no cause to worry, madame, Monsieur de Laléande does not know of your request to hear him play. I wrote asking him what days he would be free to play at my house without mentioning for whom. He replied from Biarritz that he would not be in Paris again till January. You must not thank me. My greatest joy would be to add the merest trifle to yours, etc.

                                        Grumello

There was nothing more she could do. She gave up trying and grew sadder and sadder, saddening her mother, ashamed of her sadness. She went to spend a few days in the country, then left for Trouville. She heard people discussing Monsieur de Laléande's social ambitions, and when a prince, trying his best to be agreeable to her, said: "What can I do that would please you most?" she felt almost like laughing when she thought of his surprise if she were to answer truthfully, and felt all the concentrated and bitter irony of the contrast between the great and difficult things always being done for her and the one little thing, so easy and so impossible, that would have brought back peace, health, and happiness to her, and the happiness of those dearest to her. She only knew a little relief when she was alone with the servants who waited on her, sensing her sadness. Their respectful and grieved silence spoke to her of Monsieur de Laléande. It gave her a voluptuous pleasure, and she would make them serve her luncheon slowly, lingering over it, to put off the moment when she would have to see her friends and to dissimulate her sorrow. She wanted to relish the sweet and bitter taste of the sadness that, because of him, surrounded her. She would have liked to see more people dominated by him, to feel that what took up so much room in her heart was also occupying a little of the space around her. She would have liked to possess healthy, lively animals who, gradually stricken with her ill, would go into a decline. Desperate at moments, she wanted to write to him, have someone write, demean herself. "Nothing matters any longer." But she was restrained by the thought that even in the interest of her love she must keep her position in society, since it might give her greater power over him one day, if that day ever came. And if a short intimacy with him should break the spell he had cast over her (she did not wish to believe, could not believe, or even imagine it, for an instant, but her mind, more discerning than her blind heart, foresaw the cruel eventuality), she would be left without a single support in the world. And if some other love should come to her she would lack all the resources of this power which on her return to Paris would facilitate her intimacy with Monsieur de Laléande. Trying to separate her feelings from herself and to examine them as an object, she would say to herself: "I know that he is mediocre and have always known it. That was my first opinion of him. It has not changed. Since then emotion has intervened but without, for all that, altering my opinion. He is nothing at all and it is for this nonentity I live. I live for Jacques de Laléande." But as soon as she had said his name, by an involuntary association, this time unanalyzed, she could see him again, and felt such contentment and such pain that she knew that it did not matter what a nonentity he really was, since he gave her the sensation of joys and sorrows compared to which others were as nothing. And although she realized that when she came to know him better all this would disappear, this mirage still constituted all the reality of her pain and voluptuous pleasure. A phrase from *Die Meistersinger* she had heard that evening at the Princess A—'s had the power of bringing him vividly back to her (*Dem Vogel der heut sang dem war der Schnabel hold gewachsen*). Unconsciously it had become for her the leitmotiv of Monsieur de Laléande, and, hearing it one day at a concert in Trouville, she had burst into tears. From time to time, not too often, for fear of mitigating the effect, she would lock herself in her room and, sitting at the piano (she had had it brought for no other purpose), would begin to play, closing her eyes to see him the more clearly. It was her sole intoxicating joy that ended in disillusionment, the opium she craved. Sometimes stopping to listen to the flow of her sorrow, as one leans over a spring to hear the sweet and ceaseless lamentation of the water, and thinking of the atrocious alternatives before her: either future shame and the despair of those dear to her or (if she did not yield) her own eternal sorrow—she would revile herself for having so artfully measured the doses of pleasure and pain of her love, which she had been powerless to reject at once as an invidious poison, or later to cure. Above all she reviled her eyes, or perhaps even before them her sense of curiosity and of coquetry which had made them open like flowers to tempt the young man, and had then exposed her to Monsieur de Laléande's own glances as sure as arrows and more invincibly sweet than shots of morphine. She reviled her imagination too. So tenderly had she nurtured it that she sometimes wondered if it alone had not given birth to this love which now tyrannized over its mother and tortured her. She reviled her ingenuity which had so cleverly, so well, and so ill, contrived so many romances for their meeting that their hopeless impossibility had perhaps bound her even more irrevocably to their hero; reviled the uprightness and the delicacy of her heart which would, if she should give herself, poison with remorse and shame all the joys of her guilty love; reviled her will, so impetuous, so headstrong, so bold in leaping over obstacles when her desires drove her toward an impossible goal, so weak, so soft, so broken, not only when they had to be denied, but when some other emotion seized and carried her away. Finally she reviled her mind in its divinest form, that supreme gift she had received and which is given every imaginable name without the true one ever being found—poet's intuition, ecstasy of the believer, profound sense of nature and of music—which had set up before her love infinite heights and horizons, had let it bathe in the supernatural light of her love's own charm and had, in return, lent to her love something of itself, had interested in this love, associated and confounded with it all its deepest and most secret inner life, had consecrated to it, like the treasures of the church to the Madonna, all the most precious gems of her imagination and her heart, which, in the evening or on the water, she would hear lamenting, whose melancholy and her own, at never seeing him now, were sisters; she reviled that inexpressible feeling of the mystery of things, when our spirit loses itself in the radiance of beauty like that of the sun when it sinks into the sea, for having deepened her love, for having immaterialized, broadened, infinitized it without, for all that, making it less agonizing, for as Baudelaire says (speaking of the end of autumn days), "there are certain delicious sensations which are no less intense for being vague; and there is no sharper point than that of infinity."

5

. . . and was consumed from the rising of the Sun on the seaweed by the shore, keeping in the depths of his heart like an arrow in the liver, the burning wound of the great Kypris.

THEOCRITUS: *The Cyclops*

I have just come across Madame de Breyves again here at Trouville. I have known her in happier hours. Nothing can cure her. If only she loved Monsieur de Laléande because he was handsome or because he was witty, one could hope to find a handsomer and a wittier young man to distract her. If it were his kindness or his love for her that had attracted her, someone else might try loving her with greater fidelity. But Monsieur de Laléande is neither handsome nor intelligent, has had no opportunity of proving whether he is tender or brutal, fickle or faithful. It is then really himself she loves, not his merits nor his charms, which can be found to as high a degree in others; it is really himself she loves in spite of his imperfections, in spite of his mediocrity; therefore, in spite of everything, she is doomed to love him. *Himself*, does she know what that is, except that it is something that has caused her such shudders of desolation or felicity that the rest of her life has counted for nothing, nothing else has mattered? The most beautiful physiognomy, the most original intelligence would not have that particular and mysterious essence, so unique that no human being will ever find his exact double in all the infinitude of worlds, in the whole eternity of time. If it hadn't been for Genevieve de Buivres, who innocently insisted on her going to Madame A—'s, all this would not have happened. Caught by circumstances and imprisoned, she is the victim of an ill for which there is no remedy, because it is without a reason. Certainly Monsieur de Laléande, who is probably leading a very banal life on the beach at Biarritz, indulging in harmless dreams, would be very much astonished if he knew of this other existence of his, so miraculously intense that it subordinates everything to itself, annihilates everything that is not itself, if he knew that in Madame de Breyves' soul he enjoyed an existence as continuous as his own personal existence, manifested just as effectively in actions, differing only in its heightened consciousness, less intermittent, more abundant. How surprised he would be if he knew that he, ordinarily so little sought after in his fleshly guise, is an object of interest wherever Madame de Breyves goes, among the most highly gifted people, in the most exclusive drawing rooms, amid scenery quite sufficient in itself, and that this woman, so popular everywhere, has not a thought, not a feeling, not an attention for anything but the recollection of this intruder before whom everything else fades, as though he alone were a real person and the persons present as vain as memories or shadows.

Whether Madame de Breyves takes a walk with a poet or lunches with an archduchess, whether she is alone and reading or talking with a cherished friend, whether she rides horseback or sleeps, the name, the image of Monsieur de Laléande is always over her, deliciously, cruelly, inevitably as the sky is over our heads. She has even reached the point, she who always detested Biarritz, where she finds in everything connected with that city a touching and painful charm. She is preoccupied with the people who are there, or those who are about to go and who will see him, perhaps, without knowing it, who will live with him without joy. She bears them no grudge and, without daring to give them any messages, questions them ceaselessly, wondering sometimes how, hearing her talk continually about all the things surrounding her secret, no one has guessed it. A huge photograph of Biarritz is one of the only ornaments in her room. She imagines that one of the strollers in it looks like Monsieur de Laléande. If she knew the cheap music he liked, those despised songs would without a doubt soon take the place, on her piano and in her heart, of the symphonies of Beethoven and the operas of Wagner, both because they have lowered her standards and because of the charm that he, from whom all charm and all sorrow now come, casts over them. Sometimes the image of this man whom she has seen twice only, and then only for an instant, who occupies such a tiny place in the exterior events of her life but in her heart and in her mind one so exorbitant that it absorbs them altogether, grows blurred before the tired eyes of her memory. She no longer sees him, cannot remember his features, his form, has almost forgotten even his eyes. Yet this image is all she has of him. She is beside herself at the thought that she might lose it, that her desire—which it is true tortures her but which is now her whole self, in which she has taken refuge after fleeing all the rest, to which she clings as one clings to one's own conservation, one's life, good or bad—might vanish and that he would leave her with nothing but the uneasiness and desolation of a dream, no longer knowing the object that has caused them, would no longer see him even in her mind in which she could no longer cherish him. Then suddenly, after the momentary blurring of her inner vision, his image returns. Her sorrow can begin again, and it is now almost a joy.

How will Madame de Breyves endure her return to Paris from which, until January, he will still be absent? What will she do from now until then? What will she do—what will he do—afterwards?

A dozen times I have been on the point of going to Biarritz to bring back Monsieur de Laléande. The consequences might well be terrible, but speculation is futile, since she will not hear of it. But I am desolate, seeing her little temples beaten from within, seeing her shattered by the blows without surcease of this inexplicable passion. Her whole life follows its rhythm in an anguished mode. Often she imagines that he will come to Trouville, come up to her, tell her that he loves her. She sees him; his eyes shine. He speaks to her in that colorless voice of dream which prevents our believing, while all the time forcing us to listen. It is he. He speaks the words that intoxicate even though we hear them only in dreams, when we see, radiant and touching, the divine and confident smile of two destinies uniting. And then almost at once she is awakened by the feeling that the two worlds, the world of reality and the world of her desire, are parallel, that it is as impossible for them ever to meet as a shadow the body that projected it. Then, remembering that moment by the cloakroom when her elbow rubbed his elbow, when he offered her that body which, if she had wished, if she had known, she might now be clasping to her own and which is now far away, perhaps forever, she feels cries of despair and revolt rising in her from all sides, like those one hears on sinking ships. If, sometimes, walking along the beach or in the woods, she lets the pleasure of contemplation or of reverie, or even a sweet odor, or a song brought from a distance and muffled by the breeze, gently take possession of her, make her for an instant forget her pain, all at once she feels a terrible blow and a wound in her heart—and above the waves, higher than the leaves, in the misty horizon of woods or sea, she catches sight of the vague image of her invisible and ever-present conqueror, his eyes shining through the clouds, as on the day when he offered himself to her, and sees him vanish with the quiver from which he has taken and let fly another arrow.

Translated by Louise Varese

PROUST: *The Melancholy Summer of Madame de Breyves*

1. *What are some of the unconventional elements of this love story?*

2. *What impels Madame de Breyves to flirt with a man she regards as ugly and vulgar-looking?*

3. *Is Madame de Breyves wrong not to pursue her loved one further? Would it be possible for her to do so? Does she really wish to do so any longer? Why?*

4. *According to Proust, does love convey pleasure or pain?* (*The story is taken from a volume called* Pleasures *and* Days.) *Can the situation in this story be regarded as a symbol of Proust's view of the entire world?*

Does this view have anything in common with that expressed in Mann's "Little Lizzie"?

5. In his great novel sequence, Remembrance of Things Past, *Proust is profoundly interested in memory association. We recapture and preserve the precious past, he suggests, not by any conscious mental effort, but through the accidental stimulus of an odor, a musical phrase, a movement of the body, a flavor upon the tongue. In this early story, do you see any evidence of this belief taking form?*

6. *Joseph Wood Krutch says of Proust: "His life was a retirement, step by step, from life; a penetration, step by step, into that particular world of art which was his." In what way does Madame de Breyves' existence foreshadow Proust's?*

7. *At the beginning of Part 5, a first-person narrator suddenly appears. What significance do you draw from the shift from third person to first? Who has been telling the story for the first four parts? Compare Proust's technique of narration with James's. (Proust's great novel* Remembrance *is narrated entirely in the first person, but the "I" of the narrative is a man of many selves: he is the fictionalized Marcel; in part Swann, the man of fashion; Bergotte, the man of letters; Bloch, the Jew; and others.)*

Thomas Mann

LITTLE LIZZY

Perhaps the foremost German writer of his generation, Thomas Mann was born in Lübeck, Germany, in 1875, and died in Zurich on August 12, 1955. He gained early recognition with the publication of Buddenbrooks *in 1900, when he was only twenty-five, and then for the next fifty-five years, he remained a prolific author of stories and long philosophical novels. The most famous stories are "Tonio Kröger," "Death in Venice," and "Mario and the Magician." The* Magic Mountain, *which helped him win the Nobel Prize for Literature in 1929, gave him an international reputation after its appearance in 1924. In the decade from 1933-43, Mann wrote a tetralogy based on the Biblical story of Joseph. In 1948, there appeared* Dr. Faustus, *a deeply ambitious novel which repeats in symbolic form many of Mann's major themes. "Little Lizzy," while early in Mann's career—it predates* Buddenbrooks—*nevertheless contains the dominant note of sadism and grotesqueness which are never far from his most significant work.*

ဥ❧

THERE are marriages which the imagination, even the most practiced literary one, cannot conceive. You must just accept them, as you do in the theater when you see the ancient and doddering married to the beautiful and gay, as the given premises on which the farce is mechanically built up.

Yes, the wife of Jacoby the lawyer was lovely and young, a woman of unusual charm. Some years—shall we say thirty years?—ago, she had been christened with the names of Anna, Margarete, Rosa, Amalie; but the name she went by was always Amra, composed of the initials of her four real ones; it suited to perfection her somewhat exotic personality. Her soft, heavy hair, which she wore parted on one side and brushed straight back above her ears from the narrow temples, had only the darkness of the glossy chestnut; but her skin displayed the dull, dark sallowness of the south and clothed a form which southern suns must have ripened. Her slow, voluptuous indolent presence suggested the harem; each sensuous, lazy movement of her body strengthened the impression that with her the head was entirely subordinate to the heart. She needed only to have looked at you once, with her artless brown eyes, lifting her brows in the pathetically narrow forehead, horizontally, in a quaint way she had, for you to be certain of that. But she herself was not so simple as not to know it too. Quite simply, she avoided exposing herself, she spoke seldom and little—and what is there to say against a woman who is both beautiful and silent? Yes, the word "simple" is probably the last which should be applied to her. Her glance was artless; but also it had a kind of luxurious cunning—you could see that she was not dull, also that she might be a mischief-maker. In profile her nose was rather too thick; but her full, large mouth was utterly lovely, if also lacking in any expression save sensuality.

This disturbing phenomenon was the wife of Jacoby the lawyer, a man of forty. Whoever looked at him was bound to be amazed at the fact. He was stout, Jacoby the lawyer; but stout is not the word, he was a perfect colossus of a man! His legs, in their columnar clumsiness and the slate-gray trousers he always wore, reminded one of an elephant's. His round, fat-upholstered back was that of a bear; and over the vast round of his belly his funny little gray jacket was held by a single button strained so tight that when it was unbuttoned the jacket came wide open with a pop. Scarcely anything which could be called a neck united this huge torso with the little head atop. The head had narrow watery eyes, a squabby nose, and a wee mouth between cheeks drooping with fullness. The upper lip and the round head were covered with harsh, scanty, light-colored bristles that showed the naked skin, as on an overfed dog. There was no doubt that Jacoby's fatness was not of a healthy kind. His gigantic body, tall as well as stout, was not muscular, but flabby. The blood would sometimes rush to his puffy face, then ebb away leaving it of a yellowish pallor; the mouth would be drawn and sour.

Jacoby's practice was a limited one; but he was well-to-do, partly from his wife's side; and the childless pair lived in a comfortable apartment in the Kaiserstrasse and entertained a good deal. This must have been Frau Amra's taste, for it is unthinkable that the lawyer could have cared for it; he participated with an enthusiasm of a peculiarly painful kind. This fat man's character was the oddest in the world. No human being could have been politer, more accommodating, more complaisant than he. But you unconsciously knew that this over-obligingness was somehow forced, that its true source was an inward insecurity and cowardice—the impression it gave was not very pleasant. A man who despises himself is a very ugly sight; worse still when vanity combines with his cowardice to make him wish to please. This was the case, I should say, with Jacoby: his obsequiousness was almost crawling, it went beyond the bounds of personal decency. He was quite capable of saying to a lady as he escorted her to table: "My dear lady, I am a disgusting creature, but will you do me the honor?" No humor would be mingled with the remark; it was simply cloying, bitter, self-tortured —in a word, disgusting, as he said.

The following once actually happened: the lawyer was taking a walk, and a clumsy porter with a hand-cart ran over his foot. Too late the man stopped his cart and turned round—whereupon Jacoby, quite pale and dazed, his cheeks shaking up and down, took off his hat and stuttered: "I b-beg your pardon." A thing like that is infuriating. But this extraordinary colossus seemed perpetually to suffer from a plague of conscience. When he took a walk with his wife on the Lerchenberg, the Corso of the little city, he would roll his eyes round at Amra, walking with her wonderful elastic gait at his side, and bow so anxiously, diligently, and zealously in all directions that he seemed to be begging pardon of all the lieutenants they met for being in unworthy possession of such a beautiful wife. His mouth had a pathetically ingratiating expression, as though he wanted to disarm their scorn.

I have already hinted that the reason why Amra married Jacoby is unfathomable. As for him, he was in love with her; ardently, as people of his physical make-up seldom are, and with such anxious humility as fitted the rest of his character. Sometimes, late in the evening, he would enter their large sleeping-chamber with its high windows and flowered hangings—softly, so softly that there was no sound, only the slow shaking of floor and furniture. He would come up to Amra's massive bed, where she already lay, kneel down, and with infinite caution take her hand. She would lift her brows in a level line, in the quaint way she had, and look at her husband, abject before her in the dim light, with a look of malice and sensuality combined. With his puffy, trembling hands he would softly stroke back the sleeve and press his tragic fat face into the soft brown flesh of her wrist, where little blue veins stood out. And he would speak to her, in a shaking, half-smothered voice, as a sensible man in everyday life never speaks:

"Amra, my dear Amra! I am not disturbing you? You were not asleep yet? Dear God! I have been thinking all day how beautiful you are and how much I love you. I beg you to listen, for it is so very hard to express what I feel: I love you so much that sometimes my heart contracts and I do not know where to turn. I love you beyond my strength. You do not understand that, I know; but you believe it, and you must say, just one single time, that you are a little grateful to me. For, you see, such a love as mine to you is precious, it has its value in this life of ours. And that you will never betray or deceive me, even if you cannot love me, just out of gratitude for this love. I have come to you to beg you, as seriously, as fervently as I can . . ." here the lawyer's speech would be dissolved in sobs, in low, bitter weeping, as he knelt. Amra would feel moved; she would stroke her husband's bristles and say over and over, in the soothing, contemptuous singsong one uses to a dog who comes to lick one's feet: "Yes, yes, good doggy, good doggy!"

And this behavior of Amra's was certainly not that of a moral woman. For to relieve my mind of the truth which I have so far withheld, she did already deceive her husband; she betrayed him for the embraces of a gentleman named Alfred Läutner, a gifted young musician, who at twenty-seven had made himself a small reputation with amusing little compositions. He was a slim young chap with a provocative face, a flowing blond mane, and a sunny smile in his eyes, of which he was quite aware. He belonged to the present-day race of small artists, who do not demand the utmost of themselves, whose first requirement is to be jolly and happy, who employ their pleasing little talents to heighten their personal charms. It pleases them to play in society the rôle of the naïve genius. Consciously childlike, entirely unmoral and unscrupulous, merry and self-satisfied as they are, and healthy enough to enjoy even their disorders, they are agreeable even in their vanity, so long as that has not been wounded. But woe to these wretched little poseurs when serious misfortune befalls them, with which there is no coquetting, and when they can no longer be pleasant in their own eyes. They will not know how to be wretched decently and in order, they do not know how to attack the problem of suffering. They will be destroyed. All that is a story in itself. But Herr Alfred Läutner wrote pretty things, mostly waltzes and mazurkas. They would have been rather too gay and popular to be considered music as I understand it, if each of them had not contained a passage of some originality, a modulation, a harmonic phrasing, some sort of bold effect that betrayed wit and invention, which was evidently the point of the whole and which made it interesting to genuine musicians. Often these two single measures would have a strange plaintive, melancholy tone which would come out abruptly in the midst of a piece of dance-music and as suddenly be gone.

Amra Jacoby was on fire with guilty passion for this young man, and as for him he had not enough moral fibre to resist her seductions. They met here, they met there, and for some years an immoral relation had subsisted between them, known to the whole town, who laughed at it behind the lawyer's back. But what did he think? Amra was not sensitive enough to betray herself on account of a guilty conscience, so we must take it as certain that, however the lawyer's heart, he could cherish no definite suspicions.

Spring had come, rejoicing all hearts; and Amra conceived the most charming idea.

"Christian," said she—Jacoby's name was Christian—"let us give a party, a beer party to celebrate the new beer—of course quite simple, but let's have a lot of people."

"Certainly," said the lawyer, "but could we not have it a little later?"

To which Amra made no reply, having passed on to the consideration of details.

"It will be so large that we cannot have it here, we must hire a place, some sort of outdoor restaurant where there is plenty of room and fresh air. You see that, of course. The place I am thinking of is Wendelin's big hall at the foot of the Lerchenberg. The hall is independent of the restaurant and brewery, connected by a passage only. We can decorate it for the occasion and set up long tables, drink our bocks, and dance—we must have music and even

perhaps some sort of entertainment. There is a little stage, as I happen to know, that makes it very suitable. It will be a very original
party and no end to fun."

The lawyer's face had gone a pale yellow as she spoke, and the
corners of his mouth went down. He said:

"My dear Amra! How delightful it will be! I can leave it all to
you, you are so clever. Make any arrangements you like."

And Amra made her arrangements. She took counsel of various
ladies and gentlemen, she went in person to hire the hall, she even
formed a committee of people who were invited or who volun-
teered to co-operate in the entertainment. These were exclusively
men, except for the wife of Herr Hildebrandt, an actor at the
Hoftheater, who was herself a singer. Then there was Herr Hildebrandt, an Assessor Witznagel, a young painter, Alfred Läutner
the musician, and some students brought in by Herr Witznagel,
who were to do Negro dances.

A week after Amra had made her plan, this committee met in
Amra's drawing-room in the Kaiserstrasse—a small crowded, over-
heated room, with a heavy carpet, a sofa with quantities of cushions, a fan table, English leather chairs, and a splay-legged mahogany table with a velvet cover, upon which rested several large
illustrated morocco-bound volumes. There was a fireplace too, with
a small fire still burning, and on the marble chimney-top were
plates of dainty sandwiches, glasses, and two decanters of sherry.
Amra reclined in one corner of the sofa under the fan palm, with
her legs crossed. She had the beauty of a warm summer night. A
thin blouse of light-colored silk covered her bosom, but her skirt
was of heavy dark stuff embroidered with large flowers. Sometimes
she put up one hand to brush back the chestnut hair from her narrow forehead. Frau Hildebrandt sat beside her on the sofa; she had
red hair and wore riding clothes. Opposite the two all the gentlemen formed a semicircle—among them Jacoby himself, in the lowest chair he could find. He looked unutterably wretched, kept
drawing a long breath and swallowing as though struggling against
increasing nausea. Herr Alfred Läutner was in tennis clothes—he
would not take a chair, but leaned decoratively against the chimney-piece, saying merrily that he could not sit still so long.

Herr Hildebrandt talked sonorously about English songs. He

was a most respectable gentleman, in a black suit, with a Roman head and an assured manner—in short a proper actor for a court theater, cultured, knowledgeable, and with enlightened tastes. He liked to hold forth in condemnation of Ibsen, Zola, and Tolstoi, all of whom had the same objectionable aims. But today he was benignly interested in the small affair under discussion.

"Do you know that priceless song 'That's Maria!'?" he asked. "Perhaps it is a little racy—but very effective. And then" so-and-so —he suggested other songs, upon which they came to an agreement and Frau Hildebrandt said that she would sing them. The young painter, who had sloping shoulders and a very blond beard, was to give a burlesque conjuring turn. Herr Hildebrandt offered to impersonate various famous characters. In short, everything was developing nicely, the programme was apparently arranged, when Assessor Witznagel, who had command of fluent gesture and a good many duelling scars, suddenly took the word.

"All very well, ladies and gentlemen, it looks like being most amusing. But if I may say so, it still lacks something; it wants some kind of high spot, a climax as it were, something a bit startling, perhaps, to round the thing off. I leave it to you, I have nothing particular in mind, I only think . . ."

"That is true enough!" Alfred Läutner's tenor voice came from the chimney-piece where he leaned. "Witznagel is right. We need a climax. Let us put our heads together!" He settled his red belt and looked engagingly about him.

"Well, if we do not consider the famous characters as the high spot," said Herr Hildebrandt. Everybody agreed with the Assessor. Something piquant was wanted for the principal number. Even Jacoby nodded, and murmured: "Yes, yes, something jolly and striking. . . ." They all reflected.

At the end of a minute's pause, which was broken only by stifled exclamations, an extraordinary thing happened. Amra was sitting reclined among the cushions, gnawing as busily as a mouse at the pointed nail of her little finger. She had a very odd look on her face: a vacant, almost an irresponsible smile, which betrayed a sensuality both tormented and cruel. Her eyes, very bright and wide, turned slowly to the chimney-piece, where for a second they met the musician's. Then suddenly she jerked her whole body to one side as she sat, in the direction of her husband. With both hands in her lap she stared into his face with an avid and clinging gaze, her own growing visibly paler, and said in her rich, slow voice:

"Christian, suppose you come on at the end as a *chanteuse*, in a red satin baby frock, and do a dance."

The effect of these few words was tremendous. The young painter essayed to laugh good-humoredly; Herr Hildebrandt, stony-faced, brushed a crumb from his sleeve; his wife colored up, a rare thing for her; the students coughed and used their handkerchiefs loudly; and Herr Assessor Witznagel simply left the field and got himself a sandwich. The lawyer sat huddled on his little chair, yellow in the face, with a terrified smile. He looked all around the circle, and stammered:

"But, by God . . . I—I—I am not up to—not that I—I beg pardon, but . . ."

Alfred Läutner had lost his insouciant expression; he even seemed to have reddened a little, and he thrust out his neck to peer searchingly into Amra's face. He looked puzzled and upset.

But she, Amra, holding the same persuasive pose, went on with the same impressiveness:

"And you must sing, too, Christian, a song which Herr Läutner shall compose, and he can accompany you on the piano. We could not have a better or more effective climax."

There was a pause, an oppressive pause. Then this extraordinary thing happened, that Herr Läutner, as it were seized upon and carried away by his excitement, took a step forward and his voice fairly tembled with enthusiasm as he said:

"Herr Jacoby, that is a priceless idea, and I am more than ready to compose something. You must have a dance and song, anything else is unthinkable as a wind-up to our affair. You will see, it will be the best thing I have ever written or ever shall write. In a red stain baby frock. Oh, your wife is an artist, only an artist could have hit upon the idea! Do say yes, I beg of you. I will do my part, you will see, it will be an achievement."

Here the circle broke up and the meeting became lively. Out of politeness, or out of malice, the company began to storm the lawyer with entreaties—Frau Hildebrandt went so far as to say, quite loudly, in her Brünnhilde voice:

"Herr Jacoby, after all, you are such a jolly and entertaining man!"

But the lawyer had pulled himself together and spoke, a little yellow, but with a strong effort at resolution:

"But listen to me, ladies and gentlemen—what can I say to you? It isn't my line, believe me. I have no comic gift, and besides . . . in short, no, it is quite impossible, alas!"

He stuck obstinately to his refusal, and Amra no longer insisted, but sat still with her absent look. Herr Läutner was silent too, staring in deep abstraction at a pattern in the rug. Herr Hildebrandt changed the subject, and presently the committee meeting broke up without coming to a final decision about the "climax."

On the evening of the same day Amra had gone to bed and was lying there with her eyes wide open; her husband came lumbering into the bedroom, drew a chair up beside the bed, dropped into it, and said, in a low, hesitating voice:

"Listen, Amra; to be quite frank, I am feeling very disturbed. I refused them today—I did not mean to be offensive—goodness knows I did not mean that. Or do you seriously feel that—I beg you to tell me."

Amra was silent for a moment, while her brows rose slowly. Then she shrugged her shoulders and said:

"I do not know, my dear friend, how to answer you. You behaved in a way I should not have expected from you. You were unfriendly, you refused to support our enterprise in a way which they flatteringly considered to be indispensable to it. To put it mildly, you disappointed everybody and upset the whole company with your rude lack of compliance. Whereas it was your duty as host—"

The lawyer hung his head and sighed heavily. He said:

"Believe me, Amra, I had no intention to be disobliging. I do not like to offend anybody; if I have behaved badly I am ready to make amends. It is only a joke, after all, an innocent little dressing-up— why not? I will not upset the whole affair, I am ready to . . ."

The following afternoon Amra went out again to "make preparations." She drove to Number 78 Holzstrasse and went up to the second storey, where she had an appointment. And when she lay relaxed by the expression of her love she pressed her lover's head passionately to her breast and whispered:

"Write it for four hands. We will accompany him together while he sings and dances. I will see to the costume myself."

And an extraordinary shiver, a suppressed and spasmodic burst of laughter went through the limbs of both.

For anyone who wants to give a large party out of doors Herr Wendelin's place on the slope of the Lerchenberg is to be recommended. You enter it from the pretty suburban street through a tall trellised gateway and pass into the parklike garden, in the center of which stands a large hall, connected only by a narrow passage with restaurant, kitchen, and brewery. It is a large, brightly painted wooden hall, in an amusing mixture of Chinese and Renaissance styles. It has folding doors which stand open in good weather to admit the woodland air, and it will hold a great many people.

On this evening as the carriages rolled up they were greeted from afar by the gleam of colored lights. The whole gateway, the trees, and the hall itself were set thick with lanterns, while the interior made an entrancing sight. Heavy garlands were draped across the ceiling and studded with paper lanterns. Hosts of electric lights hung among the decorations of the walls, which consisted of pine boughs, flags, and artificial flowers; the whole hall was brilliantly lighted. The stage had foliage plants grouped on either side, and a red curtain with a painted design of a presiding genius hovering in the air. A long row of decorated tables ran almost the whole length of the hall. And at these tables the guests of Attorney Jacoby were doing themselves well on cold roast veal and bock beer. There were certainly more than a hundred and fifty people: officers, lawyers, business men, artists, upper officials, with their wives and daughters. They were quite simply dressed, in black coats and light spring toilettes, for this was a jolly, informal occasion. The gentlemen carried their mugs in person to the big casks against one of the walls; the spacious, festive, brightly lighted room was filled with a heavy sweetish atmosphere of evergreen boughs, flowers, beer, food, and human beings; and there was a clatter and buzz of laughter and talk—the loud, simple talk and the high, good-natured, unrestrained, carefree laughter of the sort of people there assembled.

The attorney sat shapeless and helpless at one end of the table, near the stage. He drank little and now and then addressed a labored remark to his neighbor, Frau Regierungsrat Havermann. He breathed offensively, the corners of his mouth hung down, he stared fixedly with his bulging watery eyes into the lively scene, with a sort of melancholy remoteness, as though there resided in all this noisy merriment something inexpressively painful and perplexing.

Large fruit tarts were now being handed round for the company to cut from; they drank sweet wine with these, and the time for the speeches arrived. Herr Hildebrandt celebrated the new brew in a speech almost entirely composed of classical quotations, even Greek. Herr Witznagel, with florid gestures and ingenious turns of phrase, toasted the ladies, taking a handful of flowers from the nearest vase and comparing each flower to some feminine charm. Amra Jacoby, who sat opposite him in a pale-yellow silk frock, he called "a lovelier sister of the Maréchal Niel."

Then she nodded meaningfully to her husband, brushing back her hair from her forehead; whereupon the fat man arose and almost ruined the whole atmosphere by stammering a few words with painful effort, smiling a repulsive smile. Some half-hearted bravos rewarded him, then there was an oppressive pause, after which jollity resumed its sway. All smoking, all a little elevated by drink, they rose from table and with their own hands and a great deal of noise removed the tables from the hall to make way for the dancing.

It was after eleven and high spirits reigned supreme. Some of the guests streamed out into the brightly lighted garden to get the fresh air; others stood about the hall in groups, smoking, chatting, drawing beer from the kegs, and drinking it standing. Then a loud trumpet call sounded from the stage, summoning everybody to the entertainment. The band arrived and took its place before the curtains; rows of chairs were put in place and red programmes distributed on them; the gentlemen ranged themselves along the walls. There was an expectant hush.

The band played a noisy overture, and the curtains parted to reveal a row of Negroes horrifying to behold in their barbaric costumes and their blood-red lips, gnashing their teeth and emitting savage yells.

Certainly the entertainment was the crowning success of Amra's party. As it went on, the applause grew more and more enthusiastic. Frau Hildebrandt came on in a powdered wig, pounded with a shepherdess' crook on the floor and sang—in too large a voice—

"That's Maria!" A conjuror in a dress coat covered with orders performed the most amazing feats; Herr Hildebrandt impersonated Goethe, Bismarck, and Napoleon in an amazingly lifelike manner; and a newspaper editor, Dr. Wiesensprung, improvised a humorous lecture which had as its theme bock beer and its social significance. And now the suspense reached its height, for it was time for the last, the mysterious number which appeared on the programme framed in a laurel wreath and was entitled: *"Little Lizzy*. Song and Dance. Music by Alfred Läutner."

A movement swept through the hall, and people's eyes met as the band sat down at their instruments and Alfred Läutner came from the doorway where he had been lounging with a cigarette between his pouting lips to take his place beside Amra Jacoby at the piano, which stood in the center of the stage in front of the curtains. Herr Läutner's face was flushed and he turned over his manuscript score nervously; Amra for her part was rather pale. She leaned one arm on the back of her chair and looked loweringly at the audience. The bell rang, the pianist played a few bars of an insignificant accompaniment, the curtains parted, little Lizzy appeared.

The whole audience stiffened with amazement as that tragic and bedizened bulk shambled with a sort of bear-dance into view. It was Jacoby. A wide, shapeless garment of crimson satin, without folds, fell to his feet; it was cut out above to make a repulsive display of the fat neck, stippled with white powder. The sleeves consisted merely of a shoulder puff, but the flabby arms were covered by long lemon-colored gloves; on the head perched a high blond wig with a swaying green feather. And under the wig was a face, a puffy, pasty, unhappy, and desperately mirthful face, with cheeks that shook pathetically up and down and little red-rimmed eyes that strained in anguish towards the floor and saw nothing else at all. The fat man hoisted himself with effort from one leg to the other, while with his hands he either held up his skirts or else weakly raised his index fingers—these two gestures he had and knew no others. In a choked and gasping voice he sang, to the accompaniment of the piano.

The lamentable figure exhaled more than ever a cold breath of anguish. It killed every light-hearted enjoyment and lay like an oppressive weight upon the assembled audience. Horror was in the

depths of all these spellbound eyes, gazing at this pair at the piano
and at that husband there. The monstrous, unspeakable scandal
lasted five long minutes.

Then came a moment which none of those present will forget
as long as they live. Let us picture to ourselves what happened in
that frightful and frightfully involved little instant of time.

You know of course the absurd little jingle called "Lizzy." And
you remember the lines:

> *I can polka until I am dizzy,*
> *I can waltz with the best and beyond,*
> *I'm the popular pet, little Lizzy,*
> *Who makes all the menfolks so fond—*

which form the trivial and unlovely refrain to three longish stan-
zas. Alfred Läutner had composed a new setting to the verses I
have quoted, and it was, as he had said it would be, his masterpiece. He had, that is, brought to its highest pitch his little artifice
of introducing into a fairly vulgar and humorous piece of hackwork
a sudden phrase of genuine creative art. The melody, in C-sharp
major, had been in the first bars rather pretty and perfectly banal.
At the beginning of the refrain the rhythm became livelier and dissonances occurred, which by means of the constant accentuation
of a B-natural made one expect a transition into F-sharp major.
These dissonances went on developing until the word "beyond";
and after the "I'm the" a culmination into F-sharp major should
have followed. Instead of which the most surprising thing happened. That is, through a harsh turn, by means of an inspiration
which was almost a stroke of genius, the key changed to F-major,
and this little interlude which followed, with the use of both pedals
on the long-drawn-out first syllable of the word "Lizzy," was in-
describably, almost gruesomely effective. It was a complete surprise, an abrupt assault on the nerves, it shivered down the back,
it was a miracle, a revelation, it was like a curtain suddenly torn
away to reveal something nude.

And on the F-major chord Attorney Jacoby stopped dancing. He
stood still, he stood as though rooted to the stage with his two fore-
fingers lifted, one a little lower than the other. The word "Lizzy"
stuck in his throat, he was dumb; almost at the same time the accompaniment broke sharp off, and the incredible, absurd, and

ghastly figure stood there frozen, with his head thrust forward like a steer's, staring with inflamed eyes straight before him. He stared into the brightly lighted, decorated, crowded hall, in which, like an exhalation from all these people, the scandal hung and thickened into visibility. He stared at all these upturned faces, foreshortened and distorted by the lighting, into these hundreds of pairs of eyes all directed with the same knowing expression upon himself and the two at the piano. In a frightful stillness, unbroken by the smallest sound, his gaze traveled slowly and uneasily from the pair to the audience, from the audience to the pair, while his eyes widened more and more. Then knowledge seemed to flash across his face, like a sudden rush of blood, making it red as the frock he wore, only to give way to a waxen yellow pallor—and the fat man collapsed, making the platform creak beneath his weight.

For another moment the stillness reigned. Then there came shrieks, hubbub ensued, a few gentlemen took heart to spring upon the platform, among them a young doctor—and the curtains were drawn together.

Amra Jacoby and Alfred Läutner still sat at the piano. They had turned a little away from each other, and he, with his head bent, seemed to be listening to the echo of his F-major chord, while she, with her birdlike brain, had not yet grasped the situation, but gazed round her with vacant face.

The young doctor came back presently. He was a little Jewish gentleman with a serious face and a small pointed beard. Some people surrounded him at the door with questions—to which he replied with a shrug of the shoulders and the words:

"All over."

Translated by H. T. Lowe-Porter

MANN: *Little Lizzy*

1. *What is the theme of the story? How does Mann initially suggest it?*

2. *What is the "personality" of each of the three main characters? How is "personality" related to physique? What is the reason for this connection?*

3. *What is the real reason that Amra wants her husband to perform?*

4. Why does Jacoby go through with the performance? Does he have any choice? What causes his death?

5. Why is Läutner nervous during Jacoby's performance? Why does he add the F-major chord? (See question 2.)

6. Will the relationship between Amra and Läutner continue? What clues are there in the story?

7. Mann's experimentation with musical counterpoint in his fiction is reflected in this story. How does he use music to underline his point? (See question 1.)

8. This story also reflects Mann's interest in pathetic, frustrated, and often freakish persons who lack the ability to cope with life—in other words, with forms of human sickness. Is Jacoby sick? Amra?—Läutner? How? Is sickness a valid subject for literature? Does a writer's interest in sickness mean that he is himself sick and therefore untrustworthy as a commentator on human affairs? Compare this story to Kafka's "The Judgment." How are the two alike? Is the attitude of the author the same toward the protagonist in each story?

Hermann Hesse

WITHIN AND WITHOUT

Though Thomas Mann had eulogized his craft and T. S. Eliot had acknowledged his inspiration (in The Waste Land), *Hermann Hesse was practically a stranger in America before he received the Nobel Prize in 1946. Born in Calw, Württemberg, in 1877, Hesse drifted through a succession of occupations until two novels,* Peter Camenzind (1904) *and* Unser Rad (1905), *established him as a rival to Mann and Musil. Like the author himself, whose quest for peace took him to India in 1911, the characters of his subsequent fiction (especially in his masterpiece,* Steppenwolf (1927), *are sensitive and lonely men searching for harmony in the jungle of the world, fascinated yet perplexed by the dualism of the material and the spiritual in man. It was not until his last great novel,* Magister Ludi (1943), *that the conflict was resolved.*

❧

THERE was once a man by the name of Frederick; he devoted himself to intellectual pursuits and had a wide range of knowledge. But not all knowledge was the same to him, nor was any thought as good as any other: he loved a certain type of thinking, and disdained and abominated the others. What he loved and revered was logic —that so admirable method—and, in general, what he called "science."

"Twice two is four," he used to say. "This I believe; and man must do his thinking on the basis of this truth."

He was not unaware, to be sure, that there were other sorts of thinking and knowledge; but they were not "science," and he held a low opinion of them. Although a freethinker, he was not intolerant of religion. Religion was founded on a tacit agreement among scientists. For several centuries their science had embraced nearly everything that existed on earth and was worth knowing, with the exception of one single province: the human soul. It had become a sort of custom, as time went on, to leave this to religion, and to tolerate its speculations on the soul, though without taking them seriously. Thus Frederick too was tolerant toward religion; but everything he recognized as superstition was profoundly odious and repugnant to him. Alien, uncultured, and retarded peoples might occupy themselves with it; in remote antiquity there might have been mystical or magical thinking; but since the birth of science and logic there was no longer any sense in making use of these outmoded and dubious tools.

So he said and so he thought; and when traces of superstition came to his attention he became angry and felt as if he had been touched by something hostile.

It angered him most of all, however, if he found such traces among his own sort, among educated men who were conversant with the principles of scientific thinking. And nothing was more painful and intolerable to him than that scandalous notion which lately he had sometimes heard expressed and discussed even by men of great culture—that absurd idea that "scientific thinking" was possibly not a supreme, timeless, eternal, foreordained, and unassailable mode of thought, but merely one of many, a transient way of thinking, not impervious to change and downfall. This irreverent, destructive, poisonous notion was abroad—even Frederick could not deny it; it had cropped up here and there as a result of the distress throughout the world brought about by war, revolution, and hunger, like a warning, like a white hand's ghostly writing on a white wall.

The more Frederick suffered from the fact that this idea existed and could so deeply distress him, the more passionately he assailed it and those whom he suspected of secretly believing in it. So far only a very few from among the truly educated had openly and frankly professed their belief in this new doctrine, a doctrine that seemed destined, should it gain in circulation and power, to destroy all spiritual values on earth and call forth chaos. Well, matters had not reached that point yet, and the scattered individuals who openly embraced the idea were still so few in number that they could be considered oddities and crotchety, peculiar fellows. But a drop of the poison, an emanation of that idea, could be perceived first on this side, then on that. Among the people and the half-educated no end of new doctrines could be found anyway, esoteric doctrines, sects, and disciplineships; the world was full of them;

everywhere one could scent out superstition, mysticism, spiritualistic cults, and other mysterious forces, which it was really necessary to combat, but to which science, as if from a private feeling of weakness, had for the present given free rein.

One day Frederick went to the house of one of his friends, with whom he had often studied. It so happened that he had not seen this friend for some time. While he was climbing the stairs of the house he tried to recall when and where it was that he had last been in his friend's company; but much as he could pride himself on his good memory for other things he could not remember. Because of this he fell imperceptibly into a certain vexation and ill humor, from which, as he stood before his friend's door, he was obliged forcibly to free himself.

Hardly had he greeted Erwin, his friend, when he noticed on his genial countenance a certain, as it were forbearing, smile, which it seemed to him he had never seen there before. And hardly had he seen this smile, which despite its friendliness he at once felt to be somehow mocking or hostile, when he immediately remembered what he had just been searching his memory for in vain—his last previous meeting with Erwin. He remembered that they had parted then without having quarreled, to be sure, but yet with a sense of inner discord and dissatisfaction, because Erwin, as it had seemed to him, had given far too little support to his attacks at that time on the realm of superstition.

It was strange. How could he have forgotten that entirely? And now he also knew that this was his only reason for not having sought out his friend for so long, merely this dissatisfaction, and that he had known this all the time, although he had invented for himself a host of other excuses for his repeated postponement of this visit.

Now they confronted one another; and it seemed to Frederick as if the little rift of that day had meantime tremendously widened. He felt that in this moment something was lacking between him and Erwin that had always been there before, an aura of solidarity, of spontaneous understanding—indeed, even of affection. Instead of these there was a vacuum. They greeted each other; spoke of the weather, their acquaintances, their health; and—God knows why! with every word Frederick had the disquieting sensation that he was not quite understanding his friend, that his friend did not really know him, that his words were missing their mark, that they could find no common ground for a real conversation. Moreover Erwin still had that friendly smile on his face, which Frederick was beginning almost to hate.

During a pause in the laborious conversation Frederick looked about the studio he knew so well and saw, pinned loosely on the wall, a sheet of paper. This sight moved him strangely and awakened ancient memories; for he recalled that, long ago in their student years, this had been a habit of Erwin's, a way he sometimes chose of keeping a thinker's saying or a poet's verse fresh in his mind. He stood up and went to the wall to read the paper.

There, in Erwin's beautiful script, he read the words: "Nothing is without, nothing is within; for what is without is within."

Blanching, he stood motionless for a moment. There it was! There he stood face to face with what he feared! At another time he would have let this leaf of paper pass, would have tolerated it charitably as a whim, as a harmless foible to which anyone was entitled, perhaps as a trifling sentimentality calling for indulgence. But now it was different. He felt that these words had not been set down for the sake of a fleeting poetic mood; it was not a vagary that Erwin had returned after so many years to a practice of his youth. What stood written here, as an avowal of his friend's concern at the moment, was mysticism! Erwin was unfaithful!

Slowly he turned to face him, whose smile was again radiant.

"Explain this to me!" he demanded.

Erwin nodded, brimming with friendliness.

"Haven't you ever read this saying?"

"Certainly!" Frederick cried. "Of course I know it. It's mysticism, it's Gnosticism. It may be poetic, but—well, anyway, explain the saying to me, and why's it's hanging on your wall!"

"Gladly," Erwin said. "The saying is a first introduction to an epistemology that I've been going into lately, and which has already brought me much happiness."

Frederick restrained his temper. He asked, "A new epistemology? Is there such a thing? And what is it called?"

"Oh," Erwin answered, "it's only new to me. It's already very old and venerable. It's called magic."

The word had been uttered. Profoundly astonished and startled by so candid a confession, Frederick, with a shudder, felt that he was confronted eye to eye with the arch-enemy, in the person of his friend. He did not know whether he was nearer rage or tears; the bitter feeling of irreparable loss possessed him. For a long time he remained silent.

Then, with a pretended decision in his voice, he began, "So now you want to become a magician?"

"Yes," Erwin replied unhesitatingly.

"A sort of sorcerer's apprentice, eh?"

"Certainly."

A clock could be heard ticking in the adjoining room, it was so quiet.

Then Frederick said, "This means, you know, that you are abandoning all fellowship with serious science, and hence all fellowship with me."

"I hope that is not so," Erwin answered. "But if that's the way it has to be, what else can I do?"

"What else can you do?" Frederick burst out. "Why, break, break once and for all with this childishness, this wretched and contemptible belief in magic! That's what else you can do, if you want to keep my respect."

Erwin smiled a little, although he too no longer seemed cheerful.

"You speak as if," he said, so gently that through his quiet words Frederick's angry voice still seemed to be echoing about the room, "you speak as if that lay within my will, as if I had a choice, Frederick. That is not the case. I have no choice. It was not I that chose magic: magic chose me."

Frederick sighed deeply. "Then goodby," he said wearily, and stood up, without offering to shake hands.

"Not like that!" Erwin cried out. "No, you must not go from me like that. Pretend that one of us is lying on his deathbed—and that is so!—and that we must say farewell."

"But which of us, Erwin, is dying?"

"Today it is probably I, my friend. Whoever wishes to be born anew must be prepared to die."

Once more Frederick went up to the sheet of paper and read the saying about within and without.

"Very well," he said finally. "You are right, it won't do any good to part in anger. I'll do what you wish; I'll pretend that one of us is dying. Before I go I want to make a last request of you."

"I'm glad," Erwin said. "Tell me, what kindness can I show you on our leavetaking?"

"I repeat my first question, and this is also my request: explain this saying to me, as well as you can."

Erwin reflected a moment and then spoke:

"Nothing is without, nothing is within. You know the religious meaning of this: God is everywhere. He is in the spirit, and also in nature. All is divine, because God is all. Formerly this was called pantheism. Then the philosophic meaning: we are used to divorcing the within from the without in our thinking, but this is not necessary. Our spirit is capable of withdrawing behind the limits we have set for it, into the beyond. Beyond the pair of antitheses of which our world consists a new and different knowledge begins. . . . But, my dear friend, I must confess to you—since my thinking has changed there are no longer any unambiguous words and sayings for me: every word has tens and hundreds of meanings. And here what you fear begins—magic."

Frederick wrinkled his brow and was about to interrupt, but Erwin looked at him disarmingly and continued, speaking more distinctly, "Let me give you an example. Take something of mine along with you, any object, and examine it a little from time to time. Soon the principle of the within and the without will reveal one of its many means to you."

He glanced about the room, took a small clay figurine from a wall shelf, and gave it to Frederick, saying:

"Take this with you as my parting gift. When this thing that I am now placing in your hands ceases to be outside you and is within you, come to me again! But if it remains outside you, the way it is now, forever, then this parting of yours from me shall also be forever!"

Frederick wanted to say a great deal more; but Erwin took his hand, pressed it, and bade him farewell with an expression that permitted no further conversation.

Frederick left; descended the stairs (how prodigiously long ago he had climbed them!); went through the streets to his home, the little earthen figure in his hand, perplexed and sick of heart. In front of his house he stopped, shook the fist fiercely for a moment in which he was clutching the figurine, and felt a great urge to smash the ridiculous thing to the ground. He did not do so; he bit his lip and entered the house. Never before had he been so agitated, so tormented by conflicting emotions.

He looked for a place for his friend's gift, and put the figure on top of a bookcase. For the time being it stayed there.

Occasionally, as the days went by, he looked at it, brooding on it and on its origins, and pondering the meaning that this foolish thing was to have for him. It was a small figure of a man or a god or an idol, with two faces, like the Roman god Janus, modeled rather crudely of clay and covered with a burnt and somewhat cracked glaze. The little image looked coarse and insignificant; certainly it was not Roman or Greek workmanship; more likely it was the work of some backward, primitive race in Africa or the South Seas. The two faces, which were exactly alike, bore an apathetic, indolent faintly grinning smile—it was downright ugly the way the little gnome squandered his stupid smile.

Frederick could not get used to the figure. It was totally unpleasant and offensive to him, it got in his way, it disturbed him. The very next day he took it down and put it on the stove, and a few days later moved it to a cupboard. Again and again it got in the path of his vision, as if it were forcing itself upon him; it laughed at him coldly and dull-wittedly, put on airs, demanded attention. After a few weeks he put it in the anteroom, between the photographs of Italy and the trivial little souvenirs which no one ever looked at. Now at least he saw the idol only when he was entering or leaving, and then he passed it quickly, without examining it more closely. But here too the thing still bothered him, though he did not admit this to himself.

With this shard, this two-faced monstrosity, vexation and torment had entered his life.

One day, months later, he returned from a short trip—he undertook such excursions now from time to time, as if something were driving him restlessly about; he entered his house, went through the anteroom, was greeted by the maid, and read the letters waiting for him. But he was ill at ease, as if he had forgotten something important; no book tempted him, no chair was comfortable. He began to rack his mind—what was the cause of this? Had he neglected something important? eaten something unsettling? In reflecting it occurred to him that this disturbing feeling had come over him as he had entered the apartment. He returned to the anteroom and involuntarily his first glance sought the clay figure.

A strange fright went through him when he did not see the idol. It had disappeared. It was missing. Had it walked away on its little crockery legs? Flown away? By magic?

Frederick pulled himself together, and smiled at his nervousness. Then he began quietly to search the whole room. When he found nothing he called the maid. She came, was embarrassed, and admitted at once that she had dropped the thing while cleaning up.

"Where is it?"

It was not there any more. It had seemed so solid, that little thing; she had often had it in her hands; and yet it had shattered to a hundred little pieces and splinters, and could not be fixed. She had taken the fragments to a glazier, who had simply laughed at her; and then she had thrown them away.

Frederick dismissed the maid. He smiled. That was perfectly all right with him. He did not feel bad about the idol, God knows. The abomination was gone; now he would have peace. If only he had knocked the thing to pieces that very first day! What he had suffered in all this time! How sluggishly, strangely, craftily, evilly, satanically that idol had smiled at him! Well, now that it was gone he could admit it to himself: he had feared it, truly and sincerely feared it, this earthen god. Was it not the emblem and symbol of everything that was repugnant and intolerable to him, everything that he had recognized all along as pernicious, inimical, and worthy of suppression—an emblem of all superstitions, all darkness, all coercion of conscience and spirit? Did it not represent that ghastly power that one sometimes felt raging in the bowels of the earth, that distant earthquake, that approaching extinction of culture, that looming chaos? Had not this contemptible figure robbed him of his best friend—nay, not merely robbed, but made of the friend an enemy? Well, now the thing was gone. Vanished. Smashed to pieces. Done for. It was good so; it was much better than if he had destroyed it himself.

So he thought, or said. And he went about his affairs as before.

But it was like a curse. Now, just when he had got more or less used to that ridiculous figure, just when the sight of it in its usual place on the anteroom table had gradually become a bit familiar and unimportant to him, now its absence began to torment him! Yes, he missed it every time he went through that room; all he could see there was the empty spot where it had formerly stood, and emptiness emanated from the spot and filled the room with strangeness.

Bad days and worse nights began for Frederick. He could no longer go through the anteroom without thinking of the idol with the two faces, missing it, and feeling that his thoughts were tethered to it. This became an agonizing compulsion for him. And it was not by any means simply on the occasions when he went through that room that he was gripped by this compulsion—ah, no. Just as emptiness and desolation radiated from the now empty spot on the anteroom table, so this compulsive idea radiated within him, gradually crowded all else aside, rankling and filling him with emptiness and strangeness.

Again and again he pictured the figure with utmost distinctness, just to make it clear to himself how preposterous it was to grieve its loss. He could see it in all its stupid ugliness and barbarity, with its vacuous yet crafty smile, with its two faces—indeed, as if under duress, full of hatred and with his mouth drawn awry, he found himself attempting to reproduce that smile. The question pestered him whether the two faces were really exactly alike. Had not one of them, perhaps only because of a little roughness or a crack in the glaze, had a somewhat different expression? Something quizzical? Something sphinxlike? And how peculiar the color of that glaze had been! Green, and blue, and gray, but also red, were in it—a glaze that he now kept finding often in other objects, in a window's reflection of the sun or in the mirrorings of a wet pavement.

He brooded a great deal on this glaze, at night too. It also struck him what a strange, foreign, ill-sounding, unfamiliar, almost malignant word "glaze" was. He analyzed the word, and once he even reversed the order of its letters. Then it read "ezalg." Now where the devil did this word get its sound from? He knew this word "ezalg," certainly he knew it; moreover, it was an unfriendly and bad word, a word with ugly and disturbing connotations. For a long while he tormented himself with this question. Finally he hit upon it: "ezalg" reminded him of a book that he had bought and read many years ago on a trip, and that had dismayed, plagued, and yet secretly fascinated him; it had been entitled *Princess*

Ezalka. It was like a curse: everything connected with the figurine
—the glaze, the blue, the green, the smile—signified hostility, tormenting and poisoning him. And how very peculiarly *he*, Erwin,
his erstwhile friend, had smiled as he had given the idol into his
hand! How very peculiarly, how very significantly, how very hos-
tily.

Frederick resisted manfully—and on many days not without success—the compulsive trend of his thoughts. He sensed the danger
clearly: he did not want to go insane! No, it were better to die.
Reason was necessary, life was not. And it occurred to him that
perhaps *this* was magic, that Erwin, with the aid of that figure, had
in some way enchanted him, and that he should fall as a sacrifice,
as the defender of reason and science against these dismal powers.
But if this were so, if he could even conceive of that as possible,
then there *was* such a thing as magic, then there *was* sorcery. No,
it were better to die!

A doctor recommended walks and baths; and sometimes, in
search of amusement, he spent an evening at an inn. But it helped
very little. He cursed Erwin; he cursed himself.

One night, as he often did now, he retired early and lay restlessly
awake in bed, unable to sleep. He felt unwell and uneasy. He
wanted to meditate; he wanted to find solace, wanted to speak sentences of some sort to himself, good sentences, comforting, reassur-
ing ones, something with the straightforward serenity and lucidity
of the sentence, "Twice two is four." Nothing came to mind; but, in
a state almost of lightheadedness, he mumbled sounds and sylla-
bles to himself. Gradually words formed on his lips, and several
times, without being sensible of its meaning, he said the same short
sentence to himself, which had somehow taken form in him. He
muttered it to himself, as if it might stupefy him, as if he might
grope his way along it, as along a parapet, to the sleep that eluded
him on the narrow, narrow path that skirted the abyss.

But suddenly, when he spoke somewhat louder, the words he
was mumbling penetrated his consciousness. He knew them: they
were, "Yes, now you are within me!" And instantly he knew. He
knew what they meant—that they referred to the clay idol and
that now, in this gray night hour, he had accurately and exactly
fulfilled the prophecy Erwin had made on that unearthly day, that
now the figure, which he had held contemptuously in his fingers

then, was no longer outside him but within him! "For what is without is within."

Bounding up in a leap, he felt as if transfused with ice and fire. The world reeled about him, the planets stared at him insanely. He threw on some clothes, put on the light, left his house and ran in the middle of the night to Erwin's. There he saw a light burning in the studio window he knew so well; the door to the house was unlocked: everything seemed to be awaiting him. He rushed up the stairs. He walked unsteadily into Erwin's study, supported himself with trembling hands on the table. Erwin sat by the lamp, in its gentle light, contemplative, smiling.

Graciously Erwin arose. "You have come. That is good."

"Have you been expecting me?" Frederick whispered.

"I have been expecting you, as you know, from the moment you left here, taking my little gift with you. Has what I said then happened?"

"It has happened," Frederick said. "The idol is within me. I can't bear it any longer."

"Can I help you?" Erwin asked.

"I don't know. Do as you will. Tell me more of your magic! Tell me how the idol can get out of me again."

Erwin placed his hand on his friend's shoulder. He led him to an armchair and pressed him down in it. Then he spoke cordially to Frederick, smiling in an almost brotherly tone of voice:

"The idol will come out of you again. Have trust in me. Have trust in yourself. You have learned to believe in it. Now learn to love it! It is within you, but it is still dead, it is still a phantom to you. Awaken it, speak to it, question it! For it is you yourself! Do not hate it any longer, do not fear it, do not torment it—how you have tormented this poor idol, who was yet you yourself! How you have tormented yourself!"

"Is this the way to magic?" Frederick asked. He sat deep in the chair, as if he had grown older, and his voice was low.

"This is the way," Erwin replied, "and perhaps you have already taken the most difficult step. You have found by experience: the without can become the within. You have been beyond the pair of antitheses. It seemed hell to you; learn, my friend, it is heaven! For it is heaven that awaits you. Behold, this is magic: to interchange the without and the within, not by compulsion, not in anguish, as you have done it, but freely, voluntarily. Summon up the past, summon up the future: both are in you! Until today you have been the slave of the within. Learn to be its master. That is magic."

Translated by T. K. Brown, III

HESSE: *Within and Without*

1. *What is Hesse attacking in the scientific mind? Is it a valid attack? Compare Hesse's attack here with Lawrence's in "The Man Who Loved Islands."*

2. *Is Frederick right to be incredulous of his friend Erwin's interest in magic? How does Hesse make us share Frederick's disbelief? Is it necessary that we should?*

3. *Discuss the symbolism of the figurine. Why two faces? Why like Janus? Why does Frederick even accept it?*

4. *Why does the figurine—even after it is smashed to fragments— continue to obsess Frederick?*

5. *What happens to Frederick? What experience does he undergo? Can it be precisely explained? How does Hesse consciously avoid precision?*

6. *Does the acceptance of the figurine mean that Frederick must reject the world? What does Hesse mean by the merging of within and without? Is such a merging possible within our daily lives? Is it at all possible within Western society, or practicable only within a society that encourages asceticism and withdrawal?*

7. *Does Hesse's view have any parallels in orthodox religious terms? Why is the figurine clearly not a Christian symbol?*

8. *Compare this story with Dostoyevsky's "The Grand Inquisitor." Can you see the deep influence that Dostoyevsky had on Hesse? In what areas? Would the Frederick of the early part of the story share the attitudes of Dostoyevsky's Inquisitor?*

Robert Musil

A MAN WITHOUT CHARACTER

*Born in 1880 in Klagenfurt, Austria, Robert Musil was educated at
a military academy and then studied engineering and logic. In 1906,
his short novel* Young Torless *brought him critical acclaim, and he
gave up his academic career for writing, later serving as an officer
in the Austrian army in the First World War. In 1933, to escape the
Nazis, he fled to Vienna and then to Switzerland, where he died in
1942. His most famous fiction is the unfinished* The Man Without
Qualities, *which many continental critics have called the greatest
European novel of this century. In "A Man Without Character,"
Musil joins with his contemporaries Thomas Mann and Franz Kafka
in treating ironically the always fascinating theme of man's identity
in a world whose values are ever-changing.*

ટ્રે

To FIND people with character nowadays means searching
for them with a torch, yet going about with a burning light by day
might lay us open to ridicule. I am therefore going to tell the story
of a man who always had difficulty with his character, yes, in plain
words, someone who never really had a character. Only it troubles
me that I may merely have failed to grasp his significance in time, or
that he may in the last analysis have represented a kind of pioneer or
precursor of a new type.

We were neighbors as children. Whenever he perpetrated one
of those little pranks which are so clever that one is loath to re
count them, his mother would sigh, for the thrashing she would
give him would prove a physical strain. "Boy," she'd lament, "you
have no trace of character in you; God knows what's to become
of you!" But in more difficult cases it was Father who would be
consulted, and then the thrashing would be marked by a certain
solemnity and grave dignity—somewhat as on ceremonial occasions
at school. Before accounts were settled, my friend would himself
have to hand the Auditor-in-Chief a cane, the primary function

of which was to beat the dust out of clothes, for which it was kept in the cook's custody, while, when it was all over, the son was expected to bestow on the paternal hand a kiss with an expression of gratitude for the reprimand and an apology to the dear parents for the worries he had caused them. My friend would reverse the order. He would whine and beg pardon in advance, and continue to do so from one stroke to the next, but when it was all finished be unable to utter another word, his face turning purple as he swallowed his saliva and tears and by means of vigorous rubbing sought to erase the imprint of what he could still feel. "I don't know," his father would say, "what's to become of this boy; the fellow's completely without character!"

Thus character in our youth was something for which, even though one was without it, one would receive a thrashing. There seemed to be a certain injustice attached to this. My friend's parents, when demanding character of him and for once resorting to explanations, would explain that character was the ideological opposite of poor grades, school hours lost through truancy, tin-cups tied to dogtails, chatting and secret tomfoolery in class, obstinate subterfuges, scatterbrains, or a slingshot wantonly aimed at some innocent bird. But the natural opposite of all this was after all the terror of punishment, the fear of being found out, and the pangs of conscience which torture the soul with that sense of remorse which one would be able to feel if things should turn out to have gone awry. This was all-absorbing; to accommodate character there was neither room nor activity to spare; it was something totally superfluous. Yet it was demanded of us.

Perhaps the words spoken from time to time to my friend by way of explanation in the course of these punishments should have provided a clue, such as: "Haven't you got any pride, boy?" Or: "How can anyone be such a base liar!" But I must say I find it hard to imagine to this day how anyone can be expected to show pride when receiving a box on the ear or while under a rain of blows across someone's knees. I can imagine rage, but that was precisely what we were not supposed to feel! And it was the same with lying: what sort of liar could one be expected to be if not a base one? An unskilled one perhaps? As I think about it I imagine that what one would have liked us most to be would have been honest liars. That would have meant being charged twice over, as it were: one, you shall not lie; two, if you do lie, make sure you don't lie mendaciously. Perhaps this is something adult criminals are able to distinguish, since what is always reckoned against them as especially infamous in court is a crime committed in cold blood, with precautions, or with premeditation; but to expect such a distinction from boys would decidedly be asking too much. I'm afraid the only reason why I did not show such striking faults of character as my friend was the fact that I hadn't been so carefully brought up as he.

Of all the parental pronouncements concerning character the most illuminating were those which coupled its regrettable lack with the warning that we would be sorely in need of it as men. "And such a boy wants to become a man!" or words to that effect. Even disregarding the fact that the question of one's wanting to wasn't altogether clear, the rest still proved that character was something one would have need of only in the future; why then all those overhasty preparations now? This was exactly what we were thinking, too.

Although my friend did not possess a character at that time, he did not miss it either. This only happened later, when we were between sixteen and seventeen. It was the time when we began going to the theatre and to read novels. My friend's imagination, more receptive to the deceptive allurements of art than mine, was captured by the villain on the local stage, by the affectionate father, the heroic lover, the figure of fun, yes, even by the diabolic parlor snake, and the ravishing lady of innocence. His speech, now all fake, suddenly ran the whole gamut of what the German stage had to offer in the way of character. When he promised something, one could never be sure whether his word of honor was that of a hero or a stage villain. He might start out on a note of malice and end up being sincere; he might receive us, his friends, full of bluster, and, all at once, with the sophisticated smile of a *bon vivant*, offer us cookies and sweets or, while embracing us with a paternal hug, filch the cigarettes from our pockets.

But this was harmless and candid compared with the effect the reading of novels had on him. Novels contain descriptions of the most wonderful directions for conduct in any number of situations in life. The great drawback is that the situations in which one finds oneself in real life never quite correspond to those for which in fiction there is a provision as to how to act and what to say. World literature is an enormous magazine where millions of souls are clothed with generosity, rage, pride, love, scorn, jealousy, nobility, and meanness. When a woman we adore tramples on our feelings we know we must glance at her with a punitively soulful look; when a scoundrel maltreats an orphan we know we must fell him to the ground with one blow. But what are we to do if the adored woman, having just trampled on our feelings, slams the door of her room shut so that our soulful look can no longer reach her? Or if a table set with priceless glasses stands between us and the scoundrel maltreating the orphan? Are we to smash in the door in order to cast a soft glance through the opening; and are we carefully to clear away the expensive glasses before raising our arm for the blow? Literature invariably leaves us in the lurch in really important cases such as these. Perhaps with a greater wealth of descriptions things will have improved in a few hundred years.

Meanwhile the consequences for the well-read reader finding himself in a so-called situation of real life are especially awkward. Fully a dozen unfinished sentences, half-raised eyebrows or clenched fists, turned backs, and throbbing chests—none of them quite suited to the occasion, yet not unsuited either—are simmering in him; the corners of his mouth are simultaneously drawn up and down, his forehead frowns in gloom and is lit up by gleams of light, a vengeful look darts from his eyes even as they are retracting in shame: and this is very awkward, for what it amounts to is, so to speak, a mutual infliction of pain on the self. The result is often the familiar gulping and twitching that affect lips, eyes, hands, and throat, yes, at times to such an extent the entire body that it keeps turning like a screw to which the nut has been lost.

It was at that time that my friend discovered how much more convenient it would be to have a single character of one's own, and he began to look for it.

But he landed in new adventures. I met him again years later after he had turned to practicing law. He was wearing spectacles, had shaved off his beard, and spoke in a soft voice. "You're staring at me?" he remarked. I couldn't deny it; there was something about his appearance that made me seek for an answer. "Do I look like a lawyer?" he asked. I didn't mean to dispute it. He explained to me: "Lawyers have a very definite way of looking through their pince-nez, which is different, say, from the way doctors have. Another thing one can say about them is that all their movements and phrases are more sharply pointed or jagged than the rounded and gnarled ones of theologians. They are as different from them as a *feuilleton* is from a sermon, in other words, just as fish don't fly from tree to tree, so lawyers are immersed in an element from which they never emerge."

"Character of a career man," I said. My friend was satisfied with me. "It wasn't any too easy," he said. "When I started out I was growing a Christ's beard, but my chief forbade it, because it didn't go with the character of a lawyer. Whereupon I began walking around, looking like a painter, and when that wasn't allowed, like a seaman on leave." "For God's sake, why?" I asked. "Because of course I wanted to guard against taking on the character of a man with a career," he replied. "The trouble is there's no evading it. Of course there are lawyers who look like poets, just as there are poets who look like greengrocers, and greengrocers who have the heads of intellectuals. But they all have something of a glass-eye or false beard or poorly healed wound about them. I don't understand why, but isn't it so?" He smiled after his fashion, adding humbly: "As you know, I don't even have a personal character. . . ."

I reminded him of the numerous stage characters. "Days of our youth!" he commented with a sigh. "In becoming a man one acquires a sexual, cultural, national, class, and geographic character. Then there's the character associated with one's handwriting, the lines in one's palm, the shape of one's skull, and maybe the constellation of the stars at the moment of birth. That's too much for me. I never know which of my characters I'm to side with." Again that unobtrusive smile of his appeared. "Fortunately, my fiancée is of the opinion that I don't possess a character at all, because I haven't yet made good on my promise to marry her. That's precisely the reason I'm going to marry her; her sober judgment is indispensable to me." "Who is your fiancée?"

"According to which character? Mind you," he interrupted himself, "she knows all the same what she wants. She was originally a charmingly helpless little girl—I've known her for a long time—, but she's learned a lot from me. She thinks it's dreadful when I lie, and when I'm late getting to the office in the morning she swears I'll never be able to support a family, and when I fail to stick by something I promised I'd do, she knows only a scoundrel would behave like that."

My friend smiled once more. He was a charming person in those days, and people would look down on him with a friendly smile. Nobody seriously thought he would ever accomplish anything. What struck one even about his appearance was the fact that as soon as he began to speak every limb of his body would shift its position, his eyes would focus evasively sideways, shoulders, hands, and arms would move in directions opposite to each other, and at least one of his legs would quiver with the up-and-down swing of a letter scale in the joint of the knee. To repeat, he was an amiable person, modest, shy, respectful; and sometimes he was the opposite of all this, but one always remained fond of him if only out of curiosity.

When I saw him again he had a car and said woman for a wife now his shadow, as well as a responsible and influential position in his job. How he managed to achieve this, I don't know, but my hunch is that the whole secret was due to the fact that he was getting fat. His timid, mobile face had disappeared. Looking critically one could see it was still there, but it lay concealed under a thick layer of fat. His eyes, which in the past when he had committed some mischief could be as touching as a sad little monkey's, had not actually lost the lustre with which they shone from within, but his padded cheeks now made it difficult for them to focus sideways, hence they would stare straight ahead with a haughty expression of annoyance. The inner movements of his limbs were as jerky as ever, but their flexing was cushioned from the outside by the fatty shock absorbers at the joints, and the resulting gesturing resembled the bluntness of resolute speech. And the whole man had become like this. His will-o'-the-wisp mind had become encased in rigid walls, and was filled with heavy convictions. There would still be an occasional flash, but it no longer radiated any light in the man; rather, it was a shot fired to impress, or to fulfil a particular purpose. He had really lost a good deal compared with the past. He now talked nineteen to the dozen, though the dozen was made up of good, solid material. And he treated his past as one recalls some youthful piece of foolishness.

On one occasion I succeeded in bringing him back to our old topic of conversation—character. "I'm convinced the development of character is connected with the method of waging war," he expounded, gasping for air, "so that today one comes across it only in near-savages. Those who fight with knives and spears can't afford to do without it if they're not to get the worst of the bargain. But what character, however determined, can stand up to tanks, flamethrowers, and clouds of poison gas? Therefore, what we need today is not character, but discipline!"

I did not contradict him. But the curious thing was—and that's why I have taken the liberty of committing this reminiscence to paper—that as he stood there talking and I kept looking at him, I constantly had the feeling that he still carried his old self within him. It resided in him, enclosed in the enlarged bodily replica of the original person. The look in his eyes reflected the look in the eyes of the other, his words those of the other. It was almost uncanny. I have seen him several times since, and each time found this impression confirmed. It was evident he would have liked, if I may say so, to step up close to the window-pane, but something always prevented him.

Translated by E. M. Valk

MUSIL: *A Man Without Character*

1. *Musil's extraordinary novel,* Young Torless, *is generally regarded as a microcosmic prefiguration of the Nazi world. In "A Man Without Character," what kind of world to come does the narrator's friend foreshadow (" '. . . he may in the last analysis have represented a kind of pioneer or precursor of a new type.' ")?*

2. *Musil is saying something about a man's identity and how he acquires it. Does this slight piece bear the burden of so profound a theme?*

3. *What does the narrator's friend mean by " '. . . what we need today is not character, but discipline.' "? To what part of the story is this statement relevant?*

4. *Why does Musil make the narrator's friend a lawyer? Why is he lacking even a name? (Cf. the stories by Pirandello and Hemingway.)*

5. *Is Musil being straightforward or ironic in this tale? How do you know what he is really suggesting? Does the narrator speak for Musil, or is he, as in the Henry James story, merely a mask?*

James Joyce

COUNTERPARTS

James Joyce was born in 1882 in Dublin, the city that was to occupy his thoughts until his death in 1941 although he spent most of his adult years as a voluntary exile from his homeland. Dublin is interwoven into the fabric of his short stories, Dubliners (1914); *into his first novel,* A Portrait of the Artist as a Young Man (1916); *and into the two long works which became the keystones of his career,* Ulysses (1922) *and* Finnegans Wake (1939). *In the twenty or so years since his death, Joyce has continued to tower over the twentieth-century English novel, a literary force whose original techniques and genius with language have as yet found no equal. Although representative of Joyce's early work, "Counterparts" nevertheless suggests a view of Dublin—one composed of attachment and dismay—that was to predominate in all of his fiction.*

ह~

THE bell rang furiously and, when Miss Parker went to the tube, a furious voice called out in a piercing North of Ireland accent:

"Send Farrington here!"

Miss Parker returned to her machine, saying to a man who was writing at a desk:

"Mr. Alleyne wants you upstairs."

The man muttered *"Blast* him!" under his breath and pushed back his chair to stand up. When he stood up he was tall and of great bulk. He had a hanging face, dark wine-coloured, with fair eyebrows and moustache: his eyes bulged forward slightly and the whites of them were dirty. He lifted up the counter and, passing by the clients, went out of the office with a heavy step.

He went heavily upstairs until he came to the second landing, where a door bore a brass plate with the inscription *Mr. Alleyne.* Here he halted, puffing with labour and vexation, and knocked. The shrill voice cried:

"Come in!"

The man entered Mr. Alleyne's room. Simultaneously Mr. Alleyne, a little man wearing gold-rimmed glasses on a clean-shaven face, shot his head up over a pile of documents. The head itself was so pink and hairless it seemed like a large egg reposing on the papers. Mr. Alleyne did not lose a moment:

"Farrington? What is the meaning of this? Why have I always to complain of you? May I ask you why you haven't made a copy of that contract between Bodley and Kirwan? I told you it must be ready by four o'clock."

"But Mr. Shelley said, sir——"

"*Mr. Shelley said, sir.* . . . Kindly attend to what I say and not to what *Mr. Shelley says, sir.* You have always some excuse or another for shirking work. Let me tell you that if the contract is not copied before this evening I'll lay the matter before Mr. Crosbie. . . . Do you hear me now?"

"Yes, sir."

"Do you hear me now? . . . Ay and another little matter! I might as well be talking to the wall as talking to you. Understand once for all that you get a half an hour for your lunch and not an hour and a half. How many courses do you want, I'd like to know. . . . Do you mind me now?"

"Yes, sir."

Mr. Alleyne bent his head again upon his pile of papers. The man stared fixedly at the polished skull which directed the affairs of Crosbie & Alleyne, gauging its fragility. A spasm of rage gripped his throat for a few moments and then passed, leaving after it a sharp sensation of thirst. The man recognised the sensation and felt that he must have a good night's drinking. The middle of the month was passed and, if he could get the copy done in time, Mr. Alleyne might give him an order on the cashier. He stood still, gazing fixedly at the head upon the pile of papers. Suddenly Mr. Alleyne began to upset all the papers, searching for something. Then, as if he had been unaware of the man's presence till that moment, he shot up his head again, saying:

"Eh? Are you going to stand there all day? Upon my word, Farrington, you take things easy!"

"I was waiting to see . . ."

"Very good, you needn't wait to see. Go downstairs and do your work."

The man walked heavily towards the door and, as he went out of the room, he heard Mr. Alleyne cry after him that if the contract was not copied by evening Mr. Crosbie would hear of the matter.

He returned to his desk in the lower office and counted the sheets which remained to be copied. He took up his pen and dipped it in the ink but he continued to stare stupidly at the last words he had written: *In no case shall the said Bernard Bodley be . . .* The evening was falling and in a few minutes they would be lighting the gas: then he could write. He felt that he must slake the thirst in his throat. He stood up from his desk and, lifting the counter as before, passed out of the office. As he was passing out the chief clerk looked at him inquiringly.

"It's all right, Mr. Shelley," said the man, pointing with his finger to indicate the objective of his journey.

The chief clerk glanced at the hat-rack, but, seeing the row complete, offered no remark. As soon as he was on the landing the man pulled a shepherd's plaid cap out of his pocket, put it on his head and ran quickly down the rickety stairs. From the street door he walked on furtively on the inner side of the path towards the corner and all at once dived into a doorway. He was now safe in the dark snug of O'Neill's shop, and, filling up the little window that looked into the bar with his inflamed face, the colour of dark wine or dark meat, he called out:

"Here, Pat, give us a g.p., like a good fellow."

The curate brought him a glass of plain porter. The man drank it at a gulp and asked for a caraway seed. He put his penny on the counter and, leaving the curate to grope for it in the gloom, retreated out of the snug as furtively as he had entered it.

Darkness, accompanied by a thick fog, was gaining upon the dusk of February and the lamps in Eustace Street had been lit. The man went up by the houses until he reached the door of the office, wondering whether he could finish his copy in time. On the stairs a moist pungent odour of perfumes saluted his nose: evidently Miss Delacour had come while he was out in O'Neill's. He crammed his cap back again into his pocket and re-entered the office, assuming an air of absent-mindedness.

"Mr. Alleyne has been calling for you," said the chief clerk severely. "Where were you?"

The man glanced at the two clients who were standing at the counter as if to intimate that their presence prevented him from answering. As the clients were both male the chief clerk allowed himself a laugh.

"I know that game," he said. "Five times in one day is a little bit. . . . Well, you better look sharp and get a copy of our correspondence in the Delacour case for Mr. Alleyne."

This address in the presence of the public, his run upstairs and the porter he had gulped down so hastily confused the man and, as he sat down at his desk to get what was required, he realised how hopeless was the task of finishing his copy of the contract before half past five. The dark damp night was coming and he longed to spend it in the bars, drinking with his friends amid the glare of gas and the clatter of glasses. He got out the Delacour correspondence and passed out of the office. He hoped Mr. Alleyne would not discover that the last two letters were missing.

The moist pungent perfume lay all the way up to Mr. Alleyne's room. Miss Delacour was a middle-aged woman of Jewish appearance. Mr. Alleyne was said to be sweet on her or on her money. She came to the office often and stayed a long time when she came. She was sitting beside his desk now in an aroma of perfumes, smoothing the handle of her umbrella and nodding the great black feather in her hat. Mr. Alleyne had swivelled his chair round to face her and thrown his right foot jauntily upon his left knee. The man put the correspondence on the desk and bowed respectfully but neither Mr. Alleyne nor Miss Delacour took any notice of his bow. Mr. Alleyne tapped a finger on the correspondence and then flicked it towards him as if to say: *"That's all right: you can go."*

The man returned to the lower office and sat down again at his desk. He stared intently at the incomplete phrase: *In no case shall the said Bernard Bodley be* . . . and thought how strange it was that the last three words began with the same letter. The chief clerk began to hurry Miss Parker, saying she would never have the letters typed in time for post. The man listened to the clicking of the machine for a few minutes and then set to work to finish his copy. But his head was not clear and his mind wandered away to the glare and rattle of the public-house. It was a night for hot punches. He struggled on with his copy, but when the clock struck five he had still fourteen pages to write. Blast it! He couldn't finish it in time. He longed to execrate aloud, to bring his fist down on something violently. He was so enraged that he wrote *Bernard Bernard* instead of *Bernard Bodley* and had to begin again on a clean sheet.

He felt strong enough to clear out the whole office single-handed. His body ached to do something, to rush out and revel in violence. All the indignities of his life enraged him. . . . Could he ask the cashier privately for an advance? No, the cashier was no good, no damn good: he wouldn't give an advance. . . . He knew where he would meet the boys: Leonard and O'Halloran and Nosey Flynn. The barometer of his emotional nature was set for a spell of riot.

His imagination had so abstracted him that his name was called twice before he answered. Mr. Alleyne and Miss Delacour were standing outside the counter and all the clerks had turned round in anticipation of something. The man got up from his desk. Mr. Alleyne began a tirade of abuse, saying that two letters were missing. The man answered that he knew nothing about them, that he had made a faithful copy. The tirade continued: it was so bitter and violent that the man could hardly restrain his fist from descending upon the head of the manikin before him:

"I know nothing about any other two letters," he said stupidly.

"*You—know—nothing.* Of course you know nothing," said Mr. Alleyne. "Tell me," he added, glancing first for approval to the lady beside him, "do you take me for a fool? Do you think me an utter fool?"

The man glanced from the lady's face to the little egg-shaped head and back again; and, almost before he was aware of it, his tongue had found a felicitous moment:

"I don't think, sir," he said, "that that's a fair question to put to me."

There was a pause in the very breathing of the clerks. Everyone was astounded (the author of the witticism no less than his neighbours) and Miss Delacour, who was a stout amiable person, began to smile broadly. Mr. Alleyne flushed to the hue of a wild rose and his mouth twitched with a dwarf's passion. He shook his fist in the man's face till it seemed to vibrate like the knob of some electric machine:

"You impertinent ruffian! You impertinent ruffian! I'll make short work of you! Wait till you see! You'll apologise to me for your im-

pertinence or you'll quit the office instanter! You'll quit this, I'm telling you, or you'll apologise to me!"

. . . .

He stood in a doorway opposite the office watching to see if the
cashier would come out alone. All the clerks passed out and finally
the cashier came out with the chief clerk. It was no use trying to say
a word to him when he was with the chief clerk. The man felt that
his position was bad enough. He had been obliged to offer an abject apology to Mr. Alleyne for his impertinence but he knew what
a hornet's nest the office would be for him. He could remember the
way in which Mr. Alleyne had hounded little Peake out of the office
in order to make room for his own nephew. He felt savage and
thirsty and revengeful, annoyed with himself and with everyone
else. Mr. Alleyne would never give him an hour's rest; his life would
be a hell to him. He had made a proper fool of himself this time.
Could he not keep his tongue in his cheek? But they had never
pulled together from the first, he and Mr. Alleyne, ever since the
day Mr. Alleyne had overheard him mimicking his North of Ireland
accent to amuse Higgins and Miss Parker; that had been the beginning of it. He might have tried Higgins for the money, but sure Higgins never had anything for himself. A man with two establish-
ments to keep up, of course he couldn't. . . .

He felt his great body again aching for the comfort of the public-
house. The fog had begun to chill him and he wondered could he
touch Pat in O'Neill's. He could not touch him for more than a bob
—and a bob was no use. Yet he must get money somewhere or
other: he had spent his last penny for the g.p. and soon it would be
too late for getting money anywhere. Suddenly, as he was fingering
his watch-chain, he thought of Terry Kelly's pawn-office in Fleet
Street. That was the dart! Why didn't he think of it sooner?

He went through the narrow alley of Temple Bar quickly, mut-
tering to himself that they could all go to hell because he was going
to have a good night of it. The clerk in Terry Kelly's said *A crown!*
but the consignor held out for six shillings; and in the end the six
shillings was allowed him literally. He came out of the pawn-office
joyfully, making a little cylinder of the coins between his thumb
and fingers. In Westmoreland Street the footpaths were crowded
with young men and women returning from business and ragged
urchins ran here and there yelling out the names of the evening

editions. The man passed through the crowd, looking on the spectacle generally with proud satisfaction and staring masterfully at the office-girls. His head was full of the noises of tram-gongs and swishing trolleys and his nose already sniffed the curling fumes of punch. As he walked on he preconsidered the terms in which he would narrate the incident to the boys:

"So, I just looked at him—coolly, you know, and looked at her. Then I looked back at him again—taking my time, you know. 'I don't think that that's a fair question to put to me,' says I."

Nosey Flynn was sitting up in his usual corner of Davy Byrne's and, when he heard the story, he stood Farrington a half-one, saying it was as smart a thing as ever he heard. Farrington stood a drink in his turn. After a while O'Halloran and Paddy Leonard came in and the story was repeated to them. O'Halloran stood tailors of malt hot all round and told the story of the retort he had made to the chief clerk when he was in Callan's of Fownes's Street; but, as the retort was after the manner of the liberal shepherds in the eclogues, he had to admit that it was not as clever as Farrington's retort. At this Farrington told the boys to polish off that and have another.

Just as they were naming their poisons who should come in but Higgins! Of course he had to join in with the others. The men asked him to give his version of it, and he did so with great vivacity for the sight of five small hot whiskies was very exhilarating. Everyone roared laughing when he showed the way in which Mr. Alleyne shook his fist in Farrington's face. Then he imitated Farrington, saying, "And here was my nabs, as cool as you please," while Farrington looked at the company out of his heavy dirty eyes, smiling and at times drawing forth stray drops of liquor from his moustache with the aid of his lower lip.

When that round was over there was a pause. O'Halloran had money but neither of the other two seemed to have any; so the whole party left the shop somewhat regretfully. At the corner of Duke Street Higgins and Nosey Flynn bevelled off to the left while the other three turned back towards the city. Rain was drizzling down on the cold streets and, when they reached the Ballast Office, Farrington suggested the Scotch House. The bar was full of men and loud with the noise of tongues and glasses. The three men pushed past the whining match-sellers at the door and formed a little party at the corner of the counter. They began to exchange stories. Leonard introduced them to a young fellow named Weathers who was performing at the Tivoli as an acrobat and knockabout *artiste.* Farrington stood a drink all round. Weathers said he would take a small Irish and Apollinaris. Farrington, who had definite notions of what was what, asked the boys would they have an Apollinaris too; but the boys told Tim to make theirs hot. The talk became theatrical. O'Halloran stood a round and then Farrington stood another round, Weathers protesting that the hospitality was too Irish. He promised to get them in behind the scenes and introduce them to some nice girls. O'Halloran said that he and Leonard would go, but that Farrington wouldn't go because he was a married man; and Farrington's heavy dirty eyes leered at the company in token that he understood he was being chaffed. Weathers made them all have just one little tincture at his expense and promised to meet them later on at Mulligan's in Poolbeg Street.

When the Scotch House closed they went round to Mulligan's. They went into the parlour at the back and O'Halloran ordered small hot specials all around. They were all beginning to feel mellow. Farrington was just standing another round when Weathers came back. Much to Farrington's relief he drank a glass of bitter this time. Funds were getting low but they had enough to keep them going. Presently two young women with big hats and a young man in a check suit came in and sat at a table close by. Weathers saluted them and told the company that they were out of the Tivoli. Farrington's eyes wandered at every moment in the direction of one of the young women. There was something striking in her appearance. An immense scarf of peacock-blue muslin was wound round her hat and knotted in a great bow under her chin; and she wore bright yellow gloves, reaching to the elbow. Farrington gazed admiringly at the plump arm which she moved very often and with much grace; and when, after a little time, she answered his gaze he admired still more her large dark brown eyes. The oblique staring expression in them fascinated him. She glanced at him once or twice and, when the party was leaving the room, she brushed against his chair and said "*O, pardon!*" in a London accent. He watched her leave the room in the hope that she would look back at him, but he was disappointed. He cursed his want of money and cursed all the rounds he had stood, particularly all the whiskies and Apollinaris which he had stood to Weathers. If there was one thing that he hated it was a sponge. He was so angry that he lost count of the conversation of his friends.

When Paddy Leonard called him he found that they were talking about feats of strength. Weathers was showing his biceps muscle to the company and boasting so much that the other two had called on Farrington to uphold the national honour. Farrington pulled up his sleeve accordingly and showed his biceps muscle to the company. The two arms were examined and compared and finally it was agreed to have a trial of strength. The table was cleared and the two men rested their elbows on it, clasping hands. When Paddy Leonard said "*Go!*" each was to try to bring down the other's hand on to the table. Farrington looked very serious and determined.

The trial began. After about thirty seconds Weathers brought his opponent's hand slowly down on to the table. Farrington's dark wine-coloured face flushed darker still with anger and humiliation at having been defeated by such a stripling.

"You're not to put the weight of your body behind it. Play fair," he said.

"Who's not playing fair?" said the other.

"Come on again. The two best out of three."

The trial began again. The veins stood out on Farrington's forehead, and the pallor of Weathers' complexion changed to peony. Their hands and arms trembled under the stress. After a long struggle Weathers again brought his opponent's hand slowly on to the table. There was a murmur of applause from the spectators. The curate, who was standing beside the table, nodded his red head towards the victor and said with stupid familiarity:

"Ah! that's the knack!"

"What the hell do you know about it?" said Farrington fiercely, turning on the man. "What do you put in your gab for?"

"Sh, sh!" said O'Halloran, observing the violent expression of Farrington's face. "Pony up, boys. We'll have just one little smahan more and then we'll be off."

. . . .

A very sullen-faced man stood at the corner of O'Connell Bridge waiting for the little Sandymount tram to take him home. He was

full of smouldering anger and revengefulness. He felt humiliated
and discontented; he did not even feel drunk; and he had only two-
pence in his pocket. He cursed everything. He had done for himself
in the office, pawned his watch, spent all his money; and he had
not even got drunk. He began to feel thirsty again and he longed to
be back again in the hot reeking public-house. He had lost his reputation as a strong man, having been defeated twice by a mere boy.
His heart swelled with fury and, when he thought of the woman in
the big hat who had brushed against him and said *Pardon!* his fury
nearly choked him.

His tram let him down at Shelbourne Road and he steered his
great body along in the shadow of the wall of the barracks. He
loathed returning to his home. When he went in by the side-door
he found the kitchen empty and the kitchen fire nearly out. He
bawled upstairs:

"Ada! Ada!"

His wife was a little sharp-faced woman who bullied her husband
when he was sober and was bullied by him when he was drunk.
They had five children. A little boy came running down the stairs.

"Who is that?" said the man, peering through the darkness.

"Me, pa."

"Who are you? Charlie?"

"No, pa. Tom."

"Where's your mother?"

"She's out at the chapel."

"That's right. . . . Did she think of leaving any dinner for me?"

"Yes, pa. I——"

"Light the lamp. What do you mean by having the place in darkness? Are the other children in bed?"

The man sat down heavily on one of the chairs while the little
boy lit the lamp. He began to mimic his son's flat accent, saying half
to himself: "*At the chapel. At the chapel, if you please!*" When the
lamp was lit he banged his fist on the table and shouted:

"What's for my dinner?"

"I'm going . . . to cook it, pa," said the little boy.

The man jumped up furiously and pointed to the fire.

"On that fire! You let the fire out! By God, I'll teach you to do that
again!"

He took a step to the door and seized the walking-stick which was standing behind it.

"I'll teach you to let the fire out!" he said, rolling up his sleeve in order to give his arm free play.

The little boy cried "O, pa!" and ran whimpering round the table, but the man followed him and caught him by the coat. The little boy looked about him wildly but, seeing no way of escape, fell upon his knees.

"Now, you'll let the fire out the next time!" said the man, striking at him vigorously with the stick. "Take that, you little whelp!"

The boy uttered a squeal of pain as the stick cut his thigh. He clasped his hands together in the air and his voice shook with fright.

"O, pa!" he cried. "Don't beat me, pa! And I'll . . . I'll say a *Hail Mary* for you. . . . I'll say a *Hail Mary* for you, pa, if you don't beat me. . . . I'll say a *Hail Mary*. . . ."

JOYCE: *Counterparts*

1. The title refers to several pairings in the story. What are they?

2. "Counterparts" comes from Joyce's collection of short stories, Dub-liners. *The people and places Joyce writes about in this volume make it an excellent entry to his masterpiece,* Ulysses, *but the predominant mood is somewhat different: it is one of entrapment. Who is trapped in the story? Is Farrington? Can he help himself, or is he trapped by life, by a tedious job, without any chance of escape? If so, what is Joyce getting at? In what way is the story reminiscent of Moravia's?*

3. The story begins: "The bell rang furiously. . . ." How does this foreshadow the ending and tie the story together? How is fury related to entrapment?

4. What are some of the things which contribute to Farrington's re-tort? Why does Farrington write Bernard Bernard *instead of* Bernard Bodley? *What does this contribute to the falling-out?*

5. How does Farrington's rage naturally lead him to the pub, the scene of his second defeat?

6. Why is most of the conversation at the bar reported indirectly? What does the plain and conversational style add to the effect of the story? What is the point of the feat of strength?

7. Is there anything of what we usually call a story line here (cf. "Little Louise Roque")? How is the story constructed? (Cf. Turgenev.)

8. How do you explain the cruel ending? Is it a third defeat?

Franz Kafka

THE JUDGMENT

Franz Kafka was born in Prague in 1883, a Jew in Austrian-Czech surroundings and the son of a domineering father. He studied law, then worked in the office of the workmen's compensation division of the Austrian government. He had just become engaged when tuberculosis felled him, and he died, at forty-one, in 1924. His novels—
The Trial *(1925),* The Castle *(1926),* Amerika *(1927)—were not yet in print. Since his death, his reputation has grown into major dimension, with many critics regarding him as second to no other German prose writer. In "The Judgment," as in most of his fiction, he combined realistic detail with symbolic, dreamlike situations and scenes that reveal the anxieties and isolation of modern man.*

ଚ୍ଚ

IT WAS a Sunday morning in the very height of spring. Georg Bendemann, a young merchant, was sitting in his own room on the first floor of one of a long row of small, ramshackle houses stretching beside the river which were scarcely distinguishable from each other except in height and coloring. He had just finished a letter to an old friend of his who was now living abroad, had put it into its envelope in a slow and dreamy fashion, and with his elbows propped on the writing table was gazing out of the window at the river, the bridge and the hills on the farther bank with their tender green.

He was thinking about his friend, who had actually run away to Russia some years before, being dissatisfied with his prospects at home. Now he was carrying on a business in St. Petersburg, which had flourished to begin with but had long been going downhill, as he always complained on his increasingly rare visits. So he was wearing himself out to no purpose in a foreign country; the unfamiliar full beard he wore did not quite conceal the face Georg had known so well since childhood, and his skin was growing so yellow as to indicate some latent disease. By his own account he had no regular connection with the colony of his fellow countrymen out there and almost no social intercourse with Russian families, so that he was resigning himself to becoming a permanent bachelor.

What could one write to such a man, who had obviously run off the rails, a man one could be sorry for but could not help? Should one advise him to come home, to transplant himself and take up his old friendships again—there was nothing to hinder him—and in general to rely on the help of his friends? But that was as good as telling him, and the more kindly the more offensively, that all his efforts hitherto had miscarried, that he should finally give up, come back home, and be gaped at by everyone as a returned prodigal, that only his friends knew what was what and that he himself was just a big child who should do what his successful and home-keeping friends prescribed. And was it certain, besides, that all the pain one would have to inflict on him would achieve its object? Perhaps it would not even be possible to get him to come home at all —he said himself that he was now out of touch with commerce in his native country—and then he would still be left an alien in a foreign land embittered by his friends' advice and more than ever estranged from them. But if he did follow their advice and then didn't fit in at home—not out of malice, of course, but through force of circumstances—couldn't get on with his friends or without them, felt humiliated, couldn't be said to have either friends or a country of his own any longer, wouldn't it have been better for him to stay abroad just as he was? Taking all this into account, how could one be sure that he would make a success of life at home?

For such reasons, supposing one wanted to keep up correspondence with him, one could not send him any real news such as could frankly be told to the most distant acquaintance. It was more than three years since his last visit, and for this he offered the lame excuse that the political situation in Russia was too uncertain, which apparently would not permit even the briefest absence of a small business man while it allowed hundreds of thousands of Russians to travel peacefully abroad. But during these three years Georg's own position in life had changed a lot. Two years ago his mother had died, since when he and his father had shared the household together, and his friend had of course been informed of that and had expressed his sympathy in a letter phrased so dryly that the grief caused by such an event, one had to conclude, could not be

realized in a distant country. Since that time, however, Georg had
applied himself with greater determination to the business as well
as to everything else.

Perhaps during his mother's lifetime his father's insistence on
having everything his own way in the business had hindered him
from developing any real activity of his own, perhaps since her
death his father had become less aggressive, although he was still
active in the business, perhaps it was mostly due to an accidental
run of good fortune—which was very probable indeed—but at any
rate during those two years the business had developed in a most
unexpected way, the staff had had to be doubled, the turnover was
five times as great, no doubt about it, further progress lay just
ahead.

But Georg's friend had no inkling of this improvement. In earlier
years, perhaps for the last time in that letter of condolence, he had
tried to persuade Georg to emigrate to Russia and had enlarged
upon the prospects of success for precisely Georg's branch of trade.
The figures quoted were microscopic by comparison with the range
of Georg's present operations. Yet he shrank from letting his friend
know about his business success, and if he were to do it now retro-
spectively that certainly would look peculiar.

So Georg confined himself to giving his friend unimportant items
of gossip such as rise at random in the memory when one is idly
thinking things over on a quiet Sunday. All he desired was to leave
undisturbed the idea of the home town which his friend must have
built up to his own content during the long interval. And so it happened to Georg that three times in three fairly widely separated
letters he had told his friend about the engagement of an unimportant man to an equally unimportant girl, until indeed, quite contrary to his intentions, his friend began to show some interest in this
notable event.

Yet Georg preferred to write about things like these rather than
to confess that he himself had got engaged a month ago to a Fräulein Frieda Brandenfeld, a girl from a well-to-do family. He often
discussed this friend of his with his fiancée and the peculiar relationship that had developed between them in their correspondence.
"So he won't be coming to our wedding," said she, "and yet I have
a right to get to know all your friends." "I don't want to trouble
him," answered Georg. "Don't misunderstand me, he would prob-

ably come, at least I think so, but he would feel that his hand had been forced and he would be hurt, perhaps he would envy me and certainly he'd be discontented and without being able to do anything about his discontent he'd have to go away again alone. Alone —do you know what that means?" "Yes, but may he not hear about our wedding in some other fashion?" "I can't prevent that, of course, but it's unlikely, considering the way he lives." "Since your friends are like that, Georg, you shouldn't ever have got engaged at all." "Well, we're both to blame for that; but I wouldn't have it any other way now." And when, breathing quickly under his kisses, she still brought out: "All the same, I do feel upset," he thought it could not really involve him in trouble were he to send the news to his friend. "That's the kind of man I am and he'll just have to take me as I am," he said to himself, "I can't cut myself to another pattern that might make a more suitable friend for him."

And in fact he did inform his friend, in the long letter he had been writing that Sunday morning, about his engagement, with these words: "I have saved my best news to the end. I have got engaged to a Fräulein Frieda Brandenfeld, a girl from a well-to-do family, who only came to live here a long time after you went away, so that you're hardly likely to know her. There will be time to tell you more about her later, for today let me just say that I am very happy and as between you and me the only difference in our relationship is that instead of a quite ordinary kind of friend you will now have in me a happy friend. Besides that, you will acquire in my fiancée, who sends her warm greetings and will soon write you herself, a genuine friend of the opposite sex, which is not without importance to a bachelor. I know that there are many reasons why you can't come to see us, but would not my wedding be precisely the right occasion for giving all obstacles the go-by? Still, however that may be, do just as seems good to you without regarding any interests but your own."

With this letter in his hand Georg had been sitting a long time at the writing table, his face turned towards the window. He had barely acknowledged, with an absent smile, a greeting waved to him from the street by a passing acquaintance.

At last he put the letter in his pocket and went out of his room across a small lobby into his father's room, which he had not entered for months. There was in fact no need for him to enter it, since he saw his father daily at business and they took their mid-day meal together at an eating house; in the evening, it was true, each did as he pleased, yet even then, unless Georg—as mostly happened—went out with friends or, more recently, visited his fiancée, they always sat for a while, each with his newspaper, in their common sitting room.

It surprised Georg how dark his father's room was even on this sunny morning. So it was overshadowed as much as that by the high wall on the other side of the narrow courtyard. His father was sitting by the window in a corner hung with various mementoes of Georg's dead mother, reading a newspaper which he held to one side before his eyes in an attempt to overcome a defect of vision. On the table stood the remains of his breakfast, not much of which seemed to have been eaten.

"Ah, Georg," said his father, rising at once to meet him. His heavy dressing gown swung open as he walked and the skirts of it fluttered round him.—"My father is still a giant of a man," said Georg to himself.

"It's unbearably dark here," he said aloud.

"Yes, it's dark enough," answered his father.

"And you've shut the window, too?"

"I prefer it like that."

"Well, it's quite warm outside," said Georg, as if continuing his previous remark, and sat down.

His father cleared away the breakfast dishes and set them on a chest.

"I really only wanted to tell you," went on Georg, who had been vacantly following the old man's movements, "that I am now sending the news of my engagement to St. Petersburg." He drew the letter a little way from his pocket and let it drop back again.

"To St. Petersburg?" asked his father.

"To my friend there," said Georg, trying to meet his father's eye. —In business hours he's quite different, he was thinking. How solidly he sits here with his arms crossed.

"Oh, yes. To your friend," said his father, with peculiar emphasis.

"Well, you know, Father, that I wanted not to tell him about my engagement at first. Out of consideration for him, that was the only reason. You know yourself he's a difficult man. I said to myself that someone else might tell him about my engagement, although he's such a solitary creature that that was hardly likely—I couldn't prevent that—but I wasn't ever going to tell him myself."

"And now you've changed your mind?" asked his father, laying his enormous newspaper on the window sill and on top of it his spectacles, which he covered with one hand.

"Yes, I've been thinking it over. If he's a good friend of mine, I said to myself, my being happily engaged should make him happy too. And so I wouldn't put off telling him any longer. But before I posted the letter I wanted to let you know."

"Georg," said his father, lengthening his toothless mouth, "listen to me! You've come to me about this business, to talk it over with me. No doubt that does you honor. But it's nothing, it's worse than nothing, if you don't tell me the whole truth. I don't want to stir up matters that shouldn't be mentioned here. Since the death of our dear mother certain things have been done that aren't right. Maybe the time will come for mentioning them, and maybe sooner than we think. There's many a thing in the business I'm not aware of, maybe it's not done behind my back—I'm not going to say that it's done behind my back—I'm not equal to things any longer, my memory's failing, I haven't an eye for so many things any longer. That's the course of nature in the first place, and in the second place the death of our dear mother hit me harder than it did you.—But since we're talking about it, about this letter, I beg you, Georg, don't deceive me. It's a trivial affair, it's hardly worth mentioning, so don't deceive me. Do you really have this friend in St. Petersburg?"

Georg rose in embarrassment. "Never mind my friends. A thousand friends wouldn't make up to me for my father. Do you know what I think? You're not taking enough care of yourself. But old age must be taken care of. I can't do without you in the business, you know that very well, but if the business is going to undermine your health, I'm ready to close it down tomorrow forever. And that won't do. We'll have to make a change in your way of living. But a radical change. You sit here in the dark, and in the sitting room you would have plenty of light. You just take a bite of breakfast instead of properly keeping up your strength. You sit by a closed window, and the air would be so good for you. No, Father! I'll get the doctor to come, and we'll follow his orders. We'll change your room, you can move into the front room and I'll move in here. You won't notice the change, all your things will be moved with you. But there's time for all that later. I'll put you to bed now for a little; I'm sure you need to rest. Come, I'll help you to take off your things, you'll see I can do it. Or if you would rather go into the front room at once, you can lie down in my bed for the present. That would be the most sensible thing."

Georg stood close beside his father, who had let his head with its unkempt white hair sink on his chest.

"Georg," said his father in a low voice, without moving.

Georg knelt down at once beside his father. In the old man's weary face he saw the pupils, over-large, fixedly looking at him from the corners of the eyes.

"You have a friend in St. Petersburg. You've always been a leg-puller and you haven't even shrunk from pulling my leg. How could you have a friend out there! I can't believe it."

"Just think back a bit, Father," said Georg, lifting his father from the chair and slipping off his dressing gown as he stood feebly enough, "it'll soon be three years since my friend came to see us last. I remember that you used not to like him very much. At least twice I kept you from seeing him, although he was actually sitting with me in my room. I could quite well understand your dislike of him, my friend has his peculiarities. But then, later, you got on with him very well. I was proud because you listened to him and nodded and asked him questions. If you think back you're bound to remember. He used to tell us the most incredible stories of the Russian Revolution. For instance, when he was on a business trip to Kiev and ran into a riot, and saw a priest on a balcony who cut a broad cross in blood on the palm of his hand and held the hand up and appealed to the mob. You've told that story yourself once or twice since."

Meanwhile Georg had succeeded in lowering his father down again and carefully taking off the woollen drawers he wore over his linen underpants and his socks. The not particularly clean appearance of this underwear made him reproach himself for having been neglectful. It should have certainly been his duty to see that his father had clean changes of underwear. He had not yet explicitly discussed with his bride-to-be what arrangements should be made for his father in the future, for they had both of them silently taken it for granted that the old man would go on living alone in the old house. But now he made a quick, firm decision to take him into his own future establishment. It almost looked, on closer inspection, as if the care he meant to lavish on his father might come too late.

He carried his father to bed in his arms. It gave him a dreadful feeling to notice that while he took the few steps towards the bed the old man on his breast was playing with his watch chain. He could not lay him down on the bed for a moment, so firmly did he hang on to the watch chain.

But as soon as he was laid in bed, all seemed well. He covered himself up and even drew the blankets farther than usual over his shoulders. He looked up at Georg with a not unfriendly eye.

"You begin to remember my friend, don't you?" asked Georg, giving him an encouraging nod.

"Am I well covered up now?" asked his father, as if he were not able to see whether his feet were properly tucked in or not.

"So you find it snug in bed already," said Georg, and tucked the blankets more closely around him.

"Am I well covered up?" asked the father once more, seeming to be strangely intent upon the answer.

"Don't worry, you're well covered up."

"No!" cried his father, cutting short the answer, threw the blankets off with a strength that sent them all flying in a moment and sprang erect in bed. Only one hand lightly touched the ceiling to steady him.

"You wanted to cover me up, I know, my young sprig, but I'm far from being covered up yet. And even if this is the last strength I have, it's enough for you, too much for you. Of course I know your friend. He would have been a son after my own heart. That's why you've been playing him false all these years. Why else? Do you think I haven't been sorry for him? And that's why you had to lock yourself up in your office—the Chief is busy, mustn't be disturbed —just so that you could write your lying little letters to Russia. But thank goodness a father doesn't need to be taught how to see through his son. And now that you thought you'd got him down, so far down that you could set your bottom on him and sit on him and he wouldn't move, then my fine son makes up his mind to get married!"

Georg stared at the bogey conjured up by his father. His friend in St. Petersburg, whom his father suddenly knew too well, touched his imagination as never before. Lost in the vastness of Russia he saw him. At the door of an empty, plundered warehouse he saw him. Among the wreckage of his showcases, the slashed remnants of his wares, the falling gas brackets, he was just standing up. Why did he have to go so far away!

"But attend to me!" cried his father, and Georg almost distracted, ran towards the bed to take everything in, yet came to a stop halfway.

"Because she lifted up her skirts," his father began to flute, "because she lifted her skirts like this, the nasty creature," and mimicking her he lifted his shirt so high that one could see the scar on his thigh from his war wound, "because she lifted her skirts like this and this you made up to her, and in order to make free with her undisturbed you have disgraced your mother's memory, betrayed your friend and stuck your father into bed so that he can't move. But he can move, or can't he?"

And he stood up quite unsupported and kicked his legs out. His insight made him radiant.

Georg shrank into a corner, as far away from his father as possible. A long time ago he had firmly made up his mind to watch closely every least movement so that he should not be surprised by any indirect attack, a pounce from behind or above. At this moment he recalled this long-forgotten resolve and forgot it again, like a man drawing a short thread through the eye of a needle.

"But your friend hasn't been betrayed after all!" cried his father, emphasizing the point with stabs of his forefinger. "I've been representing him here on the spot."

"You comedian!" Georg could not resist the retort, realized at once the harm done and, his eyes starting in his head, bit his tongue back, only too late, till the pain made his knees give.

"Yes, of course I've been playing a comedy! A comedy! That's a good expression! What other comfort was left to a poor old widower? Tell me—and while you're answering me be you still my living son—what else was left to me, in my back room, plagued by a disloyal staff, old to the marrow of my bones? And my son strutting through the world, finishing off deals that I had prepared for him, bursting with triumphant glee and stalking away from his father with the closed face of a respectable business man! Do you think I didn't love you, I, from whom you are sprung?"

Now he'll lean forward, thought Georg. What if he topples and smashes himself! These words went hissing through his mind.

His father leaned forward but did not topple. Since Georg did not come any nearer, as he had expected, he straightened himself again.

"Stay where you are, I don't need you! You think you have strength enough to come over here and that you're only hanging back of your own accord. Don't be too sure! I am still much the stronger of us two. All by myself I might have had to give way, but your mother has given me so much of her strength that I've established a fine connection with your friend and I have your customers here in my pocket!"

"He has pockets even in his shirt!" said Georg to himself, and believed that with this remark he could make him an impossible figure for all the world. Only for a moment did he think so, since he kept on forgetting everything.

"Just take your bride on your arm and try getting in my way! I'll sweep her from your very side, you don't know how!"

Georg made a grimace of disbelief. His father only nodded, confirming the truth of his words, towards Georg's corner.

"How you amused me today, coming to ask me if you should tell your friend about your engagement. He knows it already, you stupid boy, he knows it all! I've been writing to him, for you forgot to take my writing things away from me. That's why he hasn't been here for years, he knows everything a hundred times better than you do yourself, in his left hand he crumples your letters unopened while in his right hand he holds up my letters to read through!"

In his enthusiasm he waved his arm over his head. "He knows everything a thousand times better!" he cried.

"Ten thousand times!" said Georg, to make fun of his father, but in his very mouth the words turned into deadly earnest.

"For years I've been waiting for you to come with some such question! Do you think I concern myself with anything else? Do you think I read my newspapers? Look!" and he threw Georg a newspaper sheet, which he had somehow taken to bed with him. An old newspaper, with a name entirely unknown to Georg.

"How long a time you've taken to grow up! Your mother had to die, she couldn't see the happy day, your friend is going to pieces in Russia, even three years ago he was yellow enough to be thrown away, and as for me, you see what condition I'm in. You have eyes in your head for that!"

"So you've been lying in wait for me!" cried Georg.

His father said pityingly, in an offhand manner: "I suppose you wanted to say that sooner. But now it doesn't matter." And in a louder voice: "So now you know what else there was in the world besides yourself, till now you've known only about yourself! An innocent child, yes, that you were, truly, but still more truly have you been a devilish human being!—And therefore take note: I sentence you now to death by drowning!"

Georg felt himself urged from the room. The crash with which his father fell on the bed behind him was still in his ears as he fled. On the staircase, which he rushed down as if its steps were an inclined plane, he ran into his charwoman on her way up to do the morning cleaning of the room. "Jesus!" she cried, and covered her face with her apron, but he was already gone. Out of the front door he rushed, across the roadway, driven towards the water. Already he was grasping at the railings as a starving man clutches food. He swung himself over, like the distinguished gymnast he had once been in his youth, to his parents' pride. With weakening grip he was still holding on when he spied between the railings a motor-bus coming which would easily cover the noise of his fall, called in a low voice: "Dear parents, I have always loved you, all the same," and let himself drop.

At this moment an unending stream of traffic was just going over the bridge.

Translated by Willa and Edwin Muir

KAFKA: *The Judgment*

1. *What is the relationship between Georg and his father? Through this relationship, what is Kafka trying to indicate?*

2. *Why does Kafka stress the role of Georg's friend? What relevance does the friend have to Georg? To his father?*

3. *Why does Georg shrink from telling his friend the truth about himself? Do you accept his explanation: "Perhaps he would envy me."?*

4. What is the relationship between Georg and his fiancée? Between his fiancée and his father? What role do these relationships have in the dénouement?

5. Why does Mr. Bendemann desire his son's death? Why by drowning?

6. Why does Georg carry out the sentence?

7. How does Kafka convey the tone of morbidity? Mention some details. Is there also an element of comedy ("I've been playing a comedy")? Mention some details. Do they clash with the dominant tone of the story?

8. A witty critic once remarked that in Dostoyevsky there is crime with punishment, in Kafka punishment without crime. Do you agree?

9. Is Kafka describing a disordered personality, a disordered society, or a disordered cosmos? Why does he do it in such orderly fashion?

10. Though dream and reality fuse in a way that obscures any neat meaning in Kafka, his language is always clear and concrete. What effect does this contrast produce?

D. H. Lawrence

THE MAN WHO LOVED ISLANDS

Like Conrad, Lawrence started out in a profession which ultimately he was to forsake, here school teaching. Born in Eastwood, Notts, on September 11, 1885, Lawrence recreated the atmosphere and some of the facts of his early home life in his third novel, Sons and Lovers *(1913). Lawrence, however, was dissatisfied with this novel, and subsequently turned to a more poetic vision of life with* The Rainbow *(1915) and* Women in Love *(1920), two of the novels on which his serious reputation rests. These two long works seemed to indicate his general direction, for in the next ten years there appeared* Aaron's Rod *(1922),* St. Mawr *(1925),* The Plumed Serpent *(1926),* Lady Chatterley's Lover *(1928), and* The Man Who Died *(1929), which he wrote shortly before his death. "The Man Who Loved Islands" fits loosely into his later work, concerned as it is with a man who destroys himself because of his inability to "connect" with other people. On March 2, 1930, Lawrence died of tuberculosis at Vence, in the south of France.*

ले

First Island

THERE was a man who loved islands. He was born on one, but it didn't suit him, as there were too many other people on it, besides himself. He wanted an island all of his own; not necessarily to be alone on it, but to make it a world of his own.

An island, if it is big enough, is no better than a continent. It has to be really quite small, before it *feels like* an island; and this story will show how tiny it has to be, before you can presume to fill it with your own personality.

Now circumstances so worked out, that this lover of islands, by the time he was thirty-five, actually acquired an island of his own. He didn't own it as freehold property, but he had a ninety-nine years' lease of it, which, as far as a man and an island are concerned,

is as good as everlasting. Since, if you are like Abraham, and want
your offspring to be numberless as the sands of the sea-shore, you
don't choose an island to start breeding on. Too soon there would
be overpopulation, overcrowding, and slum conditions. Which is a
horrid thought, for one who loves an island for its insulation. No,
an island is a nest which holds one egg, and one only. This egg is
the islander himself.

The island acquired by our potential islander was not in the remote oceans. It was quite near at home, no palm-trees nor boom of
surf on the reef, nor any of that kind of thing; but a good solid
dwelling-house, rather gloomy, above the landing-place, and beyond, a small farm-house with sheds, and a few outlying fields.
Down on the little landing bay were three cottages in a row, like
coastguards' cottages, all neat and whitewashed.

What could be more cozy and home-like? It was four miles if you
walked all round your island, through the gorse and the blackthorn
bushes, above the steep rocks of the sea and down in the little
glades where the primroses grew. If you walked straight over the
two humps of hills, the length of it, through the rocky fields where
the cows lay chewing, and through the rather sparse oats, on into
the gorse again, and so to the low cliff's edge, it took you only
twenty minutes. And when you came to the edge, you could see
another, bigger island lying beyond. But the sea was between you
and it. And as you returned over the turf where the short, down-
land cowslips nodded you saw to the east still another island, a tiny
one this time, like the calf of the cow. This tiny island also belonged
to the islander.

Thus it seems that even islands like to keep each other company.

Our islander loved his island very much. In early spring, the little
ways and glades were a snow of blackthorn, a vivid white among
the celtic stillness of close green and grey rock, blackbirds calling
out in the whiteness their first long, triumphant calls. After the
blackthorn and the nestling primroses came the blue apparition of
hyacinths, like elfin lakes and slipping sheets of blue, among the
bushes and under the glade of trees. And many birds with nests
you could peep into, on the island all your own. Wonderful what a
great world it was!

Followed summer, and the cowslips gone, the wild roses faintly
fragrant through the haze. There was a field of hay, the foxgloves

stood looking down. In a little cove, the sun was on the pale granite where you bathed, and the shadow was in the rocks. Before the mist came stealing, and you went home through the ripening oats, the glare of the sea fading from the high air as the foghorn started to moo on the other island. And then the sea-fog went, it was autumn, and oat-sheaves lying prone; the great moon, another island, rose golden out of the sea, and, rising higher, the world of the sea was white.

So autumn ended with rain, and winter came, dark skies and dampness and rain, but rarely frost. The island, your island, cowered dark, holding away from you. You could feel down in the wet, sombre hollows, the resentful spirit coiled upon itself, like a wet dog coiled in gloom, or a snake that is neither asleep nor awake. Then in the night, when the wind left off blowing in great gusts and volleys, as at sea, you felt that your island was a universe, infinite and old as the darkness; not an island at all, but an infinite dark world where all the souls from all the other bygone nights lived on, and the infinite distance was near.

Strangely, from your little island in space, you were gone forth into the dark, great realms of time, where all the souls that never die veer and swoop on their vast, strange errands. The little earthly island has dwindled, like a jumping-off place, into nothingness, for you have jumped off, you know not how, into the dark wide mystery of time, where the past is vastly alive, and the future is not separated off.

This is the danger of becoming an islander. When, in the city, you wear your white spats and dodge the traffic with the fear of death down your spine, then you are quite safe from the terrors of infinite time. The moment is your little islet in time, it is the spatial universe that careers round you.

But once isolate yourself on a little island in the sea of space, and the moment begins to heave and expand in great circles, the solid earth is gone, and your slippery, naked dark soul finds herself out in the timeless world, where the chariots of the so-called dead dash down the old streets of centuries, and souls crowd on the footways that we, in the moment, call bygone years. The souls of all the dead are alive again, and pulsating actively around you. You are out in the other infinity.

Something of this happened to our islander. Mysterious "feelings" came upon him, that he wasn't used to; strange awarenesses of old, far-gone men, and other influences; men of Gaul, with big moustaches, who had been on his island, and had vanished from the face of it, but not out of the air of night. They were there still, hurtling their big, violent, unseen bodies through the night. And there were priests, with golden knives and mistletoe; then other priests, with a crucifix; then pirates with murder on the sea.

Our islander was uneasy. He didn't believe, in the daytime, in any of this nonsense. But at night it just was so. He had reduced himself to a single point in space, and, a point being that which has neither length nor breadth, he had to step off it into somewhere else. Just as you must step into the sea, if the waters wash your foothold away, so he had, at night, to step off into the other world of undying time.

He was uncannily aware, as he lay in the dark, that the blackthorn grove that seemed a bit uncanny even in the realm of space and day, at night was crying with old men of an invisible race, around the altar stone. What was a ruin under the hornbeam trees by day, was a moaning of bloodstained priests with crucifixes, on the ineffable night. What was a cave and a hidden beach between coarse rocks, became in the invisible dark the purple-lipped imprecation of pirates.

To escape any more of this sort of awareness, our islander daily concentrated upon his material island. Why should it not be the Happy Isle at last? Why not the last small isle of the Hesperides, the perfect place, all filled with his own gracious, blossom-like spirit? A minute world of pure perfection, made by man, himself.

He began, as we begin all our attempts to regain Paradise, by spending money. The old, semi-feudal dwelling-house he restored, let in more light, put clear lovely carpets on the floor, clear, flower-petal curtains at the sullen windows, and wines in the cellars of rock. He brought over a buxom housekeeper from the world, and a soft-spoken, much-experienced butler. These too were to be islanders.

In the farm-house he put a bailiff, with two farm-hands. There were Jersey cows, tinkling a slow bell, among the gorse. There was a call to meals at midday, and the peaceful smoking of chimneys at evening, when rest descended.

A jaunty sailing-boat with a motor accessory rode in the shelter in the bay, just below the row of three white cottages. There was also a little yawl, and two row-boats drawn up on the sand. A fishing net was drying on its supports, a boat-load of new white planks stood criss-cross, a woman was going to the well with a bucket.

In the end cottage lived the skipper of the yacht, and his wife and son. He was a man from the other, large island, at home on this sea. Every fine day he went out fishing, with his son, every fine day there was fresh fish on the island.

In the middle cottage lived an old man and wife, a very faithful couple. The old man was a carpenter, and man of many jobs. He was always working, always the sound of his plane or his saw: lost in his work, he was another kind of islander.

In the third cottage was the mason, a widower with a son and two daughters. With the help of his boy, this man dug ditches and built fences, raised buttresses and erected a new outbuilding, and hewed stone from the little quarry. His daughters worked at the big house.

It was a quiet, busy little world. When the islander brought you over as his guest, you met first the dark-bearded, thin, smiling skipper, Arnold, then his boy Charles. At the house, the smooth-lipped butler who had lived all over the world valeted you, and created that curious creamy-smooth, disarming sense of luxury around you which only a perfect and rather untrustworthy servant can create. He disarmed you and had you at his mercy. The buxom housekeeper smiled and treated you with the subtly respectful familiarity, that is only dealt out to the true gentry. And the rosy maid threw a glance at you, as if you were very wonderful, coming from the great outer world. Then you met the smiling but watchful bailiff, who came from Cornwall, and the shy farm-hand from Berkshire, with his clean wife and two little children, then the rather sulky farm-hand from Suffolk. The mason, a Kent man, would talk to you by the yard, if you let him. Only the old carpenter was gruff and elsewhere absorbed.

Well then, it was a little world to itself, and everybody feeling very safe, and being very nice to you, as if you were really something special. But it was the islander's world, not yours. He was the Master. The special smile, the special attention was to the Master.

They all knew how well off they were. So the islander was no longer Mr. So-and-So. To everyone on the island, even to you yourself, he was "the Master."

Well, it was ideal. The Master was no tyrant. Ah no! He was a delicate, sensitive, handsome Master, who wanted everything perfect and everybody happy. Himself, of course, to be the fount of this happiness and perfection.

But in his way, he was a poet. He treated his guests royally, his servants liberally. Yet he was shrewd, and very wise. He never came the boss over his people. Yet he kept his eye on everything, like a shrewd, blue-eyed young Hermes. And it was amazing what a lot of knowledge he had at hand. Amazing what he knew about Jersey cows, and cheese-making, ditching and fencing, flowers and gardening, ships and the sailing of ships. He was a fount of knowledge about everything, and this knowledge he imparted to his people in an odd, half-ironical, half-portentous fashion, as if he really belonged to the quaint, half-real world of the gods.

They listened to him with their hats in their hands. He loved white clothes; or creamy white; and cloaks, and broad hats. So, in fine weather, the bailiff would see the elegant tall figure in creamy-white serge coming like some bird over the fallow, to look at the weeding of the turnips. Then there would be a doffing of hats, and a few minutes of whimsical, shrewd, wise talk, to which the bailiff answered admiringly, and the farm-hands listened in silent wonder, leaning on their hoes. The bailiff was almost tender, to the Master.

Or, on a windy morning, he would stand with his cloak blowing in the sticky sea-wind, on the edge of the ditch that was being dug to drain a little swamp, talking in the teeth of the wind to the man below, who looked up at him with steady and inscrutable eyes.

Or at evening in the rain he would be seen hurrying across the yard, the broad hat turned against the rain. And the farm-wife would hurriedly exclaim: "The Master! Get up, John, and clear him a place on the sofa." And then the door opened, and it was a cry of: "Why of all things, if it isn't the Master! Why have ye turned out then of a night like this, to come across to the like of we?" And the bailiff took his cloak, and the farm-wife his hat, the two farm-hands drew their chairs to the back, he sat on the sofa and took a child up near him. He was wonderful with children, talked to them simply wonderful, make you think of Our Saviour Himself, said the woman.

Always he was greeted with smiles, and the same peculiar deference, as if he were a higher, but also frailer being. They handled
him almost tenderly, and almost with adulation. But when he left,
or when they spoke of him, they had often a subtle, mocking smile
on their faces. There was no need to be afraid of "the Master." Just
let him have his own way. Only the old carpenter was sometimes
sincerely rude to him; so he didn't care for the old man.

It is doubtful whether any of them really liked him, man to man,
or even woman to man. But then it is doubtful if he really liked
any of them, as man to man, or man to woman. He wanted them to
be happy, and the little world to be perfect. But any one who wants
the world to be perfect must be careful not to have real likes and
dislikes. A general good-will is all you can afford.

The sad fact is, alas, that general good-will is always felt as something of an insult, by the mere object of it; and so it breeds a quite
special brand of malice. Surely general good-will is a form of ego-
ism, that it should have such a result!

Our islander, however, had his own resources. He spent long
hours in his library, for he was compiling a book of reference to all
the flowers mentioned in the Greek and Latin authors. He was not
a great classical scholar: the usual public-school equipment. But
there are such excellent translations nowadays. And it was so lovely,
tracing flower after flower as it blossomed in the ancient world.

So the first year on the island passed by. A great deal had been
done. Now the bills flooded in, and the Master, conscientious in all
things, began to study them. The study left him pale and breathless.
He was not a rich man. He knew he had been making a hole in his
capital, to get the island into running order. When he came to look,
however, there was hardly anything left but hole. Thousands and
thousands of pounds had the island swallowed into nothingness.

But surely the bulk of the spending was over! Surely the island
would now begin to be self-supporting, even if it made no profit!
Surely he was safe. He paid a good many of the bills, and took a
little heart. But he had had a shock, and the next year, the coming
year, there must be economy, frugality. He told his people so, in
simple and touching language. And they said: "Why surely!
Surely!"

So, while the wind blew and the rain lashed outside, he would
sit in his library with the bailiff over a pipe and a pot of beer, dis-

cussing farm projects. He lifted his narrow handsome face, and his
blue eye became dreamy. "*What* a wind!" It blew like cannon shots.
He thought of his island, lashed with foam, and inaccessible, and
he exulted. . . . No, he must not lose it. He turned back to the farm
projects with the zest of genius, and his hands flicked white emphasis, while the bailiff intoned: "Yes, Sir! Yes, Sir! You're right,
Master!"

But the man was hardly listening. He was looking at the Master's
blue lawn shirt and curious pink tie with the fiery red stone, at the
enamel sleeve-links, and at the ring with the peculiar scarab. The
brown searching eyes of the man of the soil glanced repeatedly over
the fine, immaculate figure of the Master, with a sort of slow, cal-
culating wonder. But if he happened to catch the Master's bright,
exalted glance, his own eye lit up with a careful cordiality and deference, as he bowed his head slightly.

Thus between them they decided what crops should be sown,
what fertilizers should be used in different places, which breed of
pigs should be imported, and which line of turkeys. That is to say,
the bailiff, by continually cautiously agreeing with the Master, kept
out of it, and let the young man have his own way.

The Master knew what he was talking about. He was brilliant at
grasping the gist of a book, and knowing how to apply his knowledge. On the whole, his ideas were sound. The bailiff even knew it.
But in the man of the soil there was no answering enthusiasm. The
brown eyes smiled their cordial deference, but the thin lips never
changed. The Master pursed his own flexible mouth in a boyish ver-
satility, as he cleverly sketched in his ideas to the other man, and
the bailiff made eyes of admiration, but in his heart he was not attending, he was only watching the Master as he would have
watched a queer, alien animal, quite without sympathy, not impli-
cated.

So, it was settled, and the Master rang for Elvery, the butler, to
bring a sandwich. He, the Master, was pleased. The butler saw it,
and came back with anchovy and ham sandwiches, and a newly
opened bottle of vermouth. There was always a newly opened bottle of something.

It was the same with the mason. The Master and he discussed the
drainage of a bit of land, and more pipes were ordered, more special bricks, more this, more that.

Fine weather came at last, there was a little lull in the hard work on the island. The Master went for a short cruise in his yacht. It was not really a yacht, just a neat little bit of a yawl. They sailed along the coast of the mainland, and put in at the ports. At every port some friend turned up, the butler made elegant little meals in the cabin. Then the Master was invited to villas and hotels, his people disembarked him as if he were a prince.

And oh, how expensive it turned out! He had to telegraph to the bank for money. And he went home again, to economize.

The marsh-marigolds were blazing in the little swamp where the ditches were being dug for drainage. He almost regretted, now, the work in hand. The yellow beauties would not blaze again.

Harvest came, and a bumper crop. There must be a harvest-home supper. The long barn was now completely restored and added to. The carpenter had made long tables. Lanterns hung from the beams of the high-pitched roof. All the people of the island were assembled. The bailiff presided. It was a gay scene.

Towards the end of the supper the Master, in a velvet jacket, appeared with his guests. Then the bailiff rose and proposed: "The Master! Long life and health to the Master!" All the people drank the health with great enthusiasm and cheering. The Master replied with a little speech: They were on an island in a little world of their own. It depended on them all to make this world a world of true happiness and content. Each must do his part. He hoped he himself did what he could, for his heart was in his island, and with the people of his island.

The butler responded: As long as the island had such a Master, it could not but be a little heaven for all the people on it.—This was seconded with virile warmth by the bailiff and the mason, the skipper was beside himself. Then there was dancing, the old carpenter was fiddler.

But under all this, things were not well. The very next morning came the farm-boy to say that a cow had fallen over the cliff. The Master went to look. He peered over the not very high declivity, and saw her lying dead, on a green ledge under a bit of late-flowering broom. A beautiful, expensive creature, already looking swollen. But what a fool, to fall so unnecessarily!

It was a question of getting several men to haul her up the

bank: and then of skinning and burying her. No one would eat the
meat. How repulsive it all was!

This was symbolic of the island. As sure as the spirits rose in the
human breast, with a movement of joy, an invisible hand struck
malevolently out of the silence. There must not be any joy, nor
even any quiet peace. A man broke a leg, another was crippled with
rheumatic fever. The pigs had some strange disease. A storm drove
the yacht on a rock. The mason hated the butler, and refused to
let his daughter serve at the house.

Out of the very air came a stony, heavy malevolence. The island
itself seemed malicious. It would go on being hurtful and evil for
weeks at a time. Then suddenly again one morning it would be fair,
lovely as a morning in Paradise, everything beautiful and flowing.
And everybody would begin to feel a great relief, and a hope for
happiness.

Then as soon as the Master was opened out in spirit like an open
flower, some ugly blow would fall. Somebody would send him an
anonymous note, accusing some other person on the island. Somebody else would come hinting things against one of his servants.

"Some folks thinks they've got an easy job out here, with all the
pickings they make!" the mason's daughter screamed at the suave
butler, in the Master's hearing. He pretended not to hear.

"My man says this island is surely one of the lean kine of Egypt,
it would swallow a sight of money, and you'd never get anything
back out of it," confided the farm-hand's wife to one of the Master's
visitors.

The people were not contented. They were not islanders. "We
feel we're not doing right by the children," said those who had children. "We feel we're not doing right by ourselves," said those who
had no children. And the various families fairly came to hate one
another.

Yet the island was so lovely. When there was a scent of honey-
suckle, and the moon brightly flickering down on the sea, then even
the grumblers felt a strange nostalgia for it. It set you yearning,
with a wild yearning; perhaps for the past, to be far back in the
mysterious past of the island, when the blood had a different throb.
Strange floods of passion came over you, strange violent lusts and
imaginations of cruelty. The blood and the passion and the lust

which the island had known. Uncanny dreams, half-dreams, half-evocated yearnings.

The Master himself began to be a little afraid of his island. He felt here strange violent feelings he had never felt before, and lustful desires that he had been quite free from. He knew quite well now that his people didn't love him at all. He knew that their spirits were secretly against him, malicious, jeering, envious, and lurking to down him. He became just as wary and secretive with regard to them.

But it was too much. At the end of the second year, several departures took place. The housekeeper went. The Master always blamed self-important women most. The mason said he wasn't going to be monkeyed about any more, so he took his departure, with his family. The rheumatic farm-hand left.

And then the year's bills came in, the Master made up his accounts. In spite of good crops, the assets were ridiculous, against the spending. The island had again lost, not hundreds but thousands of pounds. It was incredible. But you simply couldn't believe it! Where had it all gone?

The Master spent gloomy nights and days, going through accounts in the library. He was thorough. It became evident, now the housekeeper had gone, that she had swindled him. Probably everybody was swindling him. But he hated to think it, so he put the thought away.

He emerged, however, pale and hollow-eyed from his balancing of unbalanceable accounts, looking as if something had kicked him in the stomach. It was pitiable. But the money had gone, and there was an end of it. Another great hole in his capital. How could people be so heartless?

It couldn't go on, that was evident. He would soon be bankrupt. He had to give regretful notice to his butler. He was afraid to find out how much his butler had swindled him. Because the man was such a wonderful butler, after all. And the farm-bailiff had to go. The Master had no regrets in that quarter. The losses on the farm had almost embittered him.

The third year was spent in rigid cutting down of expenses. The island was still mysterious and fascinating. But it was also treacherous and cruel, secretly, fathomlessly malevolent. In spite of all its fair show of white blossom and bluebells, and the lovely dignity of foxgloves bending their rose-red bells, it was your implacable enemy.

With reduced staff, reduced wages, reduced splendour, the third year went by. But it was fighting against hope. The farm still lost a good deal. And once more, there was a hole in that remnant of capital. Another hole, in that which was already a mere remnant round the old holes. The island was mysterious in this also: it seemed to pick the very money out of your pocket, as if it were an octopus with invisible arms stealing from you in every direction.

Yet the Master still loved it. But with a touch of rancour now.

He spent, however, the second half of the fourth year intensely working on the mainland, to be rid of it. And it was amazing how difficult he found it to dispose of an island. He had thought that everybody was pining for such an island as his; but not at all. Nobody would pay any price for it. And he wanted now to get rid of it, as a man who wants a divorce at any cost.

It was not till the middle of the fifth year that he transferred it, at a considerable loss to himself, to an hotel company who were willing to speculate in it. They were to turn it into a handy honeymoon-and-golf island!

There, take that, island which didn't know when it was well off! Now be a honeymoon-and-golf island!

Second Island

The islander had to move. But he was not going to the mainland. Oh, no! He moved to the smaller island, which still belonged to him. And he took with him the faithful old carpenter and wife, the couple he never really cared for; also a widow and daughter, who had kept house for him the last year; also an orphan lad, to help the old man.

The small island was very small; but, being a hump of rock in the sea, it was bigger than it looked. There was a little track among rocks and bushes, winding and scrambling up and down around the islet, so that it took you twenty minutes to do the circuit. It was more than you would have expected.

Still, it was an island. The islander moved himself, with all his books, into the commonplace six-roomed house up to which you had to scramble from the rocky landing-place. There were also two joined-together cottages. The old carpenter lived in one, with his wife and the lad, the widow and daughter lived in the other.

At last all was in order. The Master's books filled two rooms. It was already autumn, Orion lifting out of the sea. And in the dark nights, the Master could see the lights on his late island, where the hotel company were entertaining guests who would advertise the new resort for honeymoon-golfers.

On his hump of rock, however, the Master was still master. He explored the crannies, the odd handbreadths of grassy level, the steep little cliffs where the last harebells hung, and the seeds of summer were brown above the sea, lonely and untouched. He peered down the old well. He examined the stone pen where the pig had been kept. Himself, he had a goat.

Yes, it was an island. Always, always, underneath among the rocks the celtic sea sucked and washed and smote its feathery greyness. How many different noises of the sea! deep explosions, rumblings, strange long sighs and whistling noises; then voices, real voices of people clamouring as if they were in a market, under the waters; and again, the far-off ringing of a bell, surely an actual bell! then a tremulous trilling noise, very long and alarming, and an undertone of hoarse gasping.

On this island there were no human ghosts, no ghosts of any ancient race. The sea, and the spume and the wind and the weather, had washed them all out, washed them out, so there was only the sound of the sea itself, its own ghost, myriad-voiced, communing and plotting and shouting all winter long. And only the smell of the sea, with a few bristly bushes of gorse and coarse tufts of heather, among the grey, pellucid rocks, in the grey, more pellucid air. The coldness, the greyness, even the soft, creeping fog of the sea! and the islet of rock humped up in it all, like the last point in space.

Green star Sirius stood over the sea's rim. The island was a shadow. Out at sea a ship showed small lights. Below, in the rocky cove, the row-boat and the motor-boat were safe. A light shone in the carpenter's kitchen. That was all.

Save, of course, that the lamp was lit in the house, where the widow was preparing supper, her daughter helping. The islander went in to his meal. Here he was no longer the Master, he was an islander again and he had peace. The old carpenter, the widow and daughter were all faithfulness itself. The old man worked while ever there was light to see, because he had a passion for work. The widow and her quiet, rather delicate daughter of thirty-three worked for the Master, because they loved looking after him, and they were infinitely grateful for the haven he provided them. But they didn't call him "the Master." They gave him his name: "Mr. Cathcart, Sir!" softly, and reverently. And he spoke back to them also softly, gently, like people far from the world, afraid to make a noise.

The island was no longer a "world." It was a sort of refuge. The islander no longer struggled for anything. He had no need. It was as if he and his few dependents were a small flock of sea-birds alighted on this rock, as they travelled through space, and keeping together without a word. The silent mystery of travelling birds.

He spent most of his day in his study. His book was coming along. The widow's daughter could type out his manuscript for him, she was not uneducated. It was the one strange sound on the island, the typewriter. But soon even its spattering fitted in with the sea's noises, and the wind's.

The months went by. The islander worked away in his study, the people of the island went quietly about their concerns. The goat had a little black kid with yellow eyes. There were mackerel in the sea. The old man went fishing in the rowboat, with the lad. When the weather was calm enough, they went off in the motor-boat to the biggest island, for the post. And they brought supplies, never a penny wasted. And the days went by, and the nights, without desire, without *ennui*.

The strange stillness from all desire was a kind of wonder to the islander. He didn't want anything. His soul at last was still in him, his spirit was like a dim-lit cave under water, where strange sea-foliage expands upon the watery atmosphere, and scarcely sways, and a mute fish shadowily slips in and slips away again. All still and soft and uncrying, yet alive as rooted sea-weed is alive.

The islander said to himself: "Is this happiness?" He said to himself: "I am turned into a dream. I feel nothing, or I don't know what I feel. Yet it seems to me I am happy."

Only he had to have something upon which his mental activity could work. So he spent long, silent hours in his study, working not very fast, nor very importantly, letting the writing spin softly from him as if it were drowsy gossamer. He no longer fretted whether it were good or not, what he produced. He slowly, softly spun it like gossamer, and, if it were to melt away as gossamer in autumn melts, he would not mind. It was only the soft evanescence of gossamy things which now seemed to him permanent. The very mist of eternity was in them. Whereas stone buildings, cathedrals for example, seemed to him to howl with temporary resistance, knowing they must fall at last: the tension of their long endurance seemed to howl forth from them all the time.

Sometimes he went to the mainland and to the city. Then he went elegantly, dressed in the latest style, to his club. He sat in a stall at the theatre, he shopped in Bond Street. He discussed terms for publishing his book. But over his face was that gossamy look of having dropped out of the race of progress, which made the vulgar city people feel they had won it over him, and made him glad to go back to his island.

He didn't mind if he never published his book. The years were blending into a soft mist, from which nothing obtruded. Spring came. There was never a primrose on his island, but he found a winter-aconite. There were two little sprayed bushes of blackthorn, and some wind-flowers. He began to make a list of the flowers on his islet, and that was absorbing. He noted a wild currant bush, and watched for the elder flowers on a stunted little tree, then for the first yellow rags of the broom, and wild roses. Bladder campion, orchids, stitchwort, celandine, he was prouder of them than if they had been people on his island. When he came across the golden saxifrage, so inconspicuous in a damp corner, he crouched over it in a trance, he knew not for how long, looking at it. Yet it was nothing to look at. As the widow's daughter found, when he showed it her.

He had said to her, in real triumph:

"I found the golden saxifrage this morning."

The name sounded splendid. She looked at him with fascinated brown eyes, in which was a hollow ache that frightened him a little.

"Did you, Sir? Is it a nice flower?"

He pursed his lips and tilted his brows.

"Well—not showy exactly. I'll show it you if you like."

"I should like to see it."

She was so quiet, so wistful. But he sensed in her a persistency which made him uneasy. She said she was so happy: really happy. She followed him quietly, like a shadow, on the rocky track where there was never room for two people to walk side by side. He went first, and could feel her there, immediately behind him, following so submissively, gloating on him from behind.

It was a kind of pity for her which made him become her lover: though he never realized the extent of the power she had gained over him, and how *she* willed it. But the moment he had fallen, a jangling feeling came upon him, that it was all wrong. He felt a nervous dislike of her. He had not wanted it. And it seemed to him, as far as her physical self went, she had not wanted it either. It was just her will. He went away, and climbed at the risk of his neck down to a ledge near the sea. There he sat for hours, gazing all jangled at the sea, and saying miserably to himself: "We didn't want it. We didn't really want it."

It was the automatism of sex that had caught him again. Not that he hated sex. He deemed it, as the Chinese do, one of the great life-mysteries. But it had become mechanical, automatic, and he wanted to escape that. Automatic sex shattered him, and filled him with a sort of death. He thought he had come through, to a new stillness of desirelessness. Perhaps beyond that, there was a new fresh delicacy of desire, an unentered frail communion of two people meeting on untrodden ground.

But be that as it might, this was not it. This was nothing new or fresh. It was automatic, and driven from the will. Even she, in her true self, hadn't wanted it. It was automatic in her.

When he came home, very late, and saw her face white with fear and apprehension of his feeling against her, he pitied her and spoke to her delicately, reassuringly. But he kept himself remote from her.

She gave no sign. She served him with the same silence, the same hidden hunger to serve him, to be near where he was. He felt her love following him with strange, awful persistency. She claimed nothing. Yet now, when he met her bright, brown, curiously vacant eyes, he saw in them the mute question. The question came direct at him, with a force and a power of will he never realized.

So he succumbed, and asked her again.

"Not," she said, "if it will make you hate me."

"Why should it?" he replied, nettled. "Of course not."

"You know I would do anything on earth for you."

It was only afterwards, in his exasperation, he remembered what she had said, and was more exasperated. Why should she pretend to do this *for him?* Why not for herself? But in his exasperation, he drove himself deeper in. In order to achieve some sort of satisfaction, which he never did achieve, he abandoned himself to her. Everybody on the island knew. But he did not care.

Then even what desire he had left him, and he felt only shattered. He felt that only with her will had she wanted him. Now he was shattered and full of self-contempt. His island was smirched and spoiled. He had lost his place in the rare desireless levels of Time to which he had at last arrived, and he had fallen right back. If only it had been true, delicate desire between them, and a delicate meeting on the third rare place where a man might meet a woman, when they were both true to the frail, sensitive, crocus flame of desire in them. But it had been no such thing: automatic, an act of will, not of true desire, it left him feeling humiliated.

He went away from the islet, in spite of her mute reproach. And he wandered about the continent, vainly seeking a place where he could stay. He was out of key; he did not fit in the world any more.

There came a letter from Flora—her name was Flora—to say she was afraid she was going to have a child. He sat down as if he were shot, and he remained sitting. But he replied to her: "Why be afraid? If it is so, it is so, and we should rather be pleased than afraid."

At this very moment, it happened there was an auction of islands. He got the maps, and studied them. And at the auction he bought, for very little money, another island. It was just a few acres of rock away in the north, on the outer fringe of the isles. It was low, it rose out of the great ocean. There was not a building, not even a tree on it. Only northern sea-turf, a pool of rain-water, a bit of sedge, rock, and sea-birds. Nothing else. Under the weeping wet western sky.

He made a trip to visit his new possession. For several days, owing to the seas, he could not approach it. Then, in a light sea-mist, he landed, and saw it hazy, low, stretching apparently a long way. But it was illusion. He walked over the wet, springy turf, and dark-grey sheep tossed away from him, spectral, bleating hoarsely. And he came to the dark pool, with the sedge. Then on in the dampness, to the grey sea sucking angrily among the rocks.

This was indeed an island.

So he went home to Flora. She looked at him with guilty fear, but also with a triumphant brightness in her uncanny eyes. And again he was gentle, he reassured her, even he wanted her again, with that curious desire that was almost like toothache. So he took her to the mainland, and they were married, since she was going to have his child.

They returned to the island. She still brought in his meals, her own along with them. She sat and ate with him. He would have it so. The widowed mother preferred to stay in the kitchen. And Flora slept in the guest-room of his house, mistress of his house.

His desire, whatever it was, died in him with nauseous finality. The child would still be months coming. His island was hateful to him, vulgar, a suburb. He himself had lost all his finer distinction. The weeks passed in a sort of prison, in humiliation. Yet he stuck it out, till the child was born. But he was meditating escape. Flora did not even know.

A nurse appeared, and ate at table with them. The doctor came sometimes, and, if the sea were rough, he too had to stay. He was cheery over his whisky.

They might have been a young couple in Golders Green.

The daughter was born at last. The father looked at the baby, and felt depressed, almost more than he could bear. The millstone was tied round his neck. But he tried not to show what he felt. And Flora did not know. She still smiled with a kind of half-witted triumph in her joy, as she got well again. Then she began again to look at him with those aching, suggestive, somehow impudent eyes. She adored him so.

This he could not stand. He told her that he had to go away for a time. She wept, but she thought she had got him. He told her he had settled the best part of his property on her, and wrote down for her what income it would produce. She hardly listened, only looked at him with those heavy, adoring, impudent eyes. He gave her a cheque-book, with the amount of her credit duly entered. This did arouse her interest. And he told her, if she got tired of the island, she could choose her home wherever she wished.

She followed him with those aching, persistent brown eyes, when he left, and he never even saw her weep.

He went straight north, to prepare his third island.

THE THIRD ISLAND

The third island was soon made habitable. With cement and the big pebbles from the shingle beach, two men built him a hut, and roofed it with corrugated iron. A boat brought over a bed and table, and three chairs, with a good cupboard, and a few books. He laid in a supply of coal and paraffin and food—he wanted so little.

The house stood near the flat shingle bay where he landed and where he pulled up his light boat. On a sunny day in August the men sailed away and left him. The sea was still and pale blue. On the horizon he saw the small mail-steamer slowly passing northwards, as if she were walking. She served the outer isles twice a week. He could row out to her if need be, in calm weather, and he could signal her from a flagstaff behind his cottage.

Half a dozen sheep still remained on the island, as company; and he had a cat to rub against his legs. While the sweet, sunny days of the northern autumn lasted, he would walk among the rocks, and over the springy turf of his small domain, always coming to the ceaseless, restless sea. He looked at every leaf that might be different from another, and he watched the endless expansion and contraction of the water-tossed sea-weed. He had never a tree, not even a bit of heather to guard. Only the turf, and tiny turf-plants, and the sedge by the pool, the sea-weed in the ocean. He was glad. He didn't want trees or bushes. They stood up like people, too assertive. His bare, low-pitched island in the pale blue sea was all he wanted.

He no longer worked at his book. The interest had gone. He liked to sit on the low elevation of his island, and see the sea; nothing but the pale, quiet sea. And to feel his mind turn soft and hazy, like the hazy ocean. Sometimes, like a mirage, he would see the shadow of land rise hovering to northwards. It was a big island beyond. But quite without substance.

He was soon almost startled when he perceived the steamer on the near horizon, and his heart contracted with fear, lest it were going to pause and molest him. Anxiously he watched it go, and not till it was out of sight did he feel truly relieved, himself again. The tension of waiting for human approach was cruel. He did not want to be approached. He did not want to hear voices. He was shocked by the sound of his own voice, if he inadvertently spoke to his cat. He rebuked himself for having broken the great silence. And he was irritated when his cat would look up at him and mew faintly, plaintively. He frowned at her. And she knew. She was becoming wild, lurking in the rocks, perhaps fishing.

But what he disliked most was when one of the lumps of sheep opened its mouth and baa-ed its hoarse, raucous baa. He watched it, and it looked to him hideous and gross. He came to dislike the sheep very much.

He wanted only to hear the whispering sound of the sea, and the sharp cries of the gulls, cries that came out of another world to him. And best of all, the great silence.

He decided to get rid of the sheep, when the boat came. They were accustomed to him now, and stood and stared at him with yellow or colourless eyes, in an insolence that was almost cold ridicule. There was a suggestion of cold indecency about them. He disliked them very much. And when they jumped with staccato jumps off the rocks, and their hoofs made the dry, sharp hit, and the fleece flopped on their square backs—he found them repulsive, degrading.

The fine weather passed, and it rained all day. He lay a great deal on his bed, listening to the water trickling from his roof into the zinc water-butt, looking through the open door at the rain, the dark rocks, the hidden sea. Many gulls were on the island now: many sea-birds of all sorts. It was another world of life. Many of the birds he had never seen before. His old impulse came over him, to send for a book, to know their names. In a flicker of the old passion, to know the name of everything he saw, he even decided to row out to the steamer. The names of these birds! he must know their names, otherwise he had not got them, they were not quite alive to him.

But the desire left him, and he merely watched the birds as they wheeled or walked around him, watched them vaguely, without discrimination. All interest had left him. Only there was one gull, a big handsome fellow, who would walk back and forth, back and forth in front of the open door of the cabin, as if he had some mission there. He was big, and pearl-grey, and his roundnesses were as smooth and lovely as a pearl. Only the folded wings had shut black pinions, and on the closed black feathers were three very distinct white dots, making a pattern. The islander wondered very much, why this bit of trimming on the bird out of the far, cold seas. And as the gull walked back and forth, back and forth in front of the cabin, strutting on pale-dusky gold feet, holding up his pale yellow beak, that was curved at the tip, with curious alien importance, the man wondered over him. He was portentous, he had a meaning.

Then the bird came no more. The island, which had been full of sea-birds, the flash of wings, the sound and cut of wings and sharp eerie cries in the air, began to be deserted again. No longer they sat like living eggs on the rocks and turf, moving their heads, but scarcely rising into flight round his head. No longer they ran across the turf among the sheep, and lifted themselves upon low wings. The host had gone. But some remained, always.

The days shortened, and the world grew eerie. One day the boat came: as if suddenly, swooping down. The islander found it a violation. It was torture to talk to those two men, in their homely clumsy clothes. The air of familiarity around them was very repugnant to him. Himself, he was neatly dressed, his cabin was neat and tidy. He resented any intrusion, the clumsy homeliness, the heavy-footedness of the two fishermen was really repulsive to him.

The letters they had brought, he left lying unopened in a little box. In one of them was his money. But he could not bear to open even that one. Any kind of contact was repulsive to him. Even to read his name on an envelope. He hid the letters away.

And the hustle and horror of getting the sheep caught and tied and put in the ship made him loathe with profound repulsion the whole of the animal creation. What repulsive god invented animals, and evil-smelling men? To his nostrils, the fishermen and the sheep alike smelled foul; an uncleanness on the fresh earth.

He was still nerve-racked and tortured when the ship at last lifted sail and was drawing away, over the still sea. And sometimes days after, he would start with repulsion, thinking he heard the munching of sheep.

The dark days of winter drew on. Sometimes there was no real day at all. He felt ill, as if he were dissolving, as if dissolution had already set in inside him. Everything was twilight, outside, and in his mind and soul. Once, when he went to the door, he saw black heads of men swimming in his bay. For some moments he swooned unconscious. It was the shock, the horror of unexpected human approach. The horror in the twilight! And not till the shock had undermined him and left him disembodied, did he realize that the black heads were the heads of seals swimming in. A sick relief came over him. But he was barely conscious, after the shock. Later on, he sat and wept with gratitude, because they were not men. But he never realized that he wept. He was too dim. Like some strange, ethereal animal, he no longer realized what he was doing.

Only he still derived his single satisfaction from being alone, absolutely alone, with the space soaking into him. The grey sea alone, and the footing of his sea-washed island. No other contact. Nothing human to bring its horror into contact with him. Only space, damp, twilit, sea-washed space! This was the bread of his soul.

For this reason, he was most glad when there was a storm, or when the sea was high. Then nothing could get at him. Nothing could come through to him from the outer world. True, the terrific violence of the wind made him suffer badly. At the same time, it swept the world utterly out of existence for him. He always liked the sea to be heavily rolling and tearing. Then no boat could get at him. It was like eternal ramparts round his island.

He kept no track of time, and no longer thought of opening a book. The print, the printed letters, so like the depravity of speech, looked obscene. He tore the brass label from his paraffin stove. He obliterated any bit of lettering in his cabin.

His cat had disappeared. He was rather glad. He shivered at her thin, obtrusive call. She had lived in the coal shed. And each morning he had put her a dish of porridge, the same as he ate. He washed her saucer with repulsion. He did not like her writhing about. But he fed her scrupulously. Then one day she did not come for her porridge: she always mewed for it. She did not come again.

He prowled about his island in the rain, in a big oil-skin coat, not knowing what he was looking at, nor what he went out to see. Time had ceased to pass. He stood for long spaces, gazing from a white, sharp face, with those keen, far-off blue eyes of his, gazing fiercely and almost cruelly at the dark sea under the dark sky. And if he saw the labouring sail of a fishing boat away on the cold waters, a strange malevolent anger passed over his features.

Sometimes he was ill. He knew he was ill, because he staggered as he walked, and easily fell down. Then he paused to think what it was. And he went to his stores and took out dried milk and malt, and ate that. Then he forgot again. He ceased to register his own feelings.

The days were beginning to lengthen. All winter the weather had been comparatively mild, but with much rain, much rain. He had forgotten the sun. Suddenly, however, the air was very cold, and he began to shiver. A fear came over him. The sky was level and grey, and never a star appeared at night. It was very cold. More birds began to arrive. The island was freezing. With trembling hands he made a fire in his grate. The cold frightened him.

And now it continued, day after day, a dull, deathly cold. Occasional crumblings of snow were in the air. The days were greyly longer, but no change in the cold. Frozen grey daylight. The birds passed away, flying away. Some he saw lying frozen. It was as if all life were drawing away, contracting away from the north, contracting southwards. "Soon," he said to himself, "it will all be gone, and in all these regions nothing will be alive." He felt a cruel satisfaction in the thought.

Then one night there seemed to be a relief: he slept better, did not tremble half awake, and writhe so much, half-conscious. He had become so used to the quaking and writhing of his body, he hardly noticed it. But when for once it slept deep, he noticed that.

He awoke in the morning to a curious whiteness. His window was muffled. It had snowed. He got up and opened his door, and shuddered. Ugh! how cold! All white, with a dark leaden sea, and black rocks curiously speckled with white. The foam was no longer pure. It seemed dirty. And the sea ate at the whiteness of the corpse-like land. Crumbles of snow were silting down the dead air.

On the ground the snow was a foot deep, white and smooth and soft, windless. He took a shovel to clear round his house and shed. The pallor of morning darkened. There was a strange rumbling of far-off thunder, in the frozen air, and through the newly-falling snow, a dim flash of lightning. Snow now fell steadily down, in the motionless obscurity.

He went out for a few minutes. But it was difficult. He stumbled and fell in the snow, which burned his face. Weak, faint, he toiled home. And when he recovered, he took the trouble to make hot milk.

It snowed all the time. In the afternoon again there was a muffled rumbling of thunder, and flashes of lightning blinking reddish through the falling snow. Uneasy, he went to bed and lay staring fixedly at nothing.

Morning seemed never to come. An eternity long he lay and waited for one alleviating pallor on the night. And at last it seemed the air was paler. His house was a cell faintly illuminated with white light. He realized the snow was walled outside his window. He got up, in the dead cold. When he opened his door, the motionless snow stopped him in a wall as high as his breast. Looking over the top of it, he felt the dead wind slowly driving, saw the snow-powder lift and travel like a funeral train. The blackish sea churned and champed, seeming to bite at the snow, impotent. The sky was grey, but luminous.

He began to work in a frenzy, to get at his boat. If he was to be shut in, it must be by his own choice, not by the mechanical power of the elements. He must get to the sea. He must be able to get at his boat.

But he was weak, and at times the snow overcame him. It fell on him, and he lay buried and lifeless. Yet every time, he struggled alive before it was too late, and fell upon the snow with the energy of fever. Exhausted, he would not give in. He crept indoors and made coffee and bacon. Long since he had cooked so much. Then he went at the snow once more. He must conquer the snow, this new, white brute force which had accumulated against him.

He worked in the awful, dead wind, pushing the snow aside, pressing it with his shovel. It was cold, freezing hard in the wind, even when the sun came out for a while, and showed him his white, lifeless surroundings, the black sea rolling sullen, flecked with dull spume, away to the horizons. Yet the sun had power on his face. It was **March**.

He reached the boat. He pushed the snow away, then sat down under the lee of the boat, looking at the sea, which nearly swirled to his feet, in the high tide. Curiously natural the pebbles looked, in a world gone all uncanny. The sun shone no more. Snow was falling in hard crumbs, that vanished as if by miracle as they touched the hard blackness of the sea. Hoarse waves rang in the shingle, rushing up at the snow. The wet rocks were brutally black. And all the time the myriad swooping crumbs of snow, demonish, touched the dark sea and disappeared.

During the night there was a great storm. It seemed to him he could hear the vast mass of the snow striking all the world with a ceaseless thud; and over it all, the wind roared in strange hollow volleys, in between which came a jump of blindfold lightning, then the low roll of thunder heavier than the wind. When at last the dawn faintly discoloured the dark, the storm had more or less subsided, but a steady wind drove on. The snow was up to the top of his door.

Sullenly, he worked to dig himself out. And he managed, through sheer persistency, to get out. He was in the tail of a great drift, many feet high. When he got through, the frozen snow was not more than two feet deep. But his island was gone. Its shape was all changed, great heaping white hills rose where no hills had been, inaccessible, and they fumed like volcanoes, but with snow powder. He was sickened and overcome.

His boat was in another, smaller drift. But he had not the strength to clear it. He looked at it helplessly. The shovel slipped from his hands, and he sank in the snow, to forget. In the snow itself, the sea resounded.

Something brought him to. He crept to his house. He was almost without feeling. Yet he managed to warm himself, just that part of him which leaned in snow-sleep over the coal fire. Then again, he made hot milk. After which, carefully, he built up the fire.

The wind dropped. Was it night again? In the silence, it seemed he could hear the panther-like dropping of infinite snow. Thunder rumbled nearer, crackled quick after the bleared reddened lightning. He lay in bed in a kind of stupor. The elements! The elements! His mind repeated the word dumbly. You can't win against the elements.

How long it went on, he never knew. Once, like a wraith, he got out, and climbed to the top of a white hill on his unrecognizable island. The sun was hot. "It is summer," he said to himself, "and the time of leaves." He looked stupidly over the whiteness of his foreign island, over the waste of the lifeless sea. He pretended to imagine he saw the wink of a sail. Because he knew too well there would never again be a sail on that stark sea.

As he looked, the sky mysteriously darkened and chilled. From far off came the mutter of the unsatisfied thunder, and he knew it was the signal of the snow rolling over the sea. He turned, and felt its breath on him.

LAWRENCE: *The Man Who Loved Islands*

1. The story begins: "There was a man who loved islands." Hesse's "Within and Without" opens: "There was once a man named Frederick"; Aleichem's "Tit for Tat" starts: "Once I was a rabbiner." Do you attach any significance to this phrasing of the introduction?

2. What kind of man is Cathcart? What, according to Lawrence, does he stand for? Is he a saint or a devil?

3. Why is Lawrence antagonistic and ironic toward his protagonist?

4. Why does Cathcart go from one island to another? Why are there three islands and not two or four?

5. What is the significance of his experiences on each island? How are they related?

6. What does Cathcart reject? What does he attempt to embrace?

7. Why is there such a preponderance of the color white in the story? What symbolic meaning does the snow have? If you have the chance, read Joyce's "The Dead" and Conrad Aiken's "Silent Snow, Secret Snow" and compare the use of snow as a symbol in each story. Does snow have symbolic importance in "The District Doctor"? How can you tell?

8. Lawrence's imagery helps to carry the burden of his theme. How would you describe it?

9. A persistent theme in Lawrence's earlier work is his hatred of vulgar humanity and his need to withdraw from it into isolation. For example, in a letter to Bertrand Russell, he talks about standing outside the mob and throwing bombs into it. Is this story an intensification of this doctrine or a denial of it?

Pär Lagerkvist

THE CHILDREN'S CAMPAIGN

Those who admire the haunted landscapes and dark allegories of
Ingmar Bergman should be attracted to the work of Pär Lagerkvist,
Swedish novelist, poet, and dramatist. Born in Växjö in 1891 and
schooled at Uppsala, Lagerkvist left Sweden to educate himself in
European letters; the influence of the Cubist and Expressionist
experiments is discernible especially in the collection called The
Eternal Smile, *the source of the following story. In 1930, he re-*
turned to Sweden and, according to critics, created a trend in
Swedish poetry comparable to T. S. Eliot's impact on English. His
plays have also won high praise at home, but it is as a writer of
novels with Swiftian undertones like The Hangman *(1933),* The
Dwarf *(1944), and* Barabbas *(1950) that he was awarded the*
Nobel Prize in 1951. Like his novels, "The Children's Campaign"
is an ironic tale in which Lagerkvist indicts an entire age.

EVEN the children at that time received military training,
were assembled in army units and exercised just as though on active service, had their own headquarters and annual maneuvers
when everything was conducted as in a real state of war. The
grownups had nothing directly to do with this training; the children actually exercised themselves and all command was entrusted
to them. The only use made of adult experience was to arrange
officers' training courses for especially suitable boys, who were
chosen with the greatest care and who were then put in charge
of the military education of their comrades in the ranks.

These schools were of high standing and there was hardly a boy
throughout the land who did not dream of going to them. But the
entrance tests were particularly hard; not only a perfect physique
was required but also a highly developed intelligence and character. The age of admission was six to seven years and the small
cadets then received an excellent training, both purely military and

344]   PÄR LAGERKVIST

in all other respects, chiefly the further molding of character. It was also greatly to one's credit in after life to have passed through one of these schools. It was really on the splendid foundation laid here that the quality, organization and efficiency of the child army rested.

Thereafter, as already mentioned, the grownups in no way interfered but everything was entrusted to the children themselves. No adult might meddle in the command, in organizational details or matters of promotion. Everything was managed and supervised by the children; all decisions, even the most vital, being reached by their own little general staff. No one over fourteen was allowed. The boys then passed automatically into the first age group of the regular troops with no mean military training already behind them.

The large child army, which was the object of the whole nation's love and admiration, amounted to three army corps of four divisions: infantry, light field artillery, medical and service corps. All physically fit boys were enrolled in it and a large number of girls belonged to it as nurses, all volunteers.

Now it so happened that a smaller, quite insignificant nation behaved in a high-handed and unseemly way toward its powerful neighbor, and the insult was all the greater since this nation was by no means an equal. Indignation was great and general and, since people's feelings were running high, it was necessary to rebuke the malapert and at the same time take the chance to subjugate the country in question. In this situation the child army came forward and through its high command asked to be charged with the crushing and subduing of the foe. The news of this caused a sensation and a wave of fervor throughout the country. The proposal was given serious consideration in supreme quarters and as a result the commission was given, with some hesitation, to the children. It was in fact a task well suited to this army, and the people's obvious wishes in the matter had also to be met, if possible.

The Foreign Office therefore sent the defiant country an unacceptable ultimatum and, pending the reply, the child army was mobilized within twenty-four hours. The reply was found to be unsatisfactory and war was declared immediately.

Unparalleled enthusiasm marked the departure for the front. The intrepid little youngsters had green sprigs in the barrels of their rifles and were pelted with flowers. As is so often the case, the campaign was begun in the spring, and this time the general opinion was that there was something symbolic in it. In the capital the little commander in chief and chief of general staff, in the presence of huge crowds, made a passionate speech to the troops in which he expressed the gravity of the hour and his conviction of their unswerving valor and willingness to offer their lives for their country.

The speech, made in a strong voice, aroused the greatest ecstasy. The boy—who had a brilliant career behind him and had reached his exalted position at the age of only twelve and a half—was acclaimed with wild rejoicing and from this moment was the avowed hero of the entire nation. There was not a dry eye and those of the many mothers especially shone with pride and happiness. For them it was the greatest day in their lives. The troops marched past below fluttering banners, each regiment with its music corps at the head. It was an unforgettable spectacle.

There were also many touching incidents, evincing a proud patriotism, as when a little four-year-old, who had been lifted up on his mother's arm so that he could see, howled with despair and shouted, "I want to go, too. I want to go, too!" while his mother tried to hush him, explaining that he was too small. "Small am I, eh?" he exclaimed, punching her face so that her nose bled. The evening papers were full of such episodes showing the mood of the people and of the troops who were so sure of victory. The big march past was broadcast and the c in c's speech, which had been recorded, was broadcast every evening during the days that followed at 7:15 P.M.

Military operations had already begun, however, and reports of victory began to come in at once from the front. The children had quickly taken the offensive and on one sector of the front had inflicted a heavy defeat on the enemy, seven hundred dead and wounded and over twelve hundred prisoners, while their own losses amounted to only a hundred or so fallen. The victory was celebrated at home with indescribable rejoicing and with thanksgiving services in the churches. The newspapers were filled with accounts of individual instances of valor and pictures several columns wide of the high command, of which the leading personalities, later so well-known, began to appear now for the first time. In their joy, mothers and aunts sent so much chocolate and other sweets to the army that headquarters had to issue a strict order that all such parcels were, for the time being at any rate, forbidden, since they had made whole regiments unfit for battle and these in their turn had nearly been surrounded by the enemy.

For the child army was already far inside enemy territory and still managed to keep the initiative. The advance sector did retreat slightly in order to establish contact with its wings but only improved its positions by so doing. A stalemate ensued in the theater of war for some time after this.

During July, however, troops were concentrated for a big attack along the whole line and huge reserves—the child army's, in comparison with those of its opponent, were almost inexhaustible—were mustered to the front. The new offensive, which lasted for several weeks, resulted, too, in an almost decisive victory for the whole army, even though casualties were high. The children defeated the enemy all along the line but did not manage to pursue him and thereby exploit their success to the full, because he was greatly favored by the fact that his legs were so much longer, an advantage of which he made good use. By dint of forced marches, however, the children finally succeeded in cutting the enemy's right flank to pieces. They were now in the very heart of the country and their outposts were only a few days' march from the capital.

It was a pitched battle on a big scale and the newspapers had enormous headlines every day which depicted the dramatic course of events. At set hours the radio broadcast the gunfire and a résumé of the position. The war correspondents described in rapturous words and vivid colors the state of affairs at the front—the children's incredible feats, their indomitable courage and self-sacrifice, the whole morale of the army. It was no exaggeration. The youngsters showed the greatest bravery; they really behaved like heroes. One only had to see their discipline and contempt of death during an attack, as though they had been grown-up men at least.

It was an unforgettable sight to see them storm ahead under murderous machine gun fire and the small medical orderlies dart nimbly forward and pick them up as they fell. Or the wounded and dying who were moved behind the front, those who had had a leg shot away or their bellies ripped open by a bayonet so that their entrails hung out—but without one sound of complaint crossing their small lips. The hand-to-hand fighting had been very fierce and a great number of children fell in this, while they were superior in the actual firing. Losses were estimated at 4,000 on the enemy side and 7,000 among the children, according to the secret reports. The victory had been hard won but all the more complete.

This battle became very famous and was also of far greater importance than any previously. It was now clear beyond all doubt that the children were incomparably superior in tactics, discipline and individual courage. At the same time, however, it was admitted by experts that the enemy's headlong retreat was very skillfully carried out, that his strength was evidently in defense and that he should not be underrated too much. Toward the end, also, he had unexpectedly made a stubborn resistance which had prevented any further penetration.

This observation was not without truth. In actual fact the enemy was anything but a warlike nation, and indeed his forces found it very difficult to hold their own. Nevertheless, they improved with practice during the fighting and became more efficient as time went on. This meant that they caused the children a good deal of trouble in each succeeding battle. They also had certain advantages on their side. As their opponents were so small, for instance, it was possible after a little practice to spit several of them on the bayonet at once, and often a kick was enough to fell them to the ground.

But against this, the children were so much more numerous and also braver. They were everywhere. They swarmed over one and in between one's legs and the unwarlike people were nearly demented by all these small monsters who fought like fiends. Little fiends was also what they were generally called—not without reason—and this name was even adopted in the children's homeland, but there it was a mark of honor and a pet name. The enemy troops had all their work cut out merely defending themselves. At last, however, they were able to check the others' advance and even venture on one or two counterattacks. Everything then came to a standstill for a while and there was a breathing space.

The children were now in possession of a large part of the country. But this was not always so easy. The population did not particularly like them and proved not to be very fond of children. It was alleged that snipers fired on the boys from houses and that they were ambushed when they moved in small detachments. Children had even been found impaled on stakes or with their eyes gouged out, so it was said. And in many cases these stories were no doubt true. The population had quite lost their heads, were obviously goaded into a frenzy, and as they were of little use as a warlike nation and their cruelty could therefore find no natural outlet, they tried to revenge themselves by atrocities. They felt overrun by all the foreign children as by troublesome vermin and, being at their wits' end, they simply killed whenever they had the chance. In order to put an end to these outrages the children burned one village after the other and shot hundreds of people daily, but this did not improve matters. The despicable deeds of these craven guerrillas caused them endless trouble.

At home, the accounts of all this naturally aroused the most bitter resentment. People's blood boiled to think that their small soldiers were treated in this way by those who had nothing to do with the war, by barbarous civilians who had no notion of established and judicial forms. Even greater indignation was caused, however, by an incident that occurred inside the occupied area some time after the big summer battle just mentioned.

A lieutenant who was out walking in the countryside came to a stream where a large, fat woman knelt washing clothes. He asked her the way to a village close by. The woman, who probably suspected him of evil intent, retorted, "What are you doing here? You ought to be at home with your mother." Whereupon the lieutenant drew his saber to kill her, but the woman grabbed hold of him and, putting him over her knee, thwacked him black and blue with her washboard so that he was unable to sit down for several days afterward. He was so taken aback that he did nothing, armed though he was to the teeth. Luckily no one saw the incident, but there were orders that all outrages on the part of the population were to be reported to headquarters. The lieutenant therefore duly reported what had happened to him. True, it gave him little satisfaction, but as he had to obey orders he had no choice. And so it all came out.

The incident aroused a storm of rage, particularly among those at home. The infamous deed was a humiliation for the country, an insult which nothing could wipe out. It implied a deliberate violation by this militarily ignorant people of the simplest rules of warfare. Everywhere, in the press, in propaganda speeches, in ordinary conversation, the deepest contempt and disgust for the deed was expressed. The lieutenant who had so flagrantly shamed the army had his officer's epaulettes ripped off in front of the assembled troops and was declared unworthy to serve any longer in the field. He was instantly sent home to his parents, who belonged to one of the most noted families but who now had to retire into obscurity in a remote part of the country.

The woman, on the other hand, became a heroic figure among her people and the object of their rapturous admiration. During the whole of the war she and her deed were a rallying national symbol which people looked up to and which spurred them on to further effort. She subsequently became a favorite motif in the profuse literature about their desperate struggle for freedom; a vastly popular figure, brought to life again and again as time passed, now in a rugged, everyday way which appealed to the man in the street, now in heroic female form on a grandiose scale, to become gradually more and more legendary, wreathed in saga and myth. In some versions she was shot by the enemy; in others she lived to a ripe old age, loved and revered by her people.

This incident, more than anything else, helped to increase the bad feelings between the two countries and to make them wage the war with ever greater ruthlessness. In the late summer, before the autumn rains began, both armies, ignorant of each other's plans, simultaneously launched a violent offensive, which devastated both sides. On large sectors of the front the troops completely annihilated each other so that there was not a single survivor left. Any peaceful inhabitants thereabouts who were still alive and ventured out of their cellars thought that the war was over, because all were slain.

But soon new detachments came up and began fighting again. Great confusion arose in other quarters from the fact that in the heat of attack men ran past each other and had to turn around in order to go on fighting; and that some parts of the line rushed ahead while others came behind, so that the troops were both in front of and behind where they should have been and time and again attacked each other in the rear. The battle raged in this way with extreme violence and shots were fired from all directions at once.

When at last the fighting ceased and stock was taken of the situation, it appeared that no one had won. On both sides there was an equal number of fallen, 12,924, and after all attacks and retreats the position of the armies was exactly the same as at the start of the

battle. It was agreed that both should claim the victory. Thereafter the rain set in and the armies went to earth in trenches and
put up barbed wire entanglements.

The children were the first to finish their trenches, since they had
had more to do with that kind of thing, and settled down in them
as best they could. They soon felt at home. Filthy and lousy, they
lived there in the darkness as though they had never done anything else. With the adaptability of children they quickly got into
the way of it. The enemy found this more difficult; he felt miserable
and homesick for the life above ground to which he was accustomed. Not so the children. When one saw them in their small gray
uniforms, which were caked thick with mud, and their small gas
masks, one could easily think they had been born to this existence.
They crept in and out of the holes down into the earth and scam-
pered about the passages like mice. When their burrows were attacked they were instantly up on the parapet and snapped back in
blind fury. As the months passed, this hopeless, harrowing life put
endurance to an increasingly severe test. But they never lost
courage or the will to fight.

For the enemy the strain was often too much; the glaring point-
lessness of it all made many completely apathetic. But the little
ones did not react like this. Children are really more fitted for war
and take more pleasure in it, while grownups tire of it after a while
and think it is boring. The boys continued to find the whole thing
exciting and they wanted to go on living as they were now. They
also had a more natural herd instinct; their unity and camaraderie
helped them a great deal, made it easier to hold out.

But, of course, even they suffered great hardship. Especially
when winter set in with its incessant rain, a cold sleet which made
everything sodden and filled the trenches with mud. It was enough
to unman anyone. But it would never have entered their heads to
complain. However bad things were, nothing could have made
them admit it. At home everyone was very proud of them. All the
cinemas showed parades behind the front and the little c in c and
his generals pinning medals for bravery on their soldiers' breasts.
People thought of them a great deal out there, of their little fiends,
realizing that they must be having a hard time.

At Christmas, in particular, thoughts went out to them, to the
lighted Christmas trees and all the sparkling childish eyes out in

the trenches; in every home people sat wondering how they were faring. But the children did not think of home. They were soldiers out and out, absorbed by their duty and their new life. They attacked in several places on the morning of Christmas Eve, inflicting fairly big losses on the enemy in killed and wounded, and did not stop until it was time to open their parcels. They had the real fighting spirit which might have been a lesson even to adults.

There was nothing sentimental about them. The war had hardened and developed them, made them men. It did happen that one poor little chap burst into tears when the Christmas tree was lighted, but he was made the laughing-stock of them all. "Are you homesick for your mummy, you bastard?" they said, and kept on jeering at him all evening. He was the object of their scorn all through Christmas; he behaved suspiciously and tried to keep to himself. Once he walked a hundred yards away from the post and, because he might well have been thinking of flight, he was seized and court-martialed. He could give no reason for having absented himself and since he had obviously intended to desert he was shot.

If those at home had been fully aware of the morale out there, they need not have worried. As it was, they wondered if the children could really hold their ground and half-regretted having entrusted them with the campaign, now that it was dragging on so long because of this nerve-racking stationary warfare. After the New Year help was even offered in secret, but it was rejected with proud indignation.

The morale of the enemy, on the other hand, was not so high. They did intend to fight to the last man, but the certainty of a complete victory was not so general as it should have been. They could not help thinking, either, how hopeless their fight really was; that in the long run they could not hold their own against these people who were armed to the very milk teeth, and this often dampened their courage.

Hardly had nature begun to come to life and seethe with the newly awakened forces of spring before the children started with incredible intensity to prepare for the decisive battle. Heavy mechanized artillery was brought up and placed in strong positions; huge troop movements went on night and day; all available fighting forces were concentrated in the very front lines. After murderous gunfire which lasted for six days, an attack was launched with great force and extreme skill. Individual bravery was, if possible, more dazzling than ever. The whole army was also a year older, and that means much at that age. But their opponents, too, were determined to do their utmost. They had assembled all their reserves, and their spirits, now that the rain had stopped and the weather was fine, were full of hope.

It was a terrible battle. The hospital trains immediately started going back from both sides packed with wounded and dying. Machine guns, tanks and gas played fearful havoc. For several days the outcome was impossible to foresee, since both armies appeared equally strong and the tide of battle constantly changed. The position gradually cleared, however. The enemy had expected the main attack in the center, but the child army turned out to be weakest there. Use was made of this, especially because they themselves were best prepared at this very point, and this part of the children's front was soon made to waver and was forced farther and farther back by repeated attack. Advantage was also taken of an ideal evening breeze from just the right quarter to gas the children in thousands. Encouraged by their victory, the troops pursued the offensive with all their might and with equal success.

The child army's retreat, however, turned out to be a stratagem, brilliantly conceived and carried out. Its center gave way more and more and the enemy, giving all his attention to this, forgot that at the same time he himself was wavering on both wings. In this way he ran his head into a noose. When the children considered that they had retreated far enough they halted, while the troops on the outermost wings, already far ahead, advanced swiftly until they met behind the enemy's back. The latter's entire army was thereby surrounded and in the grip of an iron hand. All the children's army had to do now was to draw the noose tighter. At last the gallant defenders had to surrender and let themselves be taken prisoner, which in fact they already were. It was the most disastrous defeat in history; not a single one escaped other than by death.

This victory became much more famous than any of the others and was eagerly studied at all military academies on account of its brilliantly executed, doubly effective encircling movement. The great general Sludelsnorp borrowed its tactics outright seventy years later at his victory over the Slivokvarks in the year 2048.

The war could not go on any longer now, because there was nothing left to fight, and the children marched to the capital with the imprisoned army between them to dictate the peace terms. These were handed over by the little commander in chief in the hall of mirrors in the stately old palace at a historic scene which was to be immortalized time and again in art and even now was reproduced everywhere in the weekly press. The film cameras whirred, the flashlights hissed and the radio broadcast the great moment to the world. The commander in chief, with austere and haughty mien and one foot slightly in front of the other, delivered the historic document with his right hand. The first and most important condition was the complete cession of the country, besides which the expenses of its capture were to be borne by the enemy, who thus had to pay the cost of the war on both sides, the last clause on account of the fact that he had been the challenging party and, according to his own admission, the cause of the war. The document was signed in dead silence, the only sound was the scratching of the fountain pen, which, according to the commentator's whisper, was solid gold and undoubtedly a future museum piece.

With this, everything was settled and the children's army returned to its own country, where it was received with indescribable rapture. Everywhere along the roads the troops were greeted with wild rejoicing; their homecoming was one long victory parade. The march into the capital and the dismissal there of the troops, which took place before vast crowds, were especially impressive. People waved and shouted in the streets as they passed, were beside themselves with enthusiasm, bands played, eyes were filled with tears of joy. Some of the loudest cheering was for the small invalids at the rear of the procession, blind and with limbs amputated, who had sacrificed themselves for their country. Many of them had already got small artificial arms and legs so that they looked just the same as before. The victory salute thundered, bayonets flashed in the sun. It was an unforgettable spectacle.

A strange, new leaf was written in the great book of history which would be read with admiration in time to come. The nation had seen many illustrious deeds performed, but never anything as proud as this. What these children had done in their devotion and fervent patriotism could never be forgotten.

Nor was it. Each spring, on the day of victory, school children marched out with flags in their hands to the cemeteries with all the small graves where the heroes rested under their small white crosses. The mounds were strewn with flowers and passionate speeches were made, reminding everyone of the glorious past, their imperishable honor and youthful, heroic spirit of self-sacrifice. The flags floated in the sun and the voices rang out clear as they sang their rousing songs, radiant childish eyes looking ahead to new deeds of glory.

Translated by Alan Blair

LAGERKVIST: *The Children's Campaign*

1. What effect does Lagerkvist's cool, detached style create? Does the story read like a fable? Explain.

2. Are children really more fitted than adults for war, as Lagerkvist develops the story? What point is he making? Should he make it directly? What would he lose by direct statement of his position?

3. What is the point of the episode involving the child-lieutenant and the fat woman who spanks him? Why the episode with the Christmas tree?

4. How does Lagerkvist tip his hand about his position? Or is this really a good way to fight small wars? Why should children not fight wars if their elders do?

5. Compare this story with Swift's "A Modest Proposal."

6. Is such training suitable for children, to build character and physique? Would you recommend it?

7. Does this story convey the horror that is intended? How? Or does it miss horror because we are accustomed to worse things?

8. Do you see any connection between Lagerkvist's point of view and that expressed in Musil's "A Man Without Character" or Lawrence's "The Man Who Loved Islands"? What do they have in common?

Ryūnosuke Akutagawa

IN A GROVE

*Ryūnosuke Akutagawa was born in 1892 and died a suicide in 1927.
He lived in Tokyo, attended the University there, later taught, and
then worked as a journalist. Among his first publications were
translations of Western writers, particularly the poetry of William
Butler Yeats and the prose of Anatole France. Characteristic of all
his work—which includes about a hundred short stories and much
incidental writing—is his precise, impersonal, restrained prose. "In
a Grove," with its conflicting testimony, raises the question of what
is fact and what is fiction, what is subjective and what objective, a
dialectic that fits perfectly Akutagawa's own tortured personality
and protean vision of reality.*

The Testimony of a Woodcutter Questioned by a High Police Commissioner

YES, SIR. Certainly, it was I who found the body. This
morning, as usual, I went to cut my daily quota of cedars, when
I found the body in a grove in a hollow in the mountains. The
exact location? About 150 meters off the Yamashina stage road.
It's an out-of-the-way grove of bamboo and cedars.

The body was lying flat on its back dressed in a bluish silk
kimono and a wrinkled head-dress of the Kyoto style. A single
sword-stroke had pierced the breast. The fallen bamboo-blades
around it were stained with bloody blossoms. No, the blood was no
longer running. The wound had dried up, I believe. And also, a gad-
fly was stuck fast there, hardly noticing my footsteps.

You ask me if I saw a sword or any such thing?

No, nothing, sir. I found only a rope at the root of a cedar near
by. And . . . well, in addition to a rope, I found a comb. That was
all. Apparently he must have made a battle of it before he was mur-

dered, because the grass and fallen bamboo-blades had been trampled down all around.

"A horse was near by?"

No, sir. It's hard enough for a man to enter, let alone a horse.

THE TESTIMONY OF A TRAVELING BUDDHIST PRIEST QUESTIONED BY A HIGH POLICE COMMISSIONER

The time? Certainly, it was about noon yesterday, sir. The unfortunate man was on the road from Sekiyama to Yamashina. He
was walking toward Sekiyama with a woman accompanying him
on horseback, who I have since learned was his wife. A scarf hanging from her head hid her face from view. All I saw was the color
of her clothes, a lilac-colored suit. Her horse was a sorrel with a fine
mane. The lady's height? Oh, about four feet five inches. Since I am
a Buddhist priest, I took little notice about her details. Well, the
man was armed with a sword as well as a bow and arrows. And I
remember that he carried some twenty odd arrows in his quiver.

Little did I expect that he would meet such a fate. Truly human
life is as evanescent as the morning dew or a flash of lightning. My
words are inadequate to express my sympathy for him.

THE TESTIMONY OF A POLICEMAN QUESTIONED BY A HIGH POLICE COMMISSIONER

The man that I arrested? He is a notorious brigand called Tajomaru. When I arrested him, he had fallen off his horse. He was
groaning on the bridge at Awataguchi. The time? It was in the early
hours of last night. For the record, I might say that the other day I
tried to arrest him, but unfortunately he escaped. He was wearing
a dark blue silk kimono and a large plain sword. And, as you see, he
got a bow and arrows somewhere. You say that this bow and these
arrows look like the ones owned by the dead man? Then Tajomaru
must be the murderer. The bow wound with leather strips, the black
lacquered quiver, the seventeen arrows with hawk feathers—these
were all in his possession I believe. Yes, sir, the horse is, as you say,
a sorrel with a fine mane. A little beyond the stone bridge I found
the horse grazing by the roadside, with his long rein dangling.

Surely there is some providence in his having been thrown by the horse.

Of all the robbers prowling around Kyoto, this Tajomaru has given the most grief to the women in town. Last autumn a wife who came to the mountain back of the Pindora of the Toribe Temple, presumably to pay a visit, was murdered, along with a girl. It has been suspected that it was his doing. If this criminal murdered the man, you cannot tell what he may have done with the man's wife. May it please your honor to look into this problem as well.

THE TESTIMONY OF AN OLD WOMAN QUESTIONED BY A HIGH POLICE COMMISSIONER

Yes, sir, that corpse is the man who married my daughter. He does not come from Kyoto. He was a samurai in the town of Kokufu in the province of Wakasa. His name was Kanazawa no Takehiko, and his age was twenty-six. He was of a gentle disposition, so I am sure he did nothing to provoke the anger of others.

My daughter? Her name is Masago, and her age is nineteen. She is a spirited, fun-loving girl, but I am sure she has never known any man except Takehiko. She has a small, oval, dark-complected face with a mole at the corner of her left eye.

Yesterday Takehiko left for Wakasa with my daughter. What bad luck it is that things should have come to such a sad end! What has become of my daughter? I am resigned to giving up my son-in-law as lost, but the fate of my daughter worries me sick. For heaven's sake leave no stone unturned to find her. I hate that robber Tajomaru, or whatever his name is. Not only my son-in-law, but my daughter . . . (Her later words were drowned in tears.)

TAJOMARU'S CONFESSION

I killed him, but not her. Where's she gone? I can't tell. Oh, wait a minute. No torture can make me confess what I don't know. Now things have come to such a head, I won't keep anything from you.

Yesterday a little past noon I met that couple. Just then a puff of wind blew, and raised her hanging scarf, so that I caught a glimpse of her face. Instantly it was again covered from my view. That may have been one reason; she looked like a Bodhisattva. At that moment I made up my mind to capture her even if I had to kill her man.

Why? To me killing isn't a matter of such great consequence as you might think. When a woman is captured, her man has to be killed anyway. In killing, I use the sword I wear at my side. Am I the only one who kills people? You, you don't use your swords. You kill people with your power, with your money. Sometimes you kill them on the pretext of working for their good. It's true they don't bleed. They are in the best of health, but all the same you've killed them. It's hard to say who is a greater sinner, you or me. (An ironical smile.)

But it would be good if I could capture a woman without killing her man. So, I made up my mind to capture her, and do my best not to kill him. But it's out of the question on the Yamashina stage road. So I managed to lure the couple into the mountains.

It was quite easy. I became their traveling companion, and I told them there was an old mound in the mountain over there, and that I had dug it open and found many mirrors and swords. I went on to tell them I'd buried the things in a grove behind the mountain, and that I'd like to sell them at a low price to anyone who would care to have them. Then . . . you see, isn't greed terrible? He was beginning to be moved by my talk before he knew it. In less than half an hour they were driving their horse toward the mountain with me.

When he came in front of the grove, I told them that the treasures were buried in it, and I asked them to come and see. The man had no objection—he was blinded by greed. The woman said she would wait on horseback. It was natural for her to say so, at the sight of a thick grove. To tell you the truth, my plan worked just as I wished, so I went into the grove with him, leaving her behind alone.

The grove is only bamboo for some distance. About fifty yards ahead there's a rather open clump of cedars. It was a convenient spot for my purpose. Pushing my way through the grove, I told him a plausible lie that the treasures were buried under the cedars. When I told him this, he pushed his laborious way toward the slender cedar visible through the grove. After a while the bamboo thinned out, and we came to where a number of cedars grew in a row. As soon as we got there, I seized him from behind. Because he was a trained, sword-bearing warrior, he was quite strong, but he was taken by surprise, so there was no help for him. I soon tied him up to the root of a cedar. Where did I get a rope? Thank heaven, being a robber, I had a rope with me, since I might have to scale a wall at any moment. Of course it was easy to stop him from calling out by gagging his mouth with fallen bamboo leaves.

When I disposed of him, I went to his woman and asked her to come and see him, because he seemed to have been suddenly taken sick. It's needless to say that this plan also worked well. The woman, her sedge hat off, came into the depths of the grove, where I led her by the hand. The instant she caught sight of her husband, she drew a small sword. I've never seen a woman of such violent temper. If I'd been off guard, I'd have got a thrust in my side. I dodged, but she kept on slashing at me. She might have wounded me deeply or killed me. But I'm Tajomaru. I managed to strike down her small sword without drawing my own. The most spirited woman is defenseless without a weapon. At least I could satisfy my desire for her without taking her husband's life.

Yes, . . . without taking his life. I had no wish to kill him. I was about to run away from the grove, leaving the woman behind in tears, when she frantically clung to my arm. In broken fragments of words, she asked that either her husband or I die. She said it was more trying than death to have her shame known to two men. She gasped out that she wanted to be the wife of whichever survived. Then a furious desire to kill him seized me. (Gloomy excitement.)

Telling you in this way, no doubt I seem a crueler man than you. But that's because you didn't see her face. Especially her burning eyes at that moment. As I saw her eye to eye, I wanted to make her my wife even if I were to be struck by lightning. I wanted to make her my wife . . . this single desire filled my mind. This was not only lust, as you might think. At that time if I'd had no other desire than lust, I'd surely not have minded knocking her down and running away. Then I wouldn't have stained my sword with his blood. But the moment I gazed at her face in the dark grove, I decided not to leave there without killing him.

But I didn't like to resort to unfair means to kill him. I untied him and told him to cross swords with me. (The rope that was found at the root of the cedar is the rope I dropped at the time.) Furious with anger, he drew his thick sword. And quick as thought, he sprang at me ferociously, without speaking a word. I needn't tell you how our fight turned out. The twenty-third stroke . . . please remember this. I'm impressed with this fact still. Nobody under the sun has ever clashed swords with me twenty strokes. (A cheerful smile.)

When he fell, I turned toward her, lowering my blood-stained sword. But to my great astonishment she was gone. I wondered to where she had run away. I looked for her in the clump of cedars. I listened, but heard only a groaning sound from the throat of the dying man.

As soon as we started to cross swords, she may have run away through the grove to call for help. When I thought of that, I decided it was a matter of life and death to me. So, robbing him of his sword, and bow and arrows, I ran out to the mountain road. There I found her horse still grazing quietly. It would be a mere waste of words to tell you the later details, but before I entered town I had already parted with the sword. That's all my confession. I know that my head will be hung in chains anyway, so put me down for the maximum penalty. (A defiant attitude.)

THE CONFESSION OF A WOMAN WHO HAS COME TO THE *Shimizu* TEMPLE

That man in the blue silk kimono, after forcing me to yield to him, laughed mockingly as he looked at my bound husband. How horrified my husband must have been! But no matter how hard he struggled in agony, the rope cut into him all the more tightly. In spite of myself I ran stumblingly toward his side. Or rather I tried to run toward him, but the man instantly knocked me down. Just at that moment I saw an indescribable light in my husband's eyes. Something beyond expression . . . his eyes make me shudder even now. That instantaneous look of my husband, who couldn't speak a word, told me all his heart. The flash in his eyes was neither anger nor sorrow . . . only a cold light, a look of loathing. More struck by the look in his eyes than by the blow of the thief, I called out in spite of myself and fell unconscious.

In the course of time I came to, and found that the man in blue silk was gone. I saw only my husband still bound to the root of the cedar. I raised myself from the bamboo-blades with difficulty, and looked into his face; but the expression in his eyes was just the same as before.

Beneath the cold contempt in his eyes, there was hatred. Shame, grief, and anger . . . I don't know how to express my heart at that time. Reeling to my feet, I went up to my husband.

"Takejiro," I said to him, "since things have come to this pass, I cannot live with you. I'm determined to die, . . . but you must die, too. You saw my shame. I can't leave you alive as you are."

This was all I could say. Still he went on gazing at me with loathing and contempt. My heart breaking, I looked for his sword. It must have been taken by the robber. Neither his sword nor his bow and arrows were to be seen in the grove. But fortunately my small sword was lying at my feet. Raising it over head, once more I said, "Now give me your life. I'll follow you right away."

When he heard these words, he moved his lips with difficulty. Since his mouth was stuffed with leaves, of course his voice could not be heard at all. But at a glance I understood his words. Despising me, his look said only, "Kill me." Neither conscious nor unconscious, I stabbed the small sword through the lilac-colored kimono into his breast.

Again at this time I must have fainted. By the time I managed to look up, he had already breathed his last—still in bonds. A streak of sinking sunlight streamed through the clump of cedars and bamboos, and shone on his pale face. Gulping down my sobs, I untied the rope from his dead body. And . . . and what has become of me since I have no more strength to tell you. Anyway I hadn't the strength to die. I stabbed my own throat with the small sword, I threw myself into a pond at the foot of the mountain, and I tried to kill myself in many ways. Unable to end my life, I am still living in dishonor. (A lonely smile.) Worthless as I am, I must have been forsaken even by the most merciful Kwannon. I killed my own husband. I was violated by the robber. Whatever can I do? Whatever can I . . . I . . . (Gradually, violent sobbing.)

THE STORY OF THE MURDERED MAN, AS TOLD THROUGH A MEDIUM

After violating my wife, the robber, sitting there, began to speak comforting words to her. Of course I couldn't speak. My whole body was tied fast to the root of a cedar. But meanwhile I winked at her many times, as much as to say "Don't believe the robber." I wanted to convey some such meaning to her. But my wife, sitting dejectedly on the bamboo leaves, was looking hard at her lap. To all appearances, she was listening to his words. I was agonized by jealousy. In the meantime the robber went on with his clever talk, from one subject to another. The robber finally made his bold, brazen proposal. "Once your virtue is stained, you won't get along well with your husband, so won't you be my wife instead? It's my love for you that made me be violent toward you."

While the criminal talked, my wife raised her face as if in a trance. She had never looked so beautiful as at that moment. What did my beautiful wife say in answer to him while I was sitting bound there? I am lost in space, but I have never thought of her answer without burning with anger and jealousy. Truly she said, . . . "Then take me away with you wherever you go."

This is not the whole of her sin. If that were all, I would not be tormented so much in the dark. When she was going out of the grove as if in a dream, her hand in the robber's, she suddenly turned pale, and pointed at me tied to the root of the cedar, and said, "Kill him! I cannot marry you as long as he lives." "Kill him!" she cried many times, as if she had gone crazy. Even now these words threaten to blow me headlong into the bottomless abyss of darkness. Has such a hateful thing come out of a human mouth ever before? Have such cursed words ever struck a human ear, even once? Even once such a . . . (A sudden cry of scorn.) At these words the robber himself turned pale. "Kill him," she cried, clinging to his arms. Looking hard at her, he answered neither yes nor no . . . but hardly had I thought about his answer before she had been knocked down into the bamboo leaves. (Again a cry of scorn.) Quietly folding his arms, he looked at me and said, "What will you do with her? Kill her or save her? You have only to nod. Kill her?" For these words alone I would like to pardon his crime.

While I hesitated, she shrieked and ran into the depths of the grove. The robber instantly snatched at her, but he failed even to grasp her sleeve.

After she ran away, he took up my sword, and my bow and arrows. With a single stroke he cut one of my bonds. I remember his mumbling, "My fate is next." Then he disappeared from the grove. All was silent after that. No, I heard someone crying. Untying the rest of my bonds, I listened carefully, and I noticed that it was my own crying. (Long silence.)

I raised my exhausted body from the root of the cedar. In front of me there was shining the small sword which my wife had dropped. I took it up and stabbed it into my breast. A bloody lump rose to my mouth, but I didn't feel any pain. When my breast grew cold, everything was as silent as the dead in their graves. What profound silence! Not a single bird-note was heard in the sky over this grave in the hollow of the mountains. Only a lonely light lingered on the cedars and mountains. By and by the light gradually grew fainter, till the cedars and bamboo were lost to view. Lying there, I was enveloped in deep silence.

Then someone crept up to me. I tried to see who it was. But darkness had already been gathering round me. Someone . . . that someone drew the small sword softly out of my breast in its invisible hand. At the same time once more blood flowed into my mouth. And once and for all I sank down into the darkness of space.

Translated by Takashi Kojima

AKUTAGAWA: *In a Grove* (*Rashomon*)

   1. *What is Akutagawa attempting to do in this story told by multiple narrators? Would the effect be spoiled if he introduced at the end the omniscient author who "knows" the truth?*

   2. *Why is this method of multiple narrators appropriate to the subject?*

   3. *Why should Tajomaru, the robber, claim that he killed the husband?*

   4. *Why should the wife claim that she killed her husband?*

   5. *Why should the husband claim to have committed suicide?*

   6. *Which version is the truth?*

   7. *The ghost of the murdered man tells his story through a medium. Does the introdution of this supernatural device disturb the realistic surface of the story?*

   8. *What elements in this Japanese story distinguish it from a Western narrative?*

9. *Osamu Shimizu writes of Akutagawa: "He hated moralists, but was himself a moralist of considerable sincerity." What if any is the "moral" of the story?*

10. *When one learns that this story was expanded into a two-hour motion picture and a three-hour play, he is reminded of Ernest Hemingway's statement: "The dignity of movement of an iceberg is due to only one-eighth of it being above water." If you were directing the motion picture, what subsurface elements would you dramatize or make more explicit? Would you be adding to or detracting from the effect of the original?*

Isaac Babel

MY FIRST GOOSE

Isaac Emmanuilovich Babel was born in Odessa, Russia, in 1894, a time when Russian oppression against the Jews was particularly severe. Nevertheless, Odessan Jews remained relatively free, and Babel was able to pick up much material there that he incorporated into Tales of Odessa *(1924). By 1915, he was ready to attempt the life of a writer and went to St. Petersburg, where his fortunes remained poor until Maxim Gorki discovered him and published two of his stories. Under Gorki's counsel, Babel sought out a life of adventure, and toward this end joined the Czar's army; his service in Poland led to his most famous collection of stories,* Red Cavalry *(1926), from which "My First Goose" is taken. Until his death, reputedly in a Russian concentration camp, in 1939 or 1940, Babel went through the vicissitudes of most Russian writers in the thirties who tried to retain their individual voices. "My First Goose" is typical of Babel's Cossack tales in that it shows how he, an intellectual and a Jew, attempted to come to terms with the violence and primitivism of these fierce soldiers who honored only a man's ability to fight.*

SAVITSKY, Commander of the VI Division, rose when he saw me, and I wondered at the beauty of his giant's body. He rose, the purple of his riding breeches and the crimson of his little tilted cap and the decorations stuck on his chest cleaving the hut as a standard cleaves the sky. A smell of scent and the sickly sweet freshness of soap emanated from him. His long legs were like girls sheathed to the neck in shining riding boots.

He smiled at me, struck his riding whip on the table, and drew toward him an order that the Chief of Staff had just finished dictating. It was an order for Ivan Chesnokov to advance on Chugunov-Dobryvodka with the regiment entrusted to him, to make contact with the enemy and destroy the same.

"For which destruction," the Commander began to write, smearing the whole sheet, "I make this same Chesnokov entirely responsible, up to and including the supreme penalty, and will if necessary strike him down on the spot; which you, Chesnokov, who have been working with me at the front for some months now, cannot doubt."

The Commander signed the order with a flourish, tossed it to his orderlies and turned upon me gray eyes that danced with merriment.

I handed him a paper with my appointment to the Staff of the Division.

"Put it down in the Order of the Day," said the Commander. "Put him down for every satisfaction save the front one. Can you read and write?"

"Yes, I can read and write," I replied, envying the flower and iron of that youthfulness. "I graduated in law from St. Petersburg University."

"Oh, are you one of those grinds?" he laughed. "Specs on your nose, too! What a nasty little object! They've sent you along without making any enquiries; and this is a hot place for specs. Think you'll get on with us?"

"I'll get on all right," I answered, and went off to the village with the quartermaster to find a billet for the night.

The quartermaster carried my trunk on his shoulder. Before us stretched the village street. The dying sun, round and yellow as a pumpkin, was giving up its roseate ghost to the skies.

We went up to a hut painted over with garlands. The quartermaster stopped, and said suddenly, with a guilty smile:

"Nuisance with specs. Can't do anything to stop it, either. Not a life for the brainy type here. But you go and mess up a lady, and a good lady too, and you'll have the boys patting you on the back."

He hesitated, my little trunk on his shoulder; then he came quite close to me, only to dart away again despairingly and run to the nearest yard. Cossacks were sitting there, shaving one another.

"Here, you soldiers," said the quartermaster, setting my little trunk down on the ground. "Comrade Savitsky's orders are that you're to take this chap in your billets, so no nonsense about it, because the chap's been through a lot in the learning line."

The quartermaster, purple in the face, left us without looking back. I raised my hand to my cap and saluted the Cossacks. A lad with long straight flaxen hair and the handsome face of the Ryazan Cossacks went over to my little trunk and tossed it out at the gate. Then he turned his back on me and with remarkable skill emitted a series of shameful noises.

"To your guns—number double-zero!" an older Cossack shouted at him, and burst out laughing. "Running fire!"

His guileless art exhausted, the lad made off. Then, crawling over the ground, I began to gather together the manuscripts and tattered garments that had fallen out of the trunk. I gathered them up and carried them to the other end of the yard. Near the hut, on a brick stove, stood a cauldron in which pork was cooking. The steam that rose from it was like the far-off smoke of home in the village, and it mingled hunger with desperate loneliness in my head. Then I covered my little broken trunk with hay, turning it into a pillow, and lay down on the ground to read in *Pravda* Lenin's speech at the Second Congress of the Comintern. The sun fell upon me from behind the toothed hillocks, the Cossacks trod on my feet, the lad made fun of me untiringly, the beloved lines came toward me along a thorny path and could not reach me. Then I put aside the paper and went out to the landlady, who was spinning on the porch.

"Landlady," I said, "I've got to eat."

The old woman raised to me the diffused whites of her purblind eyes and lowered them again.

"Comrade," she said, after a pause, "what with all this going on, I want to go and hang myself."

"Christ!" I muttered, and pushed the old woman in the chest with my fist. "You don't suppose I'm going to go into explanations with you, do you?"

And turning around I saw somebody's sword lying within reach. A severe-looking goose was waddling about the yard, inoffensively preening its feathers. I overtook it and pressed it to the ground. Its head cracked beneath my boot, cracked and emptied itself. The white neck lay stretched out in the dung, the wings twitched.

"Christ!" I said, digging into the goose with my sword. "Go and cook it for me, landlady."

Her blind eyes and glasses glistening, the old woman picked up the slaughtered bird, wrapped it in her apron, and started to bear it off toward the kitchen.

"Comrade," she said to me, after a while, "I want to go and hang myself." And she closed the door behind her.

The Cossacks in the yard were already sitting around their cauldron. They sat motionless, stiff as heathen priests at a sacrifice, and had not looked at the goose.

"The lad's all right," one of them said, winking and scooping up the cabbage soup with his spoon.

The Cossacks commenced their supper with all the elegance and restraint of peasants who respect one another. And I wiped the sword with sand, went out at the gate, and came in again, depressed. Already the moon hung above the yard like a cheap earring.

"Hey, you," suddenly said Surovkov, an older Cossack. "Sit down and feed with us till your goose is done."

He produced a spare spoon from his boot and handed it to me. We supped up the cabbage soup they had made, and ate the pork.

"What's in the newspaper?" asked the flaxen-haired lad, making room for me.

"Lenin writes in the paper," I said, pulling out *Pravda.* "Lenin writes that there's a shortage of everything."

And loudly, like a triumphant man hard of hearing, I read Lenin's speech out to the Cossacks.

Evening wrapped about me the quickening moisture of its twilight sheets; evening laid a mother's hand upon my burning forehead. I read on and rejoiced, spying out exultingly the secret curve of Lenin's straight line.

"Truth tickles everyone's nostrils," said Surovkov, when I had come to the end. "The question is, how's it to be pulled from the heap. But he goes and strikes at it straight off like a hen pecking at a grain!"

This remark about Lenin was made by Surovkov, platoon commander of the Staff Squadron; after which we lay down to sleep in the hayloft. We slept, all six of us, beneath a wooden roof that let in the stars, warming one another, our legs intermingled. I dreamed: and in my dreams saw women. But my heart, stained with bloodshed, grated and brimmed over.

Translated by Walter Morison

BABEL: *My First Goose*

1. *If we call this a story of initiation, what do we mean? Into what is the narrator initiated? What does he gain? What does he lose?*

2. *How does Babel indicate the differences between the narrator and the regular Cossacks with whom he is billeted?*

3. *What purpose is served by the lyrical description of Savitsky at the beginning of the story?*

4. *Why do the Cossacks accept the narrator only after he kills the goose?*

5. *Does Babel seem to argue that violence and brutality provide the sole possible way to exist?*

6. *What purpose does the old woman serve?*

7. *Compare the descriptions at the beginning and the end of the story: what point does Babel seem to be making about people?*

8. *Does the brutality of the story shock you? If it does not, how does Babel manage to blunt the sheer ferocity of the event?*

Ernest Hemingway

A CLEAN, WELL-LIGHTED PLACE

Born in Illinois in 1898, Ernest Hemingway began his career as a journalist. His first novel, The Sun Also Rises *(1926), as well as* A Farewell to Arms *(1929) and several dozen vigorous and terse short stories, quickly established him as a major author. His succinct prose style was soon found in the work of a hundred writers, but Hemingway's remained unique, inimitable. Although his later work, that of the 1940's and 1950's, rarely attained the clarity and power of his early novels and stories, his reputation has remained high. "A Clean, Well-Lighted Place" firmly indicates Hemingway's theme of nihilism, a negation that only a certain kind of integrity can hope to counter. That he had the flexibility of mind and spirit to move beyond this nihilism is revealed in his last major work before his tragic death in 1961,* For Whom The Bell Tolls *(1940), one of the best pieces of fiction to come out of the Spanish Civil War.*

IT WAS late and every one had left the café except an old man who sat in the shadow the leaves of the tree made against the electric light. In the day time the street was dusty, but at night the dew settled the dust and the old man liked to sit late because he was deaf and now at night it was quiet and he felt the difference. The two waiters inside the café knew that the old man was a little drunk, and while he was a good client they knew that if he became too drunk he would leave without paying, so they kept watch on him.

"Last week he tried to commit suicide," one waiter said.

"Why?"

"He was in despair."

"What about?"

"Nothing."

"How do you know it was nothing?"

"He has plenty of money."

They sat together at a table that was close against the wall near the door of the café and looked at the terrace where the tables were all empty except where the old man sat in the shadow of the leaves of the tree that moved slightly in the wind. A girl and a soldier went by in the street. The street light shone on the brass number on his collar. The girl wore no head covering and hurried beside him.

"The guard will pick him up," one waiter said.

"What does it matter if he gets what he's after?"

"He had better get off the street now. The guard will get him. They went by five minutes ago."

The old man sitting in the shadow rapped on his saucer with his glass. The younger waiter went over to him.

"What do you want?"

The old man looked at him. "Another brandy," he said.

"You'll be drunk," the waiter said. The old man looked at him. The waiter went away.

"He'll stay all night," he said to his colleague. "I'm sleepy now. I never get into bed before three o'clock. He should have killed himself last week."

The waiter took the brandy bottle and another saucer from the counter inside the café and marched out to the old man's table. He put down the saucer and poured the glass full of brandy.

"You should have killed yourself last week," he said to the deaf man. The old man motioned with his finger. "A little more," he said. The waiter poured on into the glass so that the brandy slopped over and ran down the stem into the top saucer of the pile. "Thank you," the old man said. The waiter took the bottle back inside the café. He sat down at the table with his colleague again.

"He's drunk now," he said.

"He's drunk every night."

"What did he want to kill himself for?"

"How should I know."

"How did he do it?"

"He hung himself with a rope."

"Who cut him down?"

"His niece."

"Why did they do it?"

"Fear for his soul."

"How much money has he got?"

"He's got plenty."

"He must be eighty years old."

"Anyway I should say he was eighty."

"I wish he would go home. I never get to bed before three o'clock. What kind of hour is that to go to bed?"

"He stays up because he likes it."

"He's lonely. I'm not lonely. I have a wife waiting in bed for me."

"He had a wife once too."

"A wife would be no good to him now."

"You can't tell. He might be better with a wife."

"His niece looks after him."

"I know. You said she cut him down."

"I wouldn't want to be that old. An old man is a nasty thing."

"Not always. This old man is clean. He drinks without spilling. Even now, drunk. Look at him."

"I don't want to look at him. I wish he would go home. He has no regard for those who must work."

The old man looked from his glass across the square, then over at the waiters.

"Another brandy," he said, pointing to his glass. The waiter who was in a hurry came over.

"Finished," he said, speaking with that omission of syntax stupid people employ when talking to drunken people or foreigners. 'No more tonight. Close now."

"Another," said the old man.

"No. Finished." The waiter wiped the edge of the table with a towel and shook his head.

The old man stood up, slowly counted the saucers, took a leather coin purse from his pocket and paid for the drinks, leaving half a peseta tip.

The waiter watched him go down the street, a very old man walking unsteadily but with dignity.

"Why didn't you let him stay and drink?" the unhurried waiter asked. They were putting up the shutters. "It is not half-past two."

"I want to go home to bed."

"What is an hour?"

"More to me than to him."

"An hour is the same."

"You talk like an old man yourself. He can buy a bottle and drink at home."

"It's not the same."

"No, it is not," agreed the waiter with a wife. He did not wish to be unjust. He was only in a hurry.

"And you? You have no fear of going home before your usual hour?"

"Are you trying to insult me?"

"No, hombre, only to make a joke."

"No," the waiter who was in a hurry said, rising from pulling down the metal shutters. "I have confidence. I am all confidence."

"You have youth, confidence, and a job," the older waiter said. "You have everything."

"And what do you lack?"

"Everything but work."

"You have everything I have."

"No. I have never had confidence and I am not young."

"Come on. Stop talking nonsense and lock up."

"I am of those who like to stay late at the café," the older waiter said. "With all those who do not want to go to bed. With all those who need a light for the night."

"I want to go home and into bed."

"We are of two different kinds," the older waiter said. He was now dressed to go home. "It is not only a question of youth and confidence although those things are very beautiful. Each night I am reluctant to close up because there may be some one who needs the café."

"Hombre, there are bodegas open all night long."

"You do not understand. This is a clean and pleasant café. It is well lighted. The light is very good and also, now, there are shadows of the leaves."

"Good night," said the younger waiter.

"Good night," the other said. Turning off the electric light he continued the conversation with himself. It is the light of course but it is necessary that the place be clean and pleasant. You do not want music. Certainly you do not want music. Nor can you stand before a bar with dignity although that is all that is provided for these hours. What did he fear? It was not fear or dread. It was a nothing that he knew too well. It was all a nothing and a man was nothing too. It was only that and light was all it needed and a certain cleanness and order. Some lived in it and never felt it but he knew it all was nada y pues nada y pues nada. Our nada who art in nada, nada be thy name thy kingdom nada thy will be nada in nada as it is in nada. Give us this nada our daily nada and nada us our nada as we nada our nadas and nada us not into nada but deliver us from nada; pues nada. Hail nothing full of nothing, nothing is with thee. He smiled and stood before a bar with a shining steam pressure coffee machine.

"What's yours?" asked the barman.

"Nada."

"Otro loco mas," said the barman and turned away.

"A little cup," said the waiter.

The barman poured it for him.

"The light is very bright and pleasant but the bar is unpolished," the waiter said.

The barman looked at him but did not answer. It was too late at night for conversation.

"You want another copita?" the barman asked.

"No, thank you," said the waiter and went out. He disliked bars and bodegas. A clean, well-lighted café was a very different thing. Now, without thinking further, he would go home to his room. He would lie in the bed and finally, with daylight, he would go to sleep. After all, he said to himself, it is probably only insomnia. Many must have it.

HEMINGWAY: *A Clean, Well-Lighted Place*

1. *Like much of Hemingway's fiction, this story takes place in Spain. Why is this fact never stated explicitly? Why is so much other information we would like apparently withheld?*

2. *What is the tone of the story? How does Hemingway convey it? Does the title have any significance in creating the atmosphere of the piece?*

3. *Why does the old man drink brandy after brandy? Why doesn't he try to commit suicide again?*

4. *How do the two waiters differ? How are the differences revealed? What does Hemingway mean to demonstrate through them?*

5. What is the importance of the older waiter's nada *parody?* What is Hemingway's purpose in this passage? What social comment is intended? Would this passage fit into the Pirandello story? The Sartre? The Kafka? The Moravia?

6. Can a short story be successful without real characterization, without a narrative, without a plot? Is Hemingway's story successful? If so, in doing what? How does it differ from "A District Doctor"?

7. What are the virtues of the limpid, clipped prose? What disadvantages do you discern?

8. Mark Schorer has said, "Hemingway's style is not only his subject, it is his view of life." What view is reflected in the style here?

9. How are the characters in this story related to the title of the collection from which it comes, Winner Take Nothing (1933)?

Ignazio Silone

THE TRAP

Throughout his life, Ignazio Silone has fought for humanitarian ideals, becoming in his way the conscience of his generation. Born in Italy in 1900, Silone (b. Secondo Tranquilli) early became an active Socialist. After Mussolini's march on Rome, Silone was exiled from Italy, but he returned in 1925 as a militant Communist and opposed the Fascists. In 1930, he left the party (see The God That Failed*) and settled in Switzerland. Engrossed with ethical and political problems to the same degree that the younger Moravia was with social, he was particularly suited to voice the plight of the abused peasants of his native Abruzzi. This he did in* Fontamara *(1933);* Mr. Aristotle *(1935), a collection of short stories;* Bread and Wine *(1937), his masterpiece;* A Handful of Blackberries *(1953) and* The Secret of Luca *(1956). His creativity turned almost exclusively to the field of active politics when, after the liberation, he returned to Italy. Lately,* The Fox and the Camellias *(1961) suggests that the craft of the novel has reclaimed him, even though he returns to the material of "The Trap" for his inspiration.*

ဢ

DANIEL was still out at the pig-sty, looking after the sow who was having young ones, when someone called to him from the house thirty yards away. He had much to do yet, and had told them once that he did not care to be disturbed; so he did not answer. It was Daniel's wife, Filomena; she had called him two or three times.

"Daniel! Oh, Daniel! There's someone wants to talk to you." When she received no reply, she was silent.

Daniel had done all he could to see that the sow had an easy time of it; but that is the sort of thing you can never be sure about. The night before, he had put the animal on a strict diet and, by way of further precaution, had given her a strenuous castor-oil enema. What he feared more than anything else was that she would become constipated, which might result in a paralysis of the lower regions and the drying up of her milk. He had summoned to help him one Agostino, a native of Bergamo, who had lived at Ticino for a number of years. Agostino was a mason by trade, but in the off-season he was a man of all work.

Things had started off well. Three pigs had already made their appearance, looking like three enormous rats emerging from a bloody flask. Agostino's chief concern was with finding a suitable name for each. The fourth one was slow in coming, and while Agostino held its snout, Daniel had to put his bare arm, smeared with oil, up the sow's vagina. In this fashion, he had drawn the young one out, leaving the way open for the others.

"We ought to call this one Benito," suggested Agostino.

"Nothing doing!" replied Daniel. "These pigs have already been sold to an Italian firm."

"You haven't the nerve!" said the man from Bergamo.

At this point, the voice of Daniel's younger daughter, Luisa, was heard.

"Daddy! There's someone wants to talk to you!"

Daniel meanwhile went on with the umbilical dressings of the young pigs, which was to avoid infection. Had he not already told them at the house that he did not want to be bothered by anything but his work? Again he made no reply. He put the young animals in a large wooden crate lined with straw and covered them over with a woolen blanket, while Agostino saw to the cleaning of the pig-sty and the removing of the evidences of the obstetrical operation. Silvia, Daniel's elder daughter, now called from the path which ran down to the pig-sty.

"Daddy! There's someone here who wants to speak to you!"

Silvia was accompanied by Caterina, the seamstress, an old lady from the province of Florence, who had been a dressmaker at Minusio for years, but who earned the better part of her living by going around from house to house and doing mending. When Daniel saw Caterina, he was annoyed.

"Is that why you've been yelling at me for the last hour?" he demanded. For Caterina was not exactly what you would call a person of few words.

"Caterina wants to talk to you," Silvia went on, taking no notice of her father's reproof. Agostino and Silvia went off toward the house, and Caterina was left alone with Daniel.

"You know very well," Caterina began, "that I have always attended strictly to my own business—"

"That's no business of mine," said Daniel; his tone was anything but encouraging.

"Well, you know, don't you, that all the years I've lived at Ticino I've never meddled with other people's affairs?"

"That doesn't concern me," said Daniel as he made for the house.

When she saw that he had no intention of listening to her, Caterina abandoned all preliminaries and got down to facts.

"An Italian gentleman has just been to see me," she said; "he made me a proposition; he wants me to play the spy!"

Daniel stopped short. Caterina caught her breath and then went on to tell about the call she had received from this gentleman, whom she had met once by chance in an office at Locarno.

" 'You've lived here at Ticino for a good many years,' he said to me, 'you ought to know everybody. Your business takes you everywhere, into any number of homes; you listen to any number of conversations. You're an old woman and alone in the world; no one is afraid to talk in front of you—' I told him that everybody certainly did respect me, because I've always minded my own business. He kept on talking that way, and then at last he said: 'If you've a mind to get certain information for me concerning the activities of some of the anti-Fascist Italians here in Ticino, between Ascona and Bellinzona, you can earn a little something that will make it easier for you in your old age—' "

Daniel had recovered from his surprise and was watching Caterina closely as, trembling and sighing, she went on with her story.

"Why did you come to me?" he wanted to know.

"Why did I come to you?" Caterina echoed.

"I am a native of Ticino," said Daniel, "and the affairs of these Italians don't interest me; that's the reason I'd like to know why you came to me. Who sent you?"

The old lady was taken aback.

"What do you mean?" she stammered. "You've known me for thirty years. You know that I've always been a hard worker and have always minded my own business!"

"What I want to know," Daniel broke in on her, raising his voice, "what I want to know is, who sent you here?"

"Nobody!" Caterina insisted. "I'm sorry to have bothered you; I'll be going."

Caterina took the foot-path which skirted Daniel's house and which came out on the Gordola-Minusio highway. Daniel followed her and, after a bit, resumed the discussion.

"If no one sent you, then why did you come?"

"I wanted some advice," said Caterina, and she kept on walking.

"What kind of advice?"

"Whether or not I should accept the gentleman's offer." The old lady came to a stop. "I don't know what to do. I never was in such a predicament in all my life. If I accept, I'll earn something substantial, but by doing harm to those who have never harmed me. If I refuse, they're sure to look on me as an anti-Fascist and persecute me every way they can. You've known me for thirty years. You know that I'm neither a Fascist nor an anti-Fascist. You know that I've always been a hard worker and minded my business."

Daniel was lost in thought for a moment. Caterina started to walk away again, sighing resignedly. Once more he followed her. At the end of the path, Agostino was waiting.

"I'll tell you what," Daniel suddenly said to her, "you needn't be afraid. So long as you're honest you have nothing to fear. Tell Agostino what you've just told me and do as he says."

He watched the pair as they went down the road in the direction of Gordola; then he turned back to the pig-sty, to look after the sow.

It was one morning while Daniel was at work with his daughter Silvia on the vines in the arbor that Agostino went past again for the first time. The vines were being eaten by an insect which had bored its way through the bark, and Daniel had wanted to take advantage of a free morning to get at them. He would run a metal scraper over the ailing stalks in such a manner as to remove the bark and lay bare the hidden chrysales, and Silvia would come after him to sprinkle the shoots with boiling water. It was at this time that Agostino went by upon a truck-load of brick and shouted to Daniel:

"Did you hear about it? That business is coming along!"

"What business?" Daniel answered him, although he understood well enough what Agostino meant.

"You know, that business we were talking about!" And Agostino gave a wave of his hand as the truck disappeared down the road. Daniel shook his head.

"Those Italians are all right," he remarked, turning to his daughter. "Big-hearted, impulsive, never think of danger—but they talk too much!"

"Listen, Daddy," said Silvia, plucking up courage at this point to voice a wish she had been cherishing for a long time, "I know that, though you don't say anything about it, you are doing a great deal to help free Italy, and I too would like so much to help!"

"Silvia," was her father's reply, "I wish you would pick up the pieces of bark which I have chipped off the vines, and which are lying around on the ground here, and burn them. That is all you have to do just now!"

His daughter obeyed. Daniel watched her as she went about the arbor, bending down at the foot of each vine and gathering up in her apron the tiny pieces of bark. Silvia had been twenty last November. And there was pride and trepidation in her father's glance as it rested on her. She was the dearest thing in his life, and the one over which hung the greatest threat.

Some days afterward Agostino came past a second time, one Sunday morning. Daniel and Filomena were talking with a woman who was telling them how, at Cadenazzo and at Robasacco, the night before, a number of hen-houses had been raided by foxes.

"They found fifty hens with their throats slit and their blood sucked!" The woman was precise regarding details.

"If that's the case," Daniel disagreed, "then it's not a fox but a polecat."

At this point, a chauffeur from Cadenazzo came past and they put the question up to him.

"It's a fox," declared the chauffeur, "and maybe more than one. In one hen-house, all they found left was a bunch of wing-feathers."

"We'll have to be looking after our hens," said Filomena to Daniel. "Last year they were sick, and this year, of course, it would have to be foxes!"

"The thing to do," suggested Daniel, "is to set a trap."

Agostino now arrived on the scene.

"It's coming to a head," he said to Daniel, calling him over to one side. "Caterina did what I told her to, and that fellow from the police has swallowed the hook. We'll have to be on the watch now!"

"What are you thinking about doing?" inquired Daniel.

"The thing to do is to set a trap," Agostino answered.

Daniel burst out laughing when he heard the word trap, and Filomena, who had caught nothing more than the word, now took a hand in the conversation.

"A trap's not always enough," she observed, turning to Agostino. "The fox is too wise for that. Almost always, before nibbling at the bait, he feels all around it, and he doesn't take it in his mouth right away but joggles it about and draws it over to him with his paw. It's all right to set a trap, but it's a good thing to put a little poisoned food around the hen-house at the same time."

Agostino did not get the drift at first.

"But you can't be sure of poison, even," said Daniel to his wife; "a fox has to be pretty hungry if, when he's near a hen-house, he wastes any time in picking up what's lying around on the ground. And even if he eats a piece of poisoned meat or a few chestnuts soaked in strychnine, you can't be sure then. No one has ever yet found just the right dose of strychnine to give a fox, when you don't know what kind of a fox it is. If he's big and strong, and there isn't much strychnine, all he gets is a little belly-ache, which doesn't keep him from eating the hens; but if it's a strong dose, he'll vomit it up right away, get it off his stomach, and have all the keener an appetite for chickens."

"It seems, then, there's no chance of catching a fox!" Agostino had finally realized what it was they had been talking about before he came.

"There is a chance," said Daniel, "but it's not easy. And anyway," he added, "no fox ever yet was caught by talking about it."

Filomena now went back into the house, for Luisa, the younger daughter, had called her; and the two men went out into the garden back of the house to continue their conversation.

"Caterina," Agostino was saying, "after many qualms and no end of holding back, has finally taken the job of spying on the work that we are doing here in Locarno. That fellow from the Italian police came to see her again yesterday and left her an address in Pal-

lanza to which she is to write in case she has any information to
give him."

"He didn't tell Caterina who the persons are she is supposed to
spy on?" asked Daniel.

"It seems not, for the present," said Agostino, "but he told her in
a general way that she was to get the names of all those Italian mi-
gratory workers who are all the time crossing the border into Switzerland and who there are in touch with revolutionary circles. He
told her also that she could make a nice little sum of money if she
would help him track down those who are responsible for smuggling revolutionary books and publications into Italy."

"He didn't say who it was he suspected of doing that?"

"Apparently not," said Agostino, "from the story that Caterina
gave me." And then he went on: "I had to promise Caterina that, in
case of any trouble, we'd see to it that she got out all right; I told
her we'd provide her with the means to go to Zurich and live. For
the thirty years she's been here in Ticino, as you know, that's all
she's dreamed of, to be able to live in Zurich."

"Does Caterina suspect that I have any connection with the
Italian revolutionists?"

"You can put that out of your head," Agostino assured him.
"Every time she's talked to me—you know Caterina, with a sigh
after every other word—she's told me how she has always minded
her own affairs and always means to, and how Mr. Daniel, fine man
that he is, is one Ticinese who has never meddled in politics, she
can swear to that—"

Silvia, from the window of her room, had caught sight of her
father and Agostino at the far end of the garden.

"May I come down?" she called to her father.

"Of course!" the two men replied.

The girl left the house and came down the garden path. As she
reached them, the pair changed the conversation and began talking about the weather.

Every night Daniel set a trap at the entrance to the hen-house
and put some poisoned food about, but no fox came. And Agostino's fox seemingly was in no more of a hurry to set foot in the
man from Bergamo's trap, for Daniel had heard no more about it.

"A farmer's life," he would say, "is one continual war with the weather and with animal parasites, but the hardest war of all is the one against the fox."

The work of scraping the vines had been finished, and he now began on the fruit trees. He would clean the trunks of their dried branches, dead bark, and moss, by way of uncovering the parasites' nests. Wherever there was a hole surrounded by a little streak of red, Silvia would then insert an iron wire to kill the wood-worm hidden at the bottom. When the cleaning was finished, Filomena came with a pail of lime, and each trunk was given a whitewashing to the height of a man's head.

"The trees," observed Daniel, "are now protected on the earth side, but who is going to protect them from the heavens?"

Agostino, exchanging pleasantries with Luisa, was waiting for Daniel at the door of the house.

"What's new?" was Daniel's question.

"The trap is ready!" the man from Bergamo replied.

"And the fox, what about him?"

"He'll be there tonight!"

"If only we could finish off all the foxes at once!" Daniel exclaimed.

Agostino then proceeded to inform Daniel of the way in which the provocateur was to be trapped.

"Caterina has written him that she has important information to give him, and she's made an appointment for nine o'clock tonight, at Rivapiana, down by the lake, opposite the old chapel of San Quirico. Caterina will be there, and I mean to be there too, with a couple of others."

"But don't you think," said Daniel, "that it might be well to notify the police?"

"That wouldn't be wise at all," said Agostino. "The consulate might get wind of it right away, and the fox wouldn't show up."

Daniel could not very well offer an objection to this, seeing that a number of subordinates among the police were suspected of being disloyal. The thing that worried him more than anything else was the possible trouble that might be caused the Italian emigrants.

"It ought to be done by Ticinesi!" said Daniel; but Agostino was not of this opinion.

"Too many people would be in on it then; and what's more, an Italian fox—an Italian trap!"

That evening Daniel took the train for Locarno; and along about ten o'clock he started strolling along the lake toward Saleggi, as he waited for Agostino, who was to let him know how the thing had turned out. About half-past ten, in place of Agostino, there appeared one Lucca, an Italian carpenter who lived at Minusio.

"Agostino," he told Daniel, "has been slightly wounded in one hand, and so he did not come, because he did not want to attract attention by going around with a bandaged hand."

"And what about the other man?"

"We left him lying on the ground! He came to keep the appointment with a couple of others, who went off and left him alone with Caterina, saying they would be back in an hour. We were in behind San Quirico, and we waited until they were a good distance away—they left in the direction of Navigia. In the meantime, Caterina, with her usual tears and sighs, was filling the informer with all sorts of foolishness, telling him over and over again how she had never in all her life meddled with anyone's business but her own and never would, but how all the same she had discovered, beyond any doubt, that revolutionary books and magazines to be taken into Italy were being deposited in the Franciscan Convent at Madonna del Sasso, up above Locarno."

Daniel had a good laugh at this.

"Agostino went up alone at first," Lucca went on, "leaving us there behind the church. It had been agreed that he was to make use of his revolver only in case the fellow tried to take him. He acted as if he just happened to be passing. As it was dark, he lighted a cigarette, and pretended to recognize the stranger by the glow of the match. 'Ha!' he called out, and then the rumpus began. We came out of our hiding place, while Caterina took to her heels."

"Did you have a hand in it, too?"

"Oh, there wasn't any need of that. All we did was keep a watch to see that nobody came. Agostino soon enough had the best of him. He threw him to the ground and held him with his knee and then started pounding his face as if he were crushing stone. We knew how strong Agostino was, but we never knew how much hate he had in him—"

"You mustn't forget," Daniel reminded Lucca, "that the Fascists killed Agostino's brother! You say he was wounded in the hand?"

"Yes, the spy bit him. He got Agostino's hand between his teeth and wouldn't let go. With his free hand Agostino was pounding the fellow on the jaw like a madman, but the spy held on with his teeth. Then Agostino took him by the throat and choked him just about to death."

"Did he finish him?" Daniel was alarmed.

"I think he did."

"Then Agostino in all probability will have to clear out of the country," Daniel said. "He may have to go to France—"

In view of the unforeseen turn which events had taken, Daniel made up his mind to spend the night at Locarno and to go to Bellinzona the following morning. In order that his family might not be worried about him, he went into a café and telephoned to Silvia.

"It's a lucky thing you called," his daughter said. "I've been trying for an hour to reach you, everywhere in Locarno where you're known—"

"Why, what's happened?" Daniel asked in some alarm.

"Nothing at our house," Silvia hastened to reassure him. "But not far away, on the Gordola road, there's been an automobile collision and one man was seriously injured. They got a doctor as quick as they could, and the doctor said his injuries were so serious that it would be dangerous to move him very far. They inquired in a number of houses whether they could take him in; but you know very well that, here in our neighborhood, there are nothing but hovels, like stables. And so the neighbors assured them that our house was the only possible one. Mother, to tell the truth, was rather put out about it; she said that, you being away from home, we couldn't very well take in a stranger, but I told her that I knew you would approve of it—"

"Certainly!" Daniel interrupted her. "Where did you put him?"

"In my room, on the second floor," said Silvia. "I'll sleep with Luisa; she'll be only too glad to have me."

"Is he in danger of death?"

"The doctor wouldn't say as to that. He said that he would send a nurse in this very night, although I told him that I could do everything that was necessary without any help."

"Where is he from? What's his name?" Daniel questioned her further.

"The poor fellow can't talk yet," his daughter explained. "He must come from a well-to-do family, though, for the doctor insisted that mother accept something as a deposit, to cover any expense that we might be put to."

"I'm really very sorry," said Daniel in conclusion, "that I can't come home tonight; but I'm staying over in Locarno, and tomorrow morning I'm going to Bellinzona, on some business that can't be put off. I leave everything to you; be a good girl and do whatever the doctor tells you to."

Daniel telephoned from Bellinzona the next day to find out if the injured man was still alive. It was Luisa who answered the phone, as Silvia had gone out to make a few purchases.

"He's a little better," said the young girl. "A nurse came in an automobile last night, but Silvia insisted on staying up anyway—and now the doctor's here again."

The doctor came to the telephone.

"Doctor, I want you to make yourself perfectly at home in my house," Daniel said to him. "I regret very much having to be so far from home at a time like this."

"I think the patient may be considered out of danger," the physician replied. "He's had rather a severe cerebral shake-up, but I don't look for any complications. So far as your family is concerned, I will take care of everything."

"Who is he?" inquired Daniel. "Where are his people?"

"He is Umberto Stella, an Italian engineer from Bologna. You may have heard the name. He came to Switzerland to make a study of certain hydroelectric plants."

"Whoever he may be," said Daniel, "I want you to feel that my house and my family are at your disposal."

At Bellinzona Daniel at once set about endeavoring to find out just what course the authorities might have taken in their investigation of the semi-homicidal affair at Rivapiana. He prudently refrained from bringing up the subject himself, leaving to others to speak of it first. With such an object in view, he called on his lawyer and went with him to the courthouse, by way of settling certain formalities which, as it happened, were not at all pressing. He stopped everyone he knew on the street. He bought a couple of morning newspapers but found in them not the slightest allusion to what had occurred the evening before. It was evident that nothing whatever was known of the affair at Bellinzona. Upon finding himself alone with his lawyer, he finally ventured a hint.

"I hear," he began, "that there was some kind of a political fracas among the Italians, not far from Locarno, last night—"

"Nobody's heard anything of it around here," replied the lawyer. "It must have been one that didn't get anywhere. If it had been anything serious, they would have known of it here at once. The tension between the two parties is very high in this town!"

This answer confirmed Daniel in a suspicion he already had, to the effect that Lucca's imagination had been working overtime and had dramatized a comparatively unimportant incident.

"Those Italians," said Daniel, by way of bringing the conversation to a close, "are fine fellows, big-hearted and impulsive, but they don't know when to stop talking."

"It's better the way it is," he thought to himself, "or otherwise, Agostino and Caterina would have had to leave Switzerland." Nevertheless, the fact that he had spent a night away from home and lost a day on account of such an affair annoyed him more than a little. On the train going back, he found himself in the company of a number of farmers who were talking of the fox and how it was massacring the chickens at Magadino.

"That fox is pretty clever," one of them was saying; "he's too clever for any trap!"

"But there's a new kind of trap," a second one put in, "an Italian invention—"

"It makes a lot of noise, but it doesn't catch anything!" was the first speaker's rejoinder.

"That's true enough," said Daniel, joining in the discussion, "it does make a lot of noise, and it doesn't catch a thing. All you have is a fracas that doesn't get anywhere."

Upon reaching home, Daniel went up at once to the second floor to see the patient. But on the threshold of the room Silvia barred his way, putting a finger to her lips for him to be silent.

"He has need of complete rest," the daughter whispered in her father's ear; "no visitors, no formalities, nothing that can disturb him mentally, the doctor says."

"Then there's nothing that I can do?" Daniel was a bit crestfallen.

"Before you go back downstairs, you can take your shoes off so as not to make so much noise," Silvia advised him in a hushed tone.

Daniel took off his shoes and went back down the stairs and out into the garden. He entered the toolshed and started sharpening stakes with a hedge-knife. He had no sooner begun than Silvia came running out in her slippered feet.

"Are you crazy?" she said. "Here we have a sick man in the house, and you're making all this noise."

Daniel put down the hedge-knife.

"I suppose I may at least eat?" he plaintively inquired.

Silvia nodded and ran back upstairs. Daniel took the spade and began digging up a corner of the garden. In a little while he saw Silvia leave the house with a market-basket. He then went back into the house, took off his shoes, and hastily crept up to the second floor. At the door he met the nurse, who told him that he might enter, "but only for a moment."

There in Silvia's little white bed, Daniel had a glimpse of an enormous head all bandaged in white. Although he was not naturally of a humorous turn of mind, he could not help thinking of the head of St. Nicholas of the Snows. In that huge expanse of white, there was a tiny hole for an eye, and another one a little larger which probably represented a mouth.

"There, that will do," the nurse said, ushering Daniel to the door. Going downstairs, shoes in hand, the latter met Silvia coming back.

"Where have *you* been?" Silvia demanded in a tone of reproof.

"Is that any way to speak to your father?" said Daniel, and he went back to digging in the garden. As he was digging away, Filomena came out to him.

"Silvia's lost her head!" Filomena complained to her husband. "Ever since yesterday, she hasn't shut an eye nor touched a morsel of food."

"Silvia has found her head!" Daniel answered; "she is one girl who has a heart."

"Too much of a one!" responded Silvia's mother.

"Too much of a one? You can never have too much heart," said Daniel. He was well satisfied with his daughter. His glance, always, as he gazed at her was one filled with pride and trepidation.

At the foot of the garden wall there were a few cowslips growing. Silvia came out and plucked them all, for the patient's room.

"But he can't see them! He has his eyes bandaged!" Filomena objected.

"Mother," said Silvia, "you know very well that you can see flowers with your eyes shut."

Daniel spent a good part of the following day in a vineyard which he had on the hillside. Upon coming home in the evening, he inquired after the patient's condition and learned from Silvia that their guest was improving rapidly. They had let the nurse go, and Silvia had taken the care of the patient upon herself. Daniel had a glimpse of the man only two or three times, and the impression he received was an altogether favorable one. He had, moreover, a good many other things on his mind, and so failed to notice the profound change that was taking place in the girl.

"You might give a little less thought to others and a little more to your own daughter!" his wife reproved him one evening.

"Silvia is not a child any longer, and she has a good head on her," was Daniel's curt response.

"She has a head all right, but no experience," replied his wife, who had resolved to unburden herself of what had been on her mind for a number of days past. Daniel reflected.

"You think I ought to speak to her?" he asked.

"I think you had better before it is too late!"

The next day Daniel had to go to bring a bag of seedling peas to a friend of his who lived at Comuna, in Val Verzasca, and Silvia went with him. At Comuna it did not take him long to get through with what little business he had, and he refused all invitations to go to the café.

"I prefer a little walk with my daughter," he explained to his acquaintances; "she's getting a trifle pale lately and needs the exercise."

Father and daughter then set out in silence along the road to Gordola. The wagon-road at this point ran at a considerable elevation above the stream, which could be heard tumbling down before them.

"Couldn't we walk along it?" Silvia asked.

"I don't believe so," said Daniel; but with the desire of giving in to any whim his daughter might have, he added: "We have plenty of time, though; we might go down to the river."

They found a small foot path, steep as a stair, and after many windings and turnings, they came to where the torrent was foaming against a wall of rock. The water was clear-running, and they could see every stone at the bottom. Up to this time father and daughter had exchanged only the briefest and most insignificant of words. This more than anything else gave Daniel a sense of the change which had taken place in their relations.

"Oh, look!" cried Silvia, pointing down at her feet to a strip of sand a dozen inches or so underwater, "how pretty!"

"That is spawn," her father informed her. "At the end of September the trout leave the lower part of the river and come up toward the source, and the females, full of eggs, start looking for a well-protected sandy spot. With the aid of their tails they displace the gravel and drop their eggs, which are mixed with the sand."

"And is that the way trout are born?"

"The fertilizing is done by the males, which come along after the females and sprinkle over the spot where the eggs have been deposited a thick white milky fluid. The eggs ought to be hatching about now."

Silvia looked in wonderment at the strip of sand where this mystery was accomplished.

"How beautiful," she said, "and how simple!"

"Trout, my dear girl, don't go to church!"

That was all that was said between them during this jaunt.

"Did you speak to her?" Daniel's wife asked him when they came home.

"Yes."

"What did you say?"

"Nothing."

The engineer had left his room for the first time one day and was lying stretched out on a reclining chair in the garden, when Caterina arrived from Gordola at the same time as Daniel.

"Miss Silvia!" the engineer was calling.

Caterina stopped instantly. Going up to the hedge which hid the garden from the street, she strove to see who it was that had called.

"Mr. Daniel," she said trembling all over, "that man whom you've taken in is the spy who came to Rivapiana that evening!"

"You're out of your senses!" Daniel exclaimed; and he went on to tell Caterina how it was, in his absence, the stranger had come to be brought there. Caterina went up to the hedge again and studied the convalescent intently, as he sat in the garden jesting with Silvia.

"That's the one!" she repeated; "I'm going away before he sees me."

"Very well," said Daniel, who had turned pale. "Tell Agostino to come here tomorrow at this same time; tell him, I'll make sure that no one sees him."

Sylvia came running up to meet her father.

"Now that our patient is better," she said, "I think it would be nice of you to have a little talk with him. You will see what a really fine person it is that chance has thrown our way."

"Yes, I should be very much interested in having a talk with him," said Daniel, who was doing his best to keep from showing how disturbed he was; "we can have lunch together today."

At the table, however, as he saw the man sitting there between Silvia and Luisa, the situation became unbearable to Daniel, and, pretending that he was feeling slightly ill, he excused himself and went outside. The others joined him in the garden.

"What's new in the papers?" the self-styled engineer inquired of Daniel. "It's been weeks since I've seen a newspaper."

"There's a fresh tragedy every day," replied Daniel. "Yesterday it was a big railroad wreck in France, with hundreds of dead."

"Every day a tragedy," said the alleged engineer, "but the most tragic thing of all is the way in which men go to meet their tragedies. Think of all those hundreds of persons killed in that railroad disaster. In the same train were farmers and merchants, doctors and lawyers, students, army officers, fashionable modistes, what not. They were all on the same train, and they were not on the same train. The farmer was thinking of the prices he would get from the merchant, the lawyer was thinking of the Cross of the Legion of Honor, the army officer was thinking of his wealthy fiancée, the doctor was engaged in a mental lawsuit with the mayor of his village, and the student, out of the corner of his eye, was admiring his new necktie. Each was thus traveling in his own train. And each of us has his own train in society, until, of a sudden, we all find that we are on the same train, the train of death. The student's necktie ends up under the countryman's clogs, the officer's sword is run through the traveling salesman's belly, and the modiste's latest model goes up in smoke. For all were on the same train, and they did not know it."

"But the railroad company soon enough saw to that," said Daniel; "they soon saw to it that the unity which had been reëstablished by death was broken, by putting the fur-coated corpses on one side and those in plain workmen's blouses on the other."

"Can it be," said Silvia, "that human beings are condemned to be set over against one another like that, even after death?"

"There is a vast gulf," replied the convalescent, "between man's nature, his destiny, and the thing that society makes of him. During these past days, when I was fighting off death, that subject became an obsession with me. Each of us is traveling on his own train, and we are all on the same train!"

"Present-day society," said Daniel, "is based upon keeping men divided and set against one another. The vast majority of them are separated from and set against the fruit of their own labor. For no sooner does it leave their hands than the product of men ceases to belong to those who have made it but becomes instead their enemy; the thing produced is set over against the human beings who produced it, the inanimate object becomes the fetish before which living man must bow."

"But must it always be like that?" persisted Silvia.

"When I was young," the invalid went on, "I too hoped for a society that would be different from the one we have."

Daniel rose and went back to his spading. Spring was coming on, and it was time that the work was getting under way. It was with an unwonted vigor that he sank the spade in the earth, throwing the entire weight of his body upon his right foot and tossing the clods into the air. Behind him came Filomena, breaking up the clods with a three-pronged rake. A pleasing odor of moist earth hung over the garden. The sweat was trickling down Daniel's face; internally, he was very much upset. The invalid remained in the garden, stretched out in the armchair, until the first evening stars appeared from behind Monte Ceneri.

"It's been so long," he said, half to himself, "it's been so many, many years since I've had a glimpse of the sky."

Silvia rose and returned shortly with a book.

"There is a similar case here," she told him, "in this first volume of Tolstoy's *War and Peace*. Prince Andrei, in November, 1805, had fallen wounded in the outskirts of Pratzen, in a battle between the Russian troops and those of Napoleon. Here is what Tolstoy has to say about it:

" 'Then he opened his eyes, to see what the outcome of the struggle between the two Frenchmen and the artilleryman had been, whether the red-haired artilleryman had been slain or not; he also wanted to know whether the cannon had been saved or captured. But all he could see was the high heavens up above him, no longer filled with light, but immeasurably far above, and covered over with tranquil-gliding gray clouds. "How calm and still and restful it all is," thinks Prince Andrei. "All that has no resemblance whatsoever to this running, shrieking and fighting of ours; the tranquil gliding of those clouds over the high unending heavens has nothing in common with this struggle of the Frenchmen and the artilleryman, as with grim, distorted faces they strive for the possession of a cannon swob. How does it happen that I have never seen these heavens before? How happy I am to have seen them at last. Yes, all is as naught, it is all a mistake and a lie, all except that endless expanse of blue. There is nothing, nothing beyond that. Yet even it does not exist; there is nothing but stillness and peace. And God be thanked for it!" ' "

The moon came up, flooding the Magadino plain with an eerie light.

"The moon," Luisa observed, "has eyes and a nose like us."

"Those things," Silvia explained to her younger sister, "are seas and mountains."

Their guest took it upon himself to round out the explanation.

"If the inhabitants of the moon," he said, "happen to be looking down at the earth at this moment, we probably look much the same to them as the moon does to us. Seen from up there, what are the great cities of the earth? Italy must look like a comma and Switzerland like a period."

"And how does Mussolini look from up there?" Luisa wanted to know.

"You'd better watch out," said Daniel, "or you'll be straining your eyes."

A general laugh went round at this.

The next day, when Daniel saw Agostino coming, he went out to meet him and brought him into the house from the side opposite the garden, where the engineer was seated out in the sun. The two men went up to Luisa's room, and there, from behind the Venetian shutters, Agostino was able to take a good look at the man without being seen.

"That is the one!" he said softly; and rubbing his hands, he added: "This time he's not going to get away from us!"

"What do you mean?" said Daniel with a frown.

"I mean just that, that he's not going to get away from us this time."

"You're joking." The tone of Daniel's voice took his friend from Bergamo by surprise.

"The fox is in the trap," said the latter; "do you mean to say, you're going to let him go? We've got in our hands at last, without his knowing it, one of those who in Italy have been massacring our people, in prison and on the deportation islands; and should we let him get away?" Agostino was wrought up about the matter.

"That man is a guest in my house," Daniel calmly announced.

"He's a spy!" said Agostino.

"He was a spy," answered Daniel, in the same calm voice, "but now he's a guest. He came to my house at the point of death and sought hospitality, and he has been cured in my house."

It was all Agostino could do to believe his ears.

"I can't understand such scruples as that," he said. "You know as well as I do the methods that the Fascists use against us; you know, don't you, there are no moral scruples where they are concerned?"

"I know it," was Daniel's response; "that's why I'm not a Fascist."

"And that's why we're always beaten!"

"That's why we'll win out in the end!" This was Daniel's last word. Agostino could only shake his head, in the face of such stubbornness as this.

"How long is he going to be here yet?"

"Another week, perhaps; he's not very strong yet."

"Then we'll have time to talk it over before he has a chance to get away."

Daniel decided to say nothing about it to the other members of the family, so as not to alarm them or arouse their guest's suspicions. It was at this time that one of Filomena's sisters who lived at

Vira had a child, and Daniel with his wife and Silvia went to pay her a visit, leaving Luisa at home with the invalid.

"You've been here all these weeks," said the little girl, "and you haven't yet seen our house."

"That's because I've been in bed all the time," said the engineer.

Luisa then proceeded to show him the storeroom, where they kept the potatoes, the onions, their fruit, and the garden tools. On the second floor she showed him her own room, which her sister Silvia shared with her for the time being. The guest's attention was attracted by a photograph fastened up on the wall with a tissue paper flower on either side.

"Who is that?" he asked.

"That's Matteotti," Luisa informed him.

The engineer dropped down on a chair.

"Who is Matteotti?" was his next question.

"He was the man who stuck up for the poor people, and for that reason he was killed by Mussolini."

"Are you an anti-Fascist?"

"I most certainly am!"

"And Silvia, what about her?"

"She's more of a one than I am."

"And your father?"

"More than any of us—not in what he says, but in what he does."

Luisa then showed the guest the third floor.

"This is my parents' room," she said.

"And what's this?" The engineer pointed to a small room adjoining.

"Oh, you mustn't go in there; Daddy doesn't allow it. He has a lot of papers in there, and he doesn't want us to muss them up."

Luisa and the guest went back to the garden. The invalid began striding up and down the path and kept it up for a good half hour. Then, as if he had made up his mind to something, he came up to Luisa.

"Would you mind running down with a telegram for me?" And when he had given the little girl the wording of the telegram and a few pennies, he added: "I'm tired; I am going to bed at once."

It was in vain that Silvia knocked at their guest's door the next morning, when she came to bring him his breakfast. Her repeated knocking brought not the slightest response. The door was locked.

Feeling certain that something dreadful had happened, Silvia began calling at the top of her voice, and the whole family came
running up. When Daniel had taken the door off its hinges, it was
found that the guest was not in his room. The bed had not been
slept in. His suitcases had disappeared.

"He's gone!" Silvia cried.

"He left without saying good-by!" wailed Luisa.

"He's been gone ever since yesterday," Filomena declared, pointing to the bed.

In a couple of bounds, Daniel was on the third floor, and a moment later, the other members of the family were terror-struck by
his furious outcries:

"Thief! Crook! Traitor! He's taken all my papers with him! He's
taken away all my papers!"

It was like a mortal blow to Daniel. When the women came up,
their eyes fell on the disordered room; all the drawers had been
overturned on the floor. At this point, Agostino came in. He did not
know what had happened yet, but he was very pale and he seemed
excited.

"Yesterday evening," Daniel explained to him, "the spy left the
house while I was away and took all my papers with him, among
others, those about the smuggling. Quick! There's not a minute to
lose; we must let the ones concerned know."

"This morning," said Agostino, "at Luino, a score of seasonal laborers, who are in the habit of coming over to work in Switzerland
during the daytime and going back into Italy at night, were arrested."

Silvia stood staring at her father and Agostino, as if all this were
some kind of play which they were putting on for her benefit.

"No! no!" she moaned, "it's not true! It's all a joke! Agostino, for
heaven's sake, tell me that it's not true!"

Daniel was on his feet.

"We've got to think of saving the others, before that spy gets his
hands on them!"

And he and Agostino were off in a hurry.

It was late in the evening when Daniel came home. Filomena
and Luisa were seated by the hearth, while Silvia sat on a chest,
over in one corner of the dark kitchen.

"The smugglers," announced Daniel from the kitchen door, "were

arrested early this morning. A consignment of books at Brissago
was seized at noon today. The police have been to Caterina's house.
I hear that Agostino has been arrested, and that he will probably
be expelled from the country. Haven't they been here yet?"

"No," said Filomena.

Daniel dropped down on the doorsill. The night wore slowly on,
with the slow procession of the stars. The cock crowed for the first
time, but no one so much as thought of going to bed, no one
thought of going up to the second floor where *that man* had lived
until yesterday. The cock crowed a second time. Mother and
daughter still sat by the hearth, the elder daughter on a chest over
in a corner of the kitchen, and the father there on the doorsill. It
was like a wake for the dead. The cock crowed a third time.

Then came an animal's shrill cry, like the yelp of a dog in pain,
and the squawking of hens broke in upon the silence of the night.
Daniel leaped to his feet and ran across the garden to the hen-
house. In front of it he saw a fox with one paw in the trap; plant-
ing its remaining feet upon the ground and arching its back, the
animal was doing its utmost to free the prisoned member. When
it saw the man approaching, it began leaping furiously from side
to side, tugging on the chain by which the trap was securely fastened.

"At last!" said Daniel in a ferocious tone of voice. And snatching
up an ax which lay beside the hen-house, as if he were hewing at an
oak, he began raining terrible blows upon the animal's head, its
back, its belly, its legs—blow after blow, the blows of a madman,
death-dealing blows continued to rain down, even after the little
beast had been hacked to tiny bits and reduced to nothing more
than a puddle of blood-soaked mush.

Translated by Samuel Putnam

SILONE: *The Trap*

1. *How does the title apply to the events? Is it simply a device or a
view of life? Explain how Silone makes the trap into a vast symbol.*

2. *What does the fox signify in the story? the flowers? Why does
Daniel want to call one pig "Benito"?*

3. *How does Silone make us aware of the time of the action?*

4. *What does the convalescent mean by " 'Each of us is travelling on his own train, and we are all in the same train' "? Can you see Silone's political views suggested by this statement?*

5. *Is Daniel right in permitting the convalescent to recover even though he is a Fascist opposed to everything Daniel believes in? Does one honor rules in a struggle of this sort? Do you admire Daniel for his action, or do you think him foolish?*

6. *Explain the ending in terms of the fox, of Fascism, of Daniel himself.*

7. *What values does Silone seem to honor in this story? Compare his views with Verga's in "The Orphans," and Moravia's in "The Ruin of Humanity." What does Silone share with Verga? How do they differ from Moravia? Compare the ending of this story with that of Pirandello's "The Soft Touch of Grass." Is the frustration of one character comparable to the other's?*

Graham Greene

BROTHER

*Graham Greene's early years outwardly showed little of the violence
and furious bursts of belief and unbelief which mark his serious
work, although his inner life, we learn from his essays, was tumul-
tuous. Born in Hertfordshire, England, in 1904, the son of a head-
master, Greene attended Oxford University and then took up newspaper work. In the 1930's, he began to write what he called
"entertainments" (This Gun for Hire, The Confidential Agent, The
Ministry of Fear), but his first major work, Brighton Rock (1938),
was not to appear for nearly another ten years. Then followed a series
of artistic successes: The Power and the Glory (1940), The Heart of
the Matter (1948), The End of the Affair (1951), as well as
several short stories and numerous essays and reviews. Two recent
plays that brought his name to Broadway, The Potting Shed and
The Complaisant Lover, and a novel that many critics have acclaimed as his masterpiece, The Burnt-Out Case (1961), remind
us that Greene's creative energies show no signs of flagging as he
approaches his sixties. While "Brother" lacks his characteristic
preoccupation with Catholic problems, it nevertheless does adum-
brate his social and political views.*

Ƨ☙

THE COMMUNISTS were the first to appear. They walked
quickly, a group of about a dozen, up the boulevard which runs
from Combat to Ménilmontant; a young man and a girl lagged a
little way behind because the man's leg was hurt and the girl was
helping him along. They looked impatient, harassed, hopeless, as
if they were trying to catch a train which they knew already in
their hearts they were too late to catch.

The proprietor of the café saw them coming when they were still
a long way off; the lamps at that time were still alight (it was later
that the bullets broke the bulbs and dropped darkness all over that
quarter of Paris), and the group showed up plainly in the wide

[399

barren boulevard. Since sunset only one customer had entered the café, and very soon after sunset firing could be heard from the direction of Combat; the Métro station had closed hours ago. And yet something obstinate and undefeatable in the proprietor's character prevented him from putting up the shutters; it might have been avarice; he could not himself have told what it was as he pressed his broad yellow forehead against the glass and stared this way and that, up the boulevard and down the boulevard.

But when he saw the group and their air of hurry he began immediately to close his café. First he went and warned his only customer, who was practising billiard shots, walking round and round the table, frowning and stroking a thin moustache between shots, a little green in the face under the low diffused lights.

"The Reds are coming," the proprietor said, "you'd better be off. I'm putting up the shutters."

"Don't interrupt. They won't harm me," the customer said. "This is a tricky shot. Red's in baulk. Off the cushion. Screw on spot." He shot his ball straight into a pocket.

"I knew you couldn't do anything with that," the proprietor said, nodding his bald head. "You might just as well go home. Give me a hand with the shutters first. I've sent my wife away." The customer turned on him maliciously, rattling the cue between his fingers. "It was your talking that spoilt the shot. You've cause to be frightened, I dare say. But I'm a poor man. I'm safe. I'm not going to stir." He went across to his coat and took out a dry cigar. "Bring me a bock." He walked round the table on his toes and the balls clicked and the proprietor padded back into the bar, elderly and irritated. He did not fetch the beer but began to close the shutters; every move he made was slow and clumsy. Long before he had finished the group of Communists was outside.

He stopped what he was doing and watched them with furtive dislike. He was afraid that the rattle of the shutters would attract their attention. If I am very quiet and still, he thought, they may go on, and he remembered with malicious pleasure the police barricade across the Place de la République. That will finish them. In the meanwhile I must be very quiet, very still, and he felt a kind of warm satisfaction at the idea that worldly wisdom dictated the very attitude most suited to his nature. So he stared through the edge of a shutter, yellow, plump, cautious, hearing the billiard balls crackle in the other room, seeing the young man come limping up the pavement on the girl's arm, watching them stand and stare with dubious faces up the boulevard towards Combat.

But when they came into the café he was already behind the bar, smiling and bowing and missing nothing, noticing how they had divided forces, how six of them had begun to run back the way they had come.

The young man sat down in a dark corner above the cellar stairs and the others stood round the door waiting for something to happen. It gave the proprietor an odd feeling that they should stand there in his café not asking for a drink, knowing what to expect, when he, the owner, knew nothing, understood nothing. At last the girl said "Cognac," leaving the others and coming to the bar, but when he had poured it out for her, very careful to give a fair and not a generous measure, she simply took it to the man sitting in the dark and held it to his mouth.

"Three francs," the proprietor said. She took the glass and sipped a little and turned it so that the man's lips might touch the same spot. Then she knelt down and rested her forehead against the man's forehead and so they stayed.

"Three francs," the proprietor said, but he could not make his voice bold. The man was no longer visible in his corner, only the girl's back, thin and shabby in a black cotton frock, as she knelt, leaning forward to find the man's face. The proprietor was daunted by the four men at the door, by the knowledge that they were Reds who had no respect for private property, who would drink his wine and go away without paying, who would rape his women (but there was only his wife, and she was not there), who would rob his bank, who would murder him as soon as look at him. So with fear in his heart he gave up the three francs as lost rather than attract any more attention.

Then the worst that he contemplated happened.

One of the men at the door came up to the bar and told him to pour out four glasses of cognac. "Yes, yes," the proprietor said, fumbling with the cork, praying secretly to the Virgin to send an angel, to send the police, to send the Gardes Mobiles, now, immediately, before the cork came out, "that will be twelve francs."

"Oh, no," the man said, "we are all comrades here. Share and share alike. Listen," he said, with earnest mockery, leaning across the bar, "all we have is yours just as much as it's ours, comrade," and stepping back a pace he presented himself to the proprietor, so that he might take his choice of stringy tie, of threadbare trousers, of starved features. "And it follows from that, comrade, that all you have is ours. So four cognacs. Share and share alike."

"Of course," the proprietor said, "I was only joking." Then he stood with bottle poised, and the four glasses tingled upon the counter. "A machine-gun," he said, "up by Combat," and smiled to see how for the moment the men forgot their brandy as they fidgeted near the door. Very soon now, he thought, and I shall be quit of them.

"A machine-gun," the Red said incredulously, "they're using machine-guns?"

"Well," the proprietor said, encouraged by this sign that the Gardes Mobiles were not very far away, "you can't pretend that you aren't armed yourselves." He leant across the bar in a way that was almost paternal. "After all, you know, your ideas—they wouldn't do in France. Free love."

"Who's talking of free love?" the Red said.

The proprietor shrugged and smiled and nodded at the corner. The girl knelt with her head on the man's shoulder, her back to the room. They were quite silent and the glass of brandy stood on the floor beside them. The girl's beret was pushed back on her head and one stocking was laddered and darned from knee to ankle.

"What, those two? They aren't lovers."

"I," the proprietor said, "with my bourgeois notions would have thought . . ."

"He's her brother," the Red said.

The men came clustering round the bar and laughed at him, but softly as if a sleeper or a sick person were in the house. All the time they were listening for something. Between their shoulders the proprietor could look out across the boulevard; he could see the corner of the Faubourg du Temple.

"What are you waiting for?"

"For friends," the Red said. He made a gesture with open palm as if to say, You see, we share and share alike. We have no secrets.

Something moved at the corner of the Faubourg du Temple.

"Four more cognacs," the Red said.

"What about those two?" the proprietor asked.

"Leave them alone. They'll look after themselves. They're tired."

How tired they were. No walk up the boulevard from Ménilmontant could explain the tiredness. They seemed to have come farther and fared a great deal worse than their companions. They were more starved; they were infinitely more hopeless, sitting in their dark corner away from the friendly gossip, the amicable desperate voices which now confused the proprietor's brain, until for a moment he believed himself to be a host entertaining friends.

He laughed and made a broad joke directed at the two of them; but they made no sign of understanding. Perhaps they were to be pitied, cut off from the camaraderie round the counter; perhaps they were to be envied for their deeper comradeship. The proprietor thought for no reason at all of the bare grey trees of the Tuileries like a series of exclamation marks drawn against the winter sky. Puzzled, disintegrated, with all his bearings lost, he stared out through the door towards the Faubourg.

It was as if they had not seen each other for a long while and would soon again be saying good-bye. Hardly aware of what he was doing he filled the four glasses with brandy. They stretched out worn blunted fingers for them.

"Wait," he said. "I've got something better than this"; then paused, conscious of what was happening across the boulevard. The lamplight splashed down on blue steel helmets; the Gardes Mobiles were lining out across the entrance to the Faubourg, and a machine-gun pointed directly at the café windows.

So, the proprietor thought, my prayers are answered. Now I must do my part, not look, not warn them, save myself. Have they covered the side door? I will get the other bottle. Real Napoleon brandy. Share and share alike.

He felt a curious lack of triumph as he opened the trap of the bar and came out. He tried not to walk quickly back towards the billiard room. Nothing that he did must warn these men; he tried to spur himself with the thought that every slow casual step he took was a blow for France, for his café, for his savings. He had to step over the girl's feet to pass her; she was asleep. He noted the sharp shoulder blades thrusting through the cotton, and raised his eyes and met her brother's, filled with pain and despair.

He stopped. He found he could not pass without a word. It was as if he needed to explain something, as if he belonged to the wrong party. With false bonhomie he waved the corkscrew he carried in the other's face. "Another cognac, eh?"

"It's no good talking to them," the Red said. "They're German. They don't understand a word."

"German?"

"That's what's wrong with his leg. A concentration camp."

The proprietor told himself that he must be quick, that he must put a door between him and them, that the end was very close, but he was bewildered by the hopelessness in the man's gaze. "What's he doing here?" Nobody answered him. It was as if his question were too foolish to need a reply. With his head sunk upon his breast the proprietor went past, and the girl slept on. He was like a stranger leaving a room where all the rest are friends. A German. They don't understand a word; and up, up through the heavy darkness of his mind, through the avarice and the dubious triumph, a few German words remembered from very old days climbed like spies into the light: a line from the *Lorelei* learnt at school, *Kamerad* with its war-time suggestion of fear and surrender, and oddly from nowhere the phrase *mein Bruder*. He opened the door of the billiard room and closed it behind him and softly turned the key.

"Spot in baulk," the customer explained and leant across the great green table, but while he took aim, wrinkling his narrow peevish eyes, the firing started. It came in two bursts with a rip of glass between. The girl cried out something, but it was not one of the words he knew. Then feet ran across the floor, the trap of the bar slammed. The proprietor sat back against the table and listened and listened for any further sound; but silence came in under the door and silence through the keyhole.

"The cloth. My God, the cloth," the customer said, and the proprietor looked down at his own hand which was working the corkscrew into the table.

"Will this absurdity never end?" the customer said. "I shall go home."

"Wait," the proprietor said. "Wait." He was listening to voices and footsteps in the other room. These were voices he did not recognize. Then a car drove up and presently drove away again. Somebody rattled the handle of the door.

"Who is it?" the proprietor called.

"Who are you? Open that door."

"Ah," the customer said with relief, "the police. Where was I now? Spot in baulk." He began to chalk his cue. The proprietor opened the door. Yes, the Gardes Mobiles had arrived; he was safe again, though his windows were smashed. The Reds had vanished as if they had never been. He looked at the raised trap, at the smashed electric bulbs, at the broken bottle which dripped behind the bar. The café was full of men, and he remembered with odd relief that he had not had time to lock the side door.

"Are you the owner?" the officer asked. "A bock for each of these men and a cognac for myself. Be quick about it."

The proprietor calculated: "Nine francs fifty," and watched closely with bent head the coins rattle down upon the counter.

"You see," the officer said with significance, "we pay." He nodded towards the side door. "Those others: did they pay?"

No, the proprietor admitted, they had not paid, but as he counted the coins and slipped them into the till, he caught himself silently repeating the officer's order—"A bock for each of these men." Those others, he thought, one's got to say that for them, they weren't mean about the drink. It was four cognacs with them. But, of course, they did not pay. "And my windows," he complained aloud with sudden asperity, "what about my windows?"

"Never you mind," the officer said, "the government will pay. You have only to send in your bill. Hurry up now with my cognac. I have no time for gossip."

"You can see for yourself," the proprietor said, "how the bottles have been broken. Who will pay for that?"

"Everything will be paid for," the officer said.

"And now I must go to the cellar to fetch more."

He was angry at the reiteration of the word pay. They enter my café, he thought, they smash my windows, they order me about and think that all is well if they pay, pay, pay. It occurred to him that these men were intruders.

"Step to it," the officer said and turned and rebuked one of the men who had leant his rifle against the bar.

At the top of the cellar stairs the proprietor stopped. They were in darkness, but by the light from the bar he could just make out a body half-way down. He began to tremble violently, and it was some seconds before he could strike a match. The young German lay head downwards, and the blood from his head had dropped on to the step below. His eyes were open and stared back at the proprietor with the old despairing expression of life. The proprietor would not believe that he was dead. "Kamerad," he said bending down, while the match singed his fingers and went out, trying to recall some phrase in German, but he could only remember, as he bent lower still, "mein Bruder." Then suddenly he turned and ran up the steps, waved the match-box in the officer's face, and called out in a low hysterical voice to him and his men and to the customer stooping under the low green shade, "Cochons. Cochons."

"What was that? What was that?" the officer exclaimed. "Did you say that he was your brother? It's impossible," and he frowned incredulously at the proprietor and rattled the coins in his pocket.

GREENE: *Brother*

1. *Why does Greene omit the background to the events of the story?*

2. *Greene says there was "something obstinate and undefeatable" in the proprietor. What does he mean? How is this quality related to the last two paragraphs?*

3. *What is the effect of the man practicing billiards in the background?*

4. *When does the proprietor begin to change his mind about his visitors? Why at that particular point? Do you agree with the proprietor's frame of mind at this moment? Why?*

5. *Why does the proprietor, who depends upon payment to survive, become sympathetic to the men who do not pay for their drinks and hostile to the men who do? Does the last line of the story seem relevant here?*

6. *Does the story have any significance beyond this small vignette? How does the word "Kamerad" fit into this scheme?*

7. *Should common humanity prevail over political differences? Or are the latter so great that people must put aside their humanity? What is Greene's position here?*

8. *Greene's novels are characterized by his sympathetic portrayals of outsiders and outlaws of every degree: the adulterer, the whisky priest, the*

pathological gunman, the punk hoodlum, the philandering policeman, the burnt-out case, and, in this story, the Communist refugee. Do you believe that an artist should present such outcasts, some of them enemies of society, in so sympathetic and human a light? Does it mean that he approves of their habits and practices?

9. *Is Catholic France a better setting for this story than, say, Protestant Germany or Scandinavia?*

Jean-Paul Sartre

THE WALL

Born in 1905, Jean-Paul Sartre has been not only a prolific writer of fiction, but also an influential philosopher, social commentator, and playwright. Certainly one of the most brilliant men of letters alive, his is also the most important name among the Parisian Existentialists active in the 1940's and 50's. His best-known fiction is Nausea *(1938),* The Wall *(1939), and the novels making up the incomplete tetralogy,* Roads to Freedom. *Such plays as* No Exit, Dirty Hands, *and* The Flies *have been performed often and have gained him distinction both for the cogency of their ideas and for their technical brilliance. His latest work for the theater,* The Condemned of Altona *(1960), is one of the masterpieces of modern times. "The Wall" illustrates a typical Existentialist situation, wherein men who face death must come to terms with what they are and how they have lived.*

ह

THEY pushed us into a big white room and I began to blink because the light hurt my eyes. Then I saw a table and four men behind the table, civilians, looking over the papers. They had bunched another group of prisoners in the back and we had to cross the whole room to join them. There were several I knew and some others who must have been foreigners. The two in front of me were blond with round skulls; they looked alike. I supposed they were French. The smaller one kept hitching up his pants; nerves.

It lasted about three hours; I was dizzy and my head was empty; but the room was well heated and I found that pleasant enough: for the past 24 hours we hadn't stopped shivering. The guards brought the prisoners up to the table, one after the other. The four men asked each one his name and occupation. Most of the time they didn't go any further—or they would simply ask a question here and there: "Did you have anything to do with the sabotage of munitions?" Or "Where were you the morning of the 9th and what were you doing?" They didn't listen to the answers or at least didn't seem to. They were quiet for a moment and then looking straight in front of them began to write. They asked Tom if it were true he was in the International Brigade; Tom couldn't tell them otherwise because of the papers they found in his coat. They didn't ask Juan anything but they wrote for a long time after he told them his name.

"My brother José is the anarchist," Juan said, "you know he isn't here any more. I don't belong to any party, I never had anything to do with politics."

They didn't answer. Juan went on, "I haven't done anything. I don't want to pay for somebody else."

His lips trembled. A guard shut him up and took him away. It was my turn.

"Your name is Pablo Ibbieta?"

"Yes."

The man looked at the papers and asked me, "Where's Ramon Gris?"

"I don't know."

"You hid him in your house from the 6th to the 19th."

"No."

They wrote for a minute and then the guards took me out. In the corridor Tom and Juan were waiting between two guards. We started walking. Tom asked one of the guards, "So?"

"So what?" the guard said.

"Was that the cross-examination or the sentence?"

"Sentence," the guard said.

"What are they going to do with us?"

The guard answered dryly, "Sentence will be read in your cell."

As a matter of fact, our cell was one of the hospital cellars. It was terrifically cold there because of the drafts. We shivered all night and it wasn't much better during the day. I had spent the previous five days in a cell in a monastery, a sort of hole in the wall that must have dated from the middle ages: since there were a lot of prisoners and not much room, they locked us up anywhere. I didn't miss my cell; I hadn't suffered too much from the cold but I was alone; after a long time it gets irritating. In the cellar I had company. Juan hardly ever spoke: he was afraid and he was too young

to have anything to say. But Tom was a good talker and he knew
Spanish well.

There was a bench in the cellar and four mats. When they took
us back we sat and waited in silence. After a long moment, Tom
said, "We're screwed."

"I think so too," I said, "but I don't think they'll do anything to
the kid."

"They don't have a thing against him," said Tom. "He's the
brother of a militiaman and that's all."

I looked at Juan: he didn't seem to hear. Tom went on, "You
know what they do in Saragossa? They lay the men down on the
road and run over them with trucks. A Moroccan deserter told us
that. They said it was to save ammunition."

"It doesn't save gas," I said.

I was annoyed at Tom: he shouldn't have said that.

"Then there's officers walking along the road," he went on, "su-
pervising it all. They stick their hands in their pockets and smoke
cigarettes. You think they finish off the guys? Hell no. They let them
scream. Sometimes for an hour. The Moroccan said he damned near
puked the first time."

"I don't believe they'll do that here," I said. "Unless they're really
short on ammunition."

Day was coming in through four airholes and a round opening
they had made in the ceiling on the left, and you could see the sky
through it. Through this hole, usually closed by a trap, they un-
loaded coal into the cellar. Just below the hole there was a big pile
of coal dust; it had been used to heat the hospital but since the
beginning of the war the patients were evacuated and the coal
stayed there, unused; sometimes it even got rained on because they
had forgotten to close the trap.

Tom began to shiver. "Good Jesus Christ I'm cold," he said. "Here
it goes again."

He got up and began to do exercises. At each movement his shirt
opened on his chest, white and hairy. He lay on his back, raised his
legs in the air and bicycled. I saw his great rump trembling. Tom
was husky but he had too much fat. I thought how rifle bullets or
the sharp points of bayonets would soon be sunk into this mass of
tender flesh as in a lump of butter. It wouldn't have made me feel
like that if he'd been thin.

I wasn't exactly cold, but I couldn't feel my arms and shoulders any more. Sometimes I had the impression I was missing something and began to look around for my coat and then suddenly remembered they hadn't given me a coat. It was rather uncomfortable. They took our clothes and gave them to their soldiers, leaving us only our shirts—and those canvas pants that hospital patients wear in the middle of summer. After a while Tom got up and sat next to me, breathing heavily.

"Warmer?"

"Good Christ, no. But I'm out of wind."

Around eight o'clock in the evening a major came in with two *falangistas*. He had a sheet of paper in his hand. He asked the guard, "What are the names of those three?"

"Steinbock, Ibbieta and Mirbal," the guard said.

The major put on his eyeglasses and scanned the list: "Steinbock . . . Steinbock . . . Oh yes . . . You are sentenced to death. You will be shot tomorrow morning." He went on looking. "The other two as well."

"That's not possible," Juan said. "Not me."

The major looked at him amazed. "What's your name?"

"Juan Mirbal," he said.

"Well, your name is there," said the major. "You're sentenced."

"I didn't do anything," Juan said.

The major shrugged his shoulders and turned to Tom and me.

"You're Basque?"

"Nobody is Basque."

He looked annoyed. "They told me there were three Basques. I'm not going to waste my time running after them. Then naturally you don't want a priest?"

We didn't even answer.

He said, "A Belgian doctor is coming shortly. He is authorized to spend the night with you." He made a military salute and left.

"What did I tell you," Tom said. "We get it."

"Yes," I said, "it's a rotten deal for the kid."

I said that to be decent but I didn't like the kid. His face was too thin and fear and suffering had disfigured it, twisting all his features. Three days before he was a smart sort of kid, not too bad; but now he looked like an old fairy and I thought how he'd never be young again, even if they were to let him go. It wouldn't have been too hard to have a little pity for him but pity disgusts me, or rather it horrifies me. He hadn't said anything more but he had turned grey; his face and hands were both grey. He sat down again and looked at the ground with round eyes. Tom was good hearted, he wanted to take his arm, but the kid tore himself away violently and made a face.

"Let him alone," I said in a low voice, "you can see he's going to blubber."

Tom obeyed regretfully; he would have liked to comfort the kid, it would have passed his time and he wouldn't have been tempted to think about himself. But it annoyed me: I'd never thought about death because I never had any reason to, but now the reason was here and there was nothing to do but think about it.

Tom began to talk. "So you think you've knocked guys off, do you?" he asked me. I didn't answer. He began explaining to me that he had knocked off six since the beginning of August; he didn't realize the situation and I could tell he didn't *want* to realize it. I hadn't quite realized it myself, I wondered if it hurt much, I thought of bullets, I imagined their burning hail through my body. All that was beside the real question; but I was calm: we had all night to understand. After a while Tom stopped talking and I watched him out of the corner of my eye; I saw he too had turned grey and he looked rotten; I told myself "Now it starts." It was almost dark, a dim glow filtered through the airholes and the pile of coal and made a big stain beneath the spot of sky; I could already see a star through the hole in the ceiling: the night would be pure and icy.

The door opened and two guards came in, followed by a blonde man in a tan uniform. He saluted us. "I am the doctor," he said. "I have authorization to help you in these trying hours."

He had an agreeable and distinguished voice. I said, "What do you want here?"

"I am at your disposal. I shall do all I can to make your last moments less difficult."

"What did you come here for? There are others, the hospital's full of them."

"I was sent here," he answered with a vague look. "Ah! Would you like to smoke?" he added hurriedly, "I have cigarettes and even cigars."

He offered us English cigarettes and *puros,* but we refused. I looked him in the eyes and he seemed irritated. I said to him, "You aren't here on an errand of mercy. Besides, I know you. I saw you with the fascists in the barracks yard the day I was arrested."

I was going to continue, but something surprising suddenly happened to me; the presence of this doctor no longer interested me. Generally when I'm on somebody I don't let go. But the desire to talk left me completely; I shrugged and turned my eyes away. A little later I raised my head; he was watching me curiously. The guards were sitting on a mat. Pedro, the tall thin one, was twiddling his thumbs, the other shook his head from time to time to keep from falling asleep.

"Do you want a light?" Pedro suddenly asked the doctor. The other nodded "Yes": I think he was about as smart as a log, but he surely wasn't bad. Looking in his cold blue eyes it seemed to me that his only sin was lack of imagination. Pedro went out and came back with an oil lamp which he set on the corner of the bench. It gave a bad light but it was better than nothing: they had left us in the dark the night before. For a long time I watched the circle of light the lamp made on the ceiling. I was fascinated. Then suddenly I woke up, the circle of light disappeared and I felt myself crushed under an enormous weight. It was not the thought of death or fear; it was nameless. My cheeks burned and my head ached.

I shook myself and looked at my two friends. Tom had hidden his face in his hands. I could only see the fat white nape of his neck. Little Juan was the worst; his mouth was open and his nostrils trembled. The doctor went to him and put his hand on his shoulder to comfort him, but his eyes stayed cold. Then I saw the Belgian's hand drop stealthily along Juan's arm, down to the wrist. Juan paid no attention. The Belgian took his wrist between three fingers, distractedly, the same time drawing back a little and turning his back to me. But I leaned backward and saw him take a watch from his pocket and look at it for a moment, never letting go of the wrist. After a minute he let the hand fall inert and went and leaned his back against the wall, then, as if he suddenly remembered something very important which had to be jotted down on the spot, he took a notebook from his pocket and wrote a few lines. "Bastard," I thought angrily, "let him come and take my pulse. I'll shove my fist in his rotten face."

He didn't come but I felt him watching me. I raised my head and returned his look. Impersonally, he said to me, "Doesn't it seem cold to you here?" He looked cold, he was blue.

"I'm not cold," I told him.

He never took his hard eyes off me. Suddenly I understood and my hands went to my face: I was drenched in sweat. In this cellar, in the midst of winter, in the midst of drafts, I was sweating. I ran my hands through my hair, gummed together with perspiration; at the same time I saw my shirt was damp and sticking to my skin: I had been dripping for an hour and hadn't felt it. But that swine of a Belgian hadn't missed a thing; he had seen the drops rolling down my cheeks and thought: this is the manifestation of an almost pathological state of terror; and he had felt normal and proud of being alive because he was cold. I wanted to stand up and smash his face but no sooner had I made the slightest gesture than my rage and shame were wiped out; I fell back on the bench with indifference.

I satisfied myself by rubbing my neck with my handkerchief because now I felt the sweat dropping from my hair onto my neck and it was unpleasant. I soon gave up rubbing, it was useless; my handkerchief was already soaked and I was still sweating. My buttocks were sweating too and my damp trousers were glued to the bench.

Suddenly Juan spoke. "You're a doctor?"

"Yes," the Belgian said.

"Does it hurt . . . very long?"

"Huh? When . . . ? Oh, no," the Belgian said paternally. "Not at all. It's over quickly." He acted as though he were calming a cash customer.

"But I . . . they told me . . . sometimes they have to fire twice."

"Sometimes," the Belgian said, nodding. "It may happen that the first volley reaches no vital organs."

"Then they have to reload their rifles and aim all over again?" He thought for a moment and then added hoarsely, "That takes time!"

He had a terrible fear of suffering, it was all he thought about: it was his age. I never thought much about it and it wasn't fear of suffering that made me sweat.

I got up and walked to the pile of coal dust. Tom jumped up and threw me a hateful look: I had annoyed him because my shoes squeaked. I wondered if my face looked as frightened as his: I saw he was sweating too. The sky was superb, no light filtered into the dark corner and I had only to raise my head to see the Big Dipper. But it wasn't like it had been: the night before I could see a great piece of sky from my monastery cell and each hour of the day brought me a different memory. Morning, when the sky was a hard, light blue, I thought of beaches on the Atlantic; at noon I saw the sun and I remembered a bar in Seville where I drank *manzanilla* and ate olives and anchovies; afternoons I was in the shade and I thought of the deep shadow which spreads over half a bull-ring leaving the other half shimmering in sunlight; it was really hard to see the whole world reflected in the sky like that. But now I could watch the sky as much as I pleased, it no longer evoked anything in me. I liked that better. I came back and sat near Tom. A long moment passed.

Tom began speaking in a low voice. He had to talk, without that he wouldn't have been able to recognize himself in his own mind. I thought he was talking to me but he wasn't looking at me. He was undoubtedly afraid to see me as I was, grey and sweating: we were alike and worse than mirrors of each other. He watched the Belgian, the living.

"Do you understand?" he said. "I don't understand."

I began to speak in a low voice too. I watched the Belgian.

"Why? What's the matter?"

"Something is going to happen to us that I can't understand."

There was a strange smell about Tom. It seemed to me I was more sensitive than usual to odors. I grinned. "You'll understand in a while."

"It isn't clear," he said obstinately. "I want to be brave but first I have to know . . . Listen, they're going to take us into the courtyard. Good. They're going to stand up in front of us. How many?"

"I don't know. Five or eight. Not more."

"All right. There'll be eight. Someone'll holler 'aim!' and I'll see eight rifles looking at me. I'll think how I'd like to get inside the wall, I'll push against it with my back . . . with every ounce of strength I have, but the wall will stay, like in a nightmare. I can imagine all that. If you only knew how well I can imagine it."

"All right, all right!" I said, "I can imagine it too."

"It must hurt like hell. You know, they aim at the eyes and the mouth to disfigure you," he added mechanically. "I can feel the

wounds already; I've had pains in my head and in my neck for the
past hour. Not real pains. Worse. This is what I'm going to feel to-
morrow morning. And then what?"

I well understood what he meant but I didn't want to act as if I
did. I had pains too, pains in my body like a crowd of tiny scars. I
couldn't get used to it. But I was like him, I attached no importance
to it. "After," I said, "you'll be pushing up daisies."

He began to talk to himself: he never stopped watching the Belgian. The Belgian didn't seem to be listening. I knew what he had
come to do; he wasn't interested in what we thought; he came to
watch our bodies, bodies dying in agony while yet alive.

"It's like a nightmare," Tom was saying. "You want to think of
something, you always have the impression that it's all right, that
you're going to understand and then it slips, it escapes you
and fades away. I tell myself there will be nothing afterwards. But
I don't understand what it means. Sometimes I almost can . . .
and then it fades away and I start thinking about the pains again,
bullets, explosions. I'm a materialist, I swear it to you; I'm not going crazy. But something's the matter. I see my corpse; that's not
hard but I'm the one who sees it, with my eyes. I've got to think
. . . think that I won't see anything anymore and the world will go
on for the others. We aren't made to think that, Pablo. Believe me:
I've already stayed up a whole night waiting for something. But
this isn't the same: this will creep up behind us, Pablo, and we won't
be able to prepare for it."

"Shut up," I said, "Do you want me to call a priest?"

He didn't answer. I had already noticed he had the tendency to
act like a prophet and call me Pablo, speaking in a toneless voice. I
didn't like that: but it seems all the Irish are that way. I had the
vague impression he smelled of urine. Fundamentally, I hadn't
much sympathy for Tom and I didn't see why, under the pretext
of dying together, I should have any more. It would have been different with some others. With Ramon Gris, for example. But I felt
alone between Tom and Juan. I liked that better, anyhow: with
Ramon I might have been more deeply moved. But I was terribly
hard just then and I wanted to stay hard.

He kept on chewing his words, with something like distraction.
He certainly talked to keep himself from thinking. He smelled of

urine like an old prostate case. Naturally, I agreed with him, I could
have said everything he said: it isn't *natural* to die. And since I
was going to die, nothing seemed natural to me, not this pile of coal
dust, or the bench, or Pedro's ugly face. Only it didn't please me to
think the same things as Tom. And I knew that, all through the
night, every five minutes, we would keep on thinking things at the
same time. I looked at him sideways and for the first time he
seemed strange to me: he wore death on his face. My pride was
wounded: for the past twenty-four hours I had lived next to Tom, I
had listened to him, I had spoken to him and I knew we had nothing in common. And now we looked as much alike as twin brothers, simply because we were going to die together. Tom took my
hand without looking at me.

"Pablo, I wonder . . . I wonder it it's really true that everything
ends."

I took my hand away and said, "Look between your feet, you
pig."

There was a big puddle between his feet and drops fell from his
pants-leg.

"What is it?" he asked frightened.

"You're pissing in your pants," I told him.

"It isn't true," he said furiously. "I'm not pissing. I don't feel anything."

The Belgian approached us. He asked with false solicitude, "Do
you feel ill?"

Tom did not answer. The Belgian looked at the puddle and said
nothing.

"I don't know what it is," Tom said ferociously. "But I'm not
afraid. I swear I'm not afraid."

The Belgian did not answer. Tom got up and went to piss in a
corner. He came back buttoning his fly, and sat down without a
word. The Belgian was taking notes.

All three of us watched him because he was alive. He had the
motions of a living human being, the cares of a living human being;
he shivered in the cellar the way the living are supposed to shiver;
he had an obedient, well-fed body. The rest of us hardly felt ours—
not in the same way anyhow. I wanted to feel my pants between
my legs but I didn't dare; I watched the Belgian, balancing on his

legs, master of his muscles, someone who could think about tomorrow. There we were, three bloodless shadows; we watched him and we sucked his life like vampires.

Finally he went over to little Juan. Did he want to feel his neck for some professional motive or was he obeying an impulse of charity? If he was acting by charity it was the only time during the whole night.

He caressed Juan's head and neck. The kid let himself be handled, his eyes never leaving him, then suddenly, he seized the hand and looked at it strangely. He held the Belgian's hand between his own two hands and there was nothing pleasant about them, two grey pincers gripping this fat and reddish hand. I suspected what was going to happen and Tom must have suspected it too: but the Belgian didn't see a thing, he smiled paternally. After a moment the kid brought the fat red hand to his mouth and tried to bite it. The Belgian pulled away quickly and stumbled back against the wall. For a second he looked at us with horror, he must have suddenly understood that we were not men like him. I began to laugh and one of the guards jumped up. The other was asleep, his wide open eyes were blank.

I felt relaxed and over-excited at the same time. I didn't want to think any more about what would happen at dawn, at death. It made no sense. I only found words or emptiness. But as soon as I tried to think of anything else I saw rifle barrels pointing at me. Perhaps I lived through my execution twenty times; once I even thought it was for good: I must have slept a minute. They were dragging me to the wall and I was struggling; I was asking for mercy. I woke up with a start and looked at the Belgian: I was afraid I might have cried out in my sleep. But he was stroking his moustache, he hadn't noticed anything. If I had wanted to, I think I could have slept a while; I had been awake for forty-eight hours. I was at the end of my rope. But I didn't want to lose two hours of life: they would come to wake me up at dawn, I would follow them, stupefied with sleep and I would have croaked without so much as an "Oof!"; I didn't want that, I didn't want to die like an animal, I wanted to understand. Then I was afraid of having nightmares. I got up, walked back and forth, and, to change my ideas, I began to think about my past life. A crowd of memories came back to me pell-mell. There were good and bad ones—or at least I called them that *before*. There were faces and incidents. I saw the face of a little *novillero* who was gored in Valencia during the *Feria*, the face of one of my uncles, the face of Ramon Gris. I remembered my whole life: how I was out of work for three months in 1926, how I almost starved to death. I remembered a night I spent on a bench in Grenada: I hadn't eaten for three days. I was angry, I didn't want to die. That made me smile. How madly I ran after happiness, after women, after liberty. Why? I wanted to free Spain, I admired Pi y Margall, I joined the anarchist movement, I spoke in public meetings: I took everything as seriously as if I were immortal.

At that moment I felt that I had my whole life in front of me, and I thought, "It's a damned lie." It was worth nothing because it was finished. I wondered how I'd been able to walk, to laugh with the girls: I wouldn't have moved so much as my little finger if I had only imagined I would die like this. My life was in front of me, shut, closed, like a bag and yet everything inside of it was unfinished. For an instant I tried to judge it. I wanted to tell myself, this is a beautiful life. But I couldn't pass judgment on it; it was only a sketch; I had spent my time counterfeiting eternity, I had understood nothing. I missed nothing: there were so many things I could have missed, the taste of *manzanilla* or the baths I took in summer in a little creek near Cadiz; but death had disenchanted everything.

The Belgian suddenly had a bright idea. "My friends," he told us, "I will undertake—if the military administration will allow it—to send a message for you, a souvenir to those who love you . . ."

Tom mumbled, "I don't have anybody."

I said nothing. Tom waited an instant then looked at me with curiosity. "You don't have anything to say to Concha?"

"No."

I hated this tender complicity: it was my own fault, I had talked about Concha the night before, I should have controlled myself. I was with her for a year. Last night I would have given an arm to see her again for five minutes. That was why I talked about her, it was stronger than I was. Now I had no more desire to see her, I had nothing more to say to her. I would not even have wanted to hold her in my arms: my body filled me with horror because it was grey and sweating—and I wasn't sure that her body didn't fill me with horror. Concha would cry when she found out I was dead, she would have no taste for life for months afterward. But I was still the one who was going to die. I thought of her soft, beautiful eyes. When she looked at me something passed from her to me. But I knew it was over: if she looked at me *now* the look would stay in her eyes, it wouldn't reach me. I was alone.

Tom was alone too but not in the same way. Sitting cross-legged, he had begun to stare at the bench with a sort of smile, he looked amazed. He put out his hand and touched the wood cautiously as if he were afraid of breaking something, then drew back his hand quickly and shuddered. If I had been Tom I wouldn't have amused myself by touching the bench; this was some more Irish nonsense, but I too found that objects had a funny look: they were more obliterated, less dense than usual. It was enough for me to look at the bench, the lamp, the pile of coal dust, to feel that I was going to die. Naturally I couldn't think clearly about my death but I saw it **everywhere, on things, in** the way things fell back and kept their distance, discreetly, as people who speak quietly at the bedside of a dying man. It was *his* death which Tom had just touched on the bench.

In the state I was in, if someone had come and told me I could go home quietly, that they would leave me my life whole, it would have left me cold: several hours or several years of waiting is all the same when you have lost the illusion of being eternal. I clung to nothing, in a way I was calm. But it was a horrible calm—because of my body; my body, I saw with its eyes, I heard with its ears, but it was no longer me; it sweated and trembled by itself and I didn't recognize it any more. I had to touch it and look at it to find out what was happening, as if it were the body of someone else. At times I could still feel it, I felt sinkings, and fallings, as when you're in a plane taking a nosedive, or I felt my heart beating. But that didn't reassure me. Everything that came from my body was all cock-eyed. Most of the time it was quiet and I felt no more than a sort of weight, a filthy presence against me; I had the impression of being tied to an enormous vermin. Once I felt my pants and I felt they were damp; I didn't know whether it was sweat or urine, but I went to piss on the coal pile as a precaution.

The Belgian took out his watch, looked at it. He said, "It's three-thirty."

Bastard! He must have done it on purpose. Tom jumped; we

hadn't noticed time was running out; night surrounded us like a shapeless, somber mass, I couldn't even remember that it had begun.

Little Juan began to cry. He wrung his hands, pleaded, "I don't want to die. I don't want to die."

He ran across the whole cellar waving his arms in the air, then fell sobbing on one of the mats. Tom watched him with mournful eyes, without the slightest desire to console him. Because it wasn't worth the trouble: the kid made more noise than we did, but he was less touched: he was like a sick man who defends himself against his illness by fever. It's much more serious when there isn't any fever.

He wept: I could clearly see he was pitying himself; he wasn't thinking about death. For one second, one single second, I wanted to weep myself, to weep with pity for myself. But the opposite happened: I glanced at the kid, I saw his thin sobbing shoulders and I felt inhuman: I could pity neither the others nor myself. I said to myself, "I want to die cleanly."

Tom had gotten up, he placed himself just under the round opening and began to watch for daylight. I was determined to die cleanly and I only thought of that. But ever since the doctor told us the time, I felt time flying, flowing away drop by drop.

It was still dark when I heard Tom's voice: "Do you hear them?"

Men were marching in the courtyard.

"Yes."

"What the hell are they doing? They can't shoot in the dark."

After a while we heard no more. I said to Tom, "It's day."

Pedro got up, yawning, and came to blow out the lamp. He said to his buddy, "Cold as hell."

The cellar was all grey. We heard shots in the distance.

"It's starting," I told Tom. "They must do it in the court in the rear."

Tom asked the doctor for a cigarette. I didn't want one; I didn't want cigarettes or alcohol. From that moment on they didn't stop firing.

"Do you realize what's happening," Tom said.

He wanted to add something but kept quiet, watching the door. The door opened and a lieutenant came in with four soldiers. Tom dropped his cigarette.

"Steinbock?"

Tom didn't answer. Pedro pointed him out.

"Juan Mirbal?"

"On the mat."

"Get up," the lieutenant said.

Juan did not move. Two soldiers took him under the arms and set him on his feet. But he fell as soon as they released him. The soldiers hesitated.

"He's not the first sick one," said the lieutenant. "You two carry him; they'll fix it up down there."

He turned to Tom. "Let's go."

Tom went out between two soldiers. Two others followed, carrying the kid by the armpits. He hadn't fainted; his eyes were wide open and tears ran down his cheeks. When I wanted to go out the lieutenant stopped me.

"You Ibbieta?"

"Yes."

"You wait here; they'll come for you later."

They left. The Belgian and the two jailers left too, I was alone. I did not understand what was happening to me but I would have liked it better if they had gotten it over with right away. I heard shots at almost regular intervals; I shook with each one of them. I wanted to scream and tear out my hair. But I gritted my teeth and pushed my hands in my pockets because I wanted to stay clean.

After an hour they came to get me and led me to the first floor, to a small room that smelt of cigars and where the heat was stifling. There were two officers sitting smoking in the armchairs, papers on their knees.

"You're Ibbieta?"

"Yes."

"Where is Ramon Gris?"

"I don't know."

The one questioning me was short and fat. His eyes were hard behind his glasses. He said to me, "Come here."

I went to him. He got up and took my arms, staring at me with a look that should have pushed me into the earth. At the same time he pinched my biceps with all his might. It wasn't to hurt me, it was only a game: he wanted to dominate me. He also thought he had to blow his stinking breath square in my face. We stayed for a moment like that, and I almost felt like laughing. It takes a lot to intimidate a man who is going to die; it didn't work. He pushed me back violently and sat down again. He said, "It's his life against yours. You can have yours if you tell us where he is."

These men dolled up with their riding crops and boots were still going to die. A little later than I, but not too much. They busied themselves looking for names in their crumpled papers, they ran after other men to imprison or suppress them; they had opinions on the future of Spain and on other subjects. Their little activities seemed shocking and burlesqued to me; I couldn't put myself in their place, I thought they were insane. The little man was still looking at me, whipping his boots with the riding crop. All his gestures were calculated to give him the look of a live and ferocious beast.

"So? You understand?"

"I don't know where Gris is," I answered. "I thought he was in Madrid."

The other officer raised his pale hand indolently. This indolence was also calculated. I saw through all their little schemes and I was stupefied to find there were men who amused themselves that way.

"You have a quarter of an hour to think it over," he said slowly. "Take him to the laundry, bring him back in fifteen minutes. If he still refuses he will be executed on the spot."

They knew what they were doing: I had passed the night in waiting; then they had made me wait an hour in the cellar while they shot Tom and Juan and now they were locking me up in the laundry; they must have prepared their game the night before. They told themselves that nerves eventually wear out and they hoped to get me that way.

They were badly mistaken. In the laundry I sat on a stool because I felt very weak and I began to think. But not about their proposition. Of course I knew where Gris was; he was hiding with his cousins, four kilometers from the city. I also knew that I would not reveal his hiding place unless they tortured me (but they didn't seem to be thinking about that). All that was perfectly regulated, definite and in no way interested me. Only I would have liked to understand the reasons for my conduct. I would rather die than give up Gris. Why? I didn't like Ramon Gris any more. My friendship for him had died a little while before dawn at the same time as my love for Concha, at the same time as my desire to live. Undoubtedly I thought highly of him: he was tough. But it was not for this reason that I consented to die in his place; his life had no more value than mine; no life had value. They were going to slap a man up against a wall and shoot at him until he died, whether it was I or Gris or somebody else made no difference. I knew he was more useful than I to the cause of Spain but I thought to hell with Spain and anarchy; nothing was important. Yet I was there, I could save my skin and give up Gris and I refused to do it. I found that somehow comic; it was obstinacy. I thought, "I must be stubborn!" And a droll sort of gaiety spread over me.

They came for me and brought me back to the two officers. A rat ran out from under my feet and that amused me. I turned to one of the *falangistas* and said, "Did you see the rat?"

He didn't answer. He was very sober, he took himself seriously. I wanted to laugh but I held myself back because I was afraid that once I got started I wouldn't be able to stop. The *falangista* had a moustache. I said to him again, "You ought to shave off your moustache, idiot." I thought it funny that he would let the hairs of his living being invade his face. He kicked me without great conviction and I kept quiet.

"Well," said the fat officer, "have you thought about it?"

I looked at them with curiosity, as insects of a very rare species. I told them, "I know where he is. He is hidden in the cemetery. In a vault or in the gravediggers' shack."

It was a farce. I wanted to see them stand up, buckle their belts and give orders busily.

They jumped to their feet. "Let's go. Molés, go get fifteen men from Lieutenant Lopez. You," the fat man said, "I'll let you off if you're telling the truth, but it'll cost you plenty if you're making monkeys out of us."

They left in a great clatter and I waited peacefully under the guard of *falangistas*. From time to time I smiled, thinking about the spectacle they would make. I felt stunned and malicious. I imagined them lifting up tombstones, opening the doors of the vaults one by one. I represented this situation to myself as if I had been someone else: this prisoner obstinately playing the hero, these grim *falangistas* with their moustaches and their men in uniform running among the graves; it was irresistibly funny. After half an hour the little fat man came back alone. I thought he had come to give the orders to execute me. The others must have stayed in the cemetery.

The officer looked at me. He didn't look at all sheepish. "Take him into the big courtyard with the others," he said. "After the military operations a regular court will decide what happens to him."

"Then they're not . . . not going to shoot me? . . ."

"Not now, anyway. What happens afterwards is none of my business."

I still didn't understand. I asked, "But why?"

He shrugged his shoulders without answering and the soldiers took me away. In the big courtyard there were about a hundred prisoners, women, children and a few old men. I began walking around the central grass-plot, I was stupefied. At noon they let us eat in the mess hall. Two or three people questioned me. I must have known them, but I didn't answer: I didn't even know where I was.

Around evening they pushed about ten new prisoners into the court. I recognized Garcia, the baker. He said, "What damned luck you have! I didn't think I'd see you alive."

"They sentenced me to death," I said, "and then they changed their minds. I don't know why."

"They arrested me at two o'clock," Garcia said.

"Why?" Garcia had nothing to do with politics.

"I don't know," he said. "They arrest everybody who doesn't think the way they do." He lowered his voice. "They got Gris."

I began to tremble. "When?"

"This morning. He messed it up. He left his cousin's on Tuesday because they had an argument. There were plenty of people to hide him but he didn't want to owe anything to anybody. He said, 'I'd go and hide in Ibbieta's place, but they got him, so I'll go hide in the cemetery.'"

"In the cemetery?"

"Yes. What a fool. Of course they went by there this morning, that was sure to happen. They found him in the gravediggers' shack. He shot at them and they got him."

"In the cemetery!"

Everything began to spin and I found myself sitting on the ground: I laughed so hard I cried.

Translated by Lloyd Alexander

SARTRE: *The Wall*

1. *Can you explain why Sartre puts the three men in a situation in which their doom is sealed?*

2. *Characterize the three men. Are they sufficiently differentiated?*

3. *Why does Sartre bring in the Belgian doctor? What psychological purpose does he serve? Why does Juan bite his hand?*

4. *Why does Ibbieta protect Ramon Gris when he feels little sympathy for Gris himself?*

5. *Does Ibbieta gain or lose stature by facing his death? What is Sartre's point? Do the challenge and his statement—"I want to die cleanly"—seem reminiscent of Hemingway? What else in the story reminds you of him?*

6. *What effect does imminent death have on Ibbieta's thoughts? on his physical reactions? Why does Sartre stress the physical reaction of all three men when he is evidently more concerned with the psychological?*

7. *Why does Ibbieta restrain himself from feeling pity for the suffering of the others and even for himself?*

8. *What is the point of the ending? Is it effective within the framework of the rest of the story? Is there any foreshadowing of this coincidence? Where?*

9. *Sartre has been accused of using his plays and novels to convey his own brand of Existentialist philosophy. Do you find this story suffers from over-philosophizing?*

Samuel Beckett

YELLOW

*Like Joyce, Samuel Beckett was born in Dublin (in 1906) and
then spent most of his adult life on the continent, basing himself
principally in Paris. Again like Joyce, he retained a great love for
words, an infatuation with the potentialities of language. More concerned than Joyce with seaminess and more morbid than any of his
contemporaries, Beckett has explored the underworld and come up
with his cast of isolated philosophers, tramps, bums, and madmen,
the chief characters of* Murphy *(1938),* Watt *(1953),* Molloy
(1951), Malone Dies *(1952), and* The Unnamable *(1953). The
Belacqua of "Yellow," which originally appeared in* More Pricks
Than Kicks, *is a typical Beckett "hero"—indolent, marginal to
society, aimless, yet curiously dignified and reminiscent in more
than one way of the two derelicts in that classic of the modern
theater,* Waiting for Godot.

ॐ

THE night-nurse bounced in on the tick of five and turned on
the light. Belacqua waked feeling greatly refreshed and eager to
wrestle with this new day. He had underlined, as quite a callow
boy, a phrase in Hardy's *Tess*, won by dint of cogging in the Synod:
"When grief ceases to be speculative, sleep sees her opportunity."
He had manipulated that sentence for many years now, amending
its terms, as "joy" for "grief," to answer his occasions, even calling
upon it to bear the strain of certain applications for which he
feared it had not been intended, and still it held good through it
all. He waked with it now in his mind, as though it had been there
all the time he slept, holding that fragile place against dreams.

The nurse brought a pot of tea and a glass of strong salts on a
tray.

"Pfui!" exclaimed Belacqua.

But the callous girl preferred to disregard this.

"When are they doing me?" he asked.

"You are down for twelve," she said.

Down . . . !

She took herself off.

He drank the salts and two cups of tea, and be damned to the whole of them. Then of course he was wide awake, poor fellow. But what cared he, what cared saucy Belacqua? He switched off the lamp and lay on his back in this the darkest hour, smoking.

Carry it off as he might, he was in a dreadful situation. At twelve sharp he would be sliced open—zeep!—with a bistoury. This was the idea that his mind, for the moment, was in no fit state to entertain. If this Hunnish idea once got a foothold in his little psyche in its present unready condition, topsy-turvy after yesterday's debauch of anxiety and then the good night's sleep coming on top of that, it would be annihilated. The psyche, not the idea—which was precisely the reverse of what he wished. For himself, to do him justice, he did not care. His mind might cave in for all he cared, he was tired of the old bastardo. But the unfortunate part of it was that this would appear in his behavior, he would scream and kick and bite and scratch when they came for him, beg for execution to be stayed and perhaps even wet the bed, and what a reflection on his late family that would be! The grand old Huguenot family guts, he could not do the dirty on them like that (to say nothing of his natural anxiety to be put to rights with as little fuss as possible).

"My sufferings under the anesthetic," he reflected, "will be exquisite, but I shall not remember them."

He dashed out his cigarette and put on the lamp, this not so much for the company of the light as in order to postpone daybreak until he should feel a little more sure of himself. Daybreak, with its suggestion of a nasty birth, he could not bear. Downright and all as he was, he could not bear the sight of this punctilious and almost, he sometimes felt, superfluous delivery. This was mere folly and well he knew it. He tried hard to cure himself, to frighten or laugh himself out of this weakness, but to no avail. He would grow tired and say to himself: "I am what I am." That was the end of all his meditations and endeavours: "I am what I am." He had read the phrase somewhere and liked it and made it his own.

But God at least was good—as He usually is if we only know how to take Him—in this way: that six hours separated him, Belacqua, from the ordeal, six hours were allotted to him in which to make up his mind, as a pretty drab her face for an enemy. His getting the fleam in the neck, his suffering the tortures of the damned while seeming to slumber as peacefully as a little child, were of no consequence, as hope-saved they were not, so long as his mind was master of the thought of them. What he had to do, and had with typical slackness put off doing till the last moment, was to arrange a hot reception in his mind for the thought of all the little acts of kindness that he was to endure before the day was out. Then he would be able to put a good face on it. Otherwise not. Otherwise he would bite, scratch, etc., when they came for him. Now the good face was all that concerned him, the bold devil-may-care expression (except of course that he was also anxious to be made well with the least possible ado). He did not pause to consider himself in this matter, nor the light that the coming ordeal would shed on his irrevocable self, because he really was tired of that old bastardo. No, his whole concern was with other people, the lift-boy, nurses and sisters, the local doc coming to put him off, the eminent surgeon, the handy man at hand to clean up and put the bits into the incinerator, and all the friends of his late family, who would ferret out the whole truth. It did not matter about him, he was what he was. But these outsiders, the family guts, and so on and so forth, all these things had to be considered.

An asthmatic in the room overhead was coughing his heart up. "God bless you," thought Belacqua, "you make things easier for me." But when did the unfortunate sleep? During the day, the livelong day, through the stress of the day. At twelve sharp he would be sound, or, better again, just dozing off. Meantime he coughed, as Crusoe labored to bring his gear ashore, the snugger to be.

Belacqua made a long arm and switched off the lamp. It threw shadows. He would close his eyes, he would bilk the dawn in that way. What were the eyes anyway? The posterns of the mind. They were safer closed.

If only he were well-bred or, failing that, plucky. Blue blood or gamecock! Even if he lived in his mind as much as was his boast. Then he need not be at all this pains to make himself ready. Then it would only be a question of finding a comfortable position in the strange bed, trying to sleep or reading a book, waiting calmly for the Angelus. But he was an indolent bourgeois poltroon, very talented up to a point, but not fitted for private life in the best and brightest sense, in the sense to which he referred when he bragged of how he furnished his mind and lived there, because it was the last ditch when all was said and done. But he preferred not to wait till then, he fancied it might be wiser to settle down there straight away and not wait till he was kicked into it by the world, just at the moment maybe when he was beginning to feel at home in the world. He could no more go back into his heart in that way than he could keep out of it altogether. So now there was nothing for it but to lie on his back in the dark, and exercise his talent. Unless of course he chose to distress the friends of his late family (to say nothing of perhaps jeopardizing the cure for which the friends of his late family were paying). But he had too much of the grocer's sense of honor for that. Rather than have that happen he would persist with his psyche, he would ginger up his little psyche for the occasion.

Poor Belacqua, he seems to be having a very dull, irksome morning, preparing for the fray in this manner. But he will make up for it later on, there is a good time coming for him later on, when the doctors have given him a new lease of apathy.

What were his tactics in this crisis?

In a less tight corner he might have been content to barricade his mind against the idea. But this was at the best a slipshod method, since the idea, howsoever blatant an enemy and despite the strictest guard, was almost certain to sidle in sooner or later under the skirts of a friend, and then the game was up. Still, in the ordinary run of adversity, he would doubtless have bowed to his natural indolence and adopted such a course, he would have been content merely to think of other things and hope for the best. But this was no common or garden fix, he was properly up against it this time, there could be no question of half-measures on this melancholy occasion.

His plan therefore was not to refuse admission to the idea, but to keep it at bay until his mind was ready to receive it. Then let it in and pulverize it. Obliterate the bastard. He ground his teeth in the bed. Flitter the——, tear it into pieces like a priest. So far so good. But by what means? Belacqua ransacked his mind for a suitable engine of destruction.

At this crucial point the good God came to his assistance with a phrase from a paradox of Donne: "Now among our wise men, I doubt not but many would be found, who would laugh at Heraclitus weeping, none which would weep at Democritus laughing." This was a godsend and no error. Not the phrase as a judgment, but its terms, the extremes of wisdom that it tendered to Belacqua. It is true that he did not care for these black and white alternatives as a rule. Indeed he even went so far as to hazard a little paradox on his own account, to the effect that between contraries no alternation was possible. But was it the moment for a man to be nice? Belacqua snatched eagerly at the issue. Was it to be laughter or tears? It came to the same thing in the end, but which was it to be *now?* It was too late to arrange for the luxury of both. Now in a moment he would fill his mind with one or other of these two orders of rays, shall we say ultrared and ultraviolet, and prepare to perforate his adversary.

"Really," thought Belacqua, "I cannot remember having ever spent a more dreary morning; but needs must, that was a true saying, when the devil drives."

At this all-important juncture of his delirium Belacqua found himself blinking his eyes rapidly, a regular nictation, so that little flaws of dawn gushed into his mind. This had not been done with intent, but when he found that it seemed to be benefiting him in some curious way he kept it up, until gradually the inside of his skull began to feel sore. Then he desisted and went back to the dilemma.

Here, as indeed at every crux of the enterprise, he sacrificed his sense of what was personal and proper to himself to the desirability of making a certain impression on other people, an impression almost of gallantry. He must efface himself altogether and do the little soldier. It was this paramount consideration that made him decide in favor of Bim and Bom, Crock, Democritus, whatever you are pleased to call it, and postpone its dark converse to a less public occasion. This was an abnegation if you like, for Belacqua could not resist a lachrymose philosopher, and still less when, as was the case with Heraclitus, he was obscure at the same time. He was in his element in dingy tears, and luxuriously so when these were furnished by a pre-Socratic man of acknowledged distinction. How often had he not exclaimed, skies being grey: "Another minute of this and I consecrate the remnant of my life to Heraclitus of Ephesus, I shall be that Delian diver who, after the third or fourth submersion, returns no more to the surface!"

But weeping in this charnel house would be misconstrued. All the staff, from matron to lift-boy, would make the mistake of ascribing his tears, or, perhaps better, his tragic demeanor, not to the follies of humanity at large—which of course covered themselves— but rather to the tumor the size of a brick that he had on the back of his neck. This would be a very natural mistake and Belacqua was not blaming them. No blame attached to any living person in this matter. But the news would get round that Belacqua, so far from grinning and bearing, had piped his eye, or had been on the point of doing so. Then he would be disgraced and, by extension, his late family also.

So now his course was clear. He would arm his mind with laughter—laughter is not quite the word but it will have to serve—at every point, then he would admit the idea and blow it to pieces. Smears, as after a gorge of blackberries, of hilarity—which is not quite the word either—would be adhering to his lips as he stepped smartly, *ohne Hast aber ohne Rast,* into the torture-chamber. His fortitude would be generally commended.

How did he proceed to put this plan into execution?

He has forgotten, he has no use for it any more.

The night-nurse broke in upon him at seven with another pot of tea and two cuts of toast.

"That's all you'll get now," she said.

The impertinent slut! Belacqua very nearly told her to work it up.

"Did the salts talk to you?" she said.

The sick man appraised her as she took his temperature and pulse. She was a tight, trim little bit.

"They whispered to me," he said.

When she was gone, he thought, What an all-but-flawless brunette, so spick and span too after having been on the go all night, at the beck and call of the first lousy old squaw who let fall her book or could not sleep for the roar of the traffic in Merrion Row. What the hell did anything matter anyway!

Pale wales in the east beyond the Land Commission. The day was going along nicely.

The night-nurse came back for the tray. That made her third ap-

pearance, if he was not mistaken. She would very shortly be relieved, she would eat her supper and go to bed. But not to sleep.
The place was too full of noise and light at that hour, her bed a re-
frigerator. She could not get used to this night duty, she really
could not. She lost weight and her little face became cavernous.
Also it was very difficult to arrange anything with her fiancé. What
a life!

"See you later," she said.

There was no controverting this. Belacqua cast about wildly for
a reply that would please her and do him justice at the same time.
"*Au plaisir*" was of course the very thing, but the wrong language.
Finally he settled on "I suppose so" and discharged it at her in a
very halfhearted manner, when she was more than half out of the
door. He would have been very much better advised to let it alone
and say nothing.

While he was still wasting his valuable time cursing himself for
a fool, the door burst open and the day-nurse came in with a mighty
rushing sound of starched apron. She was to have charge of him by
day. She just missed being beautiful, this Presbyterian from Aberdeen. Aberdeen!

After a little conversation *obiter,* Belacqua let fall casually, as
though the idea had only just occurred to him, whereas in fact it
had been tormenting him insidiously for some time:

"Oh nurse the W.C. perhaps it might be as well to know." Like
that, all in a rush, without any punctuation.

When she had finished telling him, he knew roughly where the
place was. But he stupidly elected to linger on in the bed with his
uneasy load, codding himself that it would be more decent not to
act incontinent on intelligence of so intimate a kind. In his anxiety
to give color to this pause he asked Miranda when he was being
done.

"Didn't the night-nurse tell you?" she said sharply. "At twelve."

So the night-nurse had split. The treacherous darling!

He got up and set out, leaving Miranda at work on the bed.
When he got back she was gone. He got back into the made bed.

Now the sun, that creature of habit, shone in through the window.

A little Aschenputtel, gummy and pert, skipped in with sticks and
coal for the fire.

"Morning," she said.

"Yes," said Belacqua. But he retrieved himself at once. "What a lovely room," he exclaimed. "All the morning sun."

No more was needed to give Aschenputtel his measure.

"Very lovely," she said bitterly, "right on me fire." She tore down the blind. "Putting out me good fire," she said.

That was certainly one way of looking at it.

"I had one old one in here," she said, "and he might be snoring but he wouldn't let the blind down."

Some old put had crossed her, that was patent.

"Not for God," she said, "so what did I do?" She screwed round on her knees from building the fire. Belacqua obliged her.

"What was that?" he said.

She turned back with a chuckle to her task. "I block it with a chair," she said, "and his shirt over the back."

"Ha," exclaimed Belacqua.

"Again he'd be up," she exulted, "don't you know." She laughed happily at the memory of this little deception. "I kep' it off all right," she said.

She talked and talked, and poor Belacqua, with his mind unfinished, had to keep his end up. Somehow he managed to create a very favorable impression.

"Well," she said at last, in an indescribable singsong, "g'bye now. See you later."

"That's right," said Belacqua.

Aschenputtel was engaged to be married to handy Andy; she had been for years. Meantime she gave him a dog's life.

Soon the fire was roaring up the chimney and Belacqua could not resist the temptation to get up and sit before it, clad only in his thin blue 100,000 Chemises pajamas. The coughing aloft had greatly abated since he first heard it. The man was gradually settling down, it did not require a Sherlock Holmes to realize that. But on the grand old yaller wall, crowding in upon his left hand, a pillar of higher tone, representing the sun, was spinning out its placid deiseal. This dribble of time, thought Belacqua, like sanies into a bucket, the world wants a new washer. He would draw the blind, both blinds.

But he was foiled by the entry of the matron with the morning paper—this, save the mark, by way of taking his mind off it. It is impossible to describe the matron. She was all right. She made him nervous the way she flung herself about.

Belacqua turned on the flow:

"What a lovely morning," he gushed, "a lovely room, all the morning sun."

The matron simply disappeared, there is no other word for it. The woman was there one moment and gone the next. It was extraordinary.

The theater sister came in. What a number of women there seemed to be in this place! She was a great raw châteaubriant of a woman, like the one on the Wincarnis bottle. She took a quick look at his neck.

"Pah," she scoffed, "that's nothing."

"Not at all," said Belacqua.

"Is that the lot?"

Belacqua did not altogether care for her tone.

"And a toe," he said, "to come off, or rather, portion of a toe."

"Top," she guffawed, "and bottom."

There was no controverting this. But he had learned his lesson. He let it pass.

This woman was found to improve on acquaintance. She had a coarse manner, but she was exceedingly gentle. She taught all her more likely patients to wind bandages. To do this well with the crazy little hand-windlass that she provided was no easy matter. The roll would become fusiform. But when one got to know the humors of the apparatus, then it could be coaxed into yielding the hard slender spools, perfect cylinders, that delighted her. All these willing slaves that passed through her hands, she blandished each one in turn. "I never had such tight, straight bandages," she would say. Then, just as the friendship established on this basis seemed about to develop into something more—how shall I say?—substantial, the patient would all of a sudden be well enough to go home. Some malignant destiny pursued this splendid woman. Years later, when the rest of the staff was forgotten, she would drift into the mind. She marked down Belacqua for the bandages.

Miranda came back, this time with the dressing tray. That voluptuous undershot cast of mouth, the clenched lips, almost *bocca romanã*, how had he failed to notice it before? Was it the same woman?

"Now," she said.

She lashed into the part with picric and ether. It beat him to understand why she should be so severe on his little bump of amativeness. It was not septic to the best of his knowledge. Then why this severity? Merely on the off-chance of its coming in for the fag end of a dig? It was very strange. It had not even been shaved. It jutted out under the short hairs like a cuckoo's bill. He trusted it would come to no harm. Really he could not afford to have it curtailed. His little bump of amativeness.

When his entire nape was as a bride's adorned (bating the obscene stain of the picric) and so tightly bandaged that he felt his eyes bulging, she transferred her compassion to the toes. She scoured the whole phalanx, top and bottom. Suddenly she began to titter. Belacqua nearly kicked her in the eye, he got such a shock. How dared she trespass on his program! He refusing to be tickled in this petty local way, trying with his teeth to reach his under lip and gouging his palms, and she forgetting herself, there was no other word for it. There were limits, he felt, to Democritus.

"Such a lang tootsy," she giggled.

Heavenly Father, the creature was bilingual. A lang tootsy! Belacqua swallowed his choler.

"Soon to be syne," he said in a loud voice. What his repartee lacked in wit it made up for in style. But it was lost on this granite Medusa.

"A long foot," he said agreeably, "I know, or a long nose. But a long toe, what does that denote?"

No answer. Was the woman then altogether cretinous? Or did she not hear him? Belting away there with her urinous picric and cooling her porridge in advance. He would try her again.

"I say," he roared, "that that toe you like so much will soon be only a memory." He could not put it plainer than that.

"Yes,"—the word died away and was repeated—"yes, his troubles are nearly over."

Belacqua broke down completely, he could not help it. This distant voice, like a *cor anglais* coming through the evening, and then the "his," the "his" was the last straw. He buried his face in his hands, he did not care who saw him.

"I would like," he sobbed, "the cat to have it, if I might."

She would never have done with her bandage, it cannot have measured less than a furlong. But of course it would never do to leave anything to chance, Belacqua could appreciate that. Still, it seemed somehow disproportioned to the length of even his toe. At last she made all fast round his shin. Then she packed her tray and left. Some people go, others leave. Belacqua felt like the rejected of these two that night in a bed. He felt he had set Miranda somehow against him. Was this then the haporth of paint? Miranda on whom so much depended. *Merde!*

It was all Lister's fault. These damned happy Victorians.

His heart gave a great leap in its box with a fulminating sense that he was all wrong, that anger would stand by him better than the other thing, the laugh seemed so feeble, so like a whinge in the end. But on second thoughts, no; anger would turn aside when it came to the point, leaving him like a sheep. Anyhow it was too late to turn back. He tried cautiously what it felt like to have the idea in his mind. . . . Nothing happened, he felt no shock. So at least he had spiked the brute, that was something.

At this point he went downstairs and had a truly military evacuation, Army Service Corps. Coming back he did not doubt that all would yet be well. He whistled a snatch outside the duty-room. There was nothing left of his room when he got back but Miranda, Miranda more prognathous than ever, loading a syringe. Belacqua tried to make light of this.

"What now?" he said.

But she had the weapon into his bottom and discharged before he realized what was happening. Not a cry escaped him.

"Did you hear what I said?" he said. "I insist, it is my right, on knowing the meaning of this, the purpose of this injection, do you hear me?"

"It is what every patient gets," she said, "before going down to the theater."

Down to the theater! Was there a conspiracy in this place to destroy him, body and soul? His tongue clave to his palate. They had desiccated his secretions. First blood to the profession!

The theater-socks were the next little bit of excitement. Really, the theater seemed to take itself very seriously. To hell with your socks, he thought, it's your mind I want.

Now events began to move more rapidly. First of all an angel of the Lord came to his assistance with a funny story, really very funny indeed—it always made Belacqua laugh till he cried—about the parson who was invited to take a small part in an amateur production. All he had to do was to snatch at his heart when the revolver went off, cry "By God! I'm shot!" and drop dead. The parson said certainly, he would be most happy, if they would have no objection to his drawing the line at "By God!" on such a secular occasion. He would replace it, if they had no objection, by "Mercy!" or "Upon my word!" or something of that kind. "Oh my! I'm shot!", how would that be?

But the production was so amateur that the revolver went off indeed and the man of God was transfixed.

"Oh!" he cried, "Oh! . . . BY CHRIST! I AM SHOT!"

It was a mercy that Belacqua was a dirty, low-down Low Church Protestant highbrow and able to laugh at this sottish jest. Laugh! How he did laugh, to be sure. Till he cried.

He got up and began to titivate himself. Now he could hear the asthmatic breathing if he listened hard. The day was out of danger, any fool could see that. A little sealed cardboard box lying on the mantelpiece caught his eye. He read the inscription: Fraisse's Ferruginous Ampoules for the Intensive Treatment of Anaemia by Intramuscular Squirtation. Registered Trademark—Mozart. The little Hexenmeister of Don Giovanni, now in his narrow cell forever mislaid, dragged into bloodlessness! How very amusing. Really, the world was in great form this morning.

Now two further women—there was no end to them—the one of a certain age, the other not, entered, ripping off their regulation cuffs as they advanced. They pounced on the bed. The precautionary oil sheet, the cradle . . . Belacqua padded up and down before the fire, the ends of his pajamas tucked like a cyclist's into the sinister socks. He would smoke one more cigarette, nor count the cost. It was astonishing, when he came to think of it, how the entire routine of this place, down to the meanest detail, was calculated to a cow's toe to promote a single end, the relief of suffering in the long run. Observe how he dots his i's now and crucifies his t's to the top of his bent. He was being put to his trumps.

Surreptitiously they searched his yellow face for signs of discomposure. In vain. It was a mask. But perhaps his voice would tremble. One, she whose life had changed, took it upon herself to say in a peevish tone:

"Sister Beamish won't bless you for soiling her good socks."

Sister Beamish would not bless him.

The voice of this person was in ruins, but she abused it further.

"Would you not stand on the mat?"

His mind was made up in a flash: he would stand on the mat. He would meet them in this matter. If he refused to stand on the mat he was lost in the eyes of these two women.

"Anything," he said, "to oblige Sister Beamish."

Miranda was having a busy morning. Now she appeared for the fourth or fifth time, he had lost count, complete with shadowy assistants. The room seemed full of grey women. It was like a dream.

"If you have any false teeth," she said, "you may remove them."

His hour was at hand, there was no blinking at the fact.

Going down in the lift with Miranda he felt his glasses under his hand. This was a blessed accident if you like, just when the silence was becoming awkward.

"Can I trust you with these?" he said.

She put them into her bosom. The divine creature! He would assault her in another minute.

"No smoking," she said, "in the operating theater."

The surgeon was washing his invaluable hands as Belacqua swaggered through the antechamber. He that hath clean hands shall be stronger. Belacqua cut the surgeon. But he flashed a dazzling smile at the Wincarnis. She would not forget that in a hurry.

He bounced up on to the table like a bridegroom. The local doc was in great form, he had just come from standing best man, he was all togged up under his vestments. He recited his exhortation and clapped on the nozzle.

"Are you right?" said Belacqua.

The mixture was too rich, there could be no question about that. His heart was running away, terrible yellow yerks in his skull. "One of the best," he heard those words that did not refer to him. The expression reassured him. The best man clawed at his tap.

By Christ! He did die!

They had clean forgotten to auscultate him!

BECKETT: *Yellow*

1. *What does the title tell you about the patient? What does it tell you about Beckett? Does it immediately indicate a point of view?*

2. *Does Beckett's wit seem appropriate in describing the emotions of a man about to undergo an operation? How does the wit function?*

3. *How does Belacqua decide to act before the operation? Why? What does his decision tell you about him? about Beckett?*

4. *What is his attitude toward the hospital personnel? Theirs toward him?*

5. *What relevance does the anecdote about the parson have to the story? Mention some of the other stories in this collection in which anecdotes are significant.*

6. *Explain the ending of the story. Why is it funny? Or is it tragic?*

7. *What view of life does Beckett suggest in this story? Is it one you agree with? What alternatives are there?*

8. *Contrast Beckett's attitudes with, say, Tolstoy's. Even though Beckett and Hesse seem vastly different in method and point of view, there are some surprising analogies. Can you see any in their stories?*

Alberto Moravia

THE RUIN OF HUMANITY

Born in 1907 to an upper middle-class family of Rome, Alberto Moravia (b. Alberto Pincherle) in the last ten years has emerged as the leading Italian novelist and short-story writer of his generation. Confined by an early illness, he educated himself through omniverous reading. From classical drama, he acquired the art of dialogue and tight structure; from Dostoyevsky and Joyce, he learned how to dramatize philosophy and psychology in fiction. These lessons he applied to depicting modern men and women against their social background, in such works as The Time of Indifference *(1929),* Two Adolescents *(1944, 1948),* The Woman of Rome *(1949),* The Conformist *(1951),* Two Women *(1958), and* The Empty Canvas *(1961). Nakedly sensual in his approach to his characters, he also catches their ennui, their sadness, their indifference, their loss of will, no less than their ability to survey what seems to overwhelm them. In its brief span, the following tale manages to embrace most of these themes, as well as to underscore the eternal war between the sexes.*

ℰ✋

ABOUT the middle of February the north wind, which had made me feel so wretched during the winter, dropped, the sky filled with clouds, and a moist breeze, which seemed to be coming from the sea, started to blow. At the soft breath of this breeze I felt myself coming to life again, although in a melancholy sort of way, as if it were whispering in my ear: "Come along, cheer up, while there's life there's hope." But, just because I felt that winter was over and spring beginning, I knew that I could no longer bear to go and work in my uncle's workshop. I had gone into the workshop a year before, like a train going into a tunnel, and I had not come out yet and I could not even see daylight at the other end. Not that the work was unpleasant or repugnant to me personally: there are worse jobs. The workshop consisted of a large shed, situated at the far end of an enclosed piece of ground which served as a depôt for a brick factory, halfway along the Via della Magliana. Inside the shed the air was always full of white, flour-like sawdust, as in a mill; and in the midst of this cloud of dust, and of the continuous humming of saws and electric lathes, we workers and my uncle, looking like floury millers, moved about, busy from morning till night making furniture and fittings. My uncle, poor man, loved me like a son, the workmen were all good chaps and, as I have already said, the work was not repugnant: first a tree-trunk, of oak or maple or chestnut, long, twisted, lean-ing up against the wall of the workshop, with all its bark upon it and even, still remaining under the bark, the ants that had inhab-ited it when it was a tree; then, after the saw had dealt with it, so many clean, white planks; then, out of these planks, with the lathe or the plane or other tools, as occasion demanded, table-legs, parts of wardrobes, cornices; and finally, after the piece of furniture had been nailed and screwed and glued together, the painting and pol-ishing. For anyone who takes pleasure in his work, this gradual progress from a tree-trunk to a piece of furniture may become a passion; it is always interesting, or, at the least, it is never boring. But evidently I am made in a different way to other people: after a few months, I could not bear the work any longer. It was not that I am not a good worker, but that I like, every little while, to pause in my work and look round me—just so as to see who I am and where I am and what point I've reached. My uncle, on the other hand, was exactly the opposite: he was always working, fiercely, passionately, never stopping to take breath or reflect; and thus, from a chair to a bracket, from a bracket to a wardrobe, from a wardrobe to a night-table, from a night-table to a chair, he had turned fifty—for that was his age—and you could see that he would go on in the same way until his death, which would be rather like the death of a lathe that falls to pieces or a saw that loses its teeth, the death, in fact, of a tool and not of a man. And on Sundays, in-deed, when he put on his best suit and walked very slowly along the pavements of the Via Arenula in company with his wife and children, his eyes half closed, his mouth twisted, and two deep lines between his mouth and his eyes, he really looked like a dis-carded, useless, broken tool; and I could not help remembering that he had acquired that appearance by stooping over his lathe and his saw and screwing up his eyes in a perpetual cloud of saw-dust; and I said to myself that life was not worth living unless you paused now and then and reflected that you *were* alive.

The bus that starts from the Trastevere station goes out into the country and back. Peasants, labourers and all sorts of poor people bring mud into it on their boots, and the smell of sweat from their working clothes, and perhaps a few insects as well. And so, at the starting-point, they spray some kind of stinking disinfectant on the floor and even on the seats, which catches you in the throat and, like an onion, makes you weep. On one of those soft February mornings, while I was waiting—my eyes full of tears because of the disinfectant—for the bus to start, the wind from the sea, com-ing in through the windows, gave me a great longing to go off on my own account, to pause for a little and reflect about myself. And so, when I got off the bus near the workshop, instead of going to the right, towards the shed, I went to the left, towards the mead-ows that lie between the main road and the Tiber. I walked off over the pallid grass, in the gentle, moist wind, facing a sky full of white clouds. The Tiber itself I could not see, because at that point it runs through a dip in the ground; away beyond it I could see abandoned factories, a big building with arches looking like a great dovecot, and a church with a dome and pillars that support noth-ing and look like the wooden pillars in a child's building game. Be-hind me was the industrial district of Rome—tall chimneys with long plumes of black smoke, factory sheds full of big windows, the low, broad cylinders of two or three gasometers and the high, nar-row ones of silos. When I thought of the workmen toiling in those factories, my leisure seemed to me even more agreeable. I felt full of cunning and watchfulness, as though I were going out hunting. And hunting indeed I was—not for game, however, but for myself.

When I reached the river, at a point where the bank is not so very steep, I slithered down the slope to the edge and sat down amongst the bushes. Only one step from my feet ran the Tiber, and I could see it twisting through the countryside like a snake, the dazzling light from the cloudy sky reflected in its yellow, wrin-kled surface. On the other side of the river were more pale green meadows and, scattered over them, sheep nibbling at the grass, sheep with puffed-out, dirty wool, and here and there a perfectly white lamb, whose wool had not yet had time to go grey. I sat clasping my knees and stared at the yellow water, which at this point formed a little whirlpool from which a black branch projected, shaggy and untidy and looking like the hair of a drowned woman. And then, in the silence, with the branch, black as ebony, quivering from the force of the current but not moving, I felt all at once as though inspired; and, not with thought but with a feeling more profound than thought, I seemed to have understood something of great importance. Or rather, to be able to understand it, if only I did my utmost to grasp it. This thing, in fact, was poised delicately; it was like having, as they say, a word on the tip of one's tongue. And, in order to hold on to it and prevent its falling back into the darkness, I said, suddenly, aloud: "My name is Gerardo Mucchietto."

Immediately a mocking voice from above said: "Commonly called Mucchio. . . . Well, well, are you talking to yourself?"

I turned round and right above me saw, standing on the edge of the bank, the daughter of the custodian of the brick-yard, Gioconda, in a black velvet skirt and a pink sweater, stockingless, her hair fluttering in the wind. Now, of all the people I knew in the whole world, Gioconda was the one I would least have wished to see at that moment. She had taken a fancy to me and she persecuted me, although I had made it plain to her in every possible way that I did not care for her. I had an immediate impulse to say something unpleasant to her, so that she should go away and leave me alone to return to the thing I had been on the point of grasping when she arrived. Without moving, I said to her: "Take care, you're showing too much leg."

But brazenly she slid down beside me. "D'you mind if I keep you company?" she asked.

"I don't know what to do with your company," I said, still without looking at her; "and besides, how can you sit on the ground here, in all this dust?"

But she lifted up her dress and sat down, well satisfied, saying: "I haven't much on underneath, anyhow." The thing I wanted to think about was still there, luckily, perched on the edge of my mind, like a bird on a window-sill. Gioconda, in the meantime, all sweet and sugary, was clinging on to my arm and saying: "Gerardo, why are you so faithless? . . . I am so fond of you."

"I'm not faithless, it's just that I don't like you, that's all."

"Why don't you like me?"

I said hastily, fearing that, as I spoke, the thing I wanted to think about might vanish: "I don't like you because you've got a big red face covered with pimples. . . . You look like a cabbage rose. . . ."

What would most women have done after a remark like that? Gone away at once. She, on the contrary, pressed herself close up against me and said coyly: "Gerardo dear, why can't you be nicer to me?"

"All right, I will be," I said desperately, "provided you go away."

"Why, were you expecting some other woman, Gerardo dear?"

"No, no one; I wanted to be alone."

"Why alone? No, let's stay together. . . . It's so lovely to be together."

This time I said nothing: the thing was still there, on the edge of my mind, but I felt that any trifle would be enough to drive it back into the darkness out of which it had come. It was at this moment that Gioconda exclaimed: "Would you like me to guess what you're thinking about?"

Stung to the quick, I answered: "You won't guess if you try for a hundred years."

"But I tell you I *can* guess. . . . Now, let's see if I'm right. I say you were thinking about these socks I'm wearing rolled down to the ankle, that match my sweater. . . . Be truthful, that's what you were thinking about." As she spoke she held out her leg, which was big and red and covered with fair hairs, displaying her foot in its strawberry-coloured sock. I could not help raising my eyes and looking at her foot, and then, all of a sudden, I became aware that the thing had fallen back over the edge, down into the darkness. I no longer felt anything, I no longer understood anything, I was empty, dead, inert, like the stakes of seasoned wood that my uncle kept propped up against the workshop wall. At the thought that I had lost sight of that most beautiful and important thing through the chatter of this stupid girl, I was seized suddenly with an immense rage and I cried out, turning brusquely towards her: "Why did you come here? . . . You're my evil genius. . . . Couldn't you have left me alone?" And, since she continued to squeeze my arm, I tore myself away from her and hit her on the head. But she clung to me obstinately, although I beat her on her big blonde head: so then I jumped up, seized her by the hair and threw her down on the gravel and trampled on her with my feet, all over her body and even on her head. Rolled up into a ball with her face in her hands, she groaned and let forth a shriek or two, but made no attempt at resistance: possibly she was pleased. However, when I was tired of trampling on her, she got up and, all covered with dust, went off sobbing. I shouted loudly after her: "You women are the ruin of humanity." Still sobbing, she went off down a track along the gravelly bed of the Tiber and disappeared.

But the thing, by this time, had taken flight, and now, although I was alone, I felt just as inert and dull and empty as when Gioconda had been there. There was nothing to be done, for that day anyhow; and there was no knowing how long it would be before I could find another opportunity like this. Seething with rage and at the same time both undecided and full of eagerness, I roamed the fields the whole morning, cursing Gioconda and cursing my fate, unable to be still, either in mind or body. In the end I realized there was nothing for me to do except go back to the workshop, so back I went. Amongst the piles of bricks Gioconda, carrying a cooking-pot, was scattering food to the hens; she greeted me from afar with a smile. I did not respond and went on into the workshop. "Better late than never," cried my uncle when he saw me. I said nothing, but put on my overalls and resumed my work at the exact point where I had left it the day before.

Translated by Angus Davidson

MORAVIA: *The Ruin of Humanity*

1. *Moravia often communicates through mood or atmosphere. What is the mood of the opening paragraph? Of the succeeding paragraphs? Of the final paragraph?*

2. *In what way does Moravia's "ear for mood" remind you of Turgenev's "ear for emotion"? Is it a substitute for plot? What other writers in this collection depend heavily upon mood?*

3. *Moravia also uses the device of "figurative foreshadowing" ("I had gone into the workshop a year before, like a train going into a tunnel") to move his story. Is it plausible that Gerardo should speak in similes? Is the naturalistic surface of the story violated by this technique?*

4. *Why does work become unbearable for Gerardo? Does his boredom seem believable?*

5. *What is Gerardo's attitude toward his uncle? Is it just?*

6. *What does the river signify to Gerardo? Compare its significance to the meaning of the river in "The Judgment."*

7. *If Gioconda had been more attractive, would Gerardo have welcomed her? Does her name have any significance?*

8. *Who or what is "the ruin of humanity"? Does Gerardo know the real answer? How is it revealed to the reader? (See questions 1, 2, and 3.)*

9. *What has Gerardo gained or lost at the end? What if anything has he learned about himself? What is Moravia's point? Is it tragic or comic? What view of society is being projected here?*

10. *What does this story have in common with "Counterparts" and with "The Man Who Loved Islands?"*